'A classic Hollywood noir ... profoundly affecting'

RUMAAN ALAM, author of *Leave the World Behind*

'A brilliant shard of California horror, worthy of Nathanael West and J.G. Ballard. Alexandra Kleeman writes fearlessly'

NATHANIEL RICH, author of *Second Nature*

'Kleeman's LA-noir eco-parable kept me constantly guessing and reading on. This is a book for our post-truth world ... or at least what's left of it'

JORDAN TANNAHILL, author of *The Listeners*

BY ALEXANDRA KLEEMAN

SOMETHING NEW UNDER THE SUN

A Novel

Alexandra Kleeman

4th ESTATE • London

4th Estate
An imprint of HarperCollins*Publishers*
1 London Bridge Street
London SE1 9GF

www.4thEstate.co.uk

HarperCollins*Publishers*
1st Floor, Watermarque Building, Ringsend Road
Dublin 4, Ireland

First published in Great Britain in 2021 by 4th Estate
First published in the United States by Hogarth in 2021
This 4th Estate paperback edition published in 2022

1

Book design by Debbie Glasserman

A catalogue record for this book is
available from the British Library

ISBN 978-0-00-833912-8

Set in Dante MT Std
Printed and bound in the UK using 100%
renewable electricity at CPI Group (UK) Ltd

THEY'RE ALL FOR GILVARRY

GUILDENSTERN: A man breaking his journey between one place and another at a third place of no name, character, population or significance, sees a unicorn cross his path and disappear. . . . "My God," says a second man, "I must be dreaming, I thought I saw a unicorn." At which point, a dimension is added that makes the experience as alarming as it will ever be.

A third witness, you understand, adds no further dimension but only spreads it thinner, and a fourth thinner still, and the more witnesses there are, the thinner it gets and the more reasonable it becomes until it is as thin as reality, the name we give to the common experience. . . .

"Look, look!" recites the crowd. "A horse with an arrow in its forehead! It must have been mistaken for a deer."

—TOM STOPPARD, *Rosencrantz and Guildenstern Are Dead*

All water has a perfect memory and is forever trying to get back to where it was.

—TONI MORRISON

SOMETHING NEW UNDER THE SUN

O n the palm-sized screen it looks curiously real, like something he's already seen. She slouches in the drugstore aisle, clawing the skin on the back of her hands, sunglasses black and gleaming in the halogen daylight. This is the girl: a bored blonde, her head at once too big and too little for her whittled-down frame. Smaller than life, shorter than expected, not as pretty, torso adrift within a pair of creased track shorts and an oversized black sweatshirt with GUCCI spelled out on front in serifed white letters. The footage has a handheld wobble; from time to time it sinks behind a shelf and you can hear the sound of close breath, the body of the camera holder hovering out of view. She keeps taking a box off the shelf, putting it back, picking it up again. Against a background of sanitary napkins, pregnancy tests, and adult diapers, she looks aimless, misplaced, like a child rehearsing an adult gesture they've seen but not fully understood.

Patrick Hamlin shields his eyes from the California sun and squints down at the miniature face on-screen, shrunken behind oversized lenses. He can't help but feel disrespected, seated off to the side of these production kids—half his age but wearing better clothes—slim-limbed youths who picked him up at the airport and then detoured without asking to this noisy poolside bar, nestled in the crotch of an overpriced hipster hotel. The potted palms by the bar all have smiles painted on their trunks, and sultry cartoonified eyes made to be photographed and uploaded to the feed. At check-in, bowls of red rubber condoms sit gratis, waiting to be snatched up by smooth-armed men and women delighted at the novelty of a cock that resembles a balloon animal. Now he's jet-lagged and dehydrated, headachy from drinking a jumbo gin-and-tonic in the glaring bright, mouth dry and tasting of stale wool as he leans over to watch their video clips on a scuffed-up smartphone, the armrest digging into his soft belly. Plastic glasses litter the tabletop, as the kids slurp from twin Bloody Marys as tall as a toy poodle.

"What is this?" Patrick asks, as the girl in the video fingers the sealed opening of the little box, her gestures halting but not unsure. "What am I seeing?"

"You have to start from the beginning to get the full effect," says one of the kids encouragingly, a Hispanic twentysomething in a short-sleeved button-up patterned with small embroidered horseshoes.

"Like a horror movie," adds the pale, smooth-faced one holding the phone. His arm drifts toward and away from Patrick randomly, making it difficult to follow the tiny happenings on the tiny screen. "You need those shots of the suburbs and hedges and mailboxes to prep for the massacre that comes later. When the violence is unleashed, the viewer can't comfort themselves by thinking it's a neighborhood fundamentally different from their own. They've already swallowed the pill."

"Like at the beginning of *Scream,* where she's making popcorn on the stovetop," says the one in the horseshoe shirt.

"Yeah, or in *Triumph of the Undead Dead,* where they're in a used-car lot arguing over the price of a station wagon right before they get devoured," says the Arm.

Devoured? Patrick has no idea what he's supposed to be looking for. The girl on-screen is famous, he knows, but he can't imagine why. She has long yellow hair and an overstuffed pout. She could be any teenager at the mall, an expensive mall, riding the escalator up and down in the afternoon stupor, clutching outsized shopping bags in both hands that swing slowly in the breeze. In the small, impossibly clear picture, her mouth is set in a stiff line, but somehow he senses that she could burst into tears at any moment. She reminds him of his daughter, or is it a combination of his daughter and his wife? On a screen in his mind, he sees their delicate mouths projected side by side, familiar lips that he's wiped with a towel, precisely etched and painfully exact, the pale, satiny pink of carnations or cooked shrimp. Back on the East Coast, three hours ahead, they must be setting the table for dinner, portioning out scoopfuls of pasta and salad, his nine-year-old daughter frowning in concentration as she folds flimsy paper napkins in half. Lately, whenever he tries to picture their faces, whether smiling or unsmiling, the image

won't hold: involuntarily, he always sees the smooth lines tremble and collapse into twists of emotion, the unbeautiful shapes
of someone about to cry.

"Skip ahead," says Horseshoe Shirt to the other. "We're losing him."

"But think about how much of the story we'll lose," the Arm
argues, "if we rush it. The ambient time, boredom, irritation,
atmosphere. The texture. The suspense. A long stasis that, like
winter blossoming into spring, reveals surprises within. What
this sort of footage lacks in plot structure, it gains back in the
quiet sorcery of something happening out of nothing, monot-
ony upended by the eruption of something new. The cinephile
in me can't abide."

"So true. But avoiding loss is impossible in a world that struggles to conjure even the basic sense of presence. Capture itself
is a form of loss, all a matter of PPI," Horseshoe replies, and
they nod at each other solemnly. The video is dragged ahead an
inch or so.

On-screen, the girl looks furtively toward the checkout counter,
then back down. Silently, she slides a finger under the flap, splits
open the little box, wriggles her hand into the aperture in the
cardstock. She's peering inside now as she pushes the contents
around with the tip of a slender manicured finger. Now the shot
is tightening, homing in on the box, which seems to be full of
tampons. The girl deftly slides three of them out and pockets
them without looking, staring straight out in front of her like
she's searching for someone all the way across the room.

"She's stealing tampons?" Patrick asks.

"Shhh," say the kids.

The camera lurches into motion, as the cameraman steps out

from behind the shelves and speaks. *Hey, Cassidy, whatcha doing? You gonna take those without paying?* His voice is cheerily unfriendly. *Is it that time of the month? You out of money? You on the rag, Cassidy? Smile into the camera—come on, baby.* Cassidy looks up, her face soft and innocent and surprised for a moment, mouth slightly parted and revealing the tips of two adorably large front teeth. Then the features rearrange. *What the fuck?* growls Cassidy, her grip tightening around the tampon box as it caves in. *You guys stake out the maxi-pad aisle now? Do you want to hide in my shower and watch me put it in?* The cameraman giggles humorlessly. *Come on, Cassidy,* says his voice behind the lens. *I don't think your fans would appreciate that kind of language. Give us a* Kassi Keene: Kid Detective *salute, can you do that? The one from the TV show. Baby, you're so moody right now. You got cramps?* Cassidy lets out a weird, strangled sound. She hurls what's in her hand right at the lens, and a mess of brightly colored cylinders bursts once, like big, clumsy confetti, as the camera whirls down to the drugstore floor and back up again, seeking her face. What it finds looks ferocious. *Press delete, cunt,* Cassidy says, her hand reaching. *Or I'm appropriating that fucking phone.*

So this is all being shot on a camera phone, Patrick thinks, scratching the side of his neck, where a stinging sensation creeps across his hot skin. Incredible resolution. Phones, he thinks, are the one thing in the world that seem always to be getting better.

Now that the two of them are in motion, the incredible resolution of the camera lens seems less equipped to handle all the physical activity. She's coming toward him with her hands out, clawlike, grabbing things off the shelves and hurling them, hard, at the arms or upper body of the man holding the phone, causing the picture to seize and tremble. He tries to keep up the nonchalant chatter, asking, *Is it 'cause* Five Moons of Triton *was a gigantic money-suck that you need to shoplift your, uh, feminine devices? Times that tough for Kassi Keene?* But it's clear from the lengthening pauses in his trash talk that he's in some degree of pain. As he backs away at an increasing speed, he's running into the sharp metal corners of the shelves, knocking down prim rows of packaged cookies and crackers. At the same time, Cassidy Carter has driven him toward the exitless back of the store, into the aisle with the household cleaners, and is battering him with a value-sized jug of hypoallergenic laundry detergent.

She grips with both hands and swings it like a sledgehammer. A little bracelet on her wrist glitters in the light. She's telling him to give her the phone, but she's saying other things too: Fuck the menstruation-industrial complex for making her buy a pack of twenty-four when all she needs is one or two to get to the end of her cycle, fuck America for being a nation-sized land-fill run by Lexus rednecks who'll never in their lives be able to comprehend the actual spiritual profundity of *Five Moons of Triton,* fuck all her fans for buying the magazines with the stolen photos of one of her old Brazilian wax sessions, her fans are creepy goblins and would chop her into little bits and eat the pieces raw if they could, and they would take a billion photos of it and probably tag her in every single one. By now, the phone is on the floor, camera pointed up at Cassidy, who looms over it with a dark expression, her legs long and bronzed and extending improbably, impossibly, up toward the sky.

As she unscrews the lid to the detergent and upends it all over the cameraman's occluded body, Patrick can't help but think that female anger has an outlandish quality to it. In a face rigorously conditioned to be beautiful, ugly feelings come as a violation of basic principles, like the monstrously large species of coconut-eating rat he had read about on the internet, discovered on a tropical island when it fell from a tree onto a passing scientist. While she was clubbing the head and back of the cameraman, the lower half of Cassidy's face had been screwed into a position of uncontrolled fury, the lower lip knotted and drawn down to expose her smooth, square teeth. At the same time, the upper half of her face, enveloped by sunglasses, seemed perfectly placid. From the nose up, there was a sort of fragile glamour that you could have fallen in love with on the spot—and it was a truly fantastic nose, actually, elegant but wholesome, lightly freckled, the tawdry bridge sleeking down to a delicate, chiseled tip. It was the sort of nose that reminded you at first of other noses you had loved in days gone by, but then began by degrees to eclipse those other noses, until all you could remember was this new nose, perfect and organic and whole.

If he was honest about it, Patrick had always sensed a disjunction, with girlfriends and mothers and even his own nine-year-old daughter, between the anger they professed to feel and the spectacular utility of that anger, to startle and confuse. He had the eerie feeling, when watching an angry woman, that he himself was being watched from someplace deep inside her— watched with the smooth, distant intelligence of a cat. Now, as he watches Cassidy shrug off the grasp of the drugstore employees who've banded together to try to restrain her, he wonders if there's a tiny, childlike version of this woman pointing and laughing within the calm center of her rage. Suddenly, Cassidy grins. With one smooth movement, she reaches down into her track shorts, pulls out the spent tampon, and slings it at the cameraman's prone body.

Namaste! she shouts, as she is led away.

"And that," says the Arm, pausing the clip, "is Cassidy Carter. I can't believe you didn't know who she was. It's as if we found you on a Micronesian island and we're teaching you, like, what a flashlight is."

"She's that famous?" Patrick asks, tilting the last drops of WAT-R from his drinking glass onto his sweaty, reddening neck.

"More. She was a Happy Meal toy. I had two when I was growing up. I used to make them karate-fight each other." Horseshoe makes rigid motions with his hands.

"Okay, she's famous, but she's clearly crazy," says Patrick. "I just don't think any serious film uses an actress who's assaulted someone in public. On video. Over feminine hygiene. How could you guarantee that she'd behave herself? It's too risky."

"Crazy is bankable," says the Arm, swiveling in his seat until he makes contact with their waitress. He lifts the empty WAT-R bottle and points to it with a hand shaped like a gun, then holds up three fingers. The waitress nods, gives a thumbs-up, and rolls her eyes. "So is free PR, like that video you just watched. So is the number-one nose in America, and the former face of Bellanex."

"Bellanex?" says Patrick.

"That acne cream that caused seizures. It made a lot of money, though," Horseshoe says, humming something that could be the Bellanex jingle.

Patrick stares down at the paused image. The girl is frozen, sandwiched between two drugstore employees in red vests, who hold her by the elbows. She's looking back toward the camera with a gigantic, diamond-hard smile. With her right hand she gives a cheery two-fingered salute, like a Girl Scout, but cuter.

"I hear you, I see your point. But I'm going to have to veto her," Patrick says with finality. He leans back in his seat and swigs his diluted gin to punctuate. Braided strands of plastic in the seatback squeal as he adjusts his mass.

There's an uncomfortable silence. When the Arm speaks, he sounds a couple years older and somberer.

"Yeah, well, with my regrets," he says, "you aren't actually attached to this film with any veto power, per se. I hope you had a chance to look over your contract and the duties and responsibilities outlined, you know, therein."

Patrick's head begins to ache a little. He squeezes his eyes open and shut. Even when his eyes are closed, the light seems to find its way in, soaking the eyelid and turning his visual field a fleshy shade of red. There's a knotty feeling in his throat, as he weighs the possibility of getting his phone out and looking up his contract right now, right in front of their bright, inquisitive twerp eyes. He looks out at the dull-turquoise pool, fully engulfed by the looming shadow of the hotel above. Neon-green pool floats shaped like hearts rotate aimlessly in the blue.

The Arm explains patiently: "Your contract stipulates that in exchange for the rights to your novel *Elsinore Lane,* the access to which is bestowed gratis, you will receive one paid production-assistant position, budget-contingent, which you may bestow at your discretion upon the individual of your choice. Including yourself, if you are your own choice."

Horseshoe Shirt pats Patrick on the back a few times. "You're one of us, man," he says in a friendly way. From his underarm comes the waft of artificial cedar.

The Arm gives him a tight smile. "Don't shoot," he says, lifting his hands up in mock surrender. "Messenger."

The waitress comes up with a tray carrying three bottles of WAT-R, each one molded into a faceted shape resembling a diamond, indicating its premium quality. California sunlight shimmies through the hard plastic, pale and golden at the same time, casting a pattern of dancing light on the bistro tabletop, like the bright mottle at the bottom of a swimming pool. She places the bottles on the surface in front of them. Slowly, one by one, she opens each bottle and sets the caps together on the far end of the table. She picks up the bottle in front of Patrick and pours it into his drinking glass. She does the same with the other two bottles and glasses. The WAT-R tumbles in, cold and transparent and odorless. She looks at the three of them sitting in silence and walks away, toward another table.

In the back of the Arm's dinged-up four-door sedan, Patrick searches on his phone for the email his agent sent him, the one with the contract attached. The subject line is *Re: Hello!* and the only text is a phone number, his agent's, so that he can call if he has any questions. He opens the contract searching for something to prove him right, but what it says is little different from what the Arm relayed at the poolside bar, where he had drunk so much gin-and-tonic that the generic techno piped in through hidden landscaping speakers lost its shape, turned to mush in his ears. As he reads, the terms of the agreement feel familiar to him, but far removed. "Approval-blind script consult," he reads, and "standard etiquette budgetary maneuvers." He remembers some of the phrases from that first read, but they don't sound as hopeful this time around. He thinks back to that first day, opening the contract, reading that term, "production assistant," and feeling such a shiver of pride that he had to put the document down and pace around the house to manage his excitement. He phoned his wife.

"Isn't that a job for a kid?" she asked, over the sound of trampoline springs squealing in the background.

"They're called PAs," he replied.

"I don't know, Patrick. You tried to break a book contract once because you didn't like the paper they were going to print it on. I think you like to be involved."

"That's what I'm saying," said Patrick. "They want me involved. On set."

There was a long screech, accompanied by a loud and violent thumping.

"What was that? It sounded terrible," he said.

"Nora just did a backflip on the trampoline. Everyone was clapping."

"If you think I should stay here at home, just say so. I don't mind. I'm sure I can give them my guidance on some things over the phone," he said, grouchily.

But Alison hadn't put up much of a fight after all. After that brief phone call in the middle of Nora's gymnastics class, the question never really came up. Patrick had signed the contract, and Nora had learned how to do her backflip on the springy, ultramarine-blue tumbling floor. Almost a year had passed since that conversation, enough time for the studio to contract out the adaptation, put together a crew, and secure a soundstage to film in—but when he stopped to think, it seemed clear that whatever was eating Alison now, making her so inexplicably sad and distant, had been nibbling even then. Though she said normal Alison things, poking at him in her invasive, cottony tone, there was a lag to everything, a second meaning, a thing she wasn't saying that only occasionally slipped out. That night, he heard a long pause on the line, followed, unexpectedly, by a burbling sound, like a small amount of water running over rocks. Patrick realized that Alison was crying. "She's so happy, Patrick," she said through a scrim of tears. "Why do I feel like she's the happiest she'll ever be?"

The city viewed from the highway has little to do with the place he had seen on the ground. It resembles an old photograph, colors faded, with a swath of flat gray rooftops close to the highway, a sea of smaller homes and buildings with reddish, quirkily tiled roofs in the middle ground. Neighborhoods pool at the base of the brown hills in the distance; tiny modernist structures stud the slopes and peaks, swaddled by smog. It looks like a diorama, three different strips of cardboard painted and stood upright to form a realistic landscape, each successive piece rendered a little hazier than the one before, articulating how vast the distance is between where they had been and where they are going. The smooth, synthetic edge of the seatbelt digs gently against Patrick's throat as he plugs Cassidy Carter's name into the search field and discovers, to his surprise, that she's starred in over twenty movies, many so famous that he recognizes their titles, though he has never actually seen any of them. He learns that she has a sister named Juneau and a father who used to sell farm equipment—the stationary kind, like silos—

until he left them all behind to try for a music career in Nashville. He learns that she was paid $195,000 per episode of *Kassi Keene: Kid Detective,* which made her the world's highest-paid child star until the end of the show's five-season run. There's a photo of her from a profile published to coincide with the show's finale—she's dressed as a sexy Sherlock Holmes, lounging on a gigantic red velvet question mark. "Who Killed Kassi Keene?" the headline reads. "It Was Miss Carter in the Studio Lot with the Hot New Film Career!"

In the front seat of the sedan, the production kids make loose, sporadic conversation, like old friends. They do each other small kindnesses: the Arm fixes the A/C vents so the cool air blows with greater precision upon Horseshoe Shirt's glistening forehead; he in turn unwraps a stick of gum the exact color and shade of a fresh tennis ball and pushes it into the Arm's mouth as he drives, both hands on the wheel, maximally alert and responsive. When the flavor has left, Horseshoe feels around on the floor for an old receipt and holds it patiently before the still-chewing mouth, waiting for the Arm to deposit his cud before tossing the little packet out the passenger-side window. All around them, the cars crawl forward fitfully, incoherently, first one lane and then another, never in unison.

"Wow," says the Arm. "I would give anything to be able to just zoom up and over all this traffic right now."

"Everyone would be gazing at you," says Horseshoe, "in wonderment."

"Remember that scene from *Back to the Future Part II* where Doc shows up in the DeLorean and then it lifts off from the ground like a spaceship and the wheels retract and it jets off into the future? Like a spaceship?"

"They would be taking videos on their phones, selling them to *TMZ*. Buying Kawasaki motorcycles and vacation packages to Los Cabos. Statues of lions and horses for their backyards. Et cetera."

Horseshoe lights a cigarette and sticks his arm out an open window and into the sunshine. Talk radio filters through the air from a Honda Civic on the passenger-side flank of the car. Today's program is about violent encounters with wildlife on the fringe of urban spaces. One of the guests is a mother of three who was attacked by a pack of raccoons while trying to return a pair of sneakers to a local Foot Locker just after closing. "They took the box from my hands and began pawing through it. They chewed at the brand detailing, the little swoosh. I think it was because of the leather scent they spray in these things, just too completely real. But if it can fool a wild animal, it must be a high-quality product." The driver of the Civic is female, in her twenties, with a lime-green streak in her hair. When she looks over, Horseshoe smiles at her and waves with his cigarette hand. She looks away.

"Do you know why we have traffic?" the Arm asks suddenly.

"There are too many cars," Horseshoe says, in a sad tone.

The Arm shakes his head, gazing out the window at small plumes of smoke in the distance, on the occluded face of the yellowing foothills. "It's because nobody can see the whole picture. There's enough road for all the cars to move along smoothly at the same speed, but even if we understand this at a rational level, we can't do anything with the knowledge. Our default is to behave as self-interested individuals. Sometimes we work against that principle and defer to another driver, but even that's just a variant on individualistic behavior. When you slow down to let someone merge in, you contribute to the worsening of the whole." He nudges the gas pedal. The car lurches forward three feet, and then rolls down to a near halt.

"Altruism is no escape. Only an exhaustive revolution could hope to alter the scale of daily existence," says Horseshoe, searching the glove compartment for more gum.

"Sometimes there are crashes. Fender benders. People lose their lives," says the Arm thoughtfully. "The victims long for a better world, a world in which the cars pass serenely in discrete space and all conflicts are indefinitely deferred. A car crash challenges scale directly. Self-driving cars were the industry's answer to that challenge, but the consumer experience wasn't in demand. The average person would rather retain control and believe themselves lucky than take on a statistically smaller risk, governed by the probabilistic Other." He puts on his signal and lurches suddenly, violently, into the right lane, the sound of horns swarming around them, muted by the chassis of the car, which shields them and holds them tight. "People don't want to place their trust in their vehicle; they want the sensation of silky, effortless agency."

"You can't repair an appetite, you can only feed it or ignore it."

"To go from one stage to another requires passage through an ungainly middle space. In this middle, human-driven cars crash into computer-driven cars, computer-driven cars crash into human-driven cars—either way, they kill the humans inside. When change happens, we want it to happen all at once. In transit, there's catastrophe."

"Catastrophe is incomplete change," says Horseshoe casually, fishing a cigarette out of the pack and tucking it behind his ear. "Change is violent for those who arrive to it late." He swivels around and offers up the opened pack to Patrick, who doesn't even notice the gesture. "The safest thing would be to remain perfectly still," he says, shrugging as he untwists, "and let the future simply arrive."

Patrick is texting Alison: *Almost at the hotel. California is paradise. These guys from the film company are genuine West Coast stoners. Call you when I'm finally alone.* He looks up from his phone, eavesdrops on the conversation for a second, and looks back down. He searches *Cassidy Carter net worth,* then *Cassidy Carter arrests.* He feels oddly unable, for some reason, to interpret the results. Is $850K a lot of money? Is three a lot of arrests? Between the lurching movement of the vehicle and the impassivity of the hills in the distance, he feels a little like he's out to sea, bobbing in a lifeboat as his body bakes beneath the heavy sun.

"I wrote a script in college about an alien invasion," the Arm says. "Small crablike creatures attach to the neural centers of cheerleaders. It begins as a slasher flick—people die in creative and ironic ways—but when the takeover is complete, it becomes a quiet, peaceful sort of thing. Then it's a movie for the aliens, full of colors, lights, moving shapes, and warm, buzzing sounds. But as long as a single human being is alive, its genre is horror."

"Was your script any good?" Horseshoe asks.

"It wasn't."

"I could see it getting made. Elle Fanning as the Last Girl. Tessa Thompson as a brilliant, corrupt scientist. Tony Hopkins as a human possessed by the alien queen."

"Thanks, man. It means a lot to me to hear that," says the Arm.

"You gotta have faith. That's why we make such heavy sacrifices, man, because we have faith in the art form. In the product. In the industry. In the ephemeral rendered luminously concrete. It's the machinery of dreams."

"But *do* we have faith in the industry? Is it a blind faith, based on nothing more concrete than the faith of other blind people who assure us that there is something there to see, if we could only see it? Is it a false faith, the belief that we who make fifteen dollars an hour will someday employ others for fifteen dollars an hour?"

Patrick looks up sharply from his phone, too sharply. Reading in a moving vehicle turns his stomach; there's a tilting feeling somewhere inside his head.

"Wait, what do we make an hour?" he asks, concerned.

"About fifteen dollars," says Horseshoe.

"My parents buy vegetables for me when they come to town," says the Arm.

Patrick stifles a groan. "What is this job?" he asks. "Is it skilled labor? Do you manage others? Do you make decisions?"

"At this stage in our careers," says Horseshoe, "I think the most accurate thing would be to say that we are managed by others and make only the simplest decisions, the sort of decisions no one else cares about. But, obviously, nobody can know, ourselves least of all, what our futures may hold in store."

Patrick grimaces and rests his head against the curve of the window. Pressed against the cool, firm glass, he stares out at the vestiges of Hollywood, far away now and muffled in haze. The sky is blue but diluted by a grayish, brownish undertone that can be found everywhere and nowhere at once—like the halfhearted presence of his wife and daughter over text or phone, like the internet, like DDT, banned in the United States but increasingly prevalent in South America, Africa, Asia. Like the omnipresent Cassidy Carter: an ambient mechanical whine coming from somewhere deep within the house that, once heard, can never again be unheard. The production kids drone on in front, talking about the fundamental correlation of the internal-combustion engine to the film projector. In the surrounding lanes of traffic, the other cars seem to move backward and forward randomly, pointlessly, going nowhere. He can't tell whether the van is moving or sitting still, but he knows that whatever is happening upends some organ deep in his torso. He is light and heavy, sunburny and chilled, dizzy and pulsing and empty like a balloon. High overhead, a hawk hangs in the air, frozen in place, as though the fact of atmosphere were only a theory, a lie. He realizes suddenly that he needs to get out of the car.

"Pull over, it's an emergency," he says weakly.

"It's a catastrophe!" says the Arm cheerfully.

"Pull over on the shoulder, or get off the highway?" Horseshoe asks, sounding concerned.

"I don't know," mumbles Patrick, his eyes squeezed shut.

The turn signal goes on, and the sedan begins its slow meander into the rightmost lane. At the side of the road, pink hibiscus in bloom. Patrick lies horizontally in the back seat, his arms crossed, trying to fit the curves of his body into seat troughs designed to cradle upright, individuated asses. He stares straight up at the car's nubby beige ceiling, tries not to think about his mouth filling uncontrollably with moisture, trying not to notice the emergency feeling growing louder like an approaching siren. Has anyone ever drowned in their own saliva, choked on it, maybe while asleep? he wonders, as the car rounds lazily through the off-ramp and pulls into the first available outlet, a large and desolate Mexican-restaurant parking lot. They slow to a stop near the turn-in, and Horseshoe gets out. The scent of parched and sunstruck vegetation fills his nostrils, and he inhales deeply with a satisfied look on his face. Then he opens the back door for Patrick, who crawls out onto a patch of vividly, electrically green grass near the front entrance and dry-heaves behind the geraniums.

"He should do child's pose," says Horseshoe, stubbing out his cigarette and lighting another.

"He should try chewing on something tough and low-calorie," says the Arm thoughtfully. "Maybe a twig."

As the kids loom above him, smoking, Patrick pulls himself into a fetal position on the ground. He wraps his arms around his middle-aged knees and tucks his head in, closes his eyes tight. It smells like mulch and quesadilla, and the clean, dry odor of the prickly lawn. He rocks gently back and forth. The sun has started to set, and the brownish tinge takes fire, igniting reds and oranges and pinks that defy summarization. Now when he closes his eyes, the fleshy red color has become even redder. The beauty of a sunset comes from the distance the light must travel in order to reach the eye of the one observing it: the greater the distance, the more encounters that light has with air particles, scattering and shifting the visible wavelength away from the familiar blue and toward exotic, desirable colors. When the breeze blows in just the right direction, Patrick can smell the scent of flowers—detergent from a laundromat across the street. Tapping their cigarette ash out onto the concrete below, the production kids stare into the sunset, squinting, shielding their eyes. They watch the indescribable colors burn over the sky, not even trying to describe them.

Off Highway 210, at the base of a hill blanketed in ivy and eucalyptus, the Hacienda Lodge offers beds and motel breakfasts to out-of-towners unfamiliar with the layout and geography of Los Angeles County. In front of the door to Room 213, Patrick slides his key card in and out of the reader at varying speeds. The reader blinks red, and then red again. The night is surprisingly dark here, despite the nearness of the highway, and the parking lot is a sea of available spaces. When the door swings open at last, it reveals two queen-sized beds a foot apart, a chair upholstered in green performance plush, a TV with no remote. The room has a yellow cast: pale-dun paint on the walls, ochre carpeting, and on each bed a quilt patterned in floral butterscotch. Through an open window in the bathroom, the whine of cars passing by at high speed mingles with the dry, green, medicinal scent of silvery trees.

Patrick lets his body fall backward onto one of the beds and lies there with his arms by his sides like a patient in a hospital bed. Of all the things that bother him about this day, the one that stings the most is the feeling of being nobody in particular, just a man middling through his forties with a body of middling fitness and three books that no one on this coast ever inquires about. Maybe this is why people have families, he thinks, so that every day, at least once, they can walk into a room and feel known by every person in it. He conjures a memory, or is it a fantasy, of home—he's with the two of them on the couch, he's tickling Nora and she's laughing brightly in slow motion, and

Alison joins in, and they laugh together for what feels like forever. It feels so real, but in actuality Nora hates to be tickled. His feet still sweaty in his leather shoes, he digs the phone out of his front pocket and calls Alison. His mood sinks a little more as he listens to the phone ring and ring and then go to voicemail. *You've reached Alison,* says the recording in a miniature version of her voice. *Do I want to be reached?*

In the bathroom, he turns both faucets, but nothing comes—only a faint scraping sound from the rotating fixtures. Crouching, he opens the cabinet beneath the sink and finds a vacated space: the pipes end abruptly; their open gullets gape above a little upright notice from the hotel, informing him that WAT-R pods are available for guest rental at an additional fee, inquire at the front desk, installation not included. He thinks he remembers seeing an article about WAT-R pods a year or so back, when California switched over from the old webwork of mains and pipes to the new, privatized system—but he can't recall whether he actually read it. Insect song blares through the open window, and he wonders if maybe his situation isn't as depressing as he thinks: he may just be dehydrated, overheated, unable to see it all clearly.

In a men's exercise magazine, he had read that hypohydration comes with a slew of mental side effects: slowed or faulty reasoning, false memories, hypersubjective judgment. The article warned that you should never make a major decision about personal relationships or employment while under-hydrated. An hour before exercising, an adult male should drink one twelve-ounce glass of water, then another one fifteen minutes before beginning the warm-up. In the first twenty minutes of activity, at least two small glasses of water should be downed quickly, and then one sixteen-ounce glass for every following hour of sustained physical activity, plus more for unusually hot or dry conditions.

On the dresser next to the TV sits an extra-large bottle of WAT-R *Pure*, WAT-R's downscale diffusion line. Unlike the bottles at the hipster hotel—thick, expensive plastic bullied into the many-faceted shape of a gem—this bottle is like any other: only the WAT-R logo in cool Helvetica remains the same. The price tag reads $4.50. Patrick twists off the cap and slopes the bulky object upward. The cheap plastic caves beneath his fingertips as smooth, clear WAT-R, the exact and mediocre temperature of his motel room, slides deep into his throat, leaving behind a stale taste, like ice that's been too long in the freezer.

He sits on the foot of his bed with the bottle between his knees and calls Alison twice. On the other line, someone picks up. There's a loud, close sound, something being rubbed over the mouthpiece. Silence, and then Alison's voice, tentative, asking "Hello?" as if it were a question.

"It's me. I called earlier," says Patrick. Hearing his own voice, he realizes that he is more annoyed than he had thought.

"Oh. I'm sorry. How long ago?"

"It doesn't matter," he says.

"Okay," she replies. He can't tell if she's annoyed at his annoyance or if, on the other hand, she is not annoyed, not thinking about him at all.

"So—I landed safely. Two kids who work for the production company picked me up. I don't think they have much access to what's going on with the picture; I'm saving my questions for when I meet with the producer tomorrow."

"Oh," she says. "All right."

"These kids, you know, they like to speak about everything as if they know all about it, but I can't imagine anyone showing them the budget for the film, asking them if it all looks right. I can't imagine anyone even telling them who the VIP they're picking up at the airport is, what his job title is—they're nice kids, but you can tell they're not in any position to see the whole picture. I have to say, it's getting on my nerves, and it's only the first day. Well, I can't complain about being driven around. There's so much traffic here it makes you want to crash your car. At least the weather's nice. It's a pure blue sky. No clouds."

"I don't know," says Alison distractedly. "I've always liked clouds. You watch them change and grow and move across the sky. They turn the sky into a sort of entertainment, like theater or cinema, when you get to know the common types they're like characters showing up again and again. My favorite was always cirrus. Ever since I was a kid."

Patrick doesn't reply.

"Patrick, are you there?"

"Yeah, I'm here," he says.

"Cirrus clouds. Do you know what I mean? Like soft, gauzy scraps of cotton wadding, stretched thin and drifting through the sky. I made some for a class project once, it must have been fourth grade. I used two whole boxes of Q-tips."

He flops back on the motel bed and exhales loudly. In the weeks leading up to this trip, he had tried to show Alison movies about Hollywood, about writers going to work in the film industry and detectives tracking down the murderers of beautiful women strangled in the hills, had sent her real-estate listings for Modernist mansions with pools and topiary perched precariously in the brown steepness. He bought Nora a book about glamorous actresses of yesteryear, hoping her fascination with historical disasters past might be cultivated into something broader, a fascination for the industry and the state where he could already almost see them living, laughing together and soaked in sunlight. The idea of a future in California, with a swimming pool and a full-sized trampoline on which Nora could hurl herself upward into the cloudless sky, seemed more real to him the closer he came to the date of his flight: his daughter could go to school with the children of Kardashians, his wife could restore her frayed nerves, become one of those women in vintage kimonos who wear their hair in a waist-length braid. But neither of them took an interest, or even seemed to notice what he was trying to do. He felt like a man slaving away, uncelebrated, digging for lost treasure in the un-marked desert.

"Can you just pretend that you care about what I'm doing here?" he says. "I'm living a literal adventure, and you make me feel like I'm sitting alone at home, imagining it all."

There's a pause on the line, and when her voice comes back it's his Alison again, more alert, more familiar.

"I'm sorry, I didn't realize you were feeling this way," she sighs. "You know how it's been for me lately, everything so blue. It's hard to wrap my head around the idea that something good could happen. And I'm not sure how the movie world works, but I know this is really exciting for you. And I'm proud, believe me. Nora is too."

"Thank you, that means a lot," says Patrick, and it's true, he feels a bit better.

"It's not your problem, Patrick," she continues. "It's really not. I know there've been times I made you worry. That thing about the lawn—I know that was so bad."

He remembers Alison on the lawn in her pajama pants and sleep tee, and shakes his head sharply, as if to make the image less clear.

"I don't know if you can understand what it's like," she says, her voice growing quieter, taking on a pale tone. "I know I've said this before. But I look out the back window of our house and I don't see the park or the trees. I see all of it dying. Part of me knows it's not—'dying' is the wrong word for it—but another part can look out and see a place that's already dead. You see? I look at Nora and I know there's no future for her, and it tears my heart in two. And what makes me feel crazy is that all around me, everywhere, people are driving cars and buying propane grills and eating double cheeseburgers, and not one of them acts like they're dying, even though they are. Not one of them sees what I see, and that means we have no chance."

"Listen," says Patrick, tense and urgent, "just listen to yourself. If you heard someone else saying this, your sister or Nora or me, what would you tell them? You would tell them to get help. To go see someone."

"Or maybe I'd listen to them. Maybe I'd think about whether there was any reality to what they were saying."

Some background chatter comes over the line. He can hear her covering the microphone with her hand, talking to someone else.

"What is that?" Patrick asks. "Who are you talking to?"

"It's Nora," Alison replies offhandedly, her mind elsewhere. "She's asking me if she needs to pack a puffy coat."

Suddenly, Patrick feels nervous. He stands up, walks to the front of the motel room, nudges the curtain aside, and stares out at the lone car at the far end of the lot below, sitting with its lights on and windshield wipers running, though there isn't a drop of water in sight, the blades whipping blindly back and forth.

"Pack for where?" he asks. "Where are you two going?"

When Alison answers, she answers slowly. She may be trying to reassure herself as much as him. "I'm taking Nora with me on a nature retreat. It's sort of a, I don't know, support group. You know, the exact thing you think I need."

"Well, where is it? What's it called?" He's raising his voice now, which she won't like. "How far away is it? And, Alison, how are you even going to get there? You don't drive."

"I *try not* to drive," she says. "And there are so many ways to avoid it—you can bike, you can carpool, you can take the bus all the way to the shopping center. But you know I used to drive an hour each way to that vet clinic outside of Philadelphia before I had my own practice. And it's just for a few days, while you're out of town. I don't want you to worry," she says in a soothing tone.

"I'm worried," he says.

"You don't need to be. It's a well-known place. They have a website."

"Well, that makes me feel better," he says sarcastically. "Does this place also have a name?"

"Earthbridge. It's called Earthbridge."

"That sounds ominous. A bridge from Earth to where?"

"I'll give you the phone number," she sighs.

Through the bathroom window, which he discovers is not

just open but missing a pane, the sweet, wet scent of night-blooming jasmine forces its way into the room. Out on the ivy-covered slope behind the Hacienda Lodge, rodents scurry up and down through the ground cover, causing the broad, dark leaves above them to jerk violently from side to side. Patrick punches the number his wife gave him into a search engine, but nothing comes up. Then he enters just the area code alone. Upstate New York, far upstate, near Oswego. Near where Cassidy Carter shot her first starring feature at age nine, a feel-good comedy set at a summer camp where all the adult counselors have been taken prisoner by a band of drug smugglers and young Cassidy has to assume the role of leader, directing a horde of preteens to hunt, forage, and scavenge for food. What was that movie called again? He takes another long swig from the plastic bottle at his bedside and then falls asleep with his mouth open to the dry, chill air. All through the night and through his formless dreams, strange sounds emanate from the hills behind the motel, sounds that could be cries of pain but could just as easily be laughter.

In the photographs posted online, the restaurant is enchanting: shady and cool in a land of so much sunlight and bare, exposed skin. In one photo, a close-up of a whole spatchcocked quail, grilled with preserved kumquat, is set against a colorful salad of shaved fennel, caraway seeds, and smoked juniper berries. The body of the quail is fragile and precise, like a tropical flower. Small crooked wings and glossy drumsticks encircle a vacated center, where the guts have been extracted with the tender skill of a model-airplane hobbyist. Past the tight-focus food, the background is a murk of charcoal grays and moody blues, indistinctly stylish. In another photo, a gray granite bar slopes a mellow S, bordered on one side by a line of gleaming gold-tone Art Nouveau barstools, on the other by a wall of artisanal tequilas reaching all the way up to the vaulted ceiling. At the right side of the image, individual dining tables in dark wood and oiled metal are cast in somber window-light and shadow, like a Vermeer painting of a high-end gastropub. In reality, the place feels like a cave: dark and in-set, with a guillotine of expensive brass lights dangling overhead.

Patrick sits in the corner of a large, steep-backed booth upholstered in cerulean velvet, with two brand-new copies of his novel *Elsinore Lane* on the table before him. He's tall enough, five foot ten, which is almost six feet, but the booth is designed to make all guests feel small and weak, regardless of their size or body type. The tufted back rises up over his head, culminating in a forward-curving cushion that pushes his head down slightly, forcing him to slouch. On the way here, his rideshare had gotten stuck in traffic, and he had spent most of the trip trying to think of how he'd play his tardiness off to Jay Arvid and Brenda Billington, the film's executive producers. Lateness, a sign of irresponsibility, could be transformed into a sign of power under the right circumstances: What if he was late because he had to take an important call from his agent? What if he had traveled farther, say from Malibu or Venice Beach, where he had been meeting with a celebrity film editor that he might want to bring on board? What if he had been on the phone with his family, a diligent and beloved father, handling one of their problems from afar?

But instead he had shown up only a few minutes late to find the restaurant nearly empty, the only people in the dining room the waitstaff and hostess, staring into the bottomless depths of their smartphones, exchanging short, flirtatious jokes that made him feel invisible. It had been forty minutes already, and Patrick was devoting himself, now, to thinking about how he might play off his earliness. What if he, too, had only just arrived a few minutes ago? What if, on entering, they found him immersed in a phone call that he wrapped up, graciously, before greeting them with a strong slap on the back? A half-hug handshake? With a raised hand toward the waiter, he requests another plate of bread and olive oil.

Arvid and Billington arrive, greeted by the maître d', the slender hostess, the bread sommelier, and the waitstaff by the door, all wishing them well. It's impossible to see them, but Patrick infers where they are from the direction in which the black-trousered bodies of waiters are turned. He's looking for the face that came up on the image search, a soft-necked man with an angular nose and a gentle chin, but the man who emerges from the throng of restaurant staffers has a more chiseled appearance. His neck has the tanned, sinewy heft of an artisanally crafted hatchet, something sold with its own hand-worked leather carrying case. He reminds Patrick of someone famously good-looking, some interchangeable leading man or a smooth, liquid blend of them all. First he thinks of Gerard Butler, then Edward Norton, then Russell Crowe, though looking at the face before him makes it harder to call any other face up for comparison. In a few seconds, Jay Arvid, who actually happens to be exactly six feet though he looks even taller, is standing next to Patrick, hoisting him up to his feet for a combination handshake-backslap. Behind him is Brenda, hair silky and mink-colored and wearing oversized red plastic eyeglasses affixed to a chintzy gold chain, the privileged art-school daughter of somebody extremely powerful. She holds her slender white hand up and gives Patrick a little wave, though she is close enough for a handshake, if she wanted one.

"So glad we could do this," says Arvid in a way that sounds both offhand and heartfelt. "It's such a pleasure to meet the author."

"It's not every day that we have dinner with a writer," says

Billington. "I guess Jay and I will have to watch our sentences. Not to give too much away, but there's a fourth coming tonight. It's a big surprise."

Billington orders red wine for the table; then Patrick calls the waitress back and asks for some water.

"WAT-R?" asks the waitress, looking from Patrick's face to Jay's to Brenda's. "No problem."

Wine glugs from the bottle. The three of them toast. Patrick toasts with WAT-R. He misjudges the rim of the hand-blown glass tumbler and ends up with WAT-R down the front of his button-down. Everything feels like it's happening at 1.5x speed, a phantom finger on the fast-forward button, dragging the scene ahead to its action point. He lifts the glass up to the light to check for holes or leaks, but all he sees are the overhead lights shifting back and forth in mottled clarity. The ice has settled in a heap at the bottom of the glass, and this seems strange to him. He tries to think of another time when he's seen this happen, but he's coming up empty.

"Don't worry, it won't bite," Brenda says, eyeing him. "You don't have much of this stuff on the East Coast, do you?" Her delivery makes him self-conscious.

Patrick takes two quick gulps and sets the glass down on the table.

"So, Hamlin. I have to tell you," says Arvid warmly, leaning toward Patrick. "When I picked your book up for the first time. I turned it over and read those words on the back. 'A ghost story,' it said, 'written in family blood.' It sent shivers down my back. What an amazing tale."

"Thanks so much," says Patrick, taking a gulp of wine. "That line was from the *Times* review."

"Ghost stories are sure bets in our industry," says Brenda, nib-bling at a piece of bread. "Audiences like them. You know there's never going to be a ghost hanging around someplace for a bor-ing reason. Where there's a ghost, there's a story."

"Well, I don't really think of the novel as a ghost story, I sup-pose," Patrick says. As he speaks about his work, he gains mo-mentum. "Or . . . it's a ghost story in the sense that *Hamlet* is a ghost story—in other words, not so much. I was really writing from personal experience—coming back to my hometown after my father passed away, finding that my mother was already be-ginning a new relationship. How quickly one's childhood is swept away by the foundation of an adulthood, hastily assem-bled. How the lifelong quest to surpass one's father is thrown into disorder by an untimely passing, leaving a life without cen-ter, without endpoint. The hurt of all that. You could say that ghost stories are fundamentally about the past, about unearth-ing a buried trauma and setting it to rest. I see my novel as an exploration of how the memory of a person, which is like a ghost in its way, can live on in the present and the future."

"Hmmm," says Brenda.

"A story with real sequel potential if I've ever seen one. No, I'm serious," Jay says, chuckling. "Maybe we'll just keep you out here with us for the long haul, you can move your family west, et cetera."

"I still haven't seen a copy of the script," says Patrick casually. "I don't know if you need me to, you know, sign off on it or anything. I'd just be curious to see what your screenwriter has done with the book."

"Do we need him to sign off, Jay?" Brenda asks, warmly. "On the changes our screenwriter made? I don't think so, right?"

Jay shakes his head.

"So maybe he can just scrounge up a copy of the script around the office?" Brenda asks. "Sometime next week? I'm sure there'll be an extra one lying around when somebody isn't using it."

The two nod at each other enthusiastically.

"How are you enjoying California?" asks Jay, warmly, turning to face him.

"I think there are coyotes living in the hill behind my hotel," replies Patrick, distracted. "In the middle of the night they cry out—they sound like hurt children."

"They sure do," says Brenda.

Jay nods. "It's how we live here, I suppose, pressed up against the underbelly of the wilderness. Just last month, a deer drowned in my swimming pool. No, really. We like to joke that we should have put the pool cover on."

"You can't blame yourself for everything bad that happens in the world, Jay," Brenda replies with sudden tenderness, placing a hand on his hand. "The world is a place where terrible things just *happen*."

She stands up unexpectedly, waving toward the mouth of the restaurant. Patrick can see that something has changed in the room. Though no one turns or stares, their bodies gravitate toward the unseen figure making her way through space dense with servers and hostesses and wait-listers angling for a table, the way the limbs of trees, bent subtly in the same direction, reflect the passage of wind and sun. Her presence makes actors of them all, as they set about doing the exact thing they had been doing before, carefully ignoring the focus of their attention. She parts the throng in a tissue-thin sweater and white jeans, the knees carefully and expensively torn. It's Cassidy Carter, her hair like a doll's and her face also like a doll's, astonishing in person, like seeing a picture come to life. Under her left arm she carries a pearlescent white motorcycle helmet, the glossy surface scuffed on one side.

"God, I'm so sorry I'm late," she says breathlessly, leaning toward Brenda and grabbing her arm to pull her into a sort of half-hug. "I was at a meeting downtown about doing some ad campaign, and it took forever to get out of there. I'm starving; did you order any apps?"

Jay stands up and envelops her in a hug. "So good to see you, Cass. Glad you could make it."

Patrick also stands up. "Hi," he says, "Patrick Hamlin. Did you come on a motorcycle?"

"No, what?" she says.

"Your helmet," he says.

"It's Chanel." On the helmet's flank, the conjoined "C"s glisten.

"Listen, Cass," Jay interjects, "what are you drinking? Tell the nice man what you want." He gestures at the waiter standing near them, holding a basket of handmade tortillas.

"I'll have a double tequila with soda and a glass of water," says Cassidy, her lips full and precise like the perfectly chiseled mouth of a Roman statue. She eyes the bottle on the table. "And I'll take a glass for a little of that red, too."

"Yes, miss," says the waiter, turning to go.

"Wait," says Cassidy. "I want water, not the knockoff, I want a hundred percent. Do you have anything nice, from Norway or Finland or something?"

"I'll bring you our menu," says the waiter, nodding slightly.

Jay slides into Patrick's side of the booth, and Cassidy slips in next to Brenda. Brenda orders the chaparral-smoked mountain trout, and Cassidy orders the kumquat-grilled quail from the photo. When the waiter gets to Patrick, Jay steps in and orders an elk steak for each of them, cooked rare. "It's his first time here," Jay explains to the waiter. "He doesn't know yet that this is exactly what he wants." When the food comes, Brenda asks if Patrick would be willing to switch places with her. He squeezes out past Jay and lets her in. As Jay leans back against the soft, spongy material of the booth, Brenda leans over and cuts his elk into neat little squares. Under the expensive lamplight, each cube looks like an ounce of blood, fixed in an impossible, unnatural shape. Patrick looks down at his steak. He imagines an elk walking through pine forest at dusk, the soft crush of hoof on pine needles, a gleaming red wedge missing from its back thigh. Cassidy is pulling the legs off her quail and turning the tiny body over onto its back to dismantle.

"So, Cassidy," Jay begins. "We were having this scheduled sitdown with Patrick here, per our contractual agreement, and then Brenda had the idea of touching base with you before the real action begins. We thought we'd combine, make it into a party. What's your mood—are you ready to start shooting next week? We have the table read tomorrow. Want somebody to pick you up?"

"Oh, don't bother, Jay," she says with a smile that flickers a little, like a lighter low on fuel, before blazing into a big toothy grin. "I'll get myself there, no problem. I love driving. And I've been getting up early every day for Bikram, anyway, so it'll be real simple. I love starting the day with a little healthy sweat, to ease out the toxins." She cocks her head and smiles like a sexy mouse.

Patrick looks over at Cassidy: she's sitting as straight as a schoolgirl, her chin tilted just slightly up so that her smooth white neck looks long, like a bird's. In her filmy, sky-blue sweater and her spotless white jeans, she looks earthy and ethereal at once. It's difficult, though not impossible, to square this poised, gracious woman with the feral girl in the video, swinging the jug of detergent like a gladiator's club. He reaches for his glass and gulps down a throatful of WAT-R. The cold liquid presses outward against the soft, inner pink tube like a stone; its mass could choke him, but it vanishes so quickly into the dark below.

"Well, let us know if you begin to feel even a whiff of fatigue and we'll send someone over there with a bottle of water and some Emergen-C, and they'll drive you straight to the office. It's no problem. Maybe Patrick here will do it."

"That's a great idea, Jay," Brenda replies. "Patrick isn't like any other PA. He's a brilliant writer, and, to be blunt, he doesn't have the experience the other PAs do, he'll be clunking around the set. He needs a special task, and Cassidy needs a special assistant. It'll be more interesting for the both of you than some nobody."

Cassidy looks bored. "I'll drive myself tomorrow," she says. "First-day-of-school stuff. I want to show off my car. After that, whatever."

Jay grins. "Then it's settled. Patrick will ferry you to the studio starting next week." He reaches forward and squeezes Patrick's biceps two times in quick succession. "Saves us a bit on payroll, anyway, if we don't need to hire a driver."

Patrick doesn't bother to remind them that he doesn't have a car. Brenda is looking at her phone. Patrick saws furtively at his steak as she types a response, emitting a blur of small clicks and beeps. Then Brenda begins to stand up. "Will you excuse us for a second?" she says to Cassidy and Patrick. "We need to get on a call," she whispers to Jay. The two of them walk away slowly into the crowd, their heads close together.

Alone in the booth, Cassidy looks at Patrick, unimpressed. She sighs and sinks down, gnawing delicately on a miniature quail wing. Her blond hair leaves a staticky golden web on the velvet upholstery.

"So," says Cassidy flatly. "They're fucking."

"Who?" asks Patrick. A moment too late, he realizes she means Jay and Brenda, of course.

"Who else?" she snaps. "Either they're sleeping together, or she's his mom. Cutting up his food. It's bad news for both of us, but worse news for you." She stares at him for several long beats. "How's that steak?" she asks.

"It tastes like it once ate a lot of tough wild roots and grasses," he replies.

Cassidy laughs a loud, flat laugh that he hasn't heard before. "Jay's made me eat that elk steak before," she confides. She grasps her wineglass around the bulb, the widest part, her nails clicking against it. "Now, instead, I do what I want. Listen, when you're the actress, they want to see you eating salads with a knife and fork. It makes you look soft, and that really gets them off. That's why I always make a point of ordering something at the high end of the price range. Something a little cruel that might make your average person feel bad if they took a moment to imagine how it died. This way, you tell them that *they're* the ones who are soft."

She looks down at his East Coast loafers.

"You're *new in town*," she says, sympathetically. Then she tosses back her entire drink. Brenda and Jay come in, their faces sobered, Jay's smile a little less smug. They slide back into their side of the booth. Brenda catches the eye of a busboy and draws a checkmark in the air.

"Are you two ready to go?" Jay asks, a tad grimly.

"Sure, Captain," replies Cassidy cheerfully. "Just one sec."

She picks up the little body of the cooked quail, just four inches long and picked clean except for the pale, slender left breast. In her delicate hand, the quail carcass is the size and shape of a human heart, a tender scrap of life that once darted through carpeting of leaf mulch in search of small bugs and hid for safety in the warm, dark rot of a hollow log. Because of their small brain-to-body ratio, quail are often described as the least intelligent of birds, useful in laboratory experiments because of the relative artlessness of their mental processes and the speed with which they gestate—with small brains and simple bodies, a quail can reach sexual maturity in just six weeks. Quail eggs hatch within sixteen to seventeen days, just a bit faster than the eighteen to twenty-one days in a mouse's gestational cycle: for this reason, the experimental quail is often called "the mouse of birds." But, unlike the mouse, the quail shares the diurnal lifestyle of human beings: it sleeps through the night in a single, unbroken stretch—except during long winter nights, when, like a human being, it sometimes wakes in the middle of the night and falls back asleep.

Jay and Brenda watch with troubled looks on their attractive, successful faces. With the slightest of winks in Patrick's direction, Cassidy brings the quail carcass to her mouth and bites into it firmly—like an apple. From deep inside its body, tiny bones snap softly in two.

In the lobby of the Hacienda Lodge, a metal rack holds rows of instant-oatmeal packets and individually packaged breakfast cereals in the less-fun flavors, like Apple Jacks and Cheerios. A pitcher of 2-percent milk sits next to a pitcher of orange juice, condensation beading on the plastic surface. The coffeemaker is making a sound like a car's engine, but nothing comes out: the pot is as empty as it was five minutes ago. Patrick stands at the waffle station, measuring out batter from a pitcher and pouring it into a Styrofoam cup. He must be hungover, because watching the batter slither out through the spout makes him want to barf. He opens the waffle maker and sprays it with a fine mist of fake butter, then pours in the batter and turns the handle to flip it. In forty-five seconds, the batter is cooked and the machine beeps. It makes a perfect waffle every time.

Last night, he stayed up until four in the morning watching Cassidy Carter's greatest hits:

Camp Do-What-Ya-Wanna, Carter's first lead role, where, in the absence of camp counselors or any other adult authorities, she quickly convinces her eight-to-twelve-year-old peers that the best form of government is not the completely unstructured anarchy that they instinctively pursue but a system of near-total social freedom tempered by collectivized labor and shared chores. In no time flat, she's incentivized the other kids not only to restore the dining hall to pristine condition after an epic food fight, but also to grow basic staple crops in a sunny field adjacent to the campground and assemble a shortwave radio from scavenged parts so that they can contact the outside world.

Happy Birthday, Miss Teen President! features Cassidy as the fourteen-year-old vegan punk-rocker Rousseau Sinclair, who assumes the role of commander-in-chief via an obscure clause in an earlier, legally primary draft of the Constitution. Shortly after her father, mother, and the entire presidential Cabinet are put into comas triggered by eating bad lobster at the inaugural dinner, Rousseau becomes not only the first female president of these United States, but the first person under the age of thirty-five to hold the highest office in the land. Despite some disturbing pro-monarchic undertones to the plot, the movie is a heartwarming ode to the possibility of compromise across political divides, as Teen President Sinclair convinces the House majority leader and minority leader to come together over a Pizza Hut dinner on a bill to ban trophy hunting in the continental United States.

In each film, Cassidy Carter, the blue-eyed outsider with a nose like a beautiful, barely remembered dream, channels her golden-haired optimism into an irresistible, idealistic rallying cry. "This land is our land, and now this skateboard is your skateboard," she tells the crabby, wizened Senate minority whip, as she teaches him how to do an ollie on the somber white steps of the Lincoln Memorial. Patrick wants to be dismissive of it all, but he can't quite muster the cynicism: what red-blooded American doesn't dream of becoming a true believer, a foot soldier for the worthiest cause? But the morning after, he's dry-mouthed and distracted, ideologically queasy, and preoccupied by how many hours of movie he watched in quick, brutal succession the night before. It feels like a hangover, but he drank only a single drink at the restaurant and nothing but WAT-R for hours after.

He still has a couple hours before the production kids show up to drive him to the studio, so he decides to walk to the Starbucks he saw when the rideshare was dropping him off last night, just a few minutes down the road. As he walks, he calls the number Alison gave him. It rings and rings without end, with no voicemail or answering machine to break the rhythm. He's walking away from the hills, toward a white and shining strip of shopping at the end of his line of sight, wavering in the heat. On the newly poured sidewalk, there are no shade trees, and no foliage overhead to deflect the sunlight that presses down on him from above, making his scalp hot and tender to the touch. To his right, small, frail oaks with sparse leaves of uncertain green, girthed like a child's arm and supported by ropes and stakes driven down into the soil. He feels a wooze of lazy despair pass through him, a feeling like suicidal ideation but lacking the specificity. Up ahead, rows of white stucco stores and offices, fading into the distance like a mirage. Though he takes step after step, somehow it doesn't feel like he's getting anywhere at all.

In front of a frozen-yogurt store, Patrick sinks down to the curb and sits there in the shadow of a parked Range Rover. He feels a vein pulsing at his temple; his tongue is cottony and dry. He used the last of the jumbo bottle of WAT-R to wash his face this morning. He needs to buy another. Crouched in this patch of shade, he reaches into his pocket and pulls out his phone. Then he calls the Oswego number ten times in a row, the spinning feeling in his stomach growing as the phone rings on and on. On the eleventh try, someone picks up.

"Hello?" says the voice of a young man, someone in his twenties, maybe.

"Hello?" asks Patrick. "Who is this?"

"Who is *this*?" says the voice on the other end of the line.

"Where are you?" he tries, growing irritable.

"Where are *you*?" says the voice, laughing, like it's a joke.

"Look," says Patrick. "I'm Alison Hamlin's husband. I want to talk to her. Put her on the phone right now."

"Whoa, man," says the voice. "Calm yeself. I just happened to be walking by and heard the pay phone ringing and I answered, as a matter of philosophy I believe in answering a call wherever and whenever it arises. That's how we tend to manage the telephone issue around here—we don't get all territorial about stuff. I don't see Alison around; she must be off in one of the cabins."

"Well, find that cabin and tell her I need to speak to her!" Patrick shouts.

"I'm actually headed out right now for a hike. But, hey, I think I see your kid. Nora, right? Hold on."

The phone receiver drops with a clatter, and Patrick hears the sound of footsteps moving farther and farther away.

"Hello?" he says, to nobody.

Sitting in the parking lot, he watches the cars pull out and drive away. A large green van pulls in and cuts its engine, the sound uncomfortably human, like a death rattle. Then, softly, a voice on the other end of the line.

"Hi?" it says, as thin as floss.

"Nora, is that you?" says Patrick. Hearing her voice is unexpectedly emotional; his throat feels chokey; he's so far from home. "How are you, sweetie?"

"Dad, are you feeling okay? You sound . . . morose, I guess." Nora's speech, crisp and articulate, has often felt a little eerie to him, coming as it did from the mouth of a nine-year-old girl. The horror, he supposed, of waking up one day to find yourself watched by another mind, a mind capable of scrutiny and judgment.

"No, honey, I'm fine. Where are you?"

"In the woods. Up near the thumb of New York State. That's what Mom says."

"What city, Nora?" Patrick presses.

"I don't know, Dad. I'm sorry. I'm not the one who does the driving." Nora's voice is calm, if a little bit confused.

"You two drove there together? How long did it take? Did you feel safe on the drive, or did anything bad happen?"

"It was a normal drive," she says quietly. "I think so. It was long, I guess, longer than I've been on before. Did we do something wrong?"

"No, it's okay. Honey, you need to tell me what you're doing up there. I mean, what's it like?"

"It's beautiful. There's life everywhere. In the morning, when it's still dark, the birds start chirping, and they fill the air with singing, so that when you walk around your ears feel full. Everyone sleeps in these tiny houses or tents. You know when it's time to wake up because the air has a morning smell and it sneaks in through the littlest cracks in the doors and windows. One of the people here has a donkey, and I watch it standing outside in the sun with its eyes closed. I brush the flies off its belly with a long piece of hay I found in the barn. I think it likes that." Nora pauses expectantly. "Life is a wonder," she adds.

"What does Mom do? Where is she now?" Patrick asks.

"She's mourning," says Nora, abstractly. He can tell that she's looking at something off in the distance, he's losing her attention.

"Wait, Nora. This is very important. What does that mean? Are you two safe?"

"Of course we are," says Nora, confused now. "Are *you* safe?"

"What?" Patrick replies.

"Dad, you sound scared. Are you in trouble? Where are you?"

"I'm nowhere," Patrick says, flustered, "I'm just fine."

"No, really, Dad, you have to tell me. What's wrong? Where are you right now? Is there someone there listening, is that why you can't say?"

Nora's voice was annoyingly like Alison's, precise and concerned, careful, like the handwriting on a get-well card. He wondered sometimes whether Nora was really as precocious as she seemed, or whether she only imitated her mother's mannerisms. How, for example, had she learned to flip his concern for her on its axis, so that he was now the one scrambling to assemble a reassuring answer? And what kind of answer could he give without revealing how unmoored he was, how little he understood? He was somewhere in Azusa or just south of it, somewhere in the eastern middle of the sprawl, an hour-plus to the studio, an hour-plus to the airport. There were no exact places in this city, and too much space. Somehow, it took an hour to get anywhere.

"I'm in a parking lot. Near a big grocery store. Completely normal."

"What's happening around you? Are you lost? You sound like I felt when I got lost in the hay maze. When I was six. You remember?" Silence on the phone as she waits patiently for an answer.

Patrick looks around him at the parking lot, incoherently strewn with cars. He sees the thin islands of diluted nature that break the lot into discrete clusters of parking spaces, each strip sown with a few square feet of sod and another sad new tree. The sky overhead is such a deep, pale blue that you could fall right into it. Then, against the background of repeated shapes, strip mall after strip mall, he notices the green van.

A man in a khaki jumpsuit, an employee maybe, is sliding the cargo door open. He leans into the dark interior, and then he's helping an old woman out and onto the asphalt. The woman wears an electric-green sweat suit that matches the van, its color vibrant against the gray-black of the parking lot. Then the man helps another person out, a middle-aged man, and another, a younger woman, all in the same green clothing. Standing near the vehicle, the three are pliant, quiescent. They stare out blankly into the distance at nothing in particular, each in their own, separate direction. The man in the jumpsuit continues unloading passengers: a gray-haired woman, a teenage boy. As they climb out of the van, he wraps an arm around each midsection to help them safely onto the ground—their healthy-looking bodies move with the extreme care and fragility of the very old or the very young. When all nine passengers are unloaded, the driver slams the doors shut. One passenger falls to the asphalt in the shock of the noise and just lies there until the driver lifts her back up to her feet. Patrick realizes with surprise that some of the people in green are young—in their twenties or thirties, not yet his age. The man in the jumpsuit fetches a rope from the trunk of the van. He moves from one person to the next, wrapping their left hands around the rope so that they look, if anything, like they are playing tug-of-war, on the same team, against nobody. He wraps the end of the rope around his own hand securely. Then he leads them all across the vast parking lot, toward the grocery store in the distance.

"Dad?" comes Nora's voice. "Are you still there?"

A retirement home for all ages, he wonders to himself. Or a psychiatric facility on a field trip? The way they cluster, unashamed to be undifferentiated, points to some shared weakness. But the group contains so many different kinds of people, with nothing visibly wrong to tie them together. He can't name what he sees, and it troubles him.

"You really have me worried, Dad," she says.

"No, don't worry, honeybee," says Patrick in a lighthearted way. "I'm just a little dehydrated, that's all. And California's not what I expected it to be. Everyone out here's a little crazy. You get the sense that what's in their head is more real to them than what's out there in the world."

He can almost hear Nora, on the other end of the line, thinking through what he's just said. "Okay," she says solemnly. "Just remember, it's not your fault if you don't strike it rich out there. I learned that during the Gold Rush everyone thought it would be easy to find gold in California just by showing up, but most of the easy gold was gone in the first four years, by about 1852.

People kept moving there because they heard you could reach into the river and pick up a gold nugget, but there wasn't any gold in the river anymore. There was only gold for the people who did hydraulic mining, where they blasted the rock with water to root out all the valuable metal, but it was bad for the rock and for the water and for everyone there who had to drink the water."

"Well, the film industry isn't like the Gold Rush, for about a million different reasons," Patrick responds.

"I'm just saying that you can always come to Earthbridge to be with us. I told Mom you might like it here, and she said maybe you wouldn't feel welcome. I thought that you would feel welcome in any place where we both are, but I guess I don't know," says Nora in a breezy voice. "I have to go now. They're about to start a tutorial on how to shear a sheep. Okay, Dad? They're starting right now."

"Okay, honey. Bye," he says. He thinks of Nora as a toddler, so helpless and so pure, staggering around the little New York City apartment where they had once lived in her bloomers, grasping at loose objects on the coffee table—a drinking glass, a TV remote—and uttering lone syllables in that baby voice still yearning to form itself. When he would pick something up off the high surfaces and hand it to her, she would regard it with an expression of pure, undiluted wonder. In those days, her brown eyes were still hazel, like Alison's.

"Oh no, wait, Nora, I need to talk to your mother—" he says, but she's already hung up.

In the dry swelter of the parking lot, Patrick stares at the green van. Such a calming color, he thinks. Like the emerald hills of Ireland, if someone plugged them into an electrical socket. He feels empty and light and a little hopeless. It occurs to him that Cassidy Carter would know what to do right now, would know exactly how to proceed. But not the real Cassidy Carter—the spunky one from those saccharine but strangely affecting movies. What had happened to the sunny, exuberant girl from all of these films? Had she been destroyed by whatever had come later in her career, or was she still lodged somewhere within, imprisoned and pleading to be set free? What was it President Rousseau Sinclair had said in her filibuster before Congress in *Happy Birthday, Miss Teen President!*—that speech about national unity? "Every one of us leads a double life," she said. "A life of the individual, and a life of the citizen. It is our lives as individuals that bring us so much trouble and so much strife—in that life, we feel ourselves alone, at odds with those around us, troubled by the dreams and desires that feel so essential to us but fail and fail again to find their footing on the steep cliffs of fortune. But there is another life within us, a life in which we are indelibly connected to one another, where our fellow citizens' well-being is tied to our own by a golden thread that I call America. Imagine a shining thread tied to your wrist, a thread that extends to that of your neighbor, and from his to that of his neighbor. And from time to time you feel a tug upon it, a tug from far away, and if you look far off into the distance you know your countryman is there, somewhere, in need of your help. I may only be fourteen going on fifteen, but I know that my life as a citizen connects me to each and every one of you sitting in this room today, and I am proud to call each of you my friend. . . ." It was drivel, of course, but even so there was something to it.

Patrick requests a rideshare to take him back to the left-hand side of the city. For fourteen minutes, he sits on the curb in the parking lot, watching a pixelated image of a car circumnavigate the surrounding roads, turning toward him and sometimes away from him, stopping at unseen traffic signals, sometimes spinning around in circles and flickering for long moments before stabilizing, pointed in the opposite direction. When the driver shows up, he's talking to someone through a headset in a throaty, unidentifiable language. With accidents clogging the 210, and reports of protesters on foot causing disruptions on the 10, he switches to local roads south and then westward, curving back up toward Glendale. Winds are low today, and the fires burn in place.

As they abandon the highway for less-congested local roads, sound-canceling walls give way to strip malls with Spanish signage and residential streets where single-story single-family homes sit square on their lots like the yolk on an over-easy egg. Windows rolled up and air conditioner roaring, he watches the blocks scroll by through glass: families with buckets and sponges out to wash the car with sudsy liquid, tawny-skinned children running barefoot on the yellow lawn. The driver brakes for a thick-braided girl riding her bicycle in loopy figure eights in the middle of the road. In front of almost every house is a bulky plastic WAT-R pod, a sky-blue box the size of a small minivan, positioned close to the road, where it blocks the sidewalk. Once a week, the tanker lumbers down these neighborhood streets, filling the receptacles of families who haven't yet paid to have WAT-R installed in their homes.

When the heat bears down, residents of West Covina fill spray bottles from the pod out front and relax beneath a backyard awning with the front door open and the back one open too, inviting the breeze to wander into their homes and out the other side. In the shade of a patio umbrella, the grandchildren take turns holding the bottle and squeezing the trigger, pointing the plastic nozzle at Grandmother's face, spritzing her with fine, cool mist. With her eyes closed, she lets her mouth fall open in relief, sighing so deeply that she feels the bottom of her lungs on the exhale. The mist settles on the surface of her hot skin, her clothing; it clings to her nostrils and enters the lungs and mouths of the children as they bask in the moisture.

As the sun sets, they padlock the pod's plastic spout, safeguarding the week's water from teenagers on bicycles who cruise the neighborhood after dark, seeking free fill-ups and bashing the plastic tankards with sticks or baseball bats or scavenged rebar, reveling in the slap of the weapon and the way its echo cuts through the peace. Some nights, vandals come with box cutters to cut messages into the thick plastic walls of the pods, inscribing their initials or the name of their girlfriend or the words FUCK and YOU. If they work their patience and muscle all through the night, a blade will chew its way through the thick plastic walls, springing the liquid beneath and letting it drain out onto the dark asphalt. In the morning, the renters phone the 1-800 number on their information packets, but all damages to pods on loan from WAT-R Corp are the responsibility of the podholder, and repairs must be done through WAT-R Corp technicians at podholder expense, and unfortunately there are no repair slots available until next week. The WAT-R pools at the base of the damaged structure, forming a moat that shines like an uncertain mirror. At dawn, the rising sun sends a fragile pink light through semiopaque polyethylene and renders the tanks briefly, fleetingly, sublime.

———

In the narrow moat of gravel winding its way around the office building, someone has planted bristling mounds of bush, interspersed by squat cacti and tall, feathery grasses. Patrick doesn't know the names of any of these plants, and it is only in this moment that he realizes how reassuring the soft, fat leaves of East Coast varietals are, their plump shapes a testament to abundance. Alison would know what these are called, Nora too, and he remembers the afternoon he spent planting tomatoes with them just a few weeks ago, in the vegetable garden that Alison started last spring as part of her recovery. Crouching in the wet grass, he jabbed a hole with the trowel his wife had given him, squinted into the dirt at small stones and weird white crumbs. Nora observed him cautiously, complimenting the width of his holes and suggesting that he dig them deeper to stabilize the floppy young stems. He left them to plant the last few after he felt he had seen everything the process had to offer, and as he walked away he turned back briefly to see them undoing his work, Alison pulling the plants up gently and holding the frenzy of dirt-covered roots suspended as Nora worked her small shovel down into the earth.

He wishes they were here now, to render intelligible the unfamiliar building's unfamiliar landscaping, to dilute the out-of-place feeling he sometimes has as a lone man in a place where he isn't certain he belongs. Patrick stares at the arrangement of plants blankly, trying to look absorbed, as Horseshoe—dressed today in a plain chambray button-up—and the Arm head into the building without him. He knows that this first arrival will make an impression in the minds of the producers, director, crew, and he wants to wait outside for a minute or two so that his entrance will register as distinct from that of the production kids, who share his job title but are not at all like him, a creator. It would have been better to enter before them, just a minute before, but the two walk too quickly with their long, lanky limbs. At ground level, small sprinkler heads spurt clear liquid at and around the graveled area, feeding a sea of green, lush grass, expensively maintained and carefully watered, thick and cool to the touch. As he stares at the landscaping, he can't help but wonder what all these plants mean: how much do they cost, is this studio large, is it small, are its finances in good order? When Patrick spots a group of five or six entering the building, clustered like high-schoolers, he slips in behind them.

The room where the reading is taking place is already full, a large square table surrounded by wheeled office chairs. In front of every setting is a bound copy of the script and a bottle of WAT-R. Patrick goes to the table to take the only open chair, but a young woman puts her palm on the seat. "This one is reserved for Cassidy Carter," she says in a voice that is apologetic, but also proud to be saying the famous name. Patrick looks at Jay and Brenda, set apart from everyone in the room, leaning over some papers that nobody else has. He drags a chair in from the periphery, into a narrow space to the right of a kid in his twenties with a short scruff of beard. His own chair is a bit lower, has no wheels, and is bright green, but he can still see everything going on at the table, including Jay and Brenda, still speaking to each other calmly, quietly, but so intently that something seems wrong. Now someone's tapping him gently, insistently, on the shoulder.

"Hey, howdy," says the kid in a low, private tone. "I'm Dillon. I'm the lead male."

He extends a hand, loose and slightly damp. Patrick grabs it too hard, then lets go too quickly.

"I'm Patrick Hamlin. I'm the writer."

"Screenwriter?" asks Dillon.

"No," he says, "I wrote the book they're basing this film on."

"Wow, that's great. You must be a proud papa."

"Thanks, I really am. It's a story that means a lot to me personally, rooted in my experience of family," Patrick replies.

"That's interesting," says Dillon. "I do a lot of realizing other people's material—not really making it 'from scratch,' as they say. I consider myself a sort of midwife, trying to deliver life rather than create it, and as such the creation process is a beautiful mystery to me. What about this story is so personal for you?"

"Well," says Patrick, awkwardly, "I suppose one answer would be that it happened to me. It's based on my life."

Dillon's handsome, untroubled face takes on a furrowed expression.

"I didn't realize it was based on something that actually happened," he says.

"Yes, well," says Patrick, gaining momentum, "you could say the entire novel is a final letter to my father, even though he was no longer with us to receive the message. I began writing the book after he passed away, on my first trip back to my hometown, in Newton, Massachusetts. Massachusetts, as you know, has always been a place where a deep sense of history is imbued in the land, it's practically everywhere you look, and so I began to think about how his presence might still be lingering around our neighborhood in the same way that those traces or scraps of lost history still seem to live in the buildings and streets. New England is a graveyard, a deeply haunted place; you could say the dead are buried seven layers deep. Native peoples, early settlers, young girls who died in childbirth, men who got their hand chopped off at the wrist for stealing turnips from land that was not their own. In the town I grew up in, you see the same names on the street signs as you do in the oldest cemetery—the old names don't disappear. That's the reality, not superstition—and still its inhabitants want to consider themselves ordinary modern Americans living in an ordinary American place. So I asked myself, why does society consider it more egregious to remember those who have gone than to forget them?"

"It sounds like you went through a crazy experience," says Dillon politely.

"I guess you could say that," Patrick responds, though he doesn't really follow.

"Do you watch a lot of horror?" Dillon asks, but before Patrick can reply, or even register the question, the girl saving Cassidy's seat raises her hand.

"Um, Jay? Brenda? I don't think Cassidy's going to make it today," she says, her arm outstretched, holding her phone. Brenda takes the phone, glances at it, and hands it back. She takes out her own phone and begins tapping on it at a furious rate. Over Dillon's shoulder, Patrick sneaks a peek at the girl's screen. It's a photo of Cassidy Carter, posted this morning, showing her beaming in the back seat of a cream-colored convertible, her arms outstretched and head tilted back triumphantly. In the background are a tangle of neon signs and shimmering buildings, all bathed in the rose-gold glow of sunrise. "There's nothing like Vegas at sunrise!!! YO TE QUIERO L.V.! #droveallnight #blessed #vegas #lasvegas," reads the caption. To have arrived in Las Vegas at sunrise, she would have left late last night, after quail and tequila, after telling all three of them how much she loved going to bed early and getting a full night's sleep and then waking up naturally with the first light of morning, which Cassidy had claimed was made of special wavelengths that actually caused the body to generate more collagen. "It's why women who farm, in Greece or Bulgaria, never even need plastic surgery," she had said. "They wake up with the first light of dawn and really soak in that light like a serum. If you could unleash all the energy of the sun to heal your physical body, you might never age. Think about it."

"Listen, everyone, I think we'd better get started," says Brenda, pushing her red eyeglasses up the bridge of her nose. "It seems like Cassidy won't be able to make it today, but she'll be with us bright and early for her fitting and then for principal photography next week." She pauses, and looks at Patrick quizzically. "Weren't you supposed to pick her up today?"

Jay jumps in. "We have Dillon Davies here, which is incredible, let's have a round of applause for Dillon."

Applause eases out mildly, as from a faucet.

"I've said it before, but I have to say it again, your work in *House of the Rising Blood* was—really, though—captivating," Jay adds. He has a way of talking, thinks Patrick, as if people are always trying to interrupt him, but they're not. "So let's just run through it from the top. Dillon, obviously you're Jacob. Brenda, could you fill in for Cassidy? And, Hela, you're the mother." A slender, light-haired woman in her late forties nods.

Patrick opens the script to the first page and begins reading silently to himself, as all around him the movie people say the lines loudly in stolid, theatrical tones. The names are the same, but the story isn't as he remembered. In his novel, a young man named Jacob sees brief and wordless glimpses of his dead father, which cause him guilt and alienate him from his mother and his beautiful ex-girlfriend Libby, who never left town but has waited patiently for him to return through years of college and grad school. Eventually, he begins acting out, and starts a bar fight with his new stepfather, in the course of which an innocent local boy is killed. This script, on the other hand, seems to be some sort of scary ghost movie, where Jacob comes home after his father's death and discovers that everyone he knows has changed in some eerie, ill-defined way. At night, when Jacob lies awake in his foreshortened teenage bed, re-examining the day's events, he peers into his mother's bedroom and finds her asleep, tossing and turning, on the ceiling. She's a ghost, and so is his best friend—even sweet Libby, an ideal love object in every other respect, has become a sort of reluctant demon. Other ghosts do scary things, particularly the stepfather, who, it becomes clear, is turning the people of the town into supernatural baddies and has his eyes set on Jacob—this seems to be more of a vampire thing, Patrick notes, and doesn't really make sense. At the end of the script, Jacob is forced to set fire to all of the other main characters, at which point his dead father's spirit appears to him, nodding approvingly and gesturing that he did a good job.

Patrick had begun writing *Elsinore Lane,* his first novel, when he was only twenty-six—grouchy and half impassioned, about to quit a Ph.D. program in English at Tulane, where he had proposed a dissertation on Shakespearean influences in early North American literature of the South, because he knew a lot about Shakespeare and knew that the program he was applying to was in the South. Toward the end of his second semester in the program, his father had died of a heart attack in the garage while trying to move several large boxes of stored clothing and obsolete appliances in order to get the lawnmower out. Patrick flew back for the funeral, then back to Louisiana to write the final papers for his seminars. That summer, he stayed away from Massachusetts, braised himself for three months in his own sweat in the shaggy heat of his screened-in apartment porch, looking out at the drooping trees. He felt that great scholarship came from the unexpected intersection of leisurely, careful reading and intense feeling, but even though he had lots of time and many reasons to feel, he didn't think anything about literature that summer that he hadn't already thought of before. He rubbed ice cubes all over his face and let the melting liquid drip down, salty, into the corners of his mouth. He knew that his father was no longer in the world, but the world didn't seem much different to him when he looked at it. The weather was the same, the university was the same, the patterns of chatter on the radio as he drove to campus were the same, though they came footnoted by loss. He wondered if some people had a more authentic relationship to reality than he did.

The next summer, he went back to Newton to stay with his mother for three weeks. He had known that she was dating a man now, but was disturbed to discover how real, how invasive the stranger's presence was. His mother's new boyfriend was unlike his father in innumerable ways: He was loud and chatty and made simple, predictable jokes. He was frank about his love for his two college-age daughters but seemed to know almost nothing about their studies, their interests. His every anecdote ended before any sort of punch line was unfurled, and he watched repeats of sitcoms that had long gone off the air and laughed as if the jokes were brand-new—as his mother dozed off next to him on the couch, just as she had done when his father was alive. It was degrading to bike around a town where he had once biked around as a skinny angry teen, depressing to go to the familiar bookstore-café and be recognized or not be recognized; either way it was like being sucked backward into a life too small that had already been lived once before. But what hurt him the most was how naturally his mother seemed to forget that his father had lived at all, and in this same house, with the same couch and refrigerator. His father's death was most real to him when he watched his mother ignore it.

This was not to say that his father was a hard person to forget. That he was easy to forget made it more painful that he had been forgotten, by his wife in particular. His father had always had a beige personality; if it were given a shape, it would be something like a beanbag chair. Patrick sometimes wondered if he had chosen to turn his father into a ghost in the novel, an absent figure appearing in visions to the son and gesturing or mouthing words he could not speak, in order to avoid having to make up a character for him to be. Patrick hated the convention of flashback and backstory as a way to pretend that characters were deeper and richer than they appeared to be in the moment—but if he hadn't hated the convention, he might have included more of his own memories of his father, most of which were ambient and cyclical, things his father tended to do rather than specific things his father had done.

For example, though his father rarely expressed emotion directly, Patrick often thought that he had a deeper, rarer emotionality than almost anybody else he had ever known. He witnessed his father's depth of feeling as an observer, almost a spy, and though these memories of his father feeling things blurred together, they all contained the image of his father in profile or three-quarters view, a remembrance of looking at someone who was looking somewhere else. When he was sitting next to his father, they would gaze silently at whatever was on the TV screen together. They liked episodic TV, detective procedurals where a murder would occur, and end up solved within the course of a single hour, and movies about people trying to do big or risky things. His father teared up during plotlines in which an ex-wife returned to her husband and asked for forgiveness, or an estranged father and son reconciled—emotions that Patrick knew were not displayed in order for him to see them, but which he thought were related to him in some way or another.

Patrick remembered watching a movie with his father about an airline pilot who crash-landed a plane safely in a risky body of water. Though the pilot was celebrated as a hero, the airline decided to sue him, arguing that he had made a dangerous and unnecessary decision to land the plane in water rather than turning it around and heading back to an airport landing strip. The pilot defended himself vigorously and nobly in court. When the court ruled in his favor, he received a standing ovation from the judge and jurors and onlookers—he walked through the cheering crowd and out of the courtroom, modestly nodding his thanks. Patrick turned to his left. Tears were wetting the cheeks of his father, his father wiping at them distractedly. "Dad?" he asked. "What's wrong?" His father turned to him with eyes pink-rimmed and watery. "It's so wonderful," he said. "So, so wonderful. He stuck to his guns and told them all how it really happened. He shoved it all in their fucking faces."

At the bottom of a dry swimming pool in the hills north of Malibu, Cassidy Carter wakes from a shallow sleep, wincing into the sun. She reaches up, her face tender, but not burnt. An inflatable pool-float in the shape of a flamingo squeals softly beneath her tan, angular little body. In other backyards all over this gated community, cerulean swimming pools are filled to the brim with thick, cold, bluish WAT-R, piped in from tankers and endlessly refilled from cisterns in the basements, so that the slow, thick liquid will slosh unceasing against the tiled rims of aqua-colored rectangles, ovals, and edgeless infinity strips. A man with a browned, chiseled face pulls his polo shirt over his head, revealing a body covered in snowy white twists of hair. Children splash one another near the pool steps, as fat, panicked bumblebees drown in the deep end.

But Cassidy's pool is a vacant hole, hard-sided and dangerous, sloped so nothing that falls in stands a chance of getting out. She's woken up to find lame geese resting, head under wing, in an inch of standing water, remnant of last week's ane- mic rain, and baby squirrels trapped and dehydrated, concealing their small bodies under a scattering of dead leaf matter. De- spite all this, she likes the empty pool. A swimming pool was the first thing she told June she was going to buy for them, the day she signed the contract for *Camp Do-What-Ya-Wanna*. It has what her first manager would have called "sentimental value," like the hand-painted good-luck sneakers June made her for her first big movie audition that he made her throw away in the parking- lot trash can because she looked "hicksville" in them. And the paradise-blue paint on the empty trough reminds her of the town she grew up in, where people painted their homes aspira- tional colors, colors that reminded them of vacations they never took. As long as she stays on the shallower end, where the faded turquoise paint still clings to the walls, there are fewer puddles and dead bugs.

Patrick pushes open the heavy Spanish-style door at the entrance to her house and steps into the cool of the foyer. The interior is all light, coldly gleaming—dove-gray stucco on the walls, pale oak for the floors, glacier-colored cushions on an eggshell linen couch—the surfaces unmarked and unloved. At the same time, with thick velveteen curtains drawn across all the windows, the dominant impression is of a vast and unyielding grayness, like a snowy plain viewed on a moonless night. Here by the front door, the house feels unused: in the living room, the plush furniture is staged with empty vases; and in the dining room to the left, twelve dining chairs upholstered in driftwood gray surround a long, empty table. The first feeling that moves through him is relief. He had expected to feel small in a movie star's home, but this expensive, lonesome space inspires as much sympathy as envy. Patrick presses in, past increasingly dark and disordered rooms—a second living room with a single couch in it, a large laundry room disheveled by brightly colored, balled-up clothes, a double-sized kitchen with two ranges and two refrigerators, chilly marble and stainless steel. A lighter and a scatter of light-colored powder on the coffee table. When he gets to the back of the house, he calls Cassidy's name, then opens the sliding glass door and calls again.

"I'm in the pool," comes the muffled reply, nearby and far away at the same time.

Patrick walks over and stares down into the trough at Cassidy Carter in her cobalt-blue one-piece, reclining amidst empty cans of Diet Coke and fallen bougainvillea. At one end of the drained pool, someone has abandoned a mural: flat figures of men and women with unnaturally pink skin dance across a span of pool wall, outlined but not filled in. At the deep end, a soccer ball rolls around in the breeze.

"You're late," she says.

"You aren't even ready?" says Patrick with a frantic note in his voice. "I told Brenda and Jay I'd have you at the fitting in twenty minutes, and it took an hour and a half just to get here."

"I hope they wait for me before they start my fitting," she says with mock earnestness.

"Get dressed," he commands. He almost shouts it.

"I don't think you understand the power dynamic here," says Cassidy. She picks a damp tee shirt up off the painted cement and drapes it over her face. "Come and get me in five. You can help yourself to a soda."

Patrick stalks off toward the house and then stops; he turns toward the pool and away again. His fists are tight white knots. He pulls out his phone, but after a moment he puts it back in his pocket. What was it Jay had said late that night, as they left their now untidy restaurant table and walked out to their cars, Cassidy and Brenda with their arms around each other, walking far ahead? "You're the only person for the job, Patrick. No, really. There's something about you, I think, that bores her a little. Tranquilizes her. Listen, we need someone like you to keep her in line. Smart, experienced, not just some green kid. A dad. I imagine she'll interest you, as a character. It's unusual, sure, but I have a good feeling about you two." Patrick curses Jay silently. Then he walks back to the pool. He doesn't see how she got down there, or how anyone could ever find their way out: the pool goes from deep end to deeper, one side about six feet deep and the other about ten. Each side has a small, chrome ladder and he imagines himself hanging from it, dropping down onto the hard concrete below, and cleaving his ankle in two. He walks around to the shallower side and tests the rungs, then turns and descends one step at a time, the metal slippery against his sweaty palms. When he gets to the part where he should jump off, he waits. A swimmy, vertiginous feeling as his bulk begins to pull him downward, the fear that something in his psyche might lean into the fall.

He looks behind him, and sees Cassidy clinging to the ladder, hoisting herself out of the pool, agile and light and skinny-armed like a lemur. As she slams the back door, he can hear the glass rattle a little within its frame.

When Patrick bursts into the house, he hears that Cassidy's already on the phone.

"Yeah, chasing me and threatening me," she says to whoever is on the line. She glances at Patrick and holds her index finger up, as if to say "One minute."

He waits, his entire face tensed.

"Brenda, what is this? Is this a film? Or is this a kidnapping? Do I deserve to be manhandled in my own home? Does that seem right to you?"

She pauses, listens.

"Of course it disturbs me," she says, sounding unusually professional. "I'm shaken up. I could hardly even hold the phone in my hand to call you. Yes, I know there's voice-activated command—I'm making a point."

Patrick lurches forward, about to do or say something, but she signals, again, that he should stop. Groaning, he collapses on the white leather couch in the second living room, clutching his head between his hands.

"Well, Brenda, I think it's an important time to revisit the terms of my payment, which seem even more essential now under these really traumatizing conditions. You know that I don't fault you for the situation. At the same time, it's definitely your legal responsibility." She nods solemnly and listens for a bit before interrupting. "Just what I asked for originally. I want to be paid every day, incrementally. We signed a contract for sixty contiguous days of shooting, so one-sixtieth per day should be fine. Overtime is double." She listens, then responds: "Well, we'll need something to transport it in, maybe a van or some kind of small truck. Blankets and padding and such, so nothing tips over or breaks." Patrick listens as a new warmth seeps into her voice: she must have gotten what she wanted. "Thank you so much for understanding," she says, her delivery innocent and sincere, her voice growing sunny. "It's really a weight off my chest, I don't know how to explain it. You know that I haven't always had much stability in my life, growing up under the industry's thumb. Well, a good friend once told me a couple of years back that I should recenter myself from time to time by doing a little breathwork and meditating on the reason why I do all this, what drives me, what makes it worth it. In my case, that's payment. It just gives me a sense of calmness and, well, mental health, when I can focus on my earnings, sitting safely in my home. It's almost meditative! Plus, you know, they can't freeze your funds when they're in a duffel under your bed. I should put some sort of video lesson together about this technique; I think I could really help people."

She turns toward Patrick and gives him a thumbs-up sign.

"Beginning today, of course," she says. "He'll help me transport it." She pauses. "You'll need to rent him something bigger to drive."

He watches incredulously as she laughs and laughs at some joke Brenda made.

"Okay, right, well, see you so soon. Give my love to Jay. Oh, he's right there? Isn't that great. And, hey, don't go too hard on this Patrick guy. I'm sure he wasn't really trying to cause me any emotional duress, he's just not from around here, doesn't know how we get things done. Okay, can't wait to see your face! Me too! Bye!" Her brilliant smile fades to one of quiet self-satisfaction as she puts the phone down on the kitchen counter.

"Win-win," she says brightly, leaning over the back of the couch.

"How did I win?" he replies sarcastically.

"Well," says Cassidy, "I negotiated the payment plan I want, and you got one free favor from me. Gratis. What do you want? An autograph for your kid?" She inspects him. "Has your kid seen my work?"

"I could call Jay up right now and tell him about the drug paraphernalia I saw all over your house," Patrick says. "He'd be interested in his famously unpredictable star returning to her famously unpredictable hobbies."

"Yeah, maybe give him a call about that," Cassidy says off-handedly, "but later. I don't think we have time for any more phone calls now, we're really late."

Cassidy grabs a wad of white from a kitchen stool overflowing with clothing and slips the mesh dress on over her swimsuit. She puts on a pair of socks from the pile and pulls a pair of sandals from a tote bag hanging on the back of a chair.

"I'm ready, let's go," she declares.

They walk out into the blinding sunlight, into the sprawl of Secret Sunset, the neighborhood a violation of scale, its homes stretched and enlarged so that the intimacy implied by the name dissolves into intimidated silence. The houses in Secret Sunset come in the styles of other houses he's seen before—a Southwestern one, a Cape Cod, a mid-century ranch, or a Spanish inspired casita—but at three times the length and twice the height, they inspire dread. They dwarf the middle-aged oaks and willows planted at their flanks and nurtured at significant expense, making cars look like toys and people look like figurines. The effect isn't neighborly: instead of sensing the other house's proximity, Patrick feels its distance.

"Let's take my car instead," says Cassidy, rooting through her handbag. "You drive, though."

"I can't leave the rental car," Patrick complains, gesturing at the matcha-green economy compact sedan he rented from the less-trafficked airport near his hotel. "I have to return it tomorrow morning."

Cassidy regards it with a look of casual repulsion. She unlocks her own vintage convertible, cream-colored and pristine but for a few dents in the passenger-side door, and tosses him the keys.

"Get one of the PAs to return it," she suggests breezily.

"I *am* a PA," he replies. "It says so in my contract."

"You said you're a writer, right? Well, if they call you an assistant and you do assistant things, you're an assistant, not a writer. If you want to move up, you have to inhabit the job you want, not the job they give you. I have a book on tape I could lend you about it." She stares at Patrick across the roof of the car—or at least he thinks she stares at him, the lenses on her sunglasses are so dark he sees nothing but his own murky shape. "Listen," she says sharply, "don't waste too much time thinking about it, we're really late already."

Patrick slides himself into the driver's seat, onto the tan leather. As he backs out, he notices for the first time that her lawn, unlike the others, is completely dead, a prickly, yellowed carpet with the dry texture of a scouring pad.

Cassidy looks up from her phone. "There's a fire in North Hollywood," she says, "so we can't take the road you came in on. We need to detour. Turn left up there."

Patrick sighs, and makes the turn. Now they're clawing their way up a mountain road, into the heart of the hills and past it, where they'll get on the 118. As the well-appointed homes and carefully watered lawns grow distant in the rearview, the terrain brambles and roughens. Twists of silvery-green scrub crawl up the hills, brownish brush and yellow grass grasping toward the cloudless sky like upward strokes of a paintbrush. Occasional trees reaching like fractures into the sky. There's the crunch of the wheels on dirt road, a fine haze of dust turning the creamy car sepia-toned. Cassidy's dangling her hand out the window like some music-video girl with no lines and no backstory, her elegant nostrils delicately flared as she sucks in the canyon air. He begins to suspect that this detour may not be wholly necessary, just another way for Cassidy Carter to get what she wants: a nice drive in the country. He looks into the sky above for signs of smoke tainting the air, but from this angle it's impossible to tell. As he stares up into the blue, it seems to telescope out and retract, some strangeness that the nine-year-old natural philosopher Nora would know how to fact-check—to tell him whether it was really happening or whether it was all in his mind.

"So," says Cassidy, staring out her window as the landscape scrolls by, "if you're a writer and you have some kind of family back in Boston or wherever, what are you doing running errands for me and Brenda? Don't you miss your kids?"

"Of course I do," Patrick responds, the anger in his voice surprising him. "Every moment I'm out here I think of using the last of my frequent-flier miles to book a same-day flight back, to people who know me. To a place where they respect what a person has achieved in their life. You realize I'm an award-winning author? That I have a carefully, lovingly built life with a wife and daughter who are very important to me, and instead of spending time with them, I'm here driving you around?" Now that he's begun venting, it's hard to stop: a pulled thread that unravels the entire rug. "You realize I created this story? That without me this movie is just a bunch of people standing around with no premise, no plot? And now, just because Jay and Brenda said so, I'm playing intern to a famously psychotic twentysome-thing."

Cassidy gives him a small smile. "I hear what you're saying. I'm a shit assignment. But maybe you should take a moment to think about what being given this assignment says about you. Maybe you're not as amazing as you think you are."

Patrick says nothing for a long moment. "I could pull over right now," he says, more quietly. "I could get out of this car and just walk away. And you might call Jay and get him to send someone else, some PA who finds your first few tantrums novel. But what about when that person quits? How many more do you think they'll send?"

For a long time nobody says anything. The noise of the en-gine leaks, diluted, into the vast, empty sky. He doesn't pull the car over to the side of the road; she doesn't argue, only sits there idly locking and unlocking the passenger-side door.

"I'm sorry you're missing your kid," says Cassidy flatly.

Patrick stares straight ahead.

"I was a kid," Cassidy says, facing away from him, staring out. "I came from the most Podunk town you've never heard of. We were famous for growing hay. People don't even eat hay. And it's not that my town was the best place to grow hay, we just made a lot of it. In the fall, hay rides and hay mazes. Scarecrows and pumpkins. The smell of living stuff drying out in the sun, gera-niums in the front yard. Whatever."

She looks at Patrick and then back out at the canyon in mo-tion.

"This was inland, an hour from Fresno. Four or five hours

from here. Nothing ever happened there, not even a hit-and-run. There just weren't enough people. And then, one day, I'm walking back from where the school bus used to let me off and this amazing car pulls up. I didn't even know what kind of car it was; probably it was some pretty humdrum bullshit, but it was shiny, and the roof was down. And inside that car was Rainer Westchapel. Do you remember him?"

Patrick reluctantly shakes his head no.

"He was in that Christmas movie, the one where Santa gives all the good children coal and all the bad children ponies by accident and one man, an ordinary IRS clerk, has to set it all straight. *Even Santa Makes Mistakes,* that movie. Well, Rainer Westchapel played the IRS guy's best friend, the abstract painter with the wise advice. I know you've seen it. They show it every year."

"Maybe," says Patrick. "I wouldn't know."

"So Rainer Westchapel pulls up next to me, and he's lost, he was trying to get to some hot spring where his buddy had a vacation house. He was house-sitting. He's not so famous, you'd only know him from *Even Santa Makes Mistakes*. But he was the biggest celebrity ever to pass through Haywood, and I got to give him directions back to the highway. Personally. It was a catastrophe for me, like a tornado or a hurricane. It changed everything. I felt like I had been diagnosed with leukemia, like one of those kids on TV where there's a number you're supposed to call to donate. I literally couldn't stay in a town where there was no chance that I'd ever see another celebrity ever again. It hurt, to think that my life would be Rainer Westchapel asking for directions, and then decade after decade of nothing, and then death. Death was right in front of me. I finally convinced my mom to move June and me closer to L.A. so that I could do auditions. It wasn't that hard; my dad had already left us."

She stares far into the distance, at the shriveled little trees.

"My sister hated it here, though," she adds, quietly.

The grass rolls by, the brush rolls by, the cripple oaks and stray, stunted chollas like visitors from another planet. The naked rock faces of small mountains roll by, and so does the road. When Cassidy Carter speaks again, her voice is curiously unemotional, like she's speaking only to herself.

"You know, after I gave him directions, Rainer Westchapel lingered there for a while with the engine running. I could hear the little pings of the machinery inside, like someone was skipping stones across the hood. He asked me how old I was and where I went to school. He asked me about my mom and my sister and what color my bedroom walls were. He had a handsome, leathery face, I guess, though I don't know if I knew it at the time. Then, suddenly, he grinned and leaned toward me, almost hanging out of the car. He licked his lower lip and said, 'Now, if you were just eight years older, I would take you with me. And I would do such things to you, little one, you wouldn't even know the words for it.' Then he sped off, toward the highway. The exhaust smelled like glue and paint thinner, mixing with the sunshine."

She's silent, then her eyes narrow. "I wonder what his net worth is today."

Patrick's still trying to think of some way to respond when he hears a shriek from the passenger seat next to him. He brakes hard, kicking up a curtain of dust. As the curtain parts he sees what Cassidy saw: a gigantic cat, dun-furred and large-pawed, the color of the hillside and the rock. He hears the sound of its exhale, like a gasket, stirring the tawny dust. Walking slowly, one paw after another, the heavy muscles like living knots, twisting beneath the skin. The mountain lion hangs its head low and takes them in from the corner of its golden eye, the tail tip twitching once to the left like a single, quickening thought.

Patrick fantasizes for a moment that seeing him would mean something to this animal, that it would remember having looked in the eyes of the human driving the car that nearly caved in its contraption of sinew and bone, the only thing an animal owns. But an animal like this exists in another world than our own, thinks Patrick to himself. The actual world, maybe, where the exact nature of a threat is as real and tangible as the stump of a tree or the engine of a Ferrari 250 GT California Spyder. Patrick is about to tell this thought to Cassidy, finally something wise and confident he can say, when, suddenly, the cat breaks into a run. "Holy Jesus hell," says Cassidy softly. They watch its heavy body turn light and elastic as it lopes smoothly, easily, up the hill and into a hidden part of the canyon, where their eyes can no longer track it.

At the studio, the indoor temperature is sixty-three degrees and the office furniture is chilly to the touch. Patrick sits in a pale-green armchair with modern lines, its back built at an angle of half-recline, making it difficult for him to hold himself in an alert, professional posture. He looks up "Oswego farm family mourning" then "Oswego nature mourning retreat" on his phone and turns up a smattering of obituaries, locals who've perished separately, unsystematically, of unrelated causes. He looks up "Oswego nature activities pay phone," "pay phone Oswego retreat," and, as a last resort, "Oswego camp donkey," but all he learns is that Oswego has many nature activities, inadequately catalogued pay phones, no public records of the locations of farm animals or livestock. The searches return thousands upon thousands of results, tranches of information peering into a small piece of someplace over two thousand miles away—but they don't show him what he's looking for. Patrick experiences a sensation of access intermingled with a deeper sense of helplessness. He searches "Earthbridge," but any useful information is buried beneath entries devoted to a natural deodorant brand of the same name. He looks up "Oswego cult," and finds a few different options: most have been defunct since the late 1990s, but there's one that still seems to be mildly active, based on local news reports from a couple years ago. He enters the purported address of the cult into a window that lets him navigate a virtual map of the neighborhood, comprising photographs that seem to have been taken during some previous Halloween. The boxy little houses, painted white and yellow and somber blue, have carved pumpkins out front and scarecrows seated on porches. He presses the arrows to walk back and forth on this virtual street, but he sees no sinister cult leaders, no pay phones, nothing to give substance to the idea that his wife and daughter are far away, mourning and surrounded by sheep.

"Wow," says Horseshoe, "you are incredibly intent upon your phone." He leans over and peers at Patrick's screen. Patrick clicks it off quickly.

"His condition," says the Arm, "is our collective malaise."

"I only have a flip phone," says Sam Sackler, the film's director, a stocky man in his forties with a thick, trim beard disguising the true shape of his face. He reaches into his pocket and pulls it out to show to the rest of the group. The four of them stare at the smooth black object in the palm of his hand, primitively shaped, like a stone.

"Sam," says Horseshoe politely after a moment has passed, "I understand why the three of us are out here waiting for someone to give us directions. But you're the director. Shouldn't you be in there with Cassidy and the costume people and Brenda and Jay?"

"This is a bit of a touchy issue," says Sam. "I, of course, agree with you fully, but Jay and Brenda said they wanted me to 'be surprised.' I told them that, as a director, surprises cause mistakes and cost money. But they insisted, and they are, after all, the ones holding the cash bag."

Horseshoe and the Arm nod sagely.

"Is it normal?" asks Patrick. "To be so secretive? Do you know that I didn't even get to see a copy of the script—the script to a movie about my book—until everyone was reading it around the table? And then, when I read the script, it's not even my story at all—it's a freak mutation, like if someone who hadn't read the book told someone else about it at a cocktail party and then that person went out and wrote a script from memory."

Everyone looks uncertain. Horseshoe shrugs.

"What, am I crazy to be bothered by this?" Patrick huffs.

"I'd rephrase that," says Sam Sackler mildly, "and ask, instead, if it's useful for you to be bothered. I've worked on probably eighty films over the course of my career, sometimes just showing up for a couple days' labor holding a piece of reflective fabric up to the light, sometimes standing at the helm of my own production. In no situation has it been useful to me to get all worked up about something, particularly when I'm planning on sticking around anyway for the cash and the résumé fodder. Sometimes, when I need to calm myself, I imagine a little boat made of folded paper, riding the rough currents of a river. That little boat is me: it goes with the flow and eventually it gets to where it's going. I flowed all the way into my first director position, and now I've made five films that have my name on them."

Horseshoe jumps in: "As for the script, why not look on the bright side? Consider Theseus's ship. A piece of wood from the hull is removed. An identical piece is set in its place. This happens thousands of times, until every piece of the ship has been removed and replaced by another identical piece. But guess what? It's still the exact same ship! They can't take that away from you."

"But the pieces aren't identical," replies Patrick. "That's my entire point."

"Let me tell you an anecdote about the evolution of consciousness," says the Arm, sitting forward in his chair. "There once was a little worm—a multicelled organism, but not by much. This worm was constructed simply, to do basic things like eating, moving toward food, moving away from enemies. But one day it encountered a negative stimulus in its environment that it couldn't escape from or alter—an increase in temperature, for example. With no recourse to change the situation or save itself from the situation, the little worm turned to the only tool it had available to itself: adaptation. It created a little organ in its body that was designed to receive the negative signals caused by the negative stimuli: we call that organ 'the brain.'"

Horseshoe is nodding exaggeratedly, deeply.

"Now, in thinking about the bad thing, it felt like it was taking an action against it, though in actuality the thing remained unchanged. It could take different stances on the terrible stimulus: it could think about how much it hated it, or question whether it was really all that bad, or even come to regard it with grudging respect as 'character-building.' In each case, the bad thing was transformed in the mind, providing an illusion of control, when in reality it remained intact. Consciousness was not created to help us solve problems; it's an invisible machine whose sole function is to internalize problems so that we can live with them forever."

"First," said Patrick, "any biologist would tell you that the way you think about evolution is incorrect."

"That doesn't bother me, because it's a parable," says the Arm.

"I thought a parable was a story where the message remains unclear, or multivalent. Your story seems to have a clear message," says Sam.

"Or does it?" the Arm replies.

"I'm just asking for some transparency," says Patrick, "for a sense of which abnormal-seeming things are actually normal and which are alarming."

In the silence, Patrick can hear the whirring of an office fridge.

"It feels like a betrayal to divulge observations that may not be to the benefit of this film," says Horseshoe.

"But to remain silent might be an even deeper betrayal," the Arm reminds him, "a betrayal of art itself."

"There is one thing," Sam Sackler interjects quietly. "We're getting ready to start filming tomorrow, and Jay tells me all necessary funds are in place, but I hear from people around town that he and Brenda are still going around looking for investors. Maybe if they were raising money for another movie it would make sense, but I know they're selling *Elsinore Lane*, because I get calls from them asking me to stop by this hotel or that so the two of them can have people inspect me. Tourists like to feed the animals, you know. I'm not complaining—as I said, complaining is not part of my philosophy of life—but if they already have what they need, why are they asking for more? And if they don't have it, why are they telling me they do?" He pauses. "But I have to say, every project is weird. And when you're in one weirdness, you kinda forget the others."

Patrick turns to the production kids. Horseshoe is looking down into his lap at his clasped hands.

"So," Patrick begins, "is it normal to be raising funds this late in the process?"

"It's just that the word 'normal,'" the Arm replies, "really complicates the question. As I see it, normal is a distribution, and it's impossible to tell, standing in one singular point within that distribution, what the shape that will emerge might be."

"Norms are always shifting," agrees Horseshoe. "First we celebrate the advent of the wheel, then we wring our hands over restricting vehicular emissions. It's what they call the march of history."

"A thing that seems abnormal today might be the first glimpse we get of a future world wherein the mores we hold dear become symptoms of mental decay or, optimistically, museum curios. We see a thing as anomaly, but that perception is only a sign of our inability to differentiate monstrosity from change."

"Sometimes a thing happening is its own prophecy," Horse-shoe says, nodding.

"A prophecy is the only thing that can be real—more real, in fact, because it's impossible to accept. Everything else is just a story told in the genre of realism," the Arm adds. "Believable because it confirms the background of our expectations against a foreground of gentle, pointless surprise."

The door to the fitting room swings open abruptly as a costume aide in a stylishly disheveled topknot emerges, her arms full of high-necked Victorian dresses, gauzy nightgowns, and somber Puritanical blouses. She has a mirthless expression on her face. Horseshoe nods at her winningly, but she ignores them all. As the heavy door swings shut, a metal arm fixed to the top hisses into action, slowing its movement. The four lean to their sides in the stiff office chairs, straining for a glimpse of what lies within. They hear the sound of laughter: Cassidy's like that of a sexy hyena and Brenda's like silvered bells, Jay's low, easy bass. There's a curved white couch in the shape of a semicircle and a sound like a champagne bottle being uncorked. Then the door clicks shut, and the office lobby is quiet once more. Patrick has a troubled expression on his face as he unscrews the lid of a bottle of WAT-R and takes a long drink.

"You know," he says slowly, "I begin to wonder if there's something going on behind the scenes of this movie, and if Cassidy could be a part of it."

For a long moment, no one says anything. Then Sam says: "Go on."

"You have this actress," Patrick says, leaning forward and lowering his voice, "who's known more for her performances off-screen than on, who's trying to get any kind of a career going again. She's probably willing to do just about anything for another chance to star in something. And then you've got this pair of producers with this weird secretive nature who kind of ooze this surreal sexual energy. Something about the whole setup feels rickety, temporary, like it's not put together to last. . . ." He trails off.

"And then?" asks Sam.

"I don't know," says Patrick.

"Your mystery lacks a plot," Sam says. He slurps at his coffee with his small pink mouth. "It would never make it past the pitch stage."

"I had a screenwriting professor back in college who used to say first you have to construct a plot, then you have to bury it, then you have to dig it back up," says Horseshoe. "The plot you describe is either too buried, not buried enough, or not sufficiently constructed."

"But Patrick puts his finger on an odd dynamic that I think we are all sensing," says the Arm. "That dynamic being a gut feeling that the people in that room over there are experiencing this project completely differently from us. That they see a completely different big picture than us, or that the picture they see is something we cannot act on or perhaps even understand. Why is their perspective so different from ours? Is it because they're so beautiful? Or because they're rich?"

"Maybe we should try to be more understanding," says Horseshoe in a ruminative way.

"Lately," says the Arm thoughtfully, "I've been wondering whether these differences go deeper than the random, unequal distribution of genetic gifts and family wealth at birth. I hypothesize that some people, a select but growing group, have evolved the ability to perceive money as a natural extension of their other sensory systems, the same way we perceive light via the photosensitive cells on the surface of the retina. To people like us, money is either an abstraction or something idiotically concrete—little rounds of metal, germ-ridden pieces of floppy paper worn down by passage from one hand to another, numbers on an ATM screen or a bank statement. But for them it's real—present in a direct, nonmetaphorical, nonsymbolic incarnation. They encounter it as a physical thing in the world, even if it's only the shimmer of money in its potentializable form. They don't have to ask themselves whether an investment will pay off, whether it's worth the risk, how much risk it involves: they simply see the money embodied in the proposition, like a piece of fruit hanging yea high above them, and they decide whether it's worth the trouble to reach up and pluck it."

The Arm pauses for a long swig of WAT-R. On the underside of his pasty white neck, the Adam's apple bobs rigidly up and down.

"How would it appear to them?" he continues, wiping the wetness from his mouth with the back of his hand. "An aura? A scent? Impossible to imagine. Capital is real to them. Collateralized debt obligation is real to them and requires no explanation or thought to appreciate. Loss is malleable as putty and compound interest is part of the world's clock, as obvious as the alternation of sun and moon. To us, this makes them wizards. But the reality is even grimmer. The last mass extinction happened two hundred fifty-two million years ago, at the end of the Paleozoic, when up to ninety-six percent of all marine species went extinct. Different theories, from global warming to meteor strike, aim to explain what paleontologists call the 'Great Dying,' but my favorite theory holds that it was the evolution of eyes in a small, select group of organisms that enabled them to hunt their blind prey to extinction. You see, even by the old rules, those individuals who understood money had a fierce advantage over everybody else. A shift like this would mean the extinction of our kind, we simple critters who believe money is produced linearly by longer, harder work."

They listen, in the office silence, to the whine of the overhead lights.

"A primitive eye is infinitely better than no eye at all," says Horseshoe glumly.

The door to the fitting room swings open again as the costume aide returns, her arms heavy with drapings of delicate metallic-mesh cocktail dresses, diaphanous white robes. Through the open door comes a tinkling of music and laughter and, ever so faintly, the sound of thin-walled glasses clinking together in a toast. As the door clicks shut, Patrick can hear Cassidy's girlish voice squealing at the sight of something the aide has brought in. The four of them sit, waiting. They watch as the Arm fumbles with a protein bar, trying to tear it open at the little notch as the plastic bends and stretches. He readjusts, gripping it like a bag of chips between his fingertips, tugging at the tenacious seam of the packaging. Horseshoe holds out his open palm, and the Arm hands it over. They take turns trying to rend the wrapper with their teeth.

Patrick stares at the door, troubled. To fill the silence, he squeezes the empty WAT-R bottle in his hand, letting it crinkle and clack. Then he decides to ask. "Hey, guys," he says with a tentative tone. "Hypothetically speaking. If your wife and your daughter had gone off somewhere in upstate New York to live in some sort of complex with people you don't know, and they wouldn't tell you where they had gone and you couldn't reliably reach them on the phone—what would you think? Would you take it as a pretty bad sign, like they were done with you?"

The four men sit in their identical armchairs and consider.

"Two parents, one kid, and a dog. I always thought that would be the perfect combination. That's what I want, someday," says Horseshoe at last.

In the parking lot, the white van sits with its back doors agape, headlights cutting through a moving haze that rolls like fog. The sun is gone but a rusty color lingers in the cold night air, like the aftertaste of blood in the mouth on a dry morning. Cassidy Carter walks a few steps ahead, a soft fluffy blanket from Jay's studio couch wrapped around her like a cape, as Patrick drags a dolly stacked high with sealed boxes. The dolly catches and twists, snagging on small concavities in the asphalt, forcing him to wrap his arm around the load as he tows, as if to comfort it. Her strappy white heels click ahead of him, punching little holes in the silence. When she reaches the open van, she mutters something under her breath. She turns to Patrick.

"There isn't any padding here, nothing to secure the cargo," she complains. She looks at him expectantly and waits.

"What are you looking at me for?" Patrick responds. He jams his foot behind a dolly wheel to keep it from moving while he squeezes one hand with the other, rubbing out a cramp. His eyes are watering, though he can't figure out why.

"Well, maybe find some?" she says.

"If I had some idea what was inside, maybe I would know how to secure them," he says. What's inside is heavy, unwieldy, irregularly shaped—he feels something slipping around when he resettles the boxes on the wheeled platform. From the jostle, he's imagining bottles of premium liquor—Tito's, Grey Goose, whatever a B-lister parties with when she's struggling to stay off the C-list.

Cassidy looks up at him, her gaze dark and pointed. "Let's just say it's valuable, not that fragile, but fragile enough that I want it cushioned and strapped in place." She lifts herself into the passenger seat while Patrick hefts box after box into the cavernous interior. Stacked on top of one another in an asymmetric cube, the seven boxes look strangely vulnerable, surrounded by feet of empty space. When he slams the doors, the sound echoes through the valley, its aftereffect larger than the event itself. He climbs into the driver's seat next to Cassidy, who's scrolling through pages of emojis on her phone.

"You know," Patrick says, "I'm going to be loading these boxes into the van for you every day after work. Eventually, I'll find out what's inside."

Cassidy looks over, her gaze intent. At this moment, she looks like one of the characters she plays on-screen, a wide-eyed girl with a tousled mane and a can-do outlook on life. She looks more beautiful, more alert and refined, he notices, now that she's paying attention to him. She stares at him longer than he thinks is polite, the blue of her eyes dark in the half-light.

"I don't share details about my salary with the public unless I want it to become Twitter bait," she says flatly.

"I don't know who I'd tell," Patrick replies. "Nobody I know would care."

"Okay," she says. She pauses a moment. "You have to guess."

"Is it solid or liquid?" he asks.

"This isn't Twenty Questions," Cassidy replies, annoyed.

"Fine. Is it alcohol? Vodka? Fancy bottles of wine? Investment wine? Human blood plasma?"

She shakes her head. "It's water. *Real* water." For the first time since he met her, Cassidy looks ill-at-ease, almost as if it matters to her what he thinks.

"Why would you get paid in water?" Patrick asks, finding it hard to hide his disbelief. "Did your money person okay this?"

"I forgot," says Cassidy pertly, "you're new to *Cal-uh-forn-ya*." The word falls from her mouth with a cartoonish growl, and she laughs loudly and too long. A crazy laugh. They drive in silence, the brake lights from the cars ahead flashing on and off, outlining their faces in unholy red.

"I feel like it's a bad idea to get paid in stuff that comes out of the faucet for pennies a gallon," he says.

"You haven't been paying attention, have you? Where you come from, WAT-R is just another bottled beverage product you can buy at the store. Here, it's all you get unless you have a lot of money and a lot of connections. Brenda and Jay have great connections," she adds, with a note of sadness. "Since you got here, every shower, every flush, every time you're thinking of—it was all WAT-R. When they first switched over, you'd see the trucks two or three times a day delivering WAT-R in big jugs, and people were always talking about it. But now, if you pay for deluxe service, they put a tank in the basement and pump it up into the plumbing once a week. You turn the faucet and it pours out, just like in the old days."

She pulls a little flask out of her bag and takes a thoughtful sip.

"I always hated the switch-over, all the cheesy slogans. 'California's homegrown liquid goodness.'" Cassidy makes a gagging sound. "Like it was invented for fun, and not because we ran out of regular water in the drought. But whatever. I use it in the plumbing like everyone does, but I don't put that stuff inside my body. There was a time when I was seriously broke and I thought I might have to give up and drink the stuff like some freaking civilian, but then I got them to give me a few more Bellanex bucks."

"Is this some sort of lifestyle choice for you? Everybody I've seen here drinks WAT-R. It's perfectly safe," says Patrick, with authority. He thinks about his hotel room, the faucets on the sink that squeak dryly and produce nothing. The shower, which gives a thin, tepid stream of water when he turns it on, and the trickly sinks in the studio restroom, the restaurant, the coffee shop.

"Brenda doesn't," Cassidy retorts. "Have you heard her do her little shtick? 'Water? I don't touch the stuff. Fish fuck in it.'"

"I just don't understand. WAT-R is water," Patrick says, looking out at the oddly illuminated sky. "It may be made in a factory, but it's the same, down to the molecular level. That's all water is, a molecule. Or a recipe for a molecule. Water in its purest form is a diagram from high-school chemistry."

Cassidy just looks out the window. Off to the side of the highway, an orange glow fades into the starless sky. She can see the roadside bramble outlined in the brownish light, the earth hot and thirsty. Just a mile or two away from here, fire crawls across the landscape, burning and burnt. Orange fronds, like a plant tossing in the wind, are the only thing seen clearly through a scrim of gray.

"You don't notice any difference?" she asks, turning to look at him. In the darkness, he can feel the intensity of her face pointed at him, unseeing, and it feels suddenly, inexplicably, like he's playing a part.

"It's water," he says, "only it comes in different bottles, different markups. All a swindle, I'm sure, an everyday injustice, but not a crime under the law of capital."

Cassidy frowns in the too-bright darkness. "It has a taste."

"You're imagining it."

"The faintest hint of marshmallow. Or baby powder, or milk. Or maybe it's that the feeling is wrong, the texture. Like touching dust on a tabletop in a room that nobody has lived in for a while. The gag of your throat when you swallow a hair. It's less a flavor than . . . the awareness of a presence."

Patrick says nothing. NPR on the radio fades in and out, crackling through the cheap speakers. The van is cozy and dark, though he feels like something bad is about to happen. Then they round the bend and see the moving, living fire: stamped on the flank of the mountain like a brand, a neon sign spelling out a single illegible word.

"They fight fires with WAT-R now," says Cassidy, gazing out at the bright wound of light on the hillside. "They say it works even better than the old stuff. Why would that be?" Patrick should be watching the road, but he can't help turning his head to stare into the blazing, catastrophic eye. The fire leaves a mark on his field of vision, a floating purple shadow like after staring at the sun. The side of his face feels warm, and he turns the van's feeble air conditioning up another notch. To be so close to disaster, to skirt its hungry edge, and at the same time feel yourself completely safe: it makes Patrick want to hold a human hand in his own, feeling the thin, long bones under the delicate skin, confirming the fragility and persistence of life. The highway curves again, and now the wildfire is in the rearview mirror, a faint afterglow.

"A vanload of luxury water every day," he says, almost to himself. "What are you going to do with all this?"

"Fill my swimming pool," she says flatly, her voice lonely and distant. He puts on the turn signal and exits, veers from the highway into Cassidy's gated community, the wide streets sleepy and dark, vacant and unburnt.

Back at the Hacienda Lodge, he parks the van beneath a cottonwood tree in the back of the lot. He checks each door manually—there are no power locks on this basic, throwaway model. When he slides the side door shut, the whole vehicle quakes. As he walks to the motel entrance, he sees a strange shape on the lawn, rounded like a stone but soft. It seems to tremble in the breeze. Patrick sinks to a crouch. The velvety mound takes on the shape of a rabbit, eerily long-limbed, with ears like a mule and legs like a gazelle. Stretched on its side in the green, thick grass like it's been paused mid-leap, its eyes are a glossy, taxidermied black.

Inside his room, he sits at the edge of the bed and calls Oswego again and again, though he knows it's close to midnight there and most likely no one will pick up. The last couple days, he's succeeded only in reaching a sampling of strange hippies, space cadets who can't seem to figure out why he's calling, or tough matrons who tell him to call back at a different time—earlier, later, on a Wednesday. Patrick pops open a bag of potato chips and twists the top off a brand-new bottle of WAT-R. Cassidy Carter doesn't know what she's talking about, thinks Patrick to himself. It's more of that New Age, crystal-healing celebrity bullshit. Money creates problems for money to solve. The crack of the cap as he breaks the seal comforts him, reminds him that the product is clean and unopened and meant for his mouth only.

Alone on a motel bedspread, meaning nothing in particular to anyone around him, Patrick looks down at his body, supine and exhausted, rising up before his gaze like a deserted island. Nobody to call, nobody to care, nobody to gaze upon his physical form with kindness, nobody to recognize the mole on his left shoulder blade and assess its size or regularity relative to prior versions. He's in the antechamber of an adventure unlike any he's experienced before, nobody he knows has ever worked a day in Hollywood, but the pride feels flimsy when it goes unwitnessed, unshared. He wonders if it wouldn't perhaps have been better if he had never had a family at all. Having known the tender pressure, the gentle crush of being loved on all sides at once, constant recipient of text messages and data points, location known, ETA known, never left to his own thoughts for more than an hour or two in the basement office, door closed, always susceptible to a call for help in the kitchen or to come see the newly completed drawing or to answer questions about the sky colored blue, the flow of small creeks, the training process involved in becoming a lawyer or a firefighter—he feels the absence of their need as rejection.

Patrick opens his laptop, stares down at the screen as it purrs atop his thighs. It's possible to stream all five seasons of *Kassi Keene: Kid Detective,* so he clicks on the first episode, "Who Killed the Cottonwood Cougar?"

The screen is racked with bright colors and the jangly sounds of the *Kassi Keene* theme song sung by a pop-punk female voice wailing over and over again: "Where's the real crime? Where's the real mystery?" In the intro, slices of Cassidy Carter in a whole season's worth of escapades are spliced together but oddly homogenous. Cassidy smiles in a yellow plaid sundress. Cassidy halts the crowning of homecoming king and queen, grabbing the microphone off its stand. Cassidy bursts through the calm surface of a lake, holding a soggy boot up in triumph. A large, furry woodchuck mascot removes its head and underneath is Cassidy's face, furrowed in concentration as she holds a magnifying glass up to her eye. There's something worrisome, from a fatherly perspective, about all these Cassidys mugging for the camera, unflaggingly perky, always giving it their energetic all. Where are the secondary characters? A best friend? Where's her TV family, her cookie-cutter TV home? A teenage love interest who plays the electric guitar, or drums, or keytar, or trombone? At the end of the intro sequence, the camera lingers on Kassi Keene's smiling face for a few long, awkward seconds, and he sits forward. Is it the loneliness that makes him think they have something in common? In the distance between her winning smile and the stiff, disappointed look in her eyes, Patrick sees a feeling he recognizes, like a tundra unmapped and uninvestigated, waiting with little optimism for the touch of the sun.

"Give yourself a promotion," reads the headline. "How to manifest a higher status by choosing who you report to!" Patrick scrolls to the bottom of the article, then back up to the top. He can't tell if the advice it offers applies to his current situation. "How to make $2,000 a week off your own cached data! How to make $500 a day using the body debris you'd usually throw in the trash can!" On the edge of the soundstage parking lot, a portable canopy shelters plastic-plattered cheese cubes and sliced fruit, a tray of skinny sandwiches on pale white bread, plastic dispensers of hot coffee and tea, and a frenzy of M&M's. The production assistants haunt the catering station, returning to it faithfully in between takes to graze on the cheese, to fold thin sandwiches into their mouths, their fingers digging into the soft colorless squares. They plunge their hands into the M&M bowl, the sound like heavy rain sifting across a metal roof. They scoop the sugary pellets straight into the mouth, or slip a handful into a pocket for later. At the far end of the folding table, bottles of WAT-R *Energy Surge,* a calorieless sweetened product with a flavor like artificial melon, wait in irregular rows to be taken.

Patrick stands off to the side of the entrance, watching the PAs come and go, their spirits animated by the fragile blessing of free food. There's something undignified, he thinks, about feeding from a trough like this, as though employee and employer alike are admitting that the most important part of a person can be satisfied like an animal. He notices that a few of the sound engineers stop by the snack table, the electricians, the tall, triangle-backed guy who holds the microphone, but they don't make a big deal of it the way the assistants do, hovering anxiously near the ravaged sandwich tray to watch for someone to come and fill it back up. In the chilly shadow of the windowless building, he decides that he won't become like them, he'll distinguish himself through behavior if not through title. He won't join them at the watering hole in between the ceaseless rushing to and from vehicles, between driving to the hardware store for staples for the staple gun or back to the office for Brenda or Jay's laptop, Zippo lighter, phone charger for the matching second cellphones they carry, which they use exclusively to communicate with each other. "Producer pagers," they call them, though in their cheap glossy plastic they look more like burners.

This morning, he's been asked to go fetch Brenda's velvet loafers with the embroidered zebras from the bottom-right drawer of her walk-in closet at home, but he swiftly delegated that to the Arm, who got stuck in traffic on the 101 and hasn't been seen since. Patrick decided in the first week that he doesn't fetch, or he only fetches important items, items with an integral part to play in the story—scripts, for example, or objects that belong in the film itself, in front of the camera. He's scanning the trickle of emerging crew for the leather jacket and trim beard of Sam Sackler: if he takes his tasks directly from the man in charge, doesn't that place him a few tiers above the other assistants, in their anonymous glom of jeans, tees, and fashion sneakers?

He drifts back and forth between the parking lot, where the crew emerges one or two at a time, to smoke cigarettes and blink into the warm sunlight, and the margins of the set, where the bodies of cast and crew turn toward the action like sunflowers toward the sun. At the center of the vast industrial space, a brilliant rectangle of color slices his gaze: the green of cartoon frogs, of a baseball field plugged into a power grid, a green like the dream of the word itself, an electric color that has never arisen without the labor of a human hand. Against the uncanny bright, the bodies of the actors are illuminated in unbelievable detail, every freckle and spot urgent under the scrutiny of the lights. He sees Dillon Davies, the alter ego of his fictional alter ego, standing in place in the bright-green field as the crew readjusts equipment. To his left, an ordinary painter's ladder is propped inexplicably in full view. The short, light-colored beard from the table read has been razored off, and now Patrick can see the young star's entire face, shockingly smooth, a brand-new face that has never been seen by his fans. In the exact center is a chiseled lower lip, as plump as a cherry. Dillon stares dully at the poured-concrete floor, chewing on a fingernail, dreamier than ever, somehow. Is this what charisma is, Patrick wonders—the skill of exuding appeal even when you appear to be exuding nothing, appear to be doing nothing at all?

Sackler isn't there among the silhouetted throng watching Dillon dismantle his hangnails; he's not bent over the electrical wires or lighting equipment or camera. Patrick looks for a director's chair, the foldable kind, iconic, clichéd—but is that too obvious? The mid-forties paunch, the thick-rimmed glasses with the thin, possibly false, lenses. He asks the pair of makeup girls by the touch-up station, but they have no idea who Sackler is. Neither does the kid with a coil of insulated cable slung over each arm, whose pockets rattle with pilfered candy as he walks away. "Can you direct me toward whoever's in charge?" Patrick asks the clustered backs, but not loudly enough for anyone to hear him. The soundstage is half lit and haphazardly peopled, like a high-school gymnasium transformed into a tornado shelter. When he sees the Arm wandering in from the sunlit outdoors, what he feels is a mixture of annoyance and relief.

"Where have you been all afternoon?" Patrick says, sighing loudly. "Wandering the desert in search of enlightenment?"

"I just had a terrible experience," says the Arm in a hushed voice.

"Do you have the pickup from the address I gave you?" Patrick asks. "Brenda will be asking about it."

"I was on the highway, driving," the Arm continues, as if Patrick hasn't even said anything. "Everything was normal. Traffic was almost at a complete standstill, I was just idling forward, braking when I needed to, watching the smoke from the fire rolling off the Malibu hills. It was beautiful. Relaxing, even. I know it doesn't sound like smoke should be that way, but if you just pretend they're clouds, dirty clouds, you can see all kinds of things. Big, puffy shapes crawling across the sky. Hippopotamus. Pirate ship. Half a dragon. Stuff like that."

"I asked you about loafers, and you're telling me about dragons."

"Dragons are what I saw," the Arm replies, "but you might see something completely different. It's subjective."

"I know what subjective is," Patrick responds.

"Well, I'm just sitting in the car, I have my music on, I'm gazing out at the natural world and at all its, you know, splendor. And then I see this gorgeous girl. She's petite, cute chin and tiny waist and all of that, and she's wearing a yellow bathing suit, it's a tankini but it's skimpy in the right ways. She's carrying a beach towel under her arm, and her hair is kind of long and kind of short. She looks like the sort of girl you'd see on the college quad, someone new to school but fitting right in. Then I see that she's not wearing any shoes and her feet are all gray, up over the ankle. Oh, and she's smiling this fantastic smile, like a face-soap billboard. She's walking on the highway, down the stripe between the lanes of traffic, which is moving slowly for the most part, but sometimes a lane starts moving a little faster and someone wings her with the edge of their rearview mirror. And then she unrolls her towel and spreads it out on the asphalt up ahead of me. She lies down right between the fast lane and the middle lane, with the cars barreling past her on both sides."

"And what did you do?" Patrick asks, uneasily interested.

"Well, I did what any good person would do," the Arm says, troubled. "I put my hazards on and went to see if she needed help. When I got out of the car, the traffic had begun to clear up, so I had to try to wave the cars away from her, and I asked her if she was okay."

"And was she okay?"

"No," he says, "she was not."

Belly-up beneath the ceaseless sunshine, she lay with her eyes closed and her midriff bared to the ultraviolet eye overhead, an expression of stark serenity carved into her pale, bronzed face. As he leaned over her, he saw her features in such incredible detail that she didn't seem real, didn't seem human: she had the incomprehensible exactness of a map. He read the contours of her unlined cheeks, the crinkles at the outer corner of her eye. Slathered with gloss, her heart-shaped mouth glinted slow as breath snaked its way up from sluggish lungs. Pulse thrumming silently in the shadow of a long, slender bone, cheekbone gleaming with man-made dew. Under the bright, prickling heat, the only thing quick in her was her eyelids, the trembling so small and so fast that it reminded him of the scutter of insects, the faint penciling of sound you hear when a housefly passes close to your ear.

But maybe that was just the vibration of the road, the humming around and beneath him as the cars picked up speed, honking to underscore their objections, and as, far ahead and out of eyesight, thousands of vehicles began their acceleration to normal speeds, tiny explosions within their engines erupting so many times a second that no human eye or ear could parse it. He slid his fingers under her neck and lifted slightly, her mouth falling open a half-inch and exposing a sliver of tongue. He was saying the words: "Miss, are you all right? Miss, are you in danger? Are you ill? Should I call the cops? An ambulance, a parent, a friend?" Someone to match face to name. But, from the un-troubled limpness of her expression, he doubted that she heard him at all.

"Don't you have something for me, Hamlin?" comes a voice from his periphery.

Patrick turns toward Brenda. Every time he sees her, he's taken aback: her beauty is vaguely inhuman, the features un-naturally even and obviously expensive. Her skin smooth and poreless, like the sexy, futuristic plastic of the modernized elec-tric toothbrushes advertised to him in the margins of his browser window. Brenda seems irritated: the smooth skin knits at the apex of her brow, creating a visible indentation.

"I delegated that task to my associate here," Patrick replies, patting the Arm's knobby shoulder.

"I was unable to complete the task," the Arm says sadly, "be-cause I became embroiled in a police emergency involving a beautiful woman."

"Forget the shoes," says Brenda breezily. "I have a pickup scheduled that Patrick can do right now. If he hurries he'll be back in time to drive Cassidy home." She hands him an invoice made out to a clinic in Oxnard, about an hour past her Malibu home. Then something catches her attention. "Oh, good," she says, her voice growing bright, "she's actually here."

From the periphery of the room, a small, alarmingly slender figure drifts toward the set in a gown of pale, stiff organza, a sort of sexed-up crinoline topped with ruffled sleeves that slump alluringly off the shoulders. The gown is too big for the body inside it; it drags after her. From this blunt angle, in the odd and spooky artificial dusk, Cassidy Carter looks like a child of eight or nine playing pretend in a grown-up's dress, her long light-colored hair wild and unbrushed. Against the half-light, her limbs are bluntly visible, stick-straight and narrow, like bones through an X-ray. Cassidy reaches the luminous green square and stops, turns around. She points at the ladder. "Is this supposed to be the 'tree'?" she asks loudly, speaking to anybody and nobody in particular. "The 'tree' I'm supposed to be climbing in this scene?" Nobody answers her. "Hellooooo," she calls, the sound echoing through the vast rectangle of trapped air, captured by this building and kept from the sky. "Who's in charge of this clown car?"

Patrick looks around. Brenda is suddenly nowhere to be seen. But Horseshoe is walking toward them, chugging a half-empty bottle of WAT-R. The lump of his throat bobs up and down rhythmically. His grin looks like a grimace as he swallows deep. From his chinos comes the rattling sound of pilfered candy.

"Hi, friends," Horseshoe says, gesturing toward the green screen with the narrowed end of the plastic bottle. "What's happening up there?"

"She's looking for the director, I think," replies the Arm. "Or someone else who has authority."

Cassidy walks over to Dillon, who looks nervous. She's standing with her arms crossed before him, the ruffles exuberantly framing her aggrieved little face, asking him questions that they can't quite hear.

"Sam was fired," says Horseshoe thoughtfully. "I heard they hired his replacement already."

"What do you mean, Sam was fired?" Patrick says, too loudly, too sharply. "By Jay? For what?"

"I'm sorry, guys, I just can't get that girl out of my head." The Arm speaks sorrowfully, and it's true, anyone can see it, he is rickety with feelings. His mouth tilts and twists; he blinks over and over and seems to have no control over it. "I remember, like, everything about her. The confusion on her face when they hauled her away. After a while, the cops showed up and blocked off a couple of the freeway lanes. They were able to get her awake somehow; they sat her up and checked her heart rate. Pointed a little green light into her eyes, gave her some WAT-R to drink. They did this thing to her that we used to do when I was a kid when we wanted the cat to swallow its medicine— they would pour a little WAT-R into her mouth and rub her throat in long downward strokes. Eventually, she started blinking, not just staring. And then she talked."

"What did she say?" asks Horseshoe.

"She said to leave her alone, because she was at the *beach*."

"What does that even mean? Was she high?"

"She kept saying the same thing: 'I'm just trying to get a little sun, it's a public beach, I'm allowed to be here.' She sounded pretty normal, or what I mean is, she would have sounded normal if she were on a beach. She was using that authoritative white-lady voice, like my mom when she's trying to return things without a receipt."

"It's a voice of extreme reason, where reason begins to tip over into irrationality," says Horseshoe, nodding. "I used to assist this woman in Echo Park who was starting a line of homemade soaps. . . ."

"Did they arrest her?" asks Patrick, uneasily.

"No," responds the Arm, staring off. "They called a Green Van, and it picked her up. They told me it was a very humane solution, to get her some treatment. But I don't know, you know? They wouldn't have listened to me, and I wouldn't have known what to say, but I still feel like I should have argued with them about it. Or at least got it on video on my phone. Something."

The three of them stare off at the set, where Cassidy is examining the ladder, her hand on a rung, jostling it to see if it'll tip. Horseshoe is chewing dully, crunching pocket candy between his young, straight teeth.

"I saw a Green Van last week," Patrick says suddenly, uncertainly. Last week feels years old. "It pulled up in front of me, and out came a whole herd of people, a random assortment. None of them seemed to know where they were or what was going on. They had to be led around on a rope, like kindergartners on a school trip."

"We call them ROADies," says Horseshoe helpfully.

"Roadies?" Patrick asks.

"They have some new kind of dementia. My mom sent me an article about it."

"Dementia is for the old," Patrick replies. "Some of these were middle-aged people, people in their thirties. One of them looked even younger, a teenager."

"The new dementia is for everybody," Horseshoe says. "In the article, they interviewed a child who had it. She couldn't remember what age she was. My mom thinks metals have something to do with it—every couple of days, she warns me not to drink from aluminum cans. When she and my dad visit my place, they'll spend the whole time emptying beers from the cans into a big pitcher. My roommate was pissed."

As the two of them talk, they begin to notice that the Arm is not joining in at all. He stares off into the middle distance, toward the remnants of a beverage cart, but doesn't seem to be looking at anything at all. When the Arm finally speaks, he sounds haunted:

"There was something really special about that girl. I feel like we connected in some major, deep, past-lives way. I only saw her the one time, for maybe five minutes tops, but I have all these images in my head of her from different angles, in different outfits. Wearing an old-fashioned blouse, like something out of a Western. The detail is completely different from a fantasy, more like a crisp, clear memory of some tiny fragment of childhood." Wetness stirs in his eyes, catches the glint of the overhead lights. "I can't help feeling that maybe, just maybe, she was The One?"

Against the supersaturated background, its color like toxic slime, Cassidy Carter climbs halfway up the ladder, pauses, dismounts. She looks at the thing, puzzled and serious, like she's trying to figure out a particularly complex math problem. She drapes her arms around it uneasily, she closes her eyes, smiles a peaceful smile, then opens them, looking up wide-eyed at the empty space, the studio nothingness. Then she begins her climb again, slower this time, and with a labored quality, readjusting her grip, sliding the hand around the underside of the flat wooden plank, registering the unseen roundness of the machine-worked slats of severed wood. Her body stretches up, out, over-mapping the width of the thing, tasting its texture with the palm of her hand, pulling herself up with a smooth release of breath, of tension, of effort. Patrick realizes that she is climbing the ladder as if it were a tree. Like the sound of electricity coursing through an overhead wire, or the scent of gasoline once it's exceeded the threshold of awareness, the tree becomes real to him with this thought, a map of holds and roughness that her body navigates with skill and grace and a measure of authentic strain.

Cassidy grunts as she heaves herself to the top of the ladder, and pauses to take in the view. She looks at the shelter of slendering boughs and branches overhead, then out into the distance, at something far away, far past the soundstage walls. She tilts her perfectly hewn chin into the inferable breeze. As she watches, her eyes narrow, her face becomes more delicate, calm, engrossed. The feeling of reality drains from his body, and all that's left is a chill beneath the skin, even in the stifling heat of the soundstage. With a shiver, Patrick realizes that it's possible for a person to believe wholly, completely, in something that's not even there.

To avoid the clogged red arteries in his navigation app, Patrick detours through the San Fernando Valley, past the brickish, brownish roofs of Santa Clarita subdivisions, cutting back down onto a smaller highway steeply bounded by strips of dust-sided cliff. Some combination of heat, stress, and cheap, mass-prepared food has altered the moisture balance of his body: he feels the loss of saliva every time he breathes in the stiff, hot air inside the van, invisibly tinged with the smoke of the wildfire still gnawing at the dry flank of Thousand Oaks, Agoura Hills, Topanga Canyon. A thin slick of life evaporates from him with each breath. There's a bloom of drab smoke to his left, and a river somewhere in that direction too—he can see it on the little map on his phone, twisting and turning in miniature as he takes the curves of the road. Somewhere beyond view, the brush is burning in the bright daylight, orange scraps of flame dulled by the sunlight. The sound of small life fleeing from the fire, scurrying toward more fire elsewhere.

Terrible, definitely. But it's not really an emergency, he thinks, putting on his signal and shifting into the fast lane, if you can drive around it. An emergency would be everywhere you looked, inescapable; some long-submerged animal intelligence would recognize it with fierce instinct. In an emergency, the mind would not drift aimlessly from daydream to distraction as his did now, in search of something to grasp. He attempts to conjure the image of his wife and daughter, but it won't hold firm: their bodies bent close together have an unreal waver, and with their backs turned toward his longing gaze, he can't make out their faces, the faces he should know so well. They're in the garden, bent together over the same spot, pushing soil into a mound with their bare, pale hands, but he can't see what they're seeing, he's missing the most important part. The background flickers, subsumed by a blankness with no color. How can he miss them, his family, if he can't even remember them clearly?

It's easier to picture Cassidy Carter, her face an amalgamation of different angles and poses gleaned from the search engine, her image animated by fresh, hot resentment and a tinge of admiration. She certainly gets what she wants, at least in his limited experience. He can almost see her—a child, aged whatever—with limbs gangly and thin, walking along dust-stricken pavement and dreaming of her future. Head down and arms out, balancing, she sets one foot in front of the other in a narrow line, her golden hair catching fire in the sunlight. As he daydreams, his foot sinks into the pedal, pushing the speed up past sixty-five, seventy, eighty, until the sound of a cassette tape rattling in the player cuts through his mind-fog and he realizes the entire van is quaking. He lifts his foot and the rattling subsides.

It reminds him of nights when Nora was still an infant— a grub of love, more animal than person, her sounds creaturely but full of sweet, unsculpted emotion. She was a fussy sleeper, and the only thing that lulled her was a late-night drive. He and Alison would pick up the pliant, astonishingly heavy body, lower it into a plastic car-seat in the back of their sedan, guide the plump legs through the straps of the seatbelt, and fasten the latch with reverence. Wordlessly, fervently, like two medieval monks working side by side, one would push shut the car door and slip into the front passenger seat as the other took the wheel; the engine sighed as key turned in ignition. The car slid into reverse with a soft moan and backed out of the driveway onto the abandoned street, and then they were crawling around the neighborhood at ten miles per hour, slow enough that the engine never crept above an idle. They drove in circles past the quiet, half-lit houses until they sensed Nora's slumber in the inky depth of her silence. Then Patrick would swivel around in his seat to peer into the darkened space and wait for gasps of streetlight to illuminate Nora's round, socked feet in the darkened space. Soft white and edgeless, they looked like sightless cartoon worms, docile and incapable of harm.

He and Alison had perfected this ritual—the careful insertion and hushed removal, the soundless transfer of weighty flesh from plastic receptacle to crib—but one day the town tore the street up to be repaved. For months, the surface was strewn with gravel and large, chassis-rattling rocks, making it impossible to drive silently at any speed. Instead of sneaking through the darkness in the hush of the engine thrum, they clung to the steering wheel or dashboard as the car rattled around them. They placed a hand, when they could, on the trembling seat. Nora never slept so well ever again, and soon Patrick returned to spending nights in his office, working on his second book—an epic novella taking place entirely during the approximately nine hours it took George Washington to cross the Delaware River. Over fifty different points of view were used, from the teenage cook preoccupied with the untimely spillage of twenty pounds of dried peas to the free, indirect musings of a muskrat down-wind who could scent the laboring humans but not see them. He called it *Hard Crossing,* and it was for a brief period of time optioned by a television studio in Denmark as "a daring meta-phor for the relation of the individual's struggle to that of the nation," though it never made it to development.

As Nora grew older, they tried different strategies to manage her insomnia: hot milk scented with cardamom, mossy-tasting herbs ground and encased in gelatin capsules, a rigid timeline of meals and rest generated by an ad-supported mindfulness app. Inevitably, she was alert until late in the night and helplessly drowsy in the day, falling asleep at her school desk in the small, dark nest of her arms. But Patrick blamed Alison for the new phase of Nora's sleeplessness: after the incident with the neigh-bor's lawn, which cost them both so many hours of apologetic planting and resodding, knocking on the doors of every house on the block and explaining that Alison was absolutely back to normal now, Nora had stayed awake for five days straight, writ-ing an unsettling document that she claimed was "a description of what I would have been dreaming if I hadn't decided to stay awake." In the handwritten text, ninety pages long, volcanic eruptions blotted out the sun, and strange spiny fishes starved in cold seas, sunk and dissolved in the soft mud. Scaly-headed birds self-birthed from thick eggs staggered toward the shadows, huge lizards crushed the bodies of lizards that were merely large between wickedly equipped jaws. Where there were people, they were blurrily seen, minuscule figures crossing the landscape on foot before being devoured by overgrown rodents with teeth like tusks.

Clearly, Patrick explained to Alison, their daughter was acting out the residue of her mother's trauma, distilling and concentrating her doomsday attitude in an effort to earn approval and possibly even make Alison happy once again. "Don't you see," he said, "our daughter telling you, 'Yes, I too see the world the way that you do. Can we please go back to normal now?'" In class, the teacher's report noted that Nora was "excessively interested in the iconography of the mushroom cloud," and a classmate's mother called to demand that Alison make her daughter stop talking about asteroids colliding with the earth, it was giving her child ominous dreams. Meanwhile, Nora wrote through the night and sometimes during the day as well, the margins of her loose-leaf cluttered with brief odes to destruction. It was only when Alison built a planting box in the backyard and assigned her the task of seeding a small garden that Nora began to fall asleep again at night—though she continued to write long apocalyptic screeds, hiding them around her room in places that they discovered when cleaning, and probably also in places that they never found at all. For his own part, Patrick was uncomfortable reading the texts or hearing about them secondhand from Alison, who devoured them all with tense, puzzled fascination. Not only were they depressing, the narratives—though they involved some overlapping, recurrent imagery—were to him largely incoherent. If there was some greater message or insight there into his daughter's mind, he was definitely not equipped to decode it. When he thinks about Alison off in her hippie sanctuary, the thing that drives him crazy is not the notion that she's making love to some shirtless, smooth-chested Woofer, but the idea of her telling some stranger all about him, all the little mistakes that misrepresent him and ought to be forgotten, poking holes in the story of their life.

A clattering squeal from somewhere beneath the car, a sound like teeth on metal. Patrick ducks his head down and around, looking for a trace of the thing he'd hit reflected in the van's large, useless side-view mirrors. He sees only the flat white flank of the van filling the mirrors, and the inexhaustible landscape stretching out behind and before him in blurry shades of ochre and tan, broom-dry and indistinct, like the component strokes of a painting when you stand too close. Up ahead, there's nothing to look at, nothing to read except the occasional WAT-R billboard, crisp hyperdetailed photographs of WAT-R bottles plunging into crystal-clear WAT-R, sending up intricate splashes in midair pause. The spurts of water resemble transparent phalluses eternally on the verge of decay, bending toward dissolution. Words float across the images, immaterial: REAL, BETTER, RIGHT AT YOUR FINGERTIPS and WATER DONE RIGHT. As he speeds by, short, steep cliffs rear up and recede, the land yawning out next to him in blotches of beige. It occurs to Patrick that it's strange to advertise WAT-R when the product has no competition. In every gas station, in every grocery store, the variegated bottles of Evian and Dasani you can still buy on the East Coast have been replaced by WAT-R *Pure*, WAT-R *Free*,

WAT-R *Clean*. What, then, do the advertisements sell? The idea
that buying WAT-R is still a choice rather than a necessity?

On the off-ramp, among soft-drink packaging and leaf litter,
a plastic bag weighed down by something heftier inside. Patrick
tries to avoid it, but as the van passes over, he feels something
burst beneath the tires, and now a sound comes from the engine, a sound like someone being slapped again and again in
calm rhythm. One left, one right, and a long cruise down broad
asphalt to the address Brenda gave him, a five-digit number at
one end of a long road. It's scrawled on a piece of torn letter-
head, two capital "B"s splayed against each other in a butterfly
shape, the high-quality paper as supple as cloth. There's no sign
on the building: it's a stucco box, taller than it is wide, uniformly
windowed in wide sheets of mirrored glass that reflect the surrounding buildings and roads in a gasoline rainbow of colors. As
he drives through the parking lot, he watches the reflection of
the white van gliding past window after window, rippling in the
uneven panes, tinted green, then blue, then gold. He knows he's
inside there, someplace, but it's difficult to pass from knowledge
to true acceptance.

He rolls down the windows and stares out at the entrance to
the unnamed, unmarked building. He tilts the bottle of WAT-R
Lite ("a fat-free beverage"), and the liquid falls out into his
mouth. It's an imperceptible weight on and around his tongue,
the bare outline of a substance rolling across the limp, soft muscle, more of a temperature than a taste. The WAT-R slips down
his throat before he even has a chance to think about swallowing
it, leaving behind the same stale, dry flavor in his maw that he
began with: motel syrup, indelible, like a tattoo on the tongue.
A dozen bright-green passenger vans are parked outside, each

identical to the one he saw in the parking lot. There's a message from Cassidy in his inbox, and it reads: *Where the f are you??? Time to drive me and my liquid paycheck back home.* He feels distraught for no good reason. Maybe it's because there's nobody within three thousand miles of his sweaty torso who cares how he feels, nobody alive to miss him back. It's like the blueness of the air above him: one color in the spectrum of colors, with nowhere to go, nothing to absorb it, so it fills the entire sky. He lifts up the bottle of WAT-R to his lips one more time, but it's empty.

At the entrance to the building, the glass doors slide open and shut on their own like matter possessed. Inside, there's a spearmint-colored counter with a plasticky, retro feel and some molded chairs that glisten dully beneath the bright lobby light. A girl behind the desk looks at him and picks up a clipboard. All around him screams a bright manic green, the exact shade of the vans parked out front, or the green screen of the movie set back in Alhambra, where he's due back, already overdue. Posters on the wall remind him in green text to remain calm and check his pockets for belongings.

"Hi there, how can I help you?" she asks, coming around the side of the wavy, sinuous desk. He takes in her green polo shirt and slacks, the tight blond ponytail—a uniform inspired by food service. Something about the middle of her face is familiar to him, but he can't quite pin it down. He squints: maybe it's her nose. She frowns slightly and puts a hand on his elbow.

"Okay, sir. Don't worry. We'll get you taken care of. We just need you to answer one question first. Are you ready?" Her voice has turned gentle and false, like she's speaking to a child, a dog, some soft and moldable mind.

"Wait," says Patrick, unsure what's happening to him.

She continues, soothingly: "Did someone drop you off here, or did you come on your own?" She stares at him. Boredom and sympathy mingle in her gaze. She holds up two clipboards. "Either one is okay—it just changes whether I give you one of the blue forms or one of the yellow ones."

He knows that the anger welling up in him is correct, though he can't explain why. Something disrespectful is happening here, with the girl and her saccharine tone and the vaguely infantilizing roundedness of everything in the room. He knows that the emotion rising to the surface of his face only makes him look weaker.

"I'm picking up for Brenda Billington," he says, coldly, emphasizing the powerful name. "I don't know who you're mistaking me for, but I'm not filling out any forms." The girl looks at him questioningly. He hardens his face, pulling everything tight, an angry customer.

"What are you picking up?" she asks.

"Look, I'm not sure," Patrick says. "Brenda just told me to come here and collect a package. I don't know how big it is, or what's in it. I'm usually involved in work on this film. I work closely with Cassidy Carter on her projects."

The girl's already wide eyes widen further, Patrick can see the white surrounding her iris as she registers this new information. "Oh, wow. Okay, hold on, I'll try to figure this out." She goes back behind the desk and looks through piles of things Patrick can't see. The sound of paper is loud in the empty room.

"So," the girl says shyly, "what's she like? Is she nice?"

Patrick doesn't answer. He's looking past her, toward the far end of the hall, out of view, where he hears the sound of figures stepping out into the corridor, a murmur of voices swiftly tamped down again. A latch on the door turns, and the space is even quieter than before.

"Right," she continues, "I mean, why would that even matter? It's not like I'm a fan because I think she's a nice person, otherwise there are tons of randos you could be a fan of. I guess I'm just asking, you know, is she *real*? Would she order a double cheeseburger without holding any of the sauce, onions, et cetera? Does she own nail-polish remover?"

"I think she would order the cheeseburger," Patrick says, distracted. It's a return of the ominous feeling he's been having all week that *nobody is in charge,* alternating with the fearful certainty that *the ones in charge are not on my side*.

"Yeah, I thought so. I read a profile of her once where it said she's the sort of girl you could grab a burger with. That really rang true to me."

Patrick leans forward, tries to peer over the counter. A mess of Post-it notes in different kinds of handwriting, a sloping heap of paperwork.

"Anyway," she says, rubbing the bridge of her nose as she looks down the short corridor at the closed door. "I need to get my manager. He'll know what's here for pickup. Almost everything here is a drop-off. Obviously."

Obviously? Patrick watches her walk off, slip past the wooden door and into an area marked EMPLOYEES ONLY. The way she warmed up to him when he said Cassidy's name made him think of calling his wife, telling her how the washed-up star he's been working with may still have some pull—though he knows if he called he'd be unlikely to reach her. More likely, he'd get Klaus again, the smarmy Midwestern woodworker whose workshop sat adjacent to the barn wall on which the public pay phone was mounted. He always seemed to have a hand free at the exact right moment, and Patrick was coming to appreciate his sense of humor and the varied woodworking-related metaphors he employed to talk about Patrick's pain, Patrick's pushiness, Patrick's ever-deferred need to pin down what exactly was happening over there in the campfire sing-along cult his wife had run off to. "Imagine that you wish to craft a tool, my friend," Klaus said, his deep voice nasalized through the tiny meshed opening in Patrick's smartphone, "in order to accomplish a very specific purpose. Let's say you have a bunch of nails and you want to make a hammer. Do you create a hammer by hammering a piece of wood? Can you hammer a piece of wood into shape? No, you need to shape the handle, cut away at the extraneous matter, chisel the place for a thumb to rest, create a smooth and sanded domicile for the hand. The beauty of creating a tool is that you perform a thousand ambient, proximate actions in order to coax out the one function you really need. And though it feels like you're beating around the bush, you are in fact preparing the bush to reveal what it holds within: a full and flourishing flock of red-winged blackbirds that burst out, full of joy, and circle the sun. Do you see what I mean, Patrick?"

While Klaus was speaking, Patrick always felt that the meanings of his little folksy stories were as clear as hospital Plexi, but afterward he'd wonder: In this analogy, was his love the hammer or the nails? Was it the thoughtfully crafted handle, or the heavy, misshapen lump of metal that formed the head of the object, a monstrous element the rest of the object struggled to support? In the empty waiting room, he can hear voices from the far end of the long corridor, the muffled rasp of one voice arguing, heavy institutional latches sliding loudly in and out of place in the stale, sun-drenched air. He can't sit still; he feels as though he's been shoved back to some lesser developmental state, a child waiting to see the dentist, powerless over his own consequences. He stands up and straightens his slacks, lets himself wander into the mouth of the long corridor leading away from the office, where the ponytailed girl argues with her manager, pushing into the heart of the building. The combination of lemon-scented cleaner and freshly unrolled carpet gives him a feeling halfway between headache and fatigue.

Deep in the corridor, there's a birth-canal feeling. *Patrick, I'm warning you,* reads the message from Cassidy that just popped up on his phone. The hallway is so narrow he can feel the walls at his flanks, dim and silent and constrictive. He suddenly realizes that this building is something other than the utilitarian office zone it presented from the road. Miles of tight walkways coiled within the deceptive boxiness of the mirrored façade, hallways funneling toward deeply remote spaces at the center of the building, far from sunlight or unforced air. A tumbleweed-blond clump of hair wobbles in a half-lit corner. He takes two right turns, until he's so deep inside the building that it gives off its own rhythm. Liquid shifts in the pipes above; air stirs slowly and comes to a halt.

Then, in the hallway before him, he sees a sudden bright rectangle lit up as vividly as a flat-screen TV. It's a window as wide as an aquarium wall, through which Patrick can see figures moving. He draws closer, stands at the edge of the glass. To his dark-adjusted eyes, the light is so bright it stings.

Inside the frame, a dozen men and women wait in a tiled room, wearing shapeless gowns the vivid, manic green of the vans and lobby. Against the supersaturated hue, the pinks and browns of their skin seem to wilt, marred by wrinkles and folds and areas where the flesh has gone loose. Their bodies come in all ages, all sizes, all races: an old man with a concave chest and a thin-legged boy whose fish-pale body makes Patrick think of middle-school locker rooms. A young Asian woman sits open-mouthed, her expensive hair tinged with streaks of honey-blond and twitching gently in unseen airflow. If this group of people were seen together in public, wearing normal clothes and smiling, their presence together would be a riddle to solve. He watches them sitting on a scatter of chairs, or silently upright with an infinitesimal sway in their stance. Their gazes point in all different directions, each one looking at nothing in particular—but at different nothings, in different places.

Then a door opens, and an assistant comes in. She wears the uniform of the Cassidy-obsessed girl at the front desk, a green polo and tan slacks. With her short-cropped hair, she reminds him of his sixth-grade art teacher, a woman who once stood at the front of the classroom and in one fluid gesture drew a flawless circle on a piece of butcher paper taped against the wall. Patrick watches as she walks over to a man with an unevenly shaved head and cups his jaw in her soft, slightly pudgy hand, tilting his gaze upward. With her other hand, she pulls a small bottle from her pocket, inverts it, and holds it above. A small nozzle hovers directly over his eyeball, an inch from the white. He sees the brief glint of liquid falling, and then the nurse shuts the man's eyelids and massages them for a few seconds before sliding them back open and moving on to the next patient.

One by one, the nurse places a drop in each eye of every man or woman or child in the room. When she rubs their closed lids, the gesture is gentle and grimly efficient. In a matter of minutes, she finishes and leaves the room. Patrick watches the inert figures fail to move, their small movements unconscious and barely perceptible, like flowers on an airless afternoon. Their moistened eyes glisten under the bright lights. Through the thick, presumably polarized pane of glass a moaning can be heard, but Patrick does not know whom to notify about this, whom to tell.

On his way out the door, the girl at the desk hands him a flier. "You can give this to a friend," she says brightly, "if you don't need it yourself!" The green paper is printed with bold black text:

ARE YOU OK?

IF YOU ARE EXPERIENCING ANY OF THESE SYMPTOMS:

- **MEMORY LOSS**
- **SWOLLEN FINGERS**
- **UNEXPECTED CLOTTING**
- **HALLUCINATION OF WATER**
- **HALLUCINATION OF BIRDS**
- **DIFFICULTY RECALLING MEMORIES**
- **UNABLE TO CRY OR SWEAT**
- **DENSE TEARS OR SWEAT**
- **UNREQUITED AFFECTION**

- **IRREGULAR OR INADEQUATE BLINKING**

- **MAN IN SUIT**

YOU MAY BE IN URGENT NEED OF TREATMENT!
VISIT YOUR NEAREST MEMODYNE CLINIC FOR
A CONSULTATION!

Standing in the cool shadow of the soundstage, Cassidy Carter presses her phone to the side of her scowling face and listens to Patrick's voicemail recording for the umpteenth time. She texts Brenda and then Jay, asking if they have an ETA on her pickup. She calls the motel in Azusa and leaves a message with the front desk: "Tell him that I've wasted almost three hours now waiting—that's worth at least a few thousand in potential income. If he pushes me too far, I'm going to bill him for the opportunity cost," she tells the apologetic front-desk boy on the other end of the line, whose teenage voice is as tender as a ripe nectarine. She scrolls through the list of contacts on her phone, names she owes a favor to and names that are good for a few hours at a club and nothing more. Her old manager's number is still in her phone—she's deleted it before, but always finds herself digging through old papers a couple days later, looking for the handwritten digits. Her high-profile exes are there, along with the secret exes she saved under innocuous aliases. She even has Rainer Westchapel's number, though she's never called. Of course he'd recognize her name, but the thought that he wouldn't remember that afternoon on the hot, inland road makes her furious.

As she swipes idly from the top of the list to the bottom and back, the only name that gives her pause is June's. Her sister's last text sits unanswered in her message inbox, two years old. She opens it up sometimes and reads it if she needs a little push for crying in a scene. *Take care of yourself Butch, please go easy on your body and your heart.* When she's down on herself and looking to feel worse, she thinks of June, whom she hasn't spoken to in almost three years, and meditates on all the happy, intact families who fuck up and still manage to forgive one another. She could phone June now, but why bother? More hushed, overly gentled questions about how she's *feeling,* whether she's being careful, whether she's treating her life like a *gift,* reminders that she's not good enough to be around until she stops drinking or doing drugs or lashing out in anger—in other words, until she starts acting more like June. Even imagining the conversation they might have fills her with the bad-news itch to call just to tell her sister that she *uses drugs when she feels like it or needs to, drugs don't use her.* Instead, she phones Kiki Bennett, a hair-dye entrepreneur turned rapper, who doesn't pick up. Scrolling down, she chooses another name, the daughter of a big-deal singer with an oversized, grating laugh. The phone rings and rings quietly in her hand. The summer sun presses down through her straw fedora, casting pin dots of bright white on her bare thighs. Between calls, she idly dials her own number, even though she knows no one is home to pick up.

Thirty-six miles away, the phones ring in seven different rooms of Cassidy Carter's seven-bedroom, eight-bathroom home, sitting unattended on its 1.3-acre lot, baking under the late-afternoon sun. As the temperature climbs, the central cooling comes on automatically, pushing new-smelling air through shiny gold vents. In the eight empty bathrooms, identical scented diffusers leak factory vetiver through oil-soaked reeds, saturating the room. In each unoccupied bedroom, a tufted queen bed frame upholstered in steely gray and adorned with decorative nail heads appears new and unused, coated in a near-imperceptible layer of dust. A vintage-look radio on the nightstand plays staticky top-forty to no one. Soft tufts of lint and old hair stir in the corners, shivering in the invisible breeze. After ten minutes, the air shuts off. In the kitchen downstairs, an internet-linked refrigerator senses the rising interior temperature and whirs into action, loudly ejecting dozens of ice cubes into a holding tank.

On mottled granite countertops, a family-sized container of Scandinavian yogurt sits lidless next to a pint of organic blueberries, gradually reaching room temperature. A fly beats itself against the plate glass. The water heater in the basement below switches on and off at fifteen-minute intervals, keeping the water at a steady middling temperature in case someone was to enter the house, make their way to one of the eight generous bathrooms, and turn on the hot-water faucet. The water heater is hooked up to a household-sized sack of WAT-R *Pure,* the liquid murky and faintly blue within a thick cloudy skin of plastic. The house a half-living thing, multi-lunged and plushly organed, steeped in electricity and suspended in a continual sigh, the rhythm of its functions too massive, too slow, for any real creature. Breathing out and never in, exhaling constantly into the world.

Out back, dark tufts of clover and nub nettles poke through the flagstones as the sprinkler starts up, broken, sputtering onto the dust. Wetness pools in the hollow around the fist-sized spigot, gathers, and overflows, trickling into a cluster of dead, embrittled rosebushes. When the wind sweeps through, the sound is dry, dry against dry: the scraping of edges paper-thin and multiple, expensive plants turned to tinder. Across the property line, the yellow brush grows thicker, thornier, and more wild. Gopher snakes slide smooth-bellied through the grasses, seeking warm, living meat in the hidden burrows; dull, palm-sized birds burst out and vanish again into the scrub. Every sound is a body moving through the world, a pair of eyes and a small trembling heart. The dust-colored birds dart in and out of the sky. Something launches from the dirt road, a grasshopper with wings that fold invisibly back into the torpedo of its body. Past a sign marking the petroleum line running beneath, bramble gives way to live oaks with small, hard leaves, nestled in the elbow of the canyon, where the water pools in the runoff.

There, by the base of the oaks, a heap of fur in ragged brown and beige: the shape like a dog's, but with a savage point to its muzzle. The coyote lies on its side in the open. Its breath comes calm and even, like that of a sleeping thing—if it's dying, it doesn't know. With eyes open and tongue trembling against the bone-white teeth, it stares straight forward, past the variegated grasses, and paddles with its feet, pawing at the air, running in place, running nowhere, as the raptors circle overhead.

Viewed from above, the parking lot of the WAT-R Super-Center on Sunset is a vast system of dark pools and narrow pathways, interconnected lakes that quench no thirst. There's one lot for families with more than two children, one for fuel-efficient and electric vehicles, one for mobility-limited customers and one for customers with compromised immune systems, a lot for Diamond Club members, who spend more than fifty thousand a year on WAT-R Solutions, and a special lot for Fusion Club cardholders, who spend three times that annually, paved in polished granite and ornamented by a lighted moving walkway that carries Fusion Elites to a private entrance, where automatic doors whoosh open with a sound like a sigh. Then there's the overflow lot, extending eight stories beneath the gleaming glass cube: like a glacier, only a fraction of the structure is visible to the unaugmented eye. Patrick guides the bulky rent-a-van down narrow subterranean channels, turning left and left again, the turns tightening, like they're spiraling down into the deep center of a nautilus shell.

"Park over there," says Horseshoe from the cargo hold, pointing at a narrow rectangular gap, better suited for a coupe. In the passenger seat, the Arm stares out the window with an emptied-out look on his face.

"We'll all have to crawl out the loading doors," Patrick gripes, but he pulls in anyway, the vehicle crawling at a speed so low that it sometimes feels like it isn't moving at all. He squeezes himself out through the driver's side as Horseshoe escorts the Arm out the back, supporting his midsection and helping him to figure out the tricky door handle. It seems to Patrick that there's something wrong with the older, taller kid, the one who seemed more in charge that first day by the pool (why can't Patrick ever remember his name?), something that can't be chalked up to unrequited love or getting baked before work. But Horseshoe insists that the Arm is simply a sensitive soul, and when his morale picks back up he's sure to have gleaned new insights from this ruminative period.

The elevator doors open onto a space so bright that the dank below-ground garage feels like a false memory, something that never existed. Bounded on all sides by pale-blue glass and pierced by shafts of cool light, the feeling is like standing in the center of a gigantic ice cube, chilly and indifferent. Families and hand-holding couples crisscross the vast interior, drifting from one sample booth to another, clutching in their fists little plastic cups filled with neon-pink vitamin-enriched WAT-R *Feminine Mystique* and banana-scented WAT-R *Rainforest Tropicale*. At the top of a twisting glass staircase sits a rooftop tasting bar, where orders of premium WAT-R by the glass come with a free shot of vodka or blue curaçao. The Arm stands in the center of the WAT-R Welcome Rotunda, near a large fountain with an ice-sculpture centerpiece of a WAT-R bottle. He looks back and forth as though trying in every direction at once. The crowd parts seamlessly around his unmoving figure, reconstituted on the other side, like water flowing around a river rock. From the fountainhead, liquid slurps forth in great slow glugs. Patrick realizes that the kid is searching the faces, every face, but for what?

"Pat, dude," Horseshoe says, placing a hand on his shoulder, "do you have the list from Brenda?"

Patrick pulls the paper from his pocket and hands it over. He's faintly ashamed to be caught gaping, like Horseshoe's poor lost friend, at this place that is ordinary to so many.

Horseshoe scans the list and hands it back. "Most of this stuff is bulk; we'll have to request it at the bulk desk. They prepare the order while we bring our vehicle around."

"So how long will it take?" Patrick asks. "I need to pick Cassidy up at five, and I was already late once this week."

"Five isn't impossible," Horseshoe replies thoughtfully, "but it isn't likely. It'll take at least an hour to make it through the different antechambers of the store, not to mention ordering and waiting at the bulk service desk. I think six-thirty is a better bet."

The Arm runs up to them, frantic, gesturing around.

"I saw a girl," he says, distraught, "I saw a girl that looked just like her." They turn around to face the crowd, but nobody looks like anyone they know. The faces fail to light up with smiles of recognition: the odd and discrepant features arranged in the same rough order as those of your loved ones, the eyes and ears and nose all present but not like theirs, not like them at all. Pop songs with the words erased seep blurrily through the speakers. A woman drops her handbag on the polished marble floor and picks it up again; she drops it a second time and wanders away. Then an employee in a tight blue WAT-R logo tee holds a megaphone up to his mouth and announces there's a new sample available at Booth Six: WAT-R *Fruit Snack Quenchers*, a chewy candy carapace filled with sweetened enriched water. The crowd murmurs, takes the shape of a parade: all Patrick can see now are backs, as the people move as one singular organism toward the exciting new product, the exciting new taste.

As they walk from the rotunda to the innards of the store, Patrick asks Horseshoe if there's any way to get to their destination faster. Shouldn't there be a path straight to the dedicated bulk-ordering station for people on tight schedules, VIPs, elderly customers who lack stamina? But Horseshoe assures him that the store is deeply democratic in design: every person, no matter how rich or poor, walks the same long path. There's wisdom in the path, which leads past countless fake rooms, even whole fake houses, each one decorated with care. There's an upscale metrosexual loft kitchen stocked with premium WAT-R in the now familiar diamond-faceted bottles, a cozy Scandinavian kitchen with bottles of WAT-R *HyggeBurst* on display next to a carved wooden bird. A petite woman with a ponytail urges shoppers to "Go with the flow!" and "Dream yourself into your own WAT-R lifestyle fantasy!" To Patrick, the naked commercialism on display here, the marketing muscle that's gone into making a basic drinking liquid aspirational, is repulsive. But when he sees the girls stripping off tee shirts to reveal genuine bikini tops, taking selfies in front of a replica Caribbean beach with bottles of tropical-infused WAT-R *Coconut Vacation!* hoisted toward the camera lens, he can't help but wish he were young again and able to join in the pageant without self-awareness, without guilt.

"Why is there a whole store for water?" the Arm asks, his head swiveling.

"It's not water," Horseshoe explains patiently, "it's WAT-R." He says the last half of the word with a harsh, downward intonation, vaguely robotic. Horseshoe is starting to look a little worried, though Patrick thinks he's trying to mask it. "You know I love you, man, but are you doing all right?"

"Why is it so big?" the Arm says, as if he hasn't heard his buddy's question. He examines a courtesy-sized bottle of WAT-R *Basic,* then shakes the liquid vigorously until a layer of faintly blue froth forms at the top. He hands it over to Patrick.

"Is he making a joke?" Patrick says to Horseshoe, who shrugs.

The plastic bottle is warm in his hands as Patrick stares at the thin blue film swirling on the surface. It reminds him of the little rafts of bubbles he would spot riding the calmer, shore-bound waves when he went to the Cape as a child: detergents from nearby factories, his mother told him.

"What's that floating on top?" he asks, handing it over to Horseshoe for inspection.

Horseshoe squints through the cheap plastic, and immediately looks bored.

"That'll go away if you just leave it alone for a while."

"But what is it?"

"I don't know what you call it," Horseshoe says. "It's fine, it'll disappear. My buddy who's in science told me that it happens because WAT-R is a little more 'social' than the old stuff. It boils at a slightly higher temperature and freezes at a slightly lower temperature. It forms stronger bonds inside the molecule, and with other molecules. So sometimes they clump together. Hence the occasional foam that doesn't really matter and that nobody cares about."

"I thought WAT-R was supposed to be the same thing, though."

"Yeah, it's the same," Horseshoe says, distracted. "It's the same as water, just a little bit more so."

The line for bulk orders stretches all the way into the showroom, so Patrick waits in place as Horseshoe and the Arm go to check out the snack bar. He takes out Brenda's instructions and reads over the list again: two dozen cooler-ready five-gallon containers of WAT-R *Pure,* two pallets each of WAT-R *Energy Surge* and *Energy Surge Plus,* five eight-gallon dispensable Quenchers of WAT-R *Basic,* along with extra spouts, and a case of WAT-R *Diamante Dreams.* In the margin, there's a note: "The *Diamante* is for the wrap party, do NOT store in main office or we will have theft!!!" He has no idea how much all of this will cost, only that it should be charged to a ten-digit account scrawled on the back of the paper in Brenda's ferociously sloppy handwriting. Over at the far end of the vast warehouse, Horseshoe and the Arm order WAT-R slushes in flavors of boysenberry and oat milk. Half-frozen WAT-R tumbles in infinite circles inside the machines, shades of fuchsia, burgundy, and ochre visible through the clear plastic casing. The Arm drops his slush on the ground and all over someone's sneakers, but Horseshoe helps him clean it up. Then they get back in line to purchase a replacement.

At the bulk desk, the bulk girl wears the same logo tee as all the other employees, but someone's written on it in marker, turning the hyphen into a sloppy, makeshift E. She logs his order with careless efficiency, asks him if he'll be paying for delivery or hauling it himself, offers him a WAT-R Solutions credit card with a 10-percent discount on today's order, and tells him that if he buys another pallet of *Energy Surge Plus,* he'll get a free pallet of *Energy Surge Pro,* which he declines. But when he hands over the account number in Brenda's scrawl, her pale forehead furrows.

"Where did you get this number?" she asks.

"My boss wrote it down for me," he says. "Brenda Billington and Jay Arvid. Film producers. This is all going to their studio in Alhambra."

"I need to ask my manager," she replies.

The manager comes over. The two ponder the ten handwritten digits, entering keystrokes into the computer system and shaking their heads. The format isn't the same as their other account numbers, explains the manager, a twentysomething with wire-frame glasses. He leans over and shows Patrick that there are ten digits in the number he gave, whereas their account numbers are supposed to be nine digits long. They'll have to call someone higher up to see what's going on. Behind Patrick, the line grumbles.

Horseshoe comes up, his mouth stained an unearthly color. "Sun's setting," he says. "Brenda and Jay are going to be pissed at us for being late." He wraps his lips around the plastic straw; hot-pink slush travels up the narrow corridor in irregular gasps.

"That sound at the end of the slushy," the Arm says in a drifting voice, "that gurgle. That's the sound the world will make when it ends." He drops his drink on the floor again, but no one moves to help.

"How long have you been drinking this WAT-R stuff? Personally, I mean?" Patrick asks.

"What's WAT-R?" the Arm asks.

"Hmm," Horseshoe says thoughtfully, ignoring the Arm. "Nobody around here asks a question like that. It must be your East Coast perspective on our situation." He pulls out his phone and scrolls through the calendar app, going back one year, then two. "I'd place it around two years three months. I was kind of an early adopter, you could say. I drank it before we had to drink it, because of the cool flavors and concepts."

"Someone told me they don't think WAT-R tastes like the real thing," Patrick says, thinking of Cassidy's profile in the dark, edged in bright fire, smelling of ashes. "What do you think? Don't you miss regular water—no decisions, no choices?"

Horseshoe tosses his emptied drink into the trash without a glance. "Again, not a thing we talk about very much here. Do you ever have convos back at home comparing the flavor of tap water in different counties? This is like that." He grows quieter. He's watching the Arm study his fallen slush with grave intensity. The Arm's eyes flicker back and forth across the trail of emerald sludge; he nudges the plastic cup with the toe of his shoe. Suddenly, he frowns. He starts scanning the crowd, as if searching for the person who left it there. Horseshoe sighs, kneads his smooth chin wearily. "You know, now that I try to remember, I can't really recall much. That's the way of regimes. My grandmother says that after Trujillo was assassinated all the music from his time began to sound faded and old-fashioned, and she could barely remember the words. Or maybe she said she didn't want to remember them. But it's like, does it matter? Water never came in flavors like *Melon Shatter* or *Tangerine*

Tango. Water didn't have different textures for different uses—I mean, I used to wash my hair with the same stuff I boiled spaghetti in. How does that even make sense?" His face lights up with a broad smile. "You know what I get when I try to conjure up that old long-lost taste of lowercase water? I taste *Tangerine Tango Energy Surge*. Have you tried that stuff? It's like an orange on LSD!"

At the edge of his vision, Patrick senses a crowd forming. Customers from the bulk-orders line are leaving their places, collecting near the checkout counters. He moves a few feet to get a glimpse, but their backs form a human wall, armored in poly-cotton and stretch jersey. From the human clot, someone shouts for an ambulance, then more join in, and soon the word rings all through the cavernous hall, stacked with WAT-R pods and WAT-R coolers from floor to ceiling. An ambulance is called; help is only six and a half minutes away, but they'll have to park it at the front entrance and make the long, convoluted journey through the different WAT-R lifestyle suites to get here. The vast room fills with a vast murmur; the line breaks. He gravitates with the rest of them toward the unseen emergency whose presence is beginning to fill every corner of the room.

At the center of the pulsing crowd, a curly-haired woman about Alison's age writhes slowly on the polished concrete floor. Belly-up and panting, she stares unblinking at the fluorescent lights overhead. With her arms she reaches slowly out and back, like she's swimming in place, like she's swimming in slow motion through dark water, the surface as still as glass. From time to time, someone bends down to grab a limb and help haul her to her feet, but the woman's body is as heavy as a corpse. When their grasp fails, she falls back to the ground with a gruesome thud. Patrick stares at her face as she squirms, rigid and set and showing no clear emotion. It's worse, he thinks, that she doesn't know she's suffering, it's more pitiful that she can't sense the pity. The mouth fixed open, the eyes still and flat, like pieces of painted plastic.

"Sir, excuse me," comes a hushed voice from behind him. It's the bulk-counter girl, with a brief hand upon his shoulder. "I just wanted to let you know that we were able to charge your account. Everything's settled now. You can get your car and come around to the pickup area; just show them your card or give them your account number. Have a happy hydration!" Patrick points toward the woman on the floor. "Is she going to be okay?" he asks, the fear giving his voice a harsh tone. The girl smiles. "Yes," she says brightly. "The ambulance is here. They're already making their way through the shopping corridor." She turns to go. "Wait," Patrick says suddenly. "What was wrong with the number?" She looks surprised. "Oh, the number was fine. It's just that none of us had seen one like that before. It's a VIP account; only founders get them. The system didn't even charge you for your items." A sharp cry from the center of the circle breaks his concentration. Another bystander has tried to help the woman up, but she's fallen again, and harder. After so many falls, her hands are blackened from the floor, her long floral skirt is torn.

Far away, at the other end of the SuperCenter, two medics push a wheeled stretcher past the model sophisticated urban loft, past the model farmhouse kitchen, past the model luxurious hotel bathroom. They wheel their empty stretcher through the model Caribbean beach and past a replica of the Statue of Liberty, assembled entirely from mint-green bottles of WAT-R

Drastic Clean!, an edible mouthwash substitute. In front of the rustic woodlands cabin model, loose bottles of WAT-R *One,* a one-calorie hydration aid, litter the plastic grass, gleaming beneath the boughs of artificial trees. At the nearby hydration station, they pause and help themselves to a complimentary bottle of WAT-R *Five,* a five-calorie thirst aid. "I like the *Five,*" says one medic to the other. "It has a crisp taste, like apples but without the apple flavor." The other takes a sip and considers. "Sure, it tastes good," he admits, "but what's the point of having five calories?" By the replica Brutalist living room, they stop again to admire the brisk, clean lines, cold stone turned to human home. There's something about the décor that implies a simpler life, just some minimalist vases and a couple of art books. It might be nice. But they press on: there's still a long way to go, and the daylight is growing dimmer through the tinted blue glass that encircles them all.

Hours late for the scheduled pickup, Patrick pulls up in front of the studio and sees a crowd gathered in front of the soundstage entrance, watching the collapsing catering tent. A few staffers struggle to straighten the sagging poles, hard metal drooping at the joints. Others try to push at the sliding brackets that support the tent's roof, though it is clear that the tent will never stand upright unless someone gets control of the tarp. They know that they aren't making much progress; dismay and boredom are struggling listlessly in their expressions as they try to hold the pieces in place. But most people are gathered around watching, drinking from catering-company coffee cups as they observe the staffers struggling amidst spilled coffee, overturned dispensers, their shoes sliding against a mulch of sandwich and pulverized candy. He's surprised at how many of the onlookers seem actually happy, actually carefree: it's fun to watch something collapse, as long as you're not beneath it.

A grip sips from a clandestine beer. Two hot girls from Wardrobe are giving each other palm readings; one spots something hopeful, and they laugh together, the highlighter on their orbital crests gleaming in the twilight. Horseshoe and the Arm climb out of the van and head into the crowd, talking and pointing, first at the tent's canopy and then at the legs. Suddenly everyone seems happy, the Arm seems normal, functional. The struggle of the tent has energized those around it, inspired them to plunge more joyfully into their catastrophe-free lives. But Patrick can't stop thinking about the woman at the SuperCenter, not much older than his wife, not much older than himself, squirming on the floor of the warehouse, her sickness bared to the crowd. He watched as one bystander bent down and blew gently on her face, clearing the thin layer of dust and debris that had settled onto her cheeks, her gaping mouth.

In the shadow of the building, he sees Cassidy leaning up against corrugated metal, her facial expression inscrutable in large, chrome-rimmed sunglasses that take up half of her little heart-shaped face. She's staring down at her phone and typing something at breakneck speed. Patrick's phone buzzes. A new message from Cassidy Carter: *Wish I were the one paying you so I could dock your pay.* Patrick parks the van in the middle of the lot and spies on her in plain sight: the indignant pucker of her lips as she texts a series of question marks that pop onto his phone a moment later, and then the letters *E, T,* and *A,* followed by another spatter of squiggles interrogating nothing, marks without a question. He watches her yellow hair twitch in the breeze as she checks the phone again and again for a response. When she finally spots him, her lips utter an inaudible curse as she stalks toward the van.

"Two hours and fifteen minutes waiting around like an asshole," she says, pulling open the passenger-side door and climbing into the sweat-scented cabin. She points at the tower of boxes propped outside, her brow smooth, white, and unlined. "Fetch," she says, but when she sees him go to do it, a haunted look on his blotchy face, she gets out and helps him heft the boxes, one by one.

It's harder for her to be angry with Patrick when he's here in front of her, silent and morose. Over the phone, she feels an exhilarated rise, like when you mix coke and tequila: the head floating high above the fray like a balloon, the body ready to fucking rage. But look into the sad man's eyes a second too long and that feeling leaks out of you. Patrick is driving like a person only half awake; he puts on the turn signal too late, drives eight miles under the speed limit. Cassidy tells him about the fight she got into today with Jay and the film's director of photography over the green screen. People always assume that she knows nothing except how to be on camera, but in fact there are many things about the production that can be seen from her position. She can read the lens and tell whether the director is mining her face or her entire body for the image; she knows whether the mic is being dropped into frame or held too far away. And from *Five Moons of Triton* and countless studio photo shoots, she knows that any background designated for erasure should be smooth and perfect—the roll of unmarred white background

paper sleeking gently down to the ground, its bend nearly unde-
tectable, like a slice of winter in the dead of July.

She pointed these things out to the DP: the sloppily painted
wall, patches of glossy and matte, with a sharp, dark crease
where green wall met green floor. The uneven lighting that cast
the leftward reach in algae-green shadow, dark and sickly. Cassidy knew she had only an imperfect sense of how money
worked in the world—the prices for nice things always seemed
hilariously random, imaginary, like the shops she and her sister,
June, used to conjure from an overturned cardboard box and
the contents of their shared closet. But cheapness was a thing
she could sense instantly and from a distance—intimate, like the
taste of vomit in the back of her throat. Cheapness was a substitute for the real thing. It was a sign that someone else, somewhere, was pocketing the difference. It offended her as an
individual who had clawed her way out of the realm of the temporary and into the sunshine of the real and lasting.

Then Jay came up and started running interference, talking
up the veritable army of animators and digital-effects wizards
who were waiting in the wings for the raw footage. Digital production had evolved since *Five Moons of Triton*, he explained, as
he placed a helpful hand on the middle of her back. Backgrounds
no longer needed to be perfect to be seamlessly replaced—in
fact, perfect was primitive. Reality was easier to override than
ever, and the substitute was much more potent, much harder to
forget. In any case, he continued, there was an important opportunity he wanted to discuss. Would Cassidy be interested in
coming to a little capital-raising party they were throwing on
Saturday at Brenda's Malibu place?

Suddenly Patrick pulls the van over to the shoulder of the

highway and buries his face in his hands. He's breathing fast and making a sound like an animal in distress, a muffled, jagged bark.

"Oh no," says Cassidy, "are you choking?"

He curls away from her, crumples, presses his head against the driver's-side window. He's still making that hacking sound; with each heave his skull strikes softly against the glass. He's coughing, Cassidy realizes, instead of crying.

"Whoa, okay. Don't worry. Take a deep breath." Cassidy exhales loudly, inhales deeply, for reference. "You messed up, but I'm not going to make a big deal about it to Jay and Brenda. People in this business say a lot of shit that doesn't mean anything in reality—I bet it's different from your book world. Just try to, you know, pick up your phone."

"You don't understand," Patrick growls, a burning pressure lodged in the space between his eyes.

"Understand what?" she asks.

"Having a family," he mutters into automotive glass, "having a family in this fucked-up world. Nothing making sense. Being responsible for all of it. Nobody listening. Being treated like a disposable, like I'm just one of those kids standing around the snack table." He feels the clench of self-consciousness: he sounds like a teenager, the self-pitying version he teases Nora about becoming, triggering her sighs. "Trying to care for the most important people in your life from the other side of the country, and not knowing where they're sleeping or whether they're warm and safe. Seeing all those comatose people in the tiled room looking so lost. And now it could be my last chance to talk to my wife and daughter and I can't do it, because I have to drive you home." Something like a sob bursts from his throat, transforms into another string of coughs.

Cassidy stares. A game she and her sister used to play when they were all living in the apartments, sharing a bunk bed in a room papered with wild-animal photos cut out of magazines, was called Switch On/Switch Off! It was a game of emotional agility, an acting exercise that never ended. You played in your real life, using your real feelings, in places both public and private. As they shopped for new audition outfits at the plastic-hanger store at the mall, Cassidy's mom might take the stretchy magenta dress right out of her hands and hang it back on the rack, telling her, "You need to get that belly under control first," and Cass would tear up, her vision overlaid by a layer of wobbling saltwater that made the mall store a wilderness of melting shapes. She'd wrangle with the feelings, losing small, steady ground, until June leaned over and whispered "Switch off!" in her ear. Then Cass would let her face go slack, neutral, like a pretty doll, until June whispered again, "Switch on!" And she would will her face to come back to life with a new emotion, a quiet, self-contained smile like that of a brave female pilot about to climb into her plane.

The challenge wasn't in shutting down the link between the feeling and the face, it was in finding something brand-new to fill the face with, a feeling distant from the one you were actually experiencing. June would play too, but Cass was the undisputed queen. When it was just the two of them, they might string the switches together for so long—ten or twelve or fifteen in a row—that they both lost track of how they had felt at the beginning, so that switching feelings and switching expressions became a feeling of its own, like floating high above yourself and seeing all the detail of your life in its precise and indifferent reality, like waves shifting on the surface of the sea.

Even now, almost twenty years later, she sometimes feels that she lives life in a vague echo of that game, searching the behavior of friends and producers and actors and staff for signs of falsity, for clues to whether they were really smiling, really shouting, without the relief of ever finding out what the underlying emotion actually was. Her ex-manager tells her with a melancholy tone that it's pathetic what's happened to her, an actress who had for many years commanded some of the highest fees in the industry for an individual under the age of twenty-five—but then he begins talking about a product-placement deal he can hook up with the tampon company, only one post a month, whenever she's bleeding, and they'll pay her a steady seven K a pop. Her ex–personal assistant waves a bright goodbye and goes off to pick up a week's supply of juice cleanse, but never returns, never sends back the money, quits her job over DM. But this display from Patrick seems genuine: it's too uncomfortable, too unnatural, too *weird* to be an effort at manipulation. He grinds his reddening face into the driver's-side window, leaving nose smudges on the curved glass. He rubs his eye sockets like he's wiping away tears, but there are no tears. Whenever a car flies past them on the highway, the stopped van shudders around their bodies, trembles beneath their feet.

Cassidy opens her door and walks around to Patrick's side. She pulls his door open and tells him to climb over into the passenger seat.

"Fine," she says, "I'll drive, so you can make your phone call. Just this one time."

As the van lurches into motion, Patrick dials the commune pay phone. It rings once, twice, five times. Then, just as he's about to despair, Alison picks up.

"Patrick, is that you?" comes the sweet, familiar voice, as clear and constant as water from a tap.

"Alison. Jesus. I can't fucking believe it. You had me so worried."

"Patrick, are you okay? What's the emergency?" Patrick can hear the nibble of fear in her voice.

"Are you kidding? *You* are the emergency, you and Nora. Do you realize we haven't spoken in eight days? I don't know if you're safe, I don't know if you're healthy. Everything can change in eight days—just look at Jonestown. And Klaus is no help. Apparently, you don't share much information with him."

"I barely know him," Alison replies.

"Listen to me," Patrick says, his voice straining. "Do you remember what it was like last spring? How worried I was? This might be worse. I'm close to tears. What are you two doing over there every day? Who's running this camp? What do you know about them, about this place you've decided has all the Big Answers?"

There's a long pause on the other end of the line, an inky silence.

"Hello?" Patrick asks. "Did we lose the call?" He holds the phone away from his head to look at the crisp display, where the screen tallies up, second by second, the duration of their connection.

"No, I'm still here," Alison answers. "I just . . ." Patrick waits. "I want to do a good job here. I want to try to put you at ease. I don't know if you'll understand. I don't think you've understood in the past."

Patrick sits silently, suddenly aware of Cassidy's presence in the seat to his left. With her large black sunglasses on, he can't tell whether she's listening in. Her pert little face is fixed on the road, as she drives into the darkening east, her back to the colors of the sunset.

"It's not a cult, it's a commune," Alison explains with a steady tone. "It's called Earthbridge; it's been around for almost eight years. This place is normal—these people were doctors, teachers, graduate students. I promise you. There's no drugs, or at least no unusual ones. There's yoga in the morning and the evening, but the evening one is a little better, less crowded. Nora and I have two beds in a cabin with a few other women, a couple kids. It's cold at night, but there's a closet-full of blankets in the lodge, big scratchy woolen ones. Probably remnants from the seventies and eighties, when this camp was booming." She pauses to listen for his response, then continues. "Nora sleeps all the way through the night; she wakes up with me, when the light breaks. She's making friends. I don't know what she's said to you, but she tells me she likes the 'idealism on display.' Though she says it's also a bit 'escapist' here."

"And the leader?" Patrick pressed.

"You mean the owners? Oh god, I don't know. This woman named Diane and her husband, Jeff? They used to work at HBO. They bought this old summer camp a few years ago, when Jeff tried to kill himself. He had just watched that viral video of the polar bear that got shot when it tried to scavenge in a grocery store. But I wouldn't say they run this place."

"What do they make you do?" He's pushing now; he feels the swaddle of Alison's carefully chosen words.

"Patrick, what are you trying to uncover?"

"Just humor me, then, if it's all so wholesome."

She sighs, and when she speaks, all the softness of her voice has been compressed into one thin line, as sharp as a blade.

"Look. We get up at seven, have hot cereal and berries in the dining hall. Then we gather at the lodge, sit on the ground pretzel-style—like children, I know, you don't have to say it. Then someone comes up to the stage, usually Talya or Linden, and they give the update. It's a list of losses we've suffered over the last twenty-four hours. A tiny silver moth indigenous to Hawaii went extinct. They started drilling off the coast of Maine, near one particular island, and if a particular bill passes the State Legislature they'll do more. We get updates on the larger things, though it's harder to put an exact date and time to their passing. This morning, they finally declared the Thwaites Glacier dead. There are pieces floating around still, but it's like looking for teeth in the ashes of a fire. The thing that had a name has been wiped off the face of the earth." She pauses. "And then we mourn."

"What does that mean, mourning? For a glacier?" Patrick can't tell whether what he said sounds serious or mocking.

"It means what you think it means," Alison replies. "We might share our thoughts, our feelings. We might cry. We might lie down and feel like dying, feel scared, we might lean or huddle or hug each other. And then someone does the eulogy. They say something like: 'Imagine how this little moth, *Philodoria auromagnifica,* lived its brief and precious life. Born into the flesh of a single kolea leaf, the plant upon which the destiny of its entire species depends. A tiny caterpillar growing each day, eating a minuscule trail through the structure on which it was born, spinning a minuscule cocoon for itself inside tunnels carved in leaf flesh. Imagine that it casts itself into the night sky for the first time, its tiny body the size of an eyelash, searching the sunless dark for a mate of its own kind. Imagine that it finds another one of its kind in the vast and unbounded air, in the undestroyable, uncontestable largeness of the world, and discovers the joy of life continuing on. How impossible it was that a creature like that should ever exist, how impossible it is that it will never come into existence again. How beautiful its life must have been to witness while it was allowed to live.'"

Alison doesn't say anything for a long time, and Patrick doesn't prod her.

"I know you don't see the point of moths, or sitting around weeping," she says crisply. "I'm just trying to give you a sense of what goes on."

"I think," says Patrick, struggling, "that we're coming up against the limits of the telephone as a medium. How can I understand where you are, whether it's as safe as you say, when all we have to communicate with are words? No matter what we say, what we do, it's only a story told over the phone. I just wish I could see the place, you know."

"Well, you'd be welcome here. You can come here any time you want."

A loud silence. Patrick looks up. The van is stopped in the middle of an empty strip-mall parking lot, engine running and headlights on. The sky is a deep, dark blue, and the stores are closed, the shadowy interior of a bead store full of strange bins and droopy materials on the walls, foreboding in the middling light. The only sound is the sound of traffic, an aimless rumbling. Cassidy is nowhere to be seen.

"I have weeks more here, weeks of work. It's crazy, unpredictable," he says. The truth is, he doesn't want to give up a nothing that could become something glamorous for a nothing that's certain to remain so. "I have so many things to tell you. But in the meantime, though, maybe you could take a few pictures with your phone and send them? Send some of where you and Nora are sleeping, the lodge and the dining hall, your beloved leaders. Then I'll have something to assess, you know?"

"I don't want to do that, Patrick," Alison responds, exasperated. "For one thing, I don't charge my phone anymore. I basically turn it on if I'm sending a letter, if I need to look up an address. For another, there's no Wi-Fi, no cell service. To send you a single photo, I would have to hike forty-five minutes to the top of See Clearly Peak, then down again. And it's the middle of the night."

Patrick makes a dismissive sound. "And you wonder why I feel like you're hiding something from me?"

"Come see for yourself," she replies.

Through the sliver of open window, the cargo van is infiltrated by the sound of cicadas. The dusky air smells of life, green and lush in the hiss of sprinklers. Where the glare of the headlights begins to soften, he sees countless insects flitting through the beams, dime-sized flutterers and long-limbed night flies bleached pale in the bright light. More life was supposed to be a beautiful thing, Patrick thinks to himself, more insects, more birds, more incomprehensible germlike animals too small to see, the planet "teeming with ineffable variety," as Nora might say in her eerily mature way. But he can't help feeling like there's something awful about all that activity, the endless increase of creatures that live somehow, grow somehow, consuming even smaller, unseen creatures to fuel their strange fragile bodies. The reality of that world unsettles his own. Now that he's heard the drone of the insects, the rhythmic in-out pulse of their alien song, it seems impossible to ignore it, to go back to the way it was before.

"Actually, no," Alison says sharply. "Don't come."

Through the dim tint of the windshield, Patrick sees a slim blond figure weaving through the empty parking lot. He feels the flow of the van's air conditioner on his face, its coolness scented dimly of plastic.

"I don't know why I keep telling you that you're welcome at Earthbridge when I know it would only make both of us miserable. Every day here, we acknowledge that the planet is dying, that the life to come, the life our children will lead, is only a shadow of the life we enjoyed ourselves. Every day, I admit to myself that the way I've lived has taken from my daughter the things we taught her to love. But I never feel as bad as I do when I remember living in that house with you and Nora, watching these same things unfold, and getting ordered by you to take my handful of pills and look away."

"You know I did every single thing I could think of to help you," Patrick says, the sense of betrayal in his voice matching the hurt in hers. "And I'm still trying."

On the other end of the line, there's a sound like a gasp and a scuffling of cloth against pay-phone receiver. He imagines tears cutting a path down the side of her nose as she pulls the phone hard to her chest, pressing bone through her scratchy fisherman's sweater. He's a little surprised that he's not crying himself—if it was going to happen at any time, this should be it. He kneads the meat of his dry eyeball through its lid, hears the shift of flesh pushing against flesh. The silence on the phone line has a hot, raspy quality.

"You change the subject," she answers at last. "You confuse me. You talk about whether the problem is actually some sort of ethical rot, the death of basic sociability, whether it all stems from that. You tell me to turn on the radio so I don't get so sad. You tell me to shape up for Nora, so I don't give her a complex. You do everything you can to tell me my feelings don't matter, short of telling me my feelings don't matter. You say everything right up to that line. We don't live in the same world." Patrick listens to the static coming over the connection, throbbing in and out like cicada song. It's a very loud silence, over the phone, when nobody speaks.

The blond figure in the parking lot stops under a streetlight, leans a bony shoulder against the lamppost, stares down at her feet for several long seconds. It's Cassidy, Patrick realizes, but with a murky look on her face and a blackish scrape across her knee. She cuts through the empty parking lot, drawing a long, scrawling arc across the painted lines and concrete medians until she seems to see the van. She approaches haltingly, her steps so slow at times that it looks as though she's drifting off to sleep. As she gets closer, Patrick sees an expression on her face that reminds him of stiff-dressed, long-braided sister wives being marched out of their compounds on the TV news, trading in a comprehensible life for one whose parameters are entirely unknown. It's an expression crafted for another world, an unimaginable place populated by peaceful and blurry things.

A latch releases, and the back doors of the van swing open, noisy and metallic.

"Now *you're* driving," Cassidy mutters vaguely, as she climbs into the cargo area. Peering back at her as she scales the horizontal flooring on hands and knees, he feels as though he's at the top of a steep cliff, looking down. She curls her body against the boxes of bottled water, lies down on the rough carpet, her face submerged in darkness. He realizes that he no longer exists for her, her mind is somewhere else. Uncovered limbs extend slender and pale from the openings of her jean shorts, as smooth as plastic, luminous, like they're gathering up all of the stray light in the parking lot for some hidden purpose.

On the other end of the line, Alison hangs the phone back on its hook. The night air on the mountain is clear and chilly, and she wraps her arms around her torso under a pooling of artificial light, feeling pulses of anger move through her body. Every time her mind comes to rest, some remembered remark from Patrick starts it back up, and suddenly she's ready to call him back, yell or cry, some unknown behavior that she knows wouldn't move him one inch. She wishes he would stop bringing up the fucking lawn. Though she accepted that it had been a mistake, a bad mistake, revisiting it made her question why she had agreed so early on to see it his way. When she thought about her period of disturbance, she heard a strong, clear voice inside telling her that she had come out of the quagmire with the help of her family's love and support—but below that dwelt a deep, wordless certainty that she had been wronged.

The crickets call from the trees in a single, dispersed voice. In the dining hall, the crafting house, the gymnasium, the windows are all dark, the other dwellers back in their assigned bunkhouse reading or telling stories, strumming loosely remembered songs on the porch. She can't go back like this, angry and unresolved. There's no real privacy here, not privacy as she knew it in their midsized suburb, where at least you could shut yourself in the bathroom and weep with the fan on to mask the noise. At Earthbridge, despite the official emphasis on mourning as the healthiest way of processing the inevitable decline of the planet, crying for your own problems is seen as indulgent, even a bit embarrassing.

Patrick was always asking her when it had started: he imagined that if he could discover the point of origin he'd know how to undo it. She found something to say each time, but it felt dishonest. As with most catastrophes, she knew it hadn't happened all at once. She remembered the day the man-made pond behind her grandparents' house ruptured during a record thunderstorm, spilling out its contents down the manicured hill and into the woodland below, the trout thrashing on the mown grass, their mouths opening and closing as they drowned in air. So much had prepared the way for the moment when the overfull reservoir inundated the weakest part of the bank: days of rain and drizzle softening the ground, seasons of silt gathering on the lacustrine bottom and reducing its holding capacity, the unchecked bloom of water weeds and lilies in the fervid humidity of that year's early summer. You couldn't say when it began, only that at one point it was certain to unfold. By the same token, even before the days when she had wept every morning while making her coffee, wept in the shower, wept when seeing Nora go off to school, wept in the parking lot of the elementary school with conditioner still in her hair, wept in her office with the door tightly shut, wept while reading the news on her computer or phone, wept for lack of sleep and lack of consolation, she had experienced other strange moments and impulses that Patrick would never have known to include in the narrative of her breakdown.

All the things he hadn't seen, things he wouldn't even have known how to look for. She grew teary-eyed in the grocery store, looking at a can of peaches in syrup. She spent three hours trying to free a white moth that had gotten trapped inside the screened-in porch. She crawled across the lawn after he had mown it, looking for survivors, afraid that she would find the bodies of insects crushed and chopped, traces of burrows destroyed and mangled rodents. And all the while, he kept buying paper towels in family packs, great pillowy bundles that he would carry into the house on his shoulder as if he were some sort of hearty, strapping lumberjack—even though they had agreed to use the reusable bamboo versions she bought online, which he threw away one afternoon by accident. She cringed when she started the car and the gasoline smell began seeping into the air. She put all the produce into a single tote bag and unloaded the pieces in random order, one by one, onto the checkout belt. They fought over the cost of solar panels. They fought over whether Nora should be raised vegetarian or whether, on the other hand, she should eat her daily fill from the limbs and torsos of big, sloe-eyed animals that had never lived a day without being destined for the slaughterhouse. Why couldn't you live life the way you wanted to? Why were you always strapped to the sinking people around you, why were you held to their standard of living, why was the only choice paper or plastic, rather than being able to choose to buy nothing at all?

Gradually, Alison realized that the lawn was a perfect illustration of her unfreedom. It had never been very nice turf, covered with fine-bladed yellowish grass that grew thin for no apparent reason in the sun-soaked front yard. It needed fertilizer made from synthetic nitrogen every couple of months, toxic herbicide to keep off the weeds, sprinklers all through the late spring and summer, and it had to be mown twice a month, severing the beginnings of the small, tidy seed pods that were, in her opinion, the only thing that made them look like real plants instead of some gaudy outdoor carpet. In February, she came up with a plan to replace their dwarfish lawn with hardier perennial grasses and a small vegetable garden that would thrive under the heavy sunlight. There would be tomatoes, cucumbers, and zucchini for dinner that summer, and they would be able to retire the weed killer for good, using the hand-weeder and trowel instead. Patrick informed her that the HOA bylaws allowed only traditional grass lawns, ornamented by tasteful flowers, bushes, and trees. They didn't allow ground covers that might spread and infect neighboring properties or overly large stretches of gravel or stone. They didn't allow fountains, fake foliage, non-American flags, or effigies of animals and people. Alison and Patrick owned the house and the land, but all they could do with it was what everyone else around them did.

It was easy, then, to fixate upon the lawn: a grotesque, unwanted presence visible from every window of the house. She thought it was symbolic, the vulgar dominance of one thing when there should be many, a fruitless, joyless labor performed

for the eyes of others. She thought possibly that it was poisoning her, making her thoughts foggy and her reasoning weak,
and she held her breath every time she walked adjacent to the
long green spans that lined both sides of this street and the next
and the next. How could it be that she had worked so hard,
saved so much money, endured long hard years building her vet-
erinary practice, and still she had no say about how she lived,
what she grew on her own damn lot? Unable to sell because the
market was down, and even if they could, they wouldn't move
because Nora loved her school. Adulthood was a curious inver-
sion of childhood helplessness; you were pinned in place by
what was below you and around you, by what you owned and
loved, rather than any sort of higher authority. She stayed up all
night looking at photos of dead whales, their stomachs bulging
with dirty plastic, acid-bleached coral the pale color of zombie
skin, the horrifying videos of animal abuse, and the equally horrifying videos of abused animals too hurt to move being lifted
up and carried away whimpering by humans seeking donations
for their South Asian animal-rescue organizations. And around
sunrise, with Patrick and Nora still asleep, she climbed out of
bed and walked around the neighborhood, looking at their lush
green lawns, tender and exposed in the sleepy hours of the
morning.

Yes, it was selfish to have been so sad. That was the first thing
they agreed on. The second was that the sadness was foreign to
her nature, it was an aberration, an invader, a weed in her berry
patch. "You used to be so happy," he told her. "Just remember
how you used to laugh when we went to feed the gulls at the
beach." She started to see a therapist, who told her that it was
unhealthy to hold on to so much guilt and pain regarding things

that were just inevitable parts of human life. We had a need to use paper, she said, to use gasoline and meat and bubble-wrap mailing envelopes and rare earth metals. Her task, said the therapist, while wearing one of her several dozen pairs of baffling, serpentine earrings, was to learn to forgive herself for living. "She wants me to forgive myself," Alison told Patrick with disdain. Quash the new impulses, fold back into society. The therapist didn't care whether Alison lived an ethical life, didn't care whether she got better, meaning became a better person. "It's not like a personal trainer at the gym," Patrick said. "A therapist doesn't make you over in whatever shape you want. They make you healthy." Nora slept with noise-canceling headphones on in case they fought after she went to bed. She brought back a magnet from school with the suicide-prevention hotline number and stuck it on the fridge. "You don't love me," Alison said, "name one thing about me that you love." Patrick said he could name a dozen. He loved how she sang along to songs when she drove without realizing she was doing it, he loved going to the movies with her where they'd get the jumbo-sized popcorn even though it was too much for anybody to finish. He loved the gentle way she touched her face when putting makeup on or taking it off. He loved how she could taste a dish at a restaurant and name every ingredient in it, down to the herbs. "What you're talking about," Alison told him, "that isn't me. That's our lifestyle. Who would I be to you without it?"

Early on a Sunday morning, Alison went outside in her bare feet wearing only a long tee shirt and began tearing up the lawn with her bare hands. She grabbed fistfuls of green, but the roots were still there, unscathed. She knew that there were sometimes native seeds in the soil below, lying dormant for years and years, waiting for a chance to grow. It was possible to free them, if only she could clear out all this bullshit. She chose the crowbar from the garage, because she thought it would be faster. After she did her own lawn, she could move on to the neighbors'. Lift the crowbar high and strike down with force, lodging the beveled end deep in the root system. Then drag that motherfucker, till that bitch, tear up big clods of white-rooted sod with a sound like hair being ripped from scalp. She wasn't wearing any makeup, no streaks ran down her face, but every so often the tears made it too hard to see, and she had to drag her soiled hand across her face to get them off. By the time Patrick came out to stop her, she had made good work of their own yard and was moving on to the Koffmans' next door. It's hard to restrain someone swinging a metal rod with one wicked end and no off-switch. By the time he pinned her to the turf, they were being watched from the stoops and through the windows of nearby houses. Back inside, he pushed her into the bathroom and propped the door shut with a chair, leaving her in there alone as the daylight grew and aged and sank away. Around dinner, he opened the bathroom door and they all ate microwaved mac and cheese in a deep, inky silence. Weeks later, when she saw Antonia Koffman in the supermarket, she continued on her path, pretending not to see her, planning to show no emotion, but when she got close, she found herself smiling and apologizing and blaming her behavior those weeks ago on a bad Ambien reaction. Afterward, she hated herself with a new sharpness, an icy, pointed pain reserved for a weak person who presented herself as even weaker than she was.

From behind, a shift in the quality of light and a sound like wood and metal moving against each other. Alison turns to find

Klaus watching her, smelling of sawdust, wiping his hands on a discolored cloth, and smiling faintly.

"Talking to your husband," he says politely, ignoring her balled-up fists and moist cheekbones.

"Oh, I was," says Alison quickly, "but it's late, I need to get back to Nora."

"I've been working on making several lazy Susans for the dining hall," he says, and pauses, like he expects her to say something.

"It'll be good," he continues, "to be able to access all the condiments or sauces from any place at the table. We have older people here, we have people who are infirm, we have children with short arms. When I'm done, everyone will be able to reach for themselves."

Alison smiles small and tight. Then she tries to smile a little bigger, to be friendly.

"Oh, that'll be nice," she says. "We won't have to pause the conversation to ask someone to pass something."

"Well, I hope people will still ask each other for help," says Klaus with a note of worry. "I believe it's good for the community to ask and to give, to rely on one another."

Alison looks off toward the bunkhouses. She can see the front lights shining in the distance, indicating that the cabins are still awake, its denizens not yet gone to bed. When the light is out above her door, she has to sneak, change her clothes in near-complete darkness, all without making a noise. Then she feels a hand heavy on her shoulder—two pats and it's over.

"It bothers me too sometimes," he says emphatically. "The contradiction between how peaceful it is here and how difficult things are in the world. I can feel guilty in moments when I think of a person I know who would thrive in this place but is still struggling out there with the sort of problems we were so glad to leave behind. For that reason, the mourning early in the day sometimes feels a bit shallow to me—as if it were a way to absolve ourselves, and enjoy the rest of the day. But I think it is all right to enjoy it here. It is all right for you to enjoy it, if you can." She dredges up a real smile for him. The moths circle the spotlight, mistaking it for a small, accessible moon.

As she walks the narrow gravel path back to her house, she thinks about his assumption that what pained her was her own contentment, how he must see her to assume this, how odd it was that his consoling gesture made her feel a bit better even though he was so far from understanding her feelings. It seems possible to Alison that if her husband were to join her here, they might understand each other at this basic, gestural level of exchange—the desire to comfort, the desire to communicate, even if the message itself came through garbled. With the time and space to focus on intention rather than outcome, they could remind each other of two people who only want the best for each other. But it seems more likely that he'll stay in California, growing ever more frantic about the distance. The path back to her cabin shines under the moonlight, and her footsteps mark the stillness with soft crunches, like boots through snow. Tomorrow she'll hike to the top of the mountain and send the photos, like he asked. Maybe she'll tell Nora to do some drawings of the campground that she can send by mail, something physical that he can hold and touch, something to put him at ease.

In the first episode of the second season of *Kassi Keene: Kid De-tective*, Kassi is a high-school junior running her own private-investigator business from out of the apartment she used to share with her still-missing father. She's turned his empty bed-room into her office, a desk with a banker's lamp and a potted fern on it where his bed used to be. During the days, she sits through calculus, U.S. history, honors English, but on the week-ends, she manages her father's landscaping company, trying to keep the few employees he still has paid up and loyal until he comes back—if he ever comes back.

In this episode, she drives the riding mower in tight, squiggly lines across the expansive back lawn of a Paradise Cove estate owned by a former talk-show host, headphones blasting her fa-vorite local band, the Lady Wolverines. Suddenly, a sound loud enough to cut through the chorus. Kassi kills the mower's en-gine, climbs off, and slides her headphones down around her neck. Through a three-inch gap in the hedgerow, she peers into the neighbor's yard, where a man in a trim charcoal-gray suit is sliding a handgun back into its holster. The owner of the house, distraught in tennis clothes and visor, cradles a small white ob-ject with both hands. "You bastard, you killed Jonesy," cries the distressed man, holding the tiny body to his chest. "I'll vote for your wicked bill. But why did you have to shoot the dog?" The gray suit slips on a pair of Ray-Bans and strolls away, slowing briefly to admire a rosebush. And as Gray Suit revs his engine and speeds off toward some unknown endpoint, we watch through the hedge gap as the remaining man looks down at the delicate mangle, the toy poodle's broken splay, blood dotting his crisp white polo knit.

Patrick pauses the episode and squints at the screen. There, in the back window of the white stucco villa, he finds the face of a sad-eyed brunette that he recognizes—from a previous episode, or from the un-screen world? Is it his imagination, or does Kassi lock eyes with her and then turn away, flinching, a rare and disturbing expression of horror disarranging the delicate, girlish face? He types *s02e01 woman back window mower scene* into the search bar of the *Kassi Keene* episode-guide Wiki, but the results are mealy and imprecise, weak cullings of summary and bland trivia, spattered with keywords from his search string. He opens a new tab and stares at the long, vacant rectangle of the search screen. He thinks of Alison in her purple yoga tank and tights, smooth-lined and side-planked, three thousand miles away, lifting one long arm elegantly up toward the ceiling, her delicate, sensitive head twisted upward in regard of nothing at all. He types, *Who is the woman watching Kassi Keene from the mansion in s02e01?* and erases it and writes *s02e01 Kassi Keene hidden meaning*. Suddenly the web unfurls.

Among the now familiar episode recaps and thinkpieces on what it means for Philip Marlowe's mantle to be taken up by a spunky blond teenager, or what Cassidy Carter's off-screen antics say about our antiquated Good Girl norms, Patrick discovers links to forums where users break down the hidden messaging in Kassi's to-camera winks and smiles, the subtle foreshadowing in the episode titles, the punny names of local businesses, and the possible puns that went unchosen. Then there's something called Kassi Keene Revelators, which boasts over twenty-three hundred members, 108 of whom are online right now, and which seems to be the only forum with new updates every day, every hour. On Revelators, they talk constantly about Missed Connections and TBR—The Big Reveal, a plot

twist they believe had been planned for the canceled sixth season, a narrative mega-event that would have cast all of Kassi's
investigations in a newer, darker, more unified light and pointed
the way to a mega-crime that exerts its lingering influence on
the town of Paradise Cove years or even decades after it first
took place.

▶ **luka_boy_ohX**

Anybody on here ever notice that the demographics of Paradise Cove
are not the same as most affluent seaside communities? My uncle
lives in a town a lot like PC (East Coast though) and the most promi-
nent group of people there are definitely the retirees. There are elder-
lies all over the place dressed in slumpy pastels, eating at fish
restaurants and lining up on the sidewalk for weekend breakfast. Old
people love the ocean. By contrast, Paradise Cove only has people who
are pretty much young, teenagers or parents of teenagers or sometimes young adults like the hot IT girl from season 3. Also no real children. I would estimate the average age in town to be around 28 y/o.

⤷ **Ntuit44player**

Interesting to note that 28 years was the average lifespan in An-
cient Egypt—the same country and people that Kassi is giving a
report on in s03e04, just before learning her father is still alive.

⤷ **diskordpro415**

I definitely have noticed this myself and would add that abnormal
population distributions often are found after major catastrophic
events like war, natural disasters, or genocides. So this all fits very
well with the HaydenStrange8 theory of the First Crime being
something pretty big and also violent, as many of us on this site are
familiar with. But with a place like PC, where almost everyone left
behind is relatively young and hot, it's not likely to be a catastrophe

like war, where young children and the elderly are more or less exempt from the culling. (Ex. one of the less-known consequences of the Black Plague was a shortage of agricultural laborers, helping to speed the decline of the feudalistic agricultural rich.)

More likely it was something like a major biohazard disaster or eco-catastrophe, where the weaker members of a community are taken out disproportionately because of their physical vulnerability.

⤷ **jonzeewhiskerz**

Reading this I feel like you guys have never seen another TV show. TV shows are all young hot people. Except for the ones made for old people that might or might not show old people in them, or the ones for kids that are usually almost all kids.

⤷ **HowDa132**

By that logic, everyone on here who watches KKKD should be a hot person 😄

⤷ **jonzeewhiskerz**

I don't follow??

⤷ **iyDkmnWU4mD**

Usually on TV shows the producers do a careful job of trying to make the people in the background look normal and show a good cross-section so that towns look average. In Kassi Keene they specifically do not do this. In fact in most TV shows there is a pressure for realism and mimicry of the outside world, i.e. the Reality Simul. What happens on Kassi Keene is intentional. They are sending a message with so much nuance in it that many people like you are sure to miss it, but those who can process and understand TBR will be positioned perfectly to hear and to accept it.

⇩ EndlingInLove71

Jonzee: I am curious if you are 100% new to this community or whether you have done your research. Of course there are some ideas on here that can seem random if you haven't been paying attention, but don't walk into the NASA control center and start complaining that you can't fly the rockets. HighrOnymussX's video-tour through s2 is a good place to start. I find her splice of different terrified expressions on the faces of Paradise Cove extras in the background of Kassi's scenes particularly convincing. There is DEFINITELY something horrifying going on in that town.

▶ 666ImpOZing

Listen, here's what we know about First Crime:

1. It involved the water supply
2. It happened either before Kassi moved to Paradise Cove or day of
3. Ron Nifton and Nifty Org were involved, possibly even the perpetrators
4. Kassi had her memory wiped at least three times but no more than 5, and others had their memory wiped a lot more
5. Lingering effects are connected to the consumption of Nifty Cola, though adults tend to feel the effect more than children, I dunno why, maybe because they are drinking more of it due to their larger body mass or having more spending money????

Everything else is just speculation!!!

Patrick clicks back to the video player. Cassidy's features fill the small, rectangular field, blurry at the edges but crisply focused on her face: the shapely, sun-kissed nose as delicate and exact as a tulip. She projects strength and determination from the nose up, but her mouth twists with something hazier. It's doubt, or maybe fear, a monstrous stitch-up of real and unreal emotions pushed into unnatural relation, a face reflecting a moment that never happened to a person that never really existed. Her lips glisten with an unreal slick that he knows, instinctively, tastes of factory-made cherry. By pressing PLAY, slipping back into this episode with the next one automatically queued, he is consciously choosing to feel the episode's emotions rather than his own, he's choosing to flush his entire system with a cleansing douche of concocted situations, concocted story, concocted feeling, and in doing so to substitute these high-gloss problems for his own, drab and all too real. When the strategy succeeds, it's almost as if he's forgotten who he is—what is he, after all, other than a temporarily unique intersection of a body and its problems?—though of course he is still there, propped on his elbows, seal-style, on the motel bedspread.

Kassi Keene finishes the mowing, dead-heads the shriveled beige globes of an out-of-season hydrangea, and collects her pay in a white envelope. Then she walks over to the neighbor's house and knocks on the door. From the front stoop, she grins her best young, harmless, professional grin, and introduces herself to the flustered man who answers. She says she was doing some yardwork next door for the Morehouses and heard a gunshot. He's changed his shirt, but there's still a spray of dog's blood across the left side of his neck. "It's a gift to see a young lady like you doing her civic duty, keeping an eye out for her community," he says brightly, a triangular smile on his expensively tanned face. "Kudos on that, which I find to be a very healthy sign of the coming generation's moral fiber. But I have to say, I don't know what you're talking about." He grins at Kassi; she narrows her eyes. "So you don't," she says, "know anything about a man in a gray suit shooting your toy poodle with a Beretta 92?" The tight smile slackens, but still he insists: "Can't say that I do, but of course I would call the police straight-away if I saw anything like that happening near me."

Kassi's face registers a sudden sadness, a disappointment, as if she can't believe that anyone could deny the reality of a be-loved pet's death less than an hour after it occurred. Her smile is a short, quick blade as she turns and heads for her truck. "Well, it's a rare treat to hear that nothing's wrong. I don't come across that so often. But be careful: Paradise Cove is the erosion capital of the world. We lose more than fifteen tons of sand per day to the waves and the wind and the foot traffic of tourists. What's been covered up around here tends to come to the surface sooner or later."

The motel air tastes of popcorn and hot dust. All afternoon, while he drove back and forth between soundstage and errands, the long afternoon sun had been pouring through the curtain-less back window in the bathroom. The fan overhead pushes around the dust, a tint of ochre, something impure. Beneath it his sweat feels unclean, his skin a magnet for whatever grit swirls unseen in the gusts of easterly wind-flow, the flavor invisi-bly tinged with burning. As Patrick rolls over onto his back, his hand brushes the slice of exposed flesh between his tee shirt and his boxer briefs, and the sensation shivers his flesh. For a mo-ment, he doesn't recognize the touch as his own. With his eyes closed, there's the familiar tremor of soft organic matter against living tissue, the irrefutable sensation of a desire not his own, a body curious about his own body, a body looking to feel. Like at a college party, when the hot whisper of a hand against his shoulder had him searching the press of young, humid flesh for the exact anatomy that had reached for his own. When he realizes what's happened, something crushes a little inside him, oozing a sad, lonely juice. It seems hopeless to wish for somebody to phone him right now, to knock on his motel-room door, but he wishes anyway. He feels like Kassi Keene, ditched by her boyfriend, ditched by her father, motherless and alone, burdened beyond her years. His body gapes, receptive and opened up to the world.

With sudden interest, he holds his arms up to the light: the bitten-down cuticles, two hands well proportioned but marred by their almost imperceptible pudginess, a quality that he had always felt gave them an unintelligent look. His gaze slides down his still-muscular forearms, mossy with dark, coarse hair. Slowly, he turns his arms over, exposing their pale undersides, traversed by a single track of faded indigo. He twists his torso to turn off the light. Then, in the dark, he rolls onto his side, cradles his right forearm in the gentle grip of his left, and brings his lips toward the warm, living surface for a kiss. Skin meets mouth, but it's a closed circle: he can't snip the cord of knowing that links his will to his action to the sensation of both. He can't un-remember himself as a man in his skivvies in an overheated motel room nursing one bristly arm, unbeloved, alone, trying to create in himself the physical sensation of someone else giving a fuck.

His phone shivers on the nightstand behind him, casts a rectangle of cool blue light. It's a message from Cassidy: *I'm ordered to go to Brenda and Jay's fucking pool party tomorrow night at the ranch. Will you play driver? I know they're expecting full persona, lots of shots, vodka luge, dancing in the fountain, all that bullshit. I don't want to fall asleep someplace fucked up again and wake up to some stranger beating it to the sight of my bare feet.*

The driveway is as dark as a backcountry road, narrow and straight, slicing the arid hills in two indistinguishable halves. In the darkness before them, patches of sage and coyote bush flare into bright view and vanish just as quickly, receding in the rear-view as Patrick and Cassidy speed by. The pale hairs on her cheeks glow white-edged in the moonlight, and he feels with sudden certainty that something might happen tonight, most likely something bad. Out in the brush, long-limbed rabbits hunch in cover of milkweed, small lakes gleam with second-hand moonlight, and all is silent except for the dingy white vehicle in the hue of a ghost, groaning through the cool evening air. The estate appears on the horizon as a lick of warm flame, a lonesome piece of light that swells as they approach, revealing its finer details: a massive steep-roofed structure sided in blackened cedar, a five-car garage with reclaimed redwood doors, and a bonfire the height of a full-grown man burning in a pit at the center of the roundabout.

Smoothing her updo, Cassidy climbs out of the van and walks through the entrance before Patrick even has time to ask whether she wants to be escorted. She wears a short strapless dress in some sort of medium blue, a simple shape drizzling with long beaded fringe that sparkles expensively in the fire-light. As she walks, the beads swing back and forth in time with her ponytail. When the valet comes to the van to take the keys, Patrick is startled to recognize him: it's one of the production assistants, dressed in a white jacket, a thin-lipped skater with a spiky haircut. Yesterday he had been standing in the parking lot taking photos of the catering-tent collapse on his phone. Patrick had watched as he captured the image of the buckling structure, applied a rainbow filter to it, and put it on loop, so that the tent fell and rose and fell and rose again, a process as natural as breathing. Now, as valet, he opens the driver's-side door and thrusts his damp palm out to receive the key.

Past the thick, overlarge door, the foyer is as big as a living room, lit by glowing curlicues of light that flicker inside expensively blown glass. The half-vacant space is strewn with furniture objects made out of some smooth-lacquered material and positioned at various heights, evocative of table, chair, console, stool, but not quite projecting the essence of any one thing. Patrick eyes the room beyond, where he sees a portion of Cassidy peeking out from behind a pair of men deep in conversation. Her skinny legs are a uniform, unnatural tan: a color like a Band-Aid. From the way the legs appear to be lengthening, extending, stretching themselves out, she must be leaning back as she talks with someone just out of view. He can't tell, with such an occluded view, whether she's enjoying herself or not.

"Could I offer you a glass of champagne as you start off this evening?" says a voice to his left.

Patrick turns and finds Horseshoe holding a gleaming brass tray. His smooth, sloping shoulders look deflated inside the large white uniform. On the tray sit a dozen asymmetrical flutes of sparkling liquid, the shade like wan gold, the glasses stemless and semi-opaque. Nothing in this place resembles itself exactly: every object a witty comment on the object category, a common shape boiled down to its gnarled core and then cast in expensive, heavy material.

"Oh, hey, Pat," Horseshoe says, his face stirring from its false, servile professionalism to form the outline of a smile. "Are you here to work? If so, you're late, and you're probably in trouble."

"I'm here to go to a party," Patrick replies, and he pauses for a moment so the next line will register with its proper weight. "I'm here with Cassidy."

"You mean as her driver?" Horseshoe asks.

"As I don't know what." He smooths down the front of his jacket. He's left the top two buttons of his shirt undone, but when he looks around the room he thinks maybe he should have gone one further. "Why are you playing waiter at Brenda's party? Is this some hazing thing?"

"A lot of us from the crew opted to work this event in the interest of making a few extra bucks," answers Horseshoe. "I wouldn't say these tasks are where our talents lie, but since flexibility and can-do spirit are prized in our industry, you could say that doing something we can't do is, in fact, the truest culmination of our profession. At least, that's what someone said back in the kitchen when we were prepping the crudités."

"Are they paying you, you know, better than on set?" Patrick asks, mystified. "Is that why you're doing this?" He takes a glass from the tray before him and downs it in four deep swallows. His throat clutches around the liquid, but it's gone all too fast.

"The pay is the same at a per-hour rate, but because we're doing more work than we would if not working, we're being paid more," he explains patiently. "We are making more pay than we would during hours in which we did not work, hours in which we would do ephemeral nonpaying activities, like polishing our own scripts or sleeping, instead. The pay increase over the unpaid scenario is practically infinity-fold if you look at it that way, an incalculability."

A few guests take glasses from Horseshoe's tray, drift on to the living room. He turns slightly and nods at them as they walk by, ignoring him. His crisp white jacket—long like a safari jacket, high-necked like a chef's—twists and bunches against the disruptive motion.

"Of course," he adds, pointing at his body, "we have to pay for the repair and cleaning of these uniforms if they sustain any damage. But if we do our tasks perfectly, they shouldn't get damaged at all."

"It's cruel to make you wear white under those conditions."

"But it's not white, it's ecru. One thing I've discovered in my admittedly brief time at this house is that there are more different shades of white than there are different shades of what we call color. There's the quartz white of the wet-bar countertop, dove white in the bathroom Corian, the linen white of the napkins, the milky eggshell color of the leather sofa over there in the living room. The lack of color is dazzling in its variety. I don't even know if my untrained eye is capable of distinguishing them all, I can barely make out a difference, but to Brenda it must be like a rainbow. I'm like a worm gazing up at the stars."

"But why," asks Patrick, "do you think they're hiring people like you, people with no experience, instead of regular servers and caterers? Did Brenda and Jay give you a reason?"

"Well, I like to think we bring a certain wide-eyed novelty to the job that might make it more exciting. To be served by someone who can still find a way to be amazed by the task, rather than some cynical, hardened champagne-slinger."

"Is that what Brenda told you?" Patrick presses. He knows that something is very wrong with how Brenda is running this party—how she and Jay are running the whole film, in fact—but he needs a reason in order to know why he feels that way.

Horseshoe lowers the tray slightly, and his eyes take on a glazed look.

"America is the land of the amateur," he begins. "The garage inventor. The jamboree dancer. The people no longer wish to watch expert chefs compete against expert chefs, creating intricate logjams of meat and vegetables. If you give uncooked food to an expert chef, all you get is expertly cooked food—we've seen it a million times. But if you give it to a retired truck driver with a heartbreaking story, an eight-year-old child with a passion for battleships, who knows what could happen? What could they discover in that reality-show pantry? What could you discover in their discovery? The surprise of success is a miracle. The possibility of failure is an aphrodisiac. What if a real-estate agent doodling random lines and triangles on the floor plan of a house were to independently re-create the discovery of the Euler line? Are you more amazed to see a beautiful flower growing in the Los Angeles County Arboretum and Botanical Garden, or from a trash heap by the side of the freeway, where cars slow down as they take the off-ramp? A glacier-white lily the size of a baby's head, its vivid green stalk reaching up toward the sky from out of the mouth of a can of Monster Energy drink."

Brenda walks up, tilts Horseshoe's tray back up so that it is flat and no longer lists toward the floor. In an oversized sweater dress of light, fluffy mauve, she tilts her head breezily to the side to reveal a single monstrously complicated earring. She looks toward Patrick as though trying to bring him into focus. In his discomfort, he swallows another glass of champagne whole.

"What are you doing here, Patrick? Are you here to work? Because, if you are, you're very late."

"Cassidy asked me to come," he responds.

"Oh, right," Brenda says, and her irritation mingles with a subtle tinge of relief. "I didn't remember inviting you to work this event. Grandpa Billington used to say that when you lose your ledger of what you've said and done, the man who picks it up off the ground becomes your master."

"I heard that your grandfather personally ordered the ending of *Citizen Kane* to be reshot," Horseshoe says with reverence.

"It's true," Brenda replies breezily, "he was a crotchety old shit. But listen, Patrick. We're very lucky you turned up. Cassidy is acting a bit wobbly now in the other room, and I think it would be good if you watched over her. Not"—and here she pauses—"in a professional capacity, but in a personal one. You probably know how emotional she can be. She uses herself as a battery, she drains herself for her work—which is beautiful, but risky too in its way." She reaches out smiling and squeezes Patrick's arm close to the elbow, three quick times between her middle finger and thumb. "Can you stick close to her tonight?"

Brenda looks at him, and her waiting face has the smoothness and consistency of butter. He knows that, if he leaned forward and licked it, it would not taste of mineral and chalk and the fake floral scent of foundation, but of something pure and young and springtime. He can tell that he is nodding because of the way the room and all the formless, over-shaped things in it seem to bob gently up and down.

In the sunken, plushly carpeted living room, an archipelago of seating meanders through the pale, ghostly space. Islands of cream in a sea of silky taupe, the organic ovaloid shapes of the furniture marred by human bodies twisted in conversation, strewn with legs crossed or knees bent, knobby and crookedly jointed. They lean in awkward semi-repose on floor pillows patterned in vaguely ethnic stripes—the human form like a broken spider, a top-heavy starfish, a fragile and imbalanced splay. There are women who look like they belong, women in graphic prints or deceptively simple clothes that reveal intricate, useless deviations up close. There are men who dress like Jay Arvid, and men who seem like they are trying to dress like him. Looking at the scattered bodies, Patrick can tell that the outfit Cassidy chose for this event is both too fancy and too cheap. Soft music seeps from an unseen opening. Dozens of small salmon toasts circle through the room on a shiny platter. An unplayed piano in the corner is a soft custom gray, the color of chinchilla.

When he finds Cassidy, it's in a remote quadrant of the room, hidden behind a large abstract sculpture. Her dress sparkles weakly in the dim light. She's sitting on a kidney-shaped sofa with two men seated on either side of her, and her expression is grimly sunny, her smile a muscle in contraction. In her hand, there's a martini glass filled with yellowish tequila.

"I love this stuff," says the guy on the right, grabbing the spangly fringe on her dress and rubbing it between his fingertips.

"I want to bat it around, like a kitty cat," says the guy on the left, and they both laugh. With their short haircuts and dark sports jackets, they have a paired look, they might be workout buddies whose schedules, diets, clothing, and slang are all beginning to converge.

"You guys are so fun," Cassidy says. She leans forward and laughs in a shiny way, like a string of mass-produced holiday bells. "How are you involved with the film again? You're both investors, right?"

"Well," says the one on the right, "Evan's an investor. I'm a maybe, depending on how convincing Brenda and Jay are tonight. I'm thinking of throwing my chips in on the sequel. Get in on the ground floor and claim a greater share of the equity."

"In my view, this film is too crowded already," says Evan. "Time to close the airplane doors and prepare for takeoff. I have a six-percent stake, but people buying in tonight are getting point-eight percent, point-forty-five percent."

"Not even a sliver of the pie," his pal interjects. "A little grocery-store sample with a toothpick stuck in it." He slurps cola-colored liquid from a heavy tumbler.

Cassidy laughs with them and brings the martini glass to her lips, her fist tight around the slender stem. Patrick feels jealousy stir within him, like an itch sliding among the soft wet organs, with no hard parts to scratch it. She looks perfectly comfortable in this contrived situation, and even if she's only acting, the performance is compelling. Her spangles shudder in the lamplight as she leans forward, giggling, and sets her glass on a large hunk of glass, a coffee table shaped like an ice cube within which a vintage rotary phone floats paralyzed, like a mosquito in amber. Suddenly her precise, girlish features light up and she begins to speak with a new confidence.

"Well, guys, if you're looking for equity," says Cassidy,

scratching her chin with a manicured hand, "I'm actually putting together a film later this year. We have a great script; it's a story about two sisters who grow apart after one of them becomes a pop star, and of course I'd play the lead, so we already have one big name signed on. I have a couple producers involved already, but you could really shape the project if you come in at this stage, not to mention carve out big slices of pie for yourself. Pie at breakfast, pie for lunch, whatever you want. This is going to be *really* big."

She leans forward for emphasis, eyebrows raised, and looks each of them square in the eye. Patrick recognizes this character: it's Kassi Keene, wide-eyed and bright, offering solutions with a big scoop of heart and just a pinch of wry wit. The two guys chuckle stiffly.

"Are you doing a bit?" the other one asks, confused. "I mean, you aren't making a movie, right?"

"Of course I am," she replies.

"I heard you were being sued by that paparazzo you beat up in the drugstore? I heard they froze all your funds. It would make it hard to get your project insured."

"Well, I can and I am," Cassidy snaps. "You know, nobody would even remember that twenty-minute span of my life if it hadn't been for the tampons. It was seriously not even a blip on the radar of the vast ocean of my life."

"It's just not a good time for me," says Evan slowly. "I've got some liquid sloshing around, but I can't afford spillage, if you know what I mean. I'm on a strictly positive-returns-investment plan."

His friend nods eagerly. "But we're big fans," he adds. "Fans for life."

"So true," Evan says. "I used to watch *Kassi Keene* in my freshman-year dorm room with a bunch of kids from our floor. We'd buy beer for cheap from the sketchy RA, and we'd drink every time Kassi said something that was clearly ironic foreshadowing. It was so fucking fun. I fucking cried when your dad went missing after the school bake-sale shoot-out and you were standing all alone by the brownie table in the rain. Such good memories."

Cassidy stands up, tilts the rest of the tequila down her slender white throat, and hands the empty to Evan's friend.

"That's fine," she says, "but some of us believe in the passage of time and not dwelling in some, like, nostalgia prison. Have a great night, guys. Enjoy the booze."

Her heels sink syrup-slow into the thick, soft carpet as she walks away, leaving little pits in her wake. Patrick watches her make her way out of the sunken room, toward the bright doorway beyond. She leans against the doorframe, swaying in place for a long moment, and then steps through.

As she makes her way through the beige, cedar-scented maze of Brenda's home, Cassidy wonders why all her luck seems to have run dry. She remembers the spells her sister used to do for her in their small, shared bedroom with the one window that looked out onto the neighbor's GrillMaster. June, so quiet at school and so shy with strangers, became someone else when she did spells: she spoke in a low voice, the voice of a woman, instructing Cassidy on what the spell they were doing was called and what it would make happen. Sometimes they did spells for money, for a hundred bucks to be found randomly by each of them within the next week. Sometimes they did spells for love, or for some girl they didn't like to break both her legs and go through lengthy physical therapy to heal them, at which point she would regret ever being mean to the Carter sisters. But mostly June insisted on spells to get Cass auditions, to promise big parts to come when she turned eighteen, spells to make her eyelashes grow longer and her hair to grow wavier. These spells June did for her career really worked. Cassidy believed it then and believes it even more today, looking back on a decade of luck and adoration that dried up almost exactly when June left her. What if she called her sister right now and demanded a spell to bring financing for a project she made herself, one all her own, a big, easy part in a franchise with a huge budget, etc.? Did magic by demand have its own power, or would June's fragile witchcraft work only when given freely, volunteered?

Patrick finds her barefoot on a Billington countertop, her silver heels overturned on the tile floor. She's crouched on the immaculate stone surface, rifling through the expansive pantry, pulling out bottles and scrutinizing the labels with an expression of cold interest. A few hard bits of sparkle gleam on the floor, casualties of the climb. Patrick can see the gooseflesh Braille on her exposed thigh where the party dress has ridden up, as chill nocturnal air flows through the open windows.

"Hamlin," she calls, turning her feline face slightly in his direction, "have you ever tasted water from the Perito Moreno Glacier? In Patagonia?"

He shakes his head no.

"How about from the Filchner-Ronne Ice Shelf?" she asks, thrusting a bluish glass bottle toward him, the craggy, long-tailed shape of Antarctica etched into its surface. A little ribbon of gold-leafed paper wrapped around the cap shows that it's pristine, unopened.

"No," he says. "What is this, just water?"

"It's fourteen hundred fifty a bottle, if you can even find a bottle to buy. I can't wrap my head around the fact that Brenda owns a shelf full of this stuff, and meanwhile, do you know how they pay out my contract?" She tears off the shiny paper and pulls off the cap, peers down into the blue slosh. "In mismatched bottles of Poland Spring, random liters of kiwi- and mango-flavored seltzer, gallon jugs with the lids taped on. Stuff that Brenda and Jay would never let touch their lips. Can you get us a couple of glasses?"

Patrick looks around the room, its vertical surfaces an intimate, fleshy pink. Small hexagonal tiles crawl across the backsplash, their color the shade of a wet tongue. Light seeps out from some unseen source underneath and behind the cabinets, falling softly upon the gray slate floor. The surfaces are smooth, seamless, with no hint of handle or knob, no sign of daily routine or personal use, not even a saltshaker left out on the countertop. It looks, he realizes, profoundly inhuman: a place built by people with the intention of leaving it unused, untouched, unloved.

"Oh god," Cassidy says, impatient. "Never mind." And she takes a long, deep drink from the thick-rimmed mouth of the bottle, the soft muscle beneath her jaw tight and slack by turns as the cool liquid slips through. She wipes her mouth with the back of her arm and hands it over.

"You know," she says as she leans back against the cabinet door, her narrow shoulders gleaming white against the strange, poreless material. "I booked my first job the week I moved to L.A. Most kids show up and do weeks or months of auditions, they go through season after season of lessons, coaching, trying out for anything, and getting nothing. I got this my third day out there. It was a commercial for that drug Optimorox: 'Are you apprehensive about the future? Do you worry that negative thoughts are beginning to drain all the good out of your life? If you suffer from inadequate or not-enough positivity, Optimorox may be able to offer something better.' I was playing the daughter of this depressed dad; we're at some kind of carnival or state fair and he can't enjoy himself, but then he pops a few Optimorox, and suddenly he's able to have a great time with his daughter again. This actor who played my dad—he was amazing. He was funny, he was good-looking in a really believable way, he smelled like roasted cinnamon almonds when you pop the top off a brand-new can. He was a dream dad. Mine had just left us all a few weeks ago, and this guy was so nice to me. He kept saying that he hoped he'd have a kid just like me someday, that he wanted to meet my mom and take us all to a real fair, a real carnival. You know, when you're playing the ring toss and eating funnel cakes for a shoot, you're still actually playing ring toss and eating funnel cakes. It's fun. I think it was the most fun I'd ever had at that point, because every moment had this extra shimmer around it, this special magic that came from the fact that it was going to be happening on TV. It was going to happen again and again, even after we stopped filming."

"Your TV dad hit on you?" He lifts the smooth rim of the bottle to his mouth and lets the cool, crisp water slide in, tasteless and pure. It moves across his tongue, quick and smooth and with an infinitesimal bitterness. But the flavor seems to vanish too fast for him to comprehend: Even as he tastes it, the taste evaporates, erases itself. He can't get the flavor of the precious, expensive water lodged in his memory. When he holds the bottle away from his lips, he can see that it's already nearly empty.

"It wasn't like that," she replies. "Anyway. We film for two days, and everyone is telling me how amazing I am, how they can't believe this is my first time acting, how I'm going to be in movies and TV shows, I'm going to have my face on a lunchbox someday. They pay me three thousand dollars, and my mom cries when the check shows up, and we all go to this diner in Marina del Rey and eat unlimited shrimp. When we leave, there's this mountain of little pink shrimp tails on the table; underneath the lights, it looks like a pile of jewels shining there. We felt rich. And then, a few weeks later, word comes back from the producers that they're reshooting the commercial because their target demographic has shifted up an income bracket, and they need a little girl who looks more upscale. So they never put me on TV. But the commercial comes on every day while my sister and I are home for the summer, and my dream dad is there, laughing and hugging and loving this little girl who looks a lot like me, but I guess richer. And even though I know that my fake dad probably doesn't love her more than he fake-loved me, even the fake version is so much more real than anything I had in my life."

There's a long pause. Patrick clears his throat.

"Do you trust Brenda and Jay?" he asks. "No offense. I know you seem close to them. But they seem like they're out for themselves."

"They probably are," says Cassidy calmly. "In this business, you sigh with relief when you realize someone's out for themselves and not out to get you."

"But they're not acting in the best interests of the film. Or the crew." He's starting to get heated. "I don't even get the sense sometimes that they expect this film to be released. I catch line-production mistakes all the time, actors saying lines that aren't what's in the script, never mind what's in my book. I don't think they care."

"And what do you want to do about it?" Cassidy looks amused, but also curious. "Are you going to make a big speech in front of everyone on set and walk out? You wouldn't be here, in this town, in this job, if you had something else you thought might work out better. You don't know how much better it feels to have a small chance than to have no chance."

"I can't just *take a chance*," says Patrick, loudly. "It's not some fun game, I need this to work out. For my family. I can't just laugh about it falling apart, I need it to work. Don't you? Do you get offered so many parts these days?"

He thinks for a moment that he's gone too far, been too rude, but Cassidy is still listening, watching him intently with a sharp look on her face.

"So what's the plan?" she says.

"If someone like you, someone indispensable, went with me," he begins, unconvincingly, "we could confront them about all these irregularities. Make them tell us the truth."

"Haven't you ever watched my show?" Cassidy laughs a little. "You don't just show up and demand the truth. You need some leverage."

"Okay, forget that. Instead, we follow the money trail. We look into how much of the budget is going into the film and how much is going . . ." He pauses. "Elsewhere. We look into the investors. Into Brenda and Jay's relationship, who knows about it, and what their plan is. And when we know something, we'll make our ask."

He pauses. In his fist, the luxurious, empty bottle feels cold and sad, like a secret. "I want to understand what's going on, at least," he says, half pleading. "Don't you?"

"Maybe. It's a nice idea. It sounds like a TV pilot. You could pitch it."

He's surprised to see her eyes shining, both darker and brighter than they had been a moment before. It could be a scrim of tears, but her voice is steady and certain, pulled as taut as plastic wrap.

"You know," she says distantly, "it takes strength to believe in what's not there. To insist that something is true when your eyes and ears and brain and heart tell you it's not. It's what I do in front of the camera. If I were better at it, I'd play my part all the goddamn time, and I'd be so much happier. Brenda, Jay, my agent, my trainer, all my quitter assistants, my fucking herbalist—everyone on that set, giving you their applause only because you pretend too. They act like they love you, and they don't really love you. But it's better when you believe they do."

Cassidy gives Patrick a filmy smile. She seems suddenly different, bereft of gusto, her beauty fragile and real. To Patrick, it's as though she's been replaced, part by part, with an entirely new person—a Cassidy with an only familial resemblance to herself, like a sister or a distant cousin. As if the person he saw all those times earlier was a photograph, a sketch, an estimate reflected back in an unsteady surface—and now the actual person has arrived. Less beautiful, he thinks, but more touchable somehow.

"Okay," she says, soberly. "I haven't been a kid detective in a long time, but the first thing I would do is find out what's inside those packages you pick up for Brenda. If there's a list or a schedule, you should make a copy of it. Have you done that yet? We can investigate tomorrow, after my scene wraps."

Something shivers close to his heart. Patrick reaches down into the shirt pocket over his left breast, draws out the heavy, trembling rectangle. A small procession of pictures crosses his screen, one photograph sliding onto the display only to be pushed off by the next. The photos are from Alison's phone number, but there are no words, no explanation. There is only the image of a broad, thick-trunked oak photographed from below, so that it towers, its bulk, its eerie largeness, overfilling the frame. Then a smear of deep-green foliage, something pink blurred within it so that each pink smear trails a tail like a comet. Another out-of-focus picture, of soft-sided blocks, cabins maybe, the right angles unnatural and therefore human. He can't tell if these photos are meant to be terrible, or if they are actually the best she could do. A final image pops up on-screen, and he recognizes Nora's small, poised hand pointing up at the sky: at the end of her fingertip is a wild, whited-out hole, a swallowing gap that could only be a bright, full summer moon. He knows that its bulk is immense, its brightness immeasurably far away—but as he peers down into the thin-glassed window to nowhere, it looks small enough to crush in his palm.

CHAPTER SIX

I n second grade, Cassidy Carter owned a parakeet named Charlene, a candy-colored creature that lived in an aquamarine cage. Though its entire body was barely six inches long, it could produce several humanlike sounds—not whole words, but soft coughs, whistles, and a noise exactly like a shy teenage girl's "um." After school, Cassidy and June would sit at the square table, doing homework, while the bird mumbled to itself nearby, flying from one short bound of the cage to another. Then, one day, the bird was dead. Cassidy searched the internet for answers: a budgie could die from dehydration, stray airborne molecules of frying-pan Teflon, paint fumes, caffeine, peanuts, avocado, parrot flu, tumors, direct sunlight and heating vents, eating too much fruit too fast, and countless other causes. "This is the whole problem with a bird," her father said. "They don't know how to ask for anything, can't call for help. Listen, that's why animals die so often, because they are no damn good at getting anyone's attention." Charlene was buried in a handkerchief beneath a purple-painted rock, never again to blink her blue-skinned eyelids in lizardlike quickness.

When Cassidy refused to sit for dinner that night (how could she eat when Charlene would never eat again?), her mother accused her of pretending. As Rita Carter would explain it to her own mother, she was blessed with one daughter who saw life as it was, and burdened by another who couldn't help but spin a web of drama around every little thing, however minor and insignificant. The first one was happy to sit silently in church, tracing the lines on her palm with a fingertip, while the other sighed and wriggled and complained of being strangled by her clothing, being about to pass out, about to have a seizure. Even at that age, she could fake a grand mal with enough gusto to stop the sermon in its tracks, lolling on the ground and shaken by invisible hands; she had learned the signs from a rerun of *ER*. Cassidy saw shallow performances all around her, and she knew that she could do better, given a chance. At home, her mother marched through scene after scene, argument and reconciliation, and her father seemed to forget his lines, going out to the garage to smoke when he couldn't think of any way to respond. She wished they would put more effort into their craft, pretend at something bigger, act out some facsimile of love until it conjured the real. But at least there was June, who could tell when Cass was putting on a show and when the real feelings were breaking through; June, who made Cass feel less fake. You only needed one other person to see what you were seeing in order to make it real: two people seeing the same thing, in fact, was more real than a whole roomful of people seeing it and sneering. After dinner was done, June brought peanut-butter toast on a plate, sprinkled with sunflower seeds, to their bedroom doorway. "I know you're really sad," June said, "but this was Charlene's favorite food and she'd want you to eat it."

At age nine, Cassidy had five auditions a week, and they were for speaking parts, multiple-sentence roles for characters written into the script with full names. When she walked into the audition room—a similar room every time, half empty and containing too many chairs—the faces turned toward her, smiling. A woman might come over, pick up handfuls of flossy blond hair, and hold them piled on top of Cassidy's skull in an ephemeral topknot, saying something like "Very pretty. With a little makeup she could play thirteen, fourteen." Later, when she was thirteen, they would tell her she could play middle-schoolers, high-schoolers, cheerleaders, and troubled teens. She auditioned for *Camp Do-What-Ya-Wanna* with a bit she had put together the week before in the two-room apartment she shared with her mom and sister. In the bit, she plays the part of herself practicing a hammy version of "Somewhere Over the Rainbow" for an audition, and also the part of her sister, bursting into the room to ask a series of humorous but increasingly dark questions about parakeets—Do parakeets sleep? Do parakeets sleep lying down? Do parakeets breathe when they sleep?—until it becomes apparent that the parakeet is dead. A hush falls over the room as the realization clouds her face, and then young Cassidy solemnly breaks the fourth wall: "That afternoon," she says, "my father sat me down and told me an important lesson: he said you have to hold on to life while you have it, but when it slips away, that's when you hold tight to the memories." Before leaving the room, the casting director exclaimed that Cassidy's emotional range was "elastic, like Silly Putty. She's Lucille Ball with the face of a future Ten!"

Cassidy waited in place as the casting director came back with one group of watchers after another. Some were older men, expensively suited, others twentysomethings in jeans and hoodies. In front of each new group, she was asked to deliver her parakeet speech with a different spin: shaky and uncertain, bold and righteously angry. "Now can you do one," the director of the film asked, straightening his glasses, intrigued, "where you don't even seem to care at all?" Cassidy nodded slowly and closed her eyes. When she opened them again, Charlene was a distant memory to her, a childish story retold by a parent decades later to a little girl that no longer existed.

Getting the part meant going to dinner with one of the producers, the casting director, and his assistant. Her mother chaperoned, while her older sister, June, stayed at home alone, watching the Thursday-night movie on TCM, sipping from a jumbo-sized bottle of Fanta. At the tablecloth restaurant, Cassidy watched her mother pick at a loose thread as she spoke rapidly about the differences between life in Haywood and life in Los Angeles, and the friendly community of child actors and actor parents they were getting to know at the Yucca Heights Apartments. How in the community building there were always free pretzels and, on the weekend, free acting lessons and seminars for the kiddies, so that the adults could finally have an afternoon alone to paint their toenails and watch a program from beginning to end. The movie people sipped from glasses of water, their faces fixed and polite, and Cassidy understood that they were not enjoying themselves at all.

She told a sad story about her father being diagnosed with

lung cancer, which had never happened, and they murmured condolences. Then she made a joke from it, and they laughed. They smiled as she told a funny story about the summer she watched *Sister Act* every day, because it was the only movie they owned, making up little games to try to make it feel new, like pretending that Whoopi Goldberg's character was a double agent and inventing a whole new situation around that once-familiar moment. She knew by some deep-lodged instinct to keep changing the mood, to offer them new pieces of her, one after another, like a tasting menu. Any actress might hold the spotlight for a moment, but keeping it meant constant change, restless shifting, becoming a plastic person, sleek and glossy, with the 360-degree flexibility of a gooseneck clamp lamp. When the waiter came, Cassidy asked in a smooth, calm voice for a double espresso, and when it came, she sipped from the bitter cup and made it look as though she loved the taste. She knew her mother was watching her from across the table, drinking deep from a glass of white Zinfandel, her stare hard enough to bruise the skin.

Cassidy looks out at the set of *Elsinore Lane*, at the assistants and techs, and sinks her fingers into thick inches of newly purchased foreign hair, feeling its fake heft slip slightly atop the genuine hair, coiled beneath. For this scene, where the audience first understands that her character is a demonic being in cahoots with the evil uncle, her look is a sort of 1960s beehive with a supernatural lift to it, an ethereal figure in a girl-group mini-dress. Cassidy practices a big smile and then a scowl, a big smile and then a scowl. Switch on, switch off. She didn't need June to say it anymore: it was second nature. Going into a scene, she should wear an expression that is tender and pliant, like a soft red skirt steak; she should feel at one with her famous face, her famous features, but she should never, ever touch them or brush her own hair out of her eyes or scratch an itch, or she might wreck the makeup department's hard work and have to go back in the seat. My face is a toxic zone, she tells herself to strengthen the injunction. Sometimes she imagines her face as a layer of Cassidy-shaped armor, the real person beginning a few millimeters down. A few millimeters down, the real her could be wearing its real expression, whatever that was.

She hears her name and walks up under the bright, hungry light of the set, her lips dry and tight with nude-colored lipstick, her eyelashes heavy with mascara, their downward drag a little like falling asleep. She shouts for someone to bring her a bottle of water, and a couple figures scurry off into the dark. A short guy in a tight black tee tells her the role of the uncle is being recast, and they may just end up CGI-ing him in anyway. He stands a six-foot-tall metal pole in front of her. There's a tennis ball glued to the top. He points at the green sphere and tells her that's her target, got it?

"Got it," she says. "I'll talk to the tennis ball. Listen, my copy of the script only has my lines, it doesn't have whatever the uncle character says in response." The photocopied pages malinger under a pox of question marks and hand-scrawled TBDs. "How do you want me to handle that? I know between the lines you're supposed to be filming my reaction, but how should I react when I don't know what he's going to be saying?"

"I'd need to check with someone about that," he says stiffly. "Can you just do a sort of generic reaction in the meantime?"

"You mean nodding and smiling or something like that?"

"Yeah, perfect," he replies.

186 / ALEXANDRA KLEEMAN

Cassidy gives him the look of someone watching a very stupid thing happen, but he doesn't seem to notice.

"The director wants a few different takes," he adds quickly, "a spooky one, a moody one, and then a more defiant, pouty one. A sultry, sad one—and then, just in case, a 'happy-go-lucky' version."

Cassidy nods once and looks around. "Who's the director today?" she asks. "Is he around here?" But the tee-shirt guy has already left. Surrounded by bright soundstage lights, she is half blinded: she can see the crowd around her, their sneakers and legs gray-scale and dim, but there are no faces. Where the director usually sits she finds a naked spotlight pointed in her direction; when she looks toward it, it leaves a neon-green bruise on her visual field, a blot she can't see through or around.

As a voice to her far right calls "Action!" she steps forward, looking the tennis ball square in the eye.

"I think he's begun to suspect what I am. What we all are," Cassidy says with an eerie slowness. She pauses, tilts her head to indicate that she's listening, then continues. "And yet," she says with a faraway tone, "something in my mortal form still remembers him. Loves him. Knows him, though I no longer know myself."

Ugh. The lines seem bad to her. But it's not worth fighting over: clock in, clock out, she tells herself, bank your water and pick your moment. The far-off voice yells, "Cut, reset!" and she looks down at the floor and back up again with a neutral expression in place. She knows all the shortcuts: to tear up, she thinks of Charlene the parakeet; to cry, she imagines the blade of a bulldozer tearing into her beloved swimming pool, halving the baby geese; and to summon a fierce expression, she thinks of her ex-manager, Toby, who dropped her and then sold photos from her invitation-only nursery-rhyme-themed birthday party to TMZ. There's a spidery feeling in the back of her throat, something she'd like to cough out or drown in water, but the water she asked for still hasn't materialized.

"I think he's begun to suspect what I am. What we all are," Cassidy purrs dangerously. She's done sexy so many times in the heavily mocked second half of her career that it's second nature: just a matter of acting a little bit sleepy, a little bit mad, and breathing exclusively through your mouth. "And yet," she continues with a petulant tone, "something in my mortal form still remembers him." The passage would be better if the lines were half the length, she thinks, but the film is already hemorrhaging words, the script shorter and shorter each day and containing more effects-loaded visual sequences that will only be assembled in postproduction. On set, the effects guys have been blocking out action zones with colorful tape, pointing into the vacant air to illustrate which figures might enter from where for the big fight scene. She watches them as they discuss in serious tones the thing that does not exist, indicating its shape and size, bringing it into hazy being through their collective belief.

Cassidy delivers her lines two more times, but as she turns to leave, they tell her the camera wasn't running and she'll have to do it all again. She curses and calls into the darkness again for her glass of water. The lines are stupid, but she can bully them into some semblance of life. "I think he's begun to suspect what I am," she says with a haunted look, as if there's a scary monster hiding in her bedroom closet. "I think he's begun to suspect what I am," she says with an eerie moan. The grips and gaffers stir in the background, their motion a whisper. "I think he's begun to suspect what I am," she says with a note of plaintive, naïve longing, a Haywood girl hoping to make it onto big-city

TV so everyone back home will see who she's become and why she will never ever be coming back. She's looking for an opening, someone she can enfold in a public scene, a distraction to give Patrick time to carry out their plan. "Is that mine?" she asks, pointing at the cup held by that skinny Latino kid Patrick is always talking to, and as he nods she lifts it from his sweaty hand and calls for a five-minute break.

As the liquid touches her lips, she flinches and drops it suddenly, as though it contains something disgusting; the cup skids across concrete. She gasps, then coughs several times, with increasing intensity. The laces of Horseshoe's vintage trainers are dark with liquid.

"Fucking assassin!" Cassidy shouts at Horseshoe, who seems flattered at first to be yelled at by the star of *Yesteryears* and *Daddy Lessons* and his personal favorite, *Daughter of Invention*, until it begins to sink in how angry she is. "I don't drink that fake water—it doesn't touch my lips. Got it?"

"But it's not fake," Horseshoe says meekly, his eyes scared but amazed. He'll be telling stories about this moment for years to come. "I got it from the dispenser with your name on it, I'm pretty sure." There's a dazed, involuntary smile on his face, something he knows he's doing but can't figure out how to stop.

"Don't try to *manage* me," she snaps. "I know the taste. I know when something's not right. Oh my god, my heart is racing. I think I'm having a reaction, I feel . . . faint." She turns to face the rest of the crew. "Listen, everyone, I'll say this once. I have a deadly allergy to fake water. Anyone who tries to feed me that hyphenated crap as some sort of sick joke is fired." She pauses, an unsteady look in her eye. "I don't feel right. Someone find Patrick. Tell him to get me some good water from Brenda and Jay's office." She turns slowly, searching the wide, vacant spaces. "I think I need to sit," she says and then she stops, breathing hard and swaying, transforming her body into a droopy flower. The crowd around her lurches into action; a folding chair is brought and unfolded, Cassidy's pale, bony body arranged for comfort and fanned with a sheaf of production schedules. She murmurs apologies as she shields her face from the weight of the bright light looming above.

At the other end of the vast structure, in front of the catering tent, Horseshoe finds Patrick by the candy bowl, his breath reeking of sugar. He tells him that Cassidy had an allergic reaction and needs some water from the executive office. "Real water," he says with emphasis, "or she'll kill you."

Patrick opens the heavy door and slips inside. Brenda and Jay share a single long, L-shaped desk, a glass pane balanced atop a spidery metal structure. He checks the files on top of the desk, memos in bolded, bullet-pointed Arial and piles of spreadsheets gridding blandly page after page. In the filing cabinets behind them, he finds eight pairs of velvet loafers embroidered with emblems of predatory animals and some jars full of prebiotics, postbiotics, herbal remedies pulverized and encapsulated. He can't find any of the packages he and the other PAs have been picking up all over the Greater Los Angeles County. But then, in the corner, where Cassidy's daily ration of water sits boxed and ready to be carted out to the big white rental van, Patrick sees manila folders with no label on the outside. Inside, invoices like the ones he's been sent out with on pickups. He pulls out his phone and takes a photo of the first document, then the next, and the next.

Meanwhile, surrounded by concerned techs, assistants, and

producers, Cassidy Carter's condition deteriorates. She tilts her head back and moans, new sweat gleaming on her brow. She asks for water, then air, then water again. And suddenly she wilts in the folding chair, her shoulders slipping down the plastic chair back like a sweater sliding off a hanger, the whole body limp and flimsy and sliding slowly onto the ground. "She's fainted," they murmur to one another, as hands reach forward to grab the slender shoulders and elevate the head, press fingers and palms to her clammy skin. "Does anybody have Jay's number?" they say, and "Who's got her water, can you check on that?" But at the moment when someone suggests that they call an ambulance, she sits up, adjusts her wig, and picks herself off the ground. "Oh, for fuck's sake," she says, "I'll get it myself," and she walks off the bright and heavily watched stage, into the chilly darkness.

Sitting in a folding chair in a dark corner of the soundstage, she watches her phone light up as the photos that Patrick took appear on her screen, one by one. You don't have to be a genius detective, she thinks, to notice that these invoices show payments owed to the film's production company, not payouts to vendors. In her decade and a half of hustling on film sets and in TV studios, this would be the first project she's seen that's collecting on debts from surrounding businesses, rather than paying them off. She feels a little giddy with the discovery, and also a little dizzy. She tries to text Patrick with the news, but for a moment she can't remember how to spell his name. It's only later that afternoon that it occurs to her that she doesn't really know what was in that plastic cup the kid handed to her on set. She meant to cause a scene, accuse him of making a mistake, but the kid was green and who knows what he gave her? It was only a sip, only for effect, but didn't it have a strange taste? Not a taste but an aftertaste, not an aftertaste but a dark omen. Didn't that sip of liquid remind her somehow of the sugar-sweet coating of a pill?

"So . . . how many of these places are we visiting tonight, boss? Don't forget about the fire—we'll be taking the long way to get anywhere." Cassidy curls into the red plastic chair, her sneakers perched on the molded lip. She reaches out for another handful of fries, her arm brushes her smooth, bare knees. In the black lenses of her sunglasses, worn indoors to minimize recognizability, Patrick can see the reflection of rows and rows of fast-food fluorescents, lights designed to beam twenty-four hours a day. Everything feels oddly wholesome here, oddly familiar but shiny and new, like he's young again. In Cassidy's company, he feels at least ten years younger—to be more precise, it feels like he's forgotten the past ten years of his life. He's standing again at the start of a career, and anything could happen, some of it bad. Behind the counter, teenagers in red hats scoop servings of French fries and chicken nuggets from large, deep vessels.

"Well," Patrick says, something fluttering in the middle space of his body, "I got about twenty-three addresses off the invoices in Brenda and Jay's office. These six are in the San Fernando Valley, not too far. I thought we could try to cross as many of these off our list tonight as we can. They're office-park locations; at least a couple seem to be memory clinics. For ROADies," he adds, the slang sitting awkwardly on his tongue.

"Okay, okay, cool," she replies. "We'll have to take the highway, and it'll be fucking slow. But it should be all right."

She grabs his vanilla milkshake, swivels the straw around to check the thickness. Plastic shrieks softly against plastic, a material wail. She pops the lid off and holds the dripping straw in her right hand, while with the left she brings the cup of cold, sweet liquid to her glossy mouth. She replaces the lid loosely and pushes the cup back across the table into Patrick's warm, empty grasp.

"Do you think we're going to go inside tonight, poke around?" Cassidy asks.

Patrick remembers the dark hallway, the window into the room where he had seen those fully grown bodies posed and helpless. Eyes open and empty of will, empty of vigor. He shudders. He doesn't want to feel the doors close behind him, shutting him in.

"I've never been inside a memo-clinic," she says, more quietly this time. "My sister worked at one for a little bit, after she quit being my assistant. She always wanted to *help people*." Cassidy's pointy fingers claw quote marks into the air. "I was, like, Help me! Help your sister! But she couldn't stand to be around the industry anymore. She said the business was rotting me like a tooth. As if there were something out there that wouldn't rot you." She laughs short, bitter. "She must have hated working at the clinic—she quit to go learn acupuncture. She had only been there a few weeks."

"Does she still do acupuncture?" Patrick asks.

"How would I know?" she replies. "Am I a psychic mind-reader?"

"You don't talk to her?" He's thinking about his own distant loved ones, gallivanting in a hippie meadow as Klaus picks up his call at the pay phone. The technology that allows you to reach anyone in the world also allows you to perceive them ignoring you in real time. "I just find that incredibly sad. Family is something irreplaceable; you can't just order another."

"If you have such a hard-on for *family*, why are you here with me, about to skulk around in dark parking lots? You could be at home sitting with your *family* in your *family room*." When Cassidy says it, the word sounds like a slur.

Suddenly she sits straight. She slaps him on the shoulder and points.

"That's my nose," she says. "Over there."

Patrick swivels in his chair. He sees girls, ponytails, a cluster of people vaguely linearized, waiting for their turn to order at the counter.

"The one with red hair," she says, her voice matter-of-fact. "In the denim skirt. Watch her when she turns around."

He watches. The girl is college-aged, short, with pillowy upper arms, a soft mass of wavy auburn hair. She talks to a couple friends as she waits in line, shifting her weight from one foot to the other. But as she turns around, Patrick seems to recognize her—there's something intimate about her face, something he finds beautiful though she's not at all his type. The strange girl gives him a creeped-out look. He's old to her, no matter how young he feels inside. And then he sees it on her face, that unforgettable appendage, the slim bridge and the tip that curves up as gentle as a flower: the girl has Cassidy's perfect nose.

"It's spooky, right?" says Cassidy. "What a succubus."

Patrick turns back to look at her. The sensation of turning away from Cassidy's nose only to encounter Cassidy's nose once again is unsettling. It seems to violate the principles of space and time, singularity, the vast and terribly lonely uniqueness of things in the world, existence a form of forced difference.

"This happens a lot?" he asks.

"I used to see one every day. I told my manager that we needed to crush it right away, either crush it or make some money off it. I tried to get a patent. The lawyers told me it was a sure thing, but the government rejected it three times. They said all the movies I had been in meant that my 'invention had already been publicly disclosed.' If I don't own my own face, who does? In the end, those lawyers set up a licensing deal for me, so, whenever a plastic surgeon does an operation for some-one who wants my name attached to it, a sort of guarantee of quality, I get about eight dollars. I used to get so many checks I never even noticed that royalty check, but now I know it shows up on the twelfth of every month, like clockwork."

He stares at her, not knowing what sort of comfort to give, what sort of joke to make. The girl with Cassidy's nose places her order at the counter and retrieves a gigantic soda. The over-sized plastic cup is as thick as her thigh.

"That nose money keeps the lights on," she says grimly, and suddenly she looks pissed off. "Are you ready to go yet? You know, I'm actually a really busy person, and I don't have infinite time to help you with your project." She grabs the empty, grease-soaked French-fry container and stalks over to the trash, crushing the stiff paper in her hand before tossing it in. She walks out to the van alone, her ankles narrow in her big white sneakers, her hair bright-edged in the streetlight glow and twitching in the breeze.

The first address is a freestanding building in an office park off the highway. The white van inches along on the GPS screen, the highway slowed by drivers up ahead who roll to a full stop to watch the living rim of fire climb the grassy knolls. The wind drives the neon line forward and into the unburnt valley, where the larger, bushier shrubs catch fire slowly, one side at a time. The burn moves from left to right, like reading a paragraph, the fresh flame reluctant at first and shy. He can hear the sound of it through the rolled-up window, feel the heat through the trickle of cool air seeping from the vents—the sound of the fire a burning muzzle, snapping vegetation in a hot, hungry mouth. Looking out at the hills, lit in intricate, mysterious designs, he feels inexplicably like he's up in an airplane at night, gazing down at the lights of a city below. As they drive, Cassidy is turned away, closed off. She ups the volume of some top-forty ballad when he tries to speak to her. Pouring through the cheap speakers, the singer's plush voice sounds fractured and moth-eaten, a disintegrating thing, and Patrick feels punished—like he's been demoted from an intriguing peer to the lame dad of a surly teenage daughter. A sense of potential has evaporated, dissolved into the suddenly chill air.

They find the building at the far end of the empty parking lot, a drab beige-bricked thing with dark-tinted windows. Patrick parks the van, and as they walk to the entrance, their footsteps echo in the vacated space. Past a row of eucalyptus trees smelling sweetly of cough drops, the red gleam of the highway is visible. He and Cassidy press their faces close to the blackish glass, but all they see are their own faces reflected back in dim, impoverished form. They walk around to the back of the building, where broken-down boxes lean against a dumpster. The trash is a mix of office supplies and junk-food wrappers: frozen burritos, instant ramen, the slimy plastic packages that once held slices of bologna. Back at the front, the door is locked, with no hours posted, and Patrick squints in through the dark. A ghostly glimpse of the interior, the outline of cheap folding chairs and a stand of pamphlets. The name MEMODYNE stenciled on the wall.

"Does that look like a waiting room to you?" he asks. "Something medical? Like a clinic?"

She gazes into the dark space and laughs loudly.

"I think we've solved the mystery," Cassidy says, falsely bright. "It's a dump. We've found a dump. Great job, Brenda. Great job, Jay."

"Have you ever heard of Memodyne?" he asks, but she says nothing, just stalks silently back toward the car. The next address is an eight-minute drive away, down broad streets scented by smoke. They pull into a strip-mall parking lot, the van crawling past shuttered storefronts at five miles per hour as Patrick checks the numbers above the door. 6830 DeSoto Avenue is a WAT-R store with two melancholy palms out front, the potted soil speckled with discarded pennies and cigarette butts. "Dump number two," says Cassidy as they park. "Dump, the sequel. Dump and dumper." The store is closed, but the tube lights stay on all night, casting a buzzing blue sheen on vats of WAT-R *Fresh* and WAT-R *Deluxe*, two lines that Patrick isn't familiar with. By the register, a double-doored refrigeration unit stocks smaller bottles for impulse buys. As he takes down notes, she texts furiously, her head bent over her phone and illuminated by the small blue light.

"This WAT-R store doesn't look like the other ones I've seen," Patrick says. The ones he's been to while picking up spare tanks for the set and returning the empties, or when the Hacienda Lodge is sold out of refills, are vast, eerily spacious showroom floors with the warehousing visible in the background. WAT-R movers whirring around the stockroom, plucking tanks and thick-walled plastic sacks from high up. "Why is this one so small?"

"Maybe it's off-market," she replies, not even looking up from her phone. "WAT-R is supposed to be cheap, but it's still more than some people are ready to pay. They can't forget how water used to come pouring out of every faucet for pennies. So some places sell samples and seconds from WAT-R Corp, or unused units of WAT-R that get consigned. Sometimes expired stuff, sometimes discontinued lines. It can be a lot cheaper, but you don't know what you're getting. That is, if you think you know what you're getting when you go to the big stores."

He takes photos of the phone number stenciled on the wall, the visible prices on the vats in the back. Behind the register is an oversized graph that shows where the different sub-brands of WAT-R figure in terms of purity and goodness. On the vertical axis, the scale goes from "Pure" to "Extremely Pure." On the horizontal axis, the graph maps a range from "Slippery" to "Sticky." Plotted all over are activities ideally suited to that particular nexus of purity and grip. Showering, for example, is best with WAT-R of moderate purity and a slippery texture. Drinking WAT-R, on the other hand, should have high purity and high stickiness, so as to aid in bodily absorption. Patrick tries to zoom in on the photo he's taken, to read the tiny printed names of sub-brands and figure out if he's been drinking and showering with the right stuff, but as the photo gets larger it dissolves into a meaningless shading of pixels and hue.

The third stop is a building four stories high at the corner of a busy road and a quiet residential lane. With its uniform windows and covered carport, the building looks like a converted chain hotel—a former Holiday Inn or La Quinta. Lights are on in the lobby, but nobody is behind the desk. Standing in front of the awning, Patrick takes a photo of the Memodyne sign out front, as Cassidy taps one message after another into the illuminated screen.

The fourth stop is in another office complex, but when they park, Cassidy refuses to get out of the van. "I need to get back home; my friend is bringing over some health supplies for me," she says. "Can we just call it a night?"

"Health supplies," Patrick says slowly, trying to make it clear through his delivery that he knows she means something else, something she won't say out loud.

"Yeah, that's right, Captain."

"It can't wait for tomorrow?"

"Why does this investigation have to be done on some emergency schedule? Did you hire me? Am I working for you?" Cassidy asks, acidly sweet.

"I thought you thought this was important," he says.

"I realize that whatever's gone rotten with Brenda and Jay, or the whole state of California, is totally new to you and feels like a very big deal. But a lot of people worked very hard to make it this rotten, and digging it all up isn't going to shock them into making things right."

"And it accomplishes more to go home and get fucked up on your white linen sectional?" He stares at her in disbelief.

She looks out the window with a smile on her face. "I get

fucked up because then I don't have to ask myself how things are. I know how they are. They're fucked up."

He turns the key in the ignition and backs out too fast. Then they're on the highway, crawling through the same traffic, their silence complete. In the burning hills, hobbled oaks keel in the flames, the twisted limbs lost in conflagration and burning swiftly. A full crown is reduced to blackened glyph, inky signs in the bright night. When the trunks are dark and smoldering, the beetles come: scenting the infrared from miles away through sensors beneath their forelimbs, they fly ten, twenty, 130 miles, drawn to the heat and the flame and the newly charred brush. They fall from the brown and smoke-choked sky, as black as bullets, mating inside the still-burning fire. Under the smoky, oscillating light, a female fire beetle crawls along the blackened craw of a burnt bush, her hard belly protected by a special wax secreted to hold in the body's moisture, to keep it from evaporating as she lays her eggs. In the months to come, her larvae will be born in the charred stump, grow in the charred stump, live off the charred stump, eating tunnels through defenseless matter, to emerge one day as a fully grown fire beetle, built to sense the heat of faraway burning and hurl its body in that direction for hours and hours of treacherous flight.

There's a dinged-up Audi with tinted windows sitting in front of Cassidy's Secret Sunset home when the van lumbers into the driveway. As she gathers her keys from the cup holder, she feels Patrick's stare hot on her cheekbones and knows that he's demanding to be looked at, acknowledged.

"Are you waiting for a good-night kiss?" she asks stiffly, trying to crack a joke.

"Maybe this doesn't seem that important to you," Patrick says slowly, his delivery pitiful, thin. "And you don't see the point. But I really do need someone here. I see all this stuff, but I don't know if I'm seeing it correctly. It looks like a conspiracy to me, but everything else in the world is telling me it's just fine, it's all normal. If I'm alone when I look into this, if nobody's around to see with me, I won't even know if I've gone crazy. It'll just happen, and then I'll be completely gone."

The smoke-scented air seeps in through the open car door. Neither of them moves; they sit there in the velour seats as the insects cry from their unseen positions in the landscaped surround.

"Okay," she says at last. "I'll see you tomorrow. Get a good night's sleep and don't go crazy. Not tonight." She leans over and squeezes his shoulder so quickly that Patrick worries he only imagined it. As he drives back to Azusa, forty-five minutes in apocalyptic wildfire traffic, he hunches his right shoulder up and lets it sink back again and again, searching the grain of his movement for any difference, any sign, any lingering evidence that she had touched his body with hers.

The next morning, Cassidy calls in sick, and Patrick drives to the studio alone. The film set doesn't resemble a film set quite as much as it did the day before. Gone are the catering tables clustered with bystanders, and the bustle of crew rushing back and forth. Now the couple dozen who remain keep apart, as though speaking about this fragile situation could destroy it. They've brought in a new director, a gaunt old hippie in plaid pants, and Jay introduces him to the whole crew as Jarrel Toback, the director of some acclaimed foreign film in the 1980s—but when Patrick tries to look him up on his phone, he can't find any trace of the guy on the internet. The Arm has taken to sitting in the darkest corner of the soundstage, the corner where they store all the extra wires, and drawing in a little black notebook. As far as Patrick can tell, all the drawings are of the crazy blond girl he saw on the highway—the Arm draws her in her bathing suit, lying on her towel, but also, more worryingly, in a formal wedding gown. Meanwhile, Horseshoe has been off set more than he's been on it, slipping in furtively and filling his pockets with catering-table candy. Even Brenda, her polish bone-deep, has begun showing up in leggings and sweatshirts—though, judging from their inscrutable taupelike color, they are probably still very expensive.

The new director gathers the techs and gaffers and grips together for a "group-building exercise," and together they form a wobbly, dented hand-holding circle. Patrick watches from afar as their new leader hoists their interlaced hands up into the air. Last night, he had returned to the motel room and binged nearly half a season of *Kassi Keene*, until he passed out mid-episode, the eerie sunrise light glowing violet through motel curtains. Though he was watching the legendary final season, the season most scrutinized by the Kassi Keene Revelators and most supposedly rife with secret clues and occult messages, he found it difficult to focus on the incremental plotlines and knew that he would probably have to watch these episodes again later, maybe later today. At five this morning, he was watching the tail end of "Joint Proportionality," an episode in which Kassi discovers that her beloved community-college economics teacher is being blackmailed about his fairly mundane marijuana habit by some nefarious enemy—probably, judging from the grammar and syntax of the random notes, a disgruntled Paradise Cove Community College student. He remembers the first half of the episode more or less—the questioning of various students with motive, the trip to the IT expert. But after that it gets fuzzy, it's all fuzzy except for Kassi's face, or does he mean Cassidy's face, the big blue eyes and bubble-gum-colored lipstick so clear in his memory that he could have sworn he was there, standing in the room, the day those episodes were being filmed.

Patrick takes out his phone and navigates to the /Kassi-KeeneTBR forum, checking the Big Reveal summary guide thread for the episode. As always, he starts out skeptical about the idea of a shadow storyline undergirding the flippant, cheery forty-five-minute narratives, but becomes more convinced as the various posters present their evidence. He's absorbed the different acronyms and code words—RH for "red herring" and AH for "actual herring," NCA for "Nifty-controlled agent" and TKO for "Team Kassi Overall." He's learned the vocabulary they use for discussing different types of clues: "signs" for little inadvertent hints left by the show's creators, "signals" for things they want you to follow up and investigate on your own, "flares" for huge, mind-blowing discoveries.

▶ **diskordpro415**

Ok so though this episode is not one of my all-time favorites, I do think it is one of the richest in TBR nuggets and does a lot to clarify the threads that serious watchers were following throughout previous episodes. Just to give you all some of the top signals and flares I spotted while watching:

- When Prof. Cabrillo receives the blackmail e-mail he shows to Kassi, there's a GIF of his face pasted onto a dancing bear image, which hearkens back to the ransom note Kassi received in s02e17 w the donkey-bear GIF and shows that there is a link between the two crimes. Because the kidnapper in that ep (Bonnie Tasker) was killed with the other a-capella club kids at the beginning of season 4, the link can't be literal—instead it's a meta-link, the show telling us it sees a connection between these two diff crimes.

- The "blackmailer" uses language that is simplistic, but peppered with internet slang & shortened "words" that could be acronyms: ENUF, LTR, 4EVA. We've already established that acronyms have a secret life in Paradise Cove, and we should get deciphering the blackmail note because it could be a breakthrough.

- When Kassi and Prof. Cabrillo finally confront the blackmailer (Prof. Dickson, Cabrillo's nemesis from the English department), you would expect the blackmailer to give some sort of defense or explanation of their actions—it's what you could call a convention of the genre. But when they confront Prof. Dickson, he doesn't do this, he goes on a rant about how something evil is happening in PC and then he throws himself off the cliff. I think this is a signal that his goal really wasn't to blackmail Cabrillo, it was to draw Kassi's attention to some important piece of the TBR puzzle. And he kills himself right before the cops show up—meaningful?? Did he have knowledge of double agents on the police force?

↳ **JCtheDestroyer**

Great job on all of this, I agree w/everything—and also I would add that Dickson is pictured in his classroom holding a copy of Hamlet. Hamlet is a play about a man who knows there is "something rotten in the state of Denmark." Dickson knows too—and his death causes his message (the speech he gives on the cliff) to live on for long after his death, just like Shakespeare's masterwork.

⤓ **BBGunn40x**

Dickson was definitely TKO. The actor who played him was already breaking through with a big role in the Marvel Universe. They always lure bigger actors to the show with hero roles, not villains.

⤓ **jonzeewhiskerz**

He was TKO??? He shot a gun at Kassi on the cliff. I think you got it twisted.

⤓ **HaydenStrange8**

The show intends for us to make bold connections between disparate elements: it knows that we, not Kassi, are the real detectives and that we have a view of TBR that she can never possibly achieve, because she is part of the flawed and corrupt system. She sees what the system shows her, but we have the bird's eye view and can see so much more, including those things that lie in the system's subconscious, things it is not even aware it knows.

For this reason, I prefer not to use the term TBR, which refers to a plot reveal that may or may not ever have been planned for the show. I use the term TBP, The Big Picture, which stands for the actuality of Paradise Cove, a thing that can perhaps only be uncovered from the audience's vantage point, through analysis and deep thought. TBR may or may not be real, and certainly never happened. But TBP is as real as the ground (we think) we walk on, the water (we think) we drink.

↓ GMB21078

What is this, more TBR IRL bullshit? Some of us trust the writers and actors on this show. Some of us actually love the show and believe they know what they're doing.

↓ Taxxxonomi

Many of u can't wrap your mind around IRL b/c it would imply that u have a Real Life to be In, and that's just way too much for most ppl on here :P

↓ SheeplessInSeattle

HaydenStrange8 is like the kid who comes along and knocks your sandcastle down so that you'll be forced to build one with him. He destroys everyone else's game because he doesn't like to play alone.

↓ EndlingInLove71

LOL . . . no kidding I knew a kid who would do that! Wonder where that asshole is today.

▶ DezasterPeace

What caught my eye in this episode was the similarity between how the English lit professor died and this news article about a crewmember who fell to his death on the season 2 set of Kassi Keene. Just a few of the similarities: Peter Guerrera, the crew member who died, was working on a lighting repair about 63 feet above the point of impact. Estimated height of Paradise Cliffs, based on long shots and exterior footage? 68 feet. Guerrera was a snappy dresser and you can see what he's wearing in the obituary photo—a striped blue button-down shirt, just like Prof. Dickson. The kicker? Guerrera was also an English major in college. So where does the line between fact and fiction truly exist? Doesn't this scene resemble a finger pointing at the moon? Only a fool looks at the finger.

↴ PDX_DDavis

If you want to peddle this conspiracy theory BS, take it to /Kassi-KeeneTBR_IRL. This is a forum for serious-minded fans of the show to engage in some deep reading and analysis, and try to reconstruct the missing information that would have been given in the following season's true series finale. We're seeking closure, not a tinfoil hat.

↴ GMB21078

So you're saying one random crew member had a completely random accident, the kind that happen all the time in workplaces, and the writers and producers of the show wrote it into some totally random episode years later as a way of—what? Calling attention to it? Memorializing him years later? Or are you saying there was foul play? Are you saying that it wasn't an accident, it was a suicide? Just say what you mean. Stop being all ominous about it.

↴ ChZhChan05

Correction: NOTHING is completely random

↴ EndlingInLove71

As a computer scientist, I can confirm this. Randomness is not a property of the universe, connections are. Randomness is an illusion that projects sometimes when the links are too numerous to comprehend.

Patrick feels the phone spasm in his hot palm. A message from Cassidy slides onto the screen: *Good morning, sunshine. . . . When are we meeting up for recon pt. 2? I'm out of bed but you can assume it'll take me a few hours to wake up.* He looks at the clock—it's almost three-thirty. The director and all the techies are lying down on the floor in the center of the space cleared for the exercises. They lie on their sides, bodies limp and relaxed and curled into a loose fetal position, while a woman standing with a stopwatch slowly counts up. She hits one hundred, then two hundred, and then, much later, seven hundred. Patrick texts back: *It's kind of a dead day on set. I think Brenda and Jay will let me off if I say I'm doing errands for you. Want a pickup?*

Pulling into the triple-wide driveway, Patrick sees no black Audi, no sign that anyone was ever there or had ever stayed over. He watches through the windshield as Cassidy steps out in sunglasses and a striped dress, her light-colored hair catching the sunshine and refracting it, drawing a golden halo around her heartlike face. She's showing up with no complaints, none of the usual stalling tactics, and he can't help but think she was waiting for him on the other side of that door, staring out the window, and wondering when he'd show—her face holding that peculiar mixture of innocence and awareness that he finds so strangely affecting in season five of *Kassi Keene: Kid Detective*, where her acting starts to leave behind the Nancy Drew tropes and show some real sophistication.

"Are you ready for a tour of the picturesque parking lots of the San Fernando Valley?" she asks, eyebrows raised.

"Well, we can start somewhere else on the list," Patrick replies self-consciously. "I mean, there's the San Gabriel Valley, Anaheim, Huntington Beach, even a couple of sites in Bakersfield. It's not like the San Fernando Valley is the only place—we have options."

"I was kidding," Cassidy says. "I could care less where we go, as long as we see some parking lots."

"Another joke," he says. She's being so agreeable. It occurs to him that, if she's not invested in the mission, maybe she's simply invested in spending time with him. Could it be that she feels a connection to him, something that he failed to notice?

"Well, I think we could be doing more. I can get into places you wouldn't imagine; I can get people to talk to me who really shouldn't." Through the dark shades he can see the focus of her eyes, boring straight into him. "People always want to please celebrities. Sometimes, when I worry that I'm really finally over, I go to a restaurant and order something crazy, something that's probably never been on the menu. When it shows up, I know that I've still got it."

"Okay. If you're willing to do the talking, I know where we should go next," he says, starting the engine and beginning to back out of the driveway. He only feels a tinge of dread as he points the bulky vehicle in the direction of the clinic he visited last week where the Cassidy fan behind the front desk mistook him for a patient, and whose address he found in Brenda's documents.

As the building comes into view, Patrick feels the strangest sensation come over him, as though time is a piece of paper folded in half and some unseen hand is drawing its finger across his heart to make the crease. He looks out to his left and sees the white van sliding across the mirror panes of glass, its whiteness reflected back in gold, teal, and orange. Somewhere deep in his chest, like a lump of something swallowed and stuck in place, a voice is shrieking that it's not right for it all to happen again: If he walks into that building and sees himself standing at the counter, he knows it'll be his end. He'll cease to exist, he'll ignite, he'll return to vapor and dust.

As they pass through the sliding doors, a figure behind the

counter screams and ducks. A moment later, the head pops back up, yellow hair disheveled but still silky and soft. Her hands cover her mouth, but he can tell it's the girl he talked to on his previous trip to the clinic, wearing an expression that looks like terror, but is full of joy.

"Oh my god, I can't believe it's you!" she says, looking past him, and Patrick notices for the first time that her unplaceable familiarity actually has an exact source: her nose, which is Cassidy's. She smiles from a differently shaped mouth, but the nose wrinkles in the exact same way. It's like looking at an old photograph or a badly drawn portrait, the resemblance inexact but intended to be identical.

"Hey, girl," Cassidy chirps with an easy, unforced friendliness, "I'm so glad to meet you! My friend Pat here told me that you were a fan, and I said I wanted to come and meet you too and hear about your life and this fascinating place you work in."

"I am so completely honored," the girl gushes. "Did I win a contest or something?" She looks to Patrick now, searching for answers in his eyes, but he gives her none. "I swear, I think I'm your biggest fan. I mean, I swear, I basically learned to read so that I could read the novelization of *Camp Do-What-Ya-Wanna*. I love you. I actually was you—like, I dressed up as you from *Five Moons of Triton* for Halloween. This is so freaking cool!"

"It *is* freaking cool! What's your name?"

"I'm Ashley," says Ashley.

"Hi, Ashley," Cassidy says, smiling. "I love this." She reaches forward and lays one pale fingertip on the girl's nose. "I just think it's so cute when I meet one of my nose siblings out in the real world. We're like a little family."

Patrick coughs, and they both turn to look at him. "Sorry to interrupt, but I told Cassidy that you'd be able to tell her a little about this facility, what you guys are doing here. She's researching a role. She's supposed to be playing an inmate."

"An inmate?" Ashley asks innocently.

"Well, a sort of patient, someone with an illness," Cassidy says quickly. "It's tricky. It's one of these roles where if you're good there's awards chatter, and if you're bad they publish a bunch of pieces saying your career is over."

"Your career could never be over," Ashley replies beatifically.

"Awww," Cassidy says. "Do you think you could give me a little tour? I'm so enchanted by this place and by what you do. I think helping people is the greatest thing anyone can do with their life."

"I think," Ashley says, "that would be possible. But maybe I should call my manager and confirm it's okay?"

"Oh sure," Cassidy replies quickly, "whatever you need to do. But, like, from my end, from the perspective of the project, it's so important that word doesn't get out too early. Can you trust your manager to keep this *completely* under wraps?"

"Completely?" Ashley repeats, with an anxious smile. Patrick watches as Cassidy whispers something in her ear; the two of them giggle at each other. Ashley exits and is back a couple moments later with the keys, motioning for them to follow.

She leads them down the long hallway to the left, the same dark and flickering space that Patrick found himself in on his last visit. This time, she turns on all the hall lights, and the narrow space shivers with brightness, every detail gratingly visible, from the television-static pattern of the carpeting to the small geometric confetti print on the walls. She points out the intake room, where potential patients come when they've been referred to the facility. There's an examination table, several spiral-bound booklets, and a series of colorful objects—a red ball, a blue pyramid, a green cylinder—dead-end toys from which all the fun has been wrung out. Next she shows them the dressing room, where patients who've passed through the intake process go to leave their personal clothing and put on the facility-issued green sweat suit. She pops open one of the lockers so that they can see the sneakers and slacks stacked up neatly inside. On top of the little stack is a brown wallet, a set of keys, and a bottle of WAT-R *Extra*. "I actually have to clear that one out later today," she says, moving on quickly.

"Can I ask," Patrick says, "what you treat here?"

"Sure, I guess that's common knowledge," Ashley says slowly. "Even if not a lot of people know it." Her face takes on a professional expression, though he can see her look briefly around her, searching for someone to hand the question off to. "We specialize in Random-Onset Acute Dementia. So . . . it's a degenerative mental disease that affects a different demographic from Alzheimer's or vascular dementia. Actually, it affects all demographics. It can basically happen to anyone. We have all kinds of people here, doctors and retirees and personal trainers and even some high-school students. We even have a Golden Globe winner."

"And what do they do all day?" Cassidy asks. "Can I meet some of them?"

"All of our patients are on a twenty-four-hour treatment cycle," Ashley replies, looking uncomfortable, "so they can't really be disturbed. But we can look in on them through the window. There's a lot you can see through the window."

She takes them up a flight of stairs to a long viewing window that opens up onto a sort of playroom. More colorful geometric blocks, sports equipment, human figurines of different sizes and styles, all laid out on rubberized gymnasium flooring. Some adult-sized domestic play sets are lined up alongside of the wall, a fake kitchen with appliances made out of wood with real, turnable knobs, and a fake living room with a real TV. Two women in their twenties sit in the model living room, watching an amateur ninja competition on the vivid, extraordinarily detailed screen. In the model kitchen, an elderly man with a mournful face stirs the imagined contents of a wooden pot with a Barbie doll. Sitting on a folding chair facing the chalkboard is a heavier-set man whom Patrick thinks he might recognize. The beard, the short fingers, the small and compact mouth—it could be Sam Sackler, the director Brenda and Jay suddenly replaced. Sam had seemed perfectly fine just a couple weeks ago, but a couple weeks were like months these days. Or does he mean years? He looks to Cassidy to see if she's recognized him too, but she's absorbed in Ashley's diligent explanation of the different treatment cycles.

"The tricky thing about ROAD is that it's a little different for each person depending on where their forgetting begins first, and it's hard to give twenty different people with twenty different kinds of sick the right treatment all at the same time. Some people lose old memories, some people forget who they are, some people forget what things are called, others forget how to use the stuff in their house. Some get weird obsessions, they fall in love, they say they're swimming in a lake when they've been sitting in a chair all day. There are hallucinations, but most of them are pretty boring—a guy will see a bird flying overhead when there is no bird, or they'll start yapping about the sea when it has nothing to do with anything. So many people think they can see the ocean or smell it. Our pamphlets say it's because of primeval ancestral memories lodged in our deep memory, but I think maybe it's just because a lot of good times that you'd want to remember happen on a beach," Ashley says quietly, moving them along to another area. "There's just one hallucination they all have in common. I mean, not that I know, since I don't have ROAD, but it's what a lot of patients report."

"What is it?" Cassidy asks, her voice hot and curious.

"It gives me the heebie-jeebies," Ashley says, and shudders.

"Tell me," Cassidy says, like it's a tasty bit of gossip about a girl they both know.

"They see a guy. A guy in a gray suit."

"A gray suit?"

"They all say gray."

"What's so scary about a guy in a gray suit?"

"Just that he's not there," Ashley says, and they look at each other silently.

The next window opens onto an empty room, a sort of classroom: a rectangular space with an erasable whiteboard at one end and rows of long tables with chairs lined up all around. On the walls, posters showing farm animals and some, but not all, of the letters of the alphabet.

"Do they forget the alphabet?" Cassidy asks, a serious expression on her face.

"Well"—Ashley hesitates—"it's hard to tell what they forget or remember sometimes. We try to give them a better life, provide them with things to think about or remember. If we can't push them in the recovery direction, we try to make their descent smooth and pleasant. We mostly focus on trying to get them to share reality with us, to see what we see. Or that's what other people focus on: I focus on answering the phones."

"What do you mean," says Patrick, "by descent?"

Ashley looks intently at his face, like she's trying to remember something. It occurs to him that she may not recall meeting him the other day.

"Well, the disease is progressive," she says matter-of-factly. "It starts with the memories that are like thoughts. Then it takes your memories of what you are—how to eat, how to swallow, how to blink. At the end, they forget how to breathe. It starts shallow and goes deep. That's when people need us the most. Nobody wants to squirt eye drops in their family member's eye every fifteen minutes, but if you don't, they really dry up."

"What about," Patrick says, "some sort of tiled room where the patients are waiting? What's that room for?

"Is there . . ." he begins, and then stops. He tries to remember what he saw, how to describe it, but the words edge away from him as he tries to grasp them. "A green room. Long. Lights. Tiles everywhere with their cold feel. Men and women with these destroyed expressions on their faces. A window too, as big as a tank at the aquarium, like looking straight into the water. But the water is air. What do you use that for?"

Both Cassidy and Ashley are staring at him.

"Wait, can you slow down and say that again? It got a little blurry," Ashley says, looking toward Cassidy for clarification, or confirmation. He feels something rise in him, some reddening feeling, frustration or indignation. It occurs to him, suddenly, that he doesn't know how he looks or sounds, doesn't know whether he's giving off angry or weak or disjointed. Ashley moves toward him with an open hand that she tries to press to his forehead, but he lurches back, out of her reach.

"Patrick?" asks Cassidy with genuine bewilderment. When he looks at her face, he realizes that she is worried about him, worried with no sarcasm, irony, or spin. The surprise of her genuine concern is almost enough to make him feel located again, like a person who knows his place in the world.

Just then, the phone starts buzzing in the pocket of his chinos, frightening him. He pulls it out, and for a moment he doesn't know what to expect, he knows nothing at all. Then he sees the Earthbridge pay-phone number lighting up the face of his phone and feels a rush of gratitude, knowing that it must be someone who knows him, someone who loves him, someone who can tell him he's not crazy. "I have to take this call," he says sharply, and stalks off toward where he thinks he remembers the exit once was.

On the phone, Nora's voice pours through with the liquid clarity of a wind chime.

"Dad? Are you there?"

"Yes, honey," he says, relieved to be free from the stickiness of concern, relieved to be in control again. "I'm here, little bug. You know I'm always here to help you, don't you, even if I'm on the other side of the country. No matter what you need. And I'm so glad you called."

There's a pause.

"Um, is that you, Dad? You sound different."

"Never mind," Patrick says. "Tell me how you're doing. Are you shearing some sheep? Are you, you know, mourning and praying?"

"We finished shearing all the sheep a few weeks ago. Once you shear them, it's months before you can shear them again. But I've been doing vermiculture instead. I have my own vermiculture bin, and now I teach other kids how to do it."

"What sort of bin?" Patrick asks. The word tangles in his ear, he can't seem to straighten it out long enough to decipher it.

"It's a worm farm," Nora replies. "I feed them and turn the soil every day. Last week I noticed a lot of flies, so I put a carnivorous plant nearby. Worms are the heartbeat of the earth. That's what I realized last month."

"Okay, Nora," he says absently, squinting into the half-dim corridor. "Just remember to wash your hands." The path he's taking looked familiar at first, but now he realizes that the building looks the same everywhere, each hallway, each stairwell an allusion to the ones that have come before. The design is constricting, he thinks; it closes tight around him, mazelike and intestinal.

"That's not what I called about anyway. Dad, I wanted to tell you something. You were in one of my visions, I saw you."

"A vision?" he says, turning, trying to remember which door he had come from.

"Yes. I saw you in the driver's seat of a white car, a convertible, with the top down. It was California, I think, with brown hills on all sides and tough little bushes clinging to the slopes. There was a blond woman next to you. You two were coming up the road fast, with the dust billowing out behind you, and suddenly you hit the brakes. The car stops in the haze, and both of you are just staring forward with this surprised expression on your face, looking right at me. Does this sound like anything to you? The woman was pretty."

"No, I don't think so," says Patrick, the kindness he wants to project blurred by distraction. In fact, the question annoys him: He never minded being roused in the middle of the night to soothe his daughter when she was tormented by dreams that had become too lifelike; even before he had become a father, this was one of the things he imagined himself doing with pride, with gladness. But in practice, talking Nora out of her fears was laborious and time-consuming, and after a couple rounds of debate he always felt crabby, worried about how the missing sleep would affect his writing the next day.

"Are you sure, Dad? The scene doesn't remind you of anything? The vision was so clear in my mind, I could even smell the grass and the trees and something burning far off in the distance. You don't know who the woman could be or what she might represent?"

"I think she represents your imagination listening to your mother talk about my life here, working with Cassidy Carter," he replies, patiently. "It's probably your subconscious telling you that you miss your dad and wish you could be here with me. Honey, you call these visions, and I know they feel real and important to you, but they're mirages. They're imaginings of what you wish you could see, guided by what your heart misses or fears."

When Nora responds, her speech is measured, careful.

"But my visions aren't things I want to see or things I wish for, most of the time I don't even know what they are or whether they're supposed to be things from the past or from the future. I don't want them, I just write them down so they don't crowd my head. And also, when you see a mirage, other people can see it just like you do, if they're standing where you are. It's not something you imagine, it's an optical illusion that happens when light is refracting a special way. You can take a photo of a mirage."

"You can't take a photo of a mirage, Nora, that's ridiculous."

"And I don't even know if it's true that I want to be in California with you," says Nora's wispy voice over the phone. "It feels like something bad is happening there. You were in our mourning memorial today, the fires that are happening right near you. Linden read this whole report: Forty-seven thousand acres burned so far. Loss of hundreds of homes, thousands and thousands of animals. There are horses that fled the fire and had to run all the way to the beach, and now they're trapped down there, with no fresh water to drink. Can you imagine what it's like to be that thirsty when your body's that big?"

"Honey," Patrick says, looking around him for the emergency exit, "I wouldn't worry about that. They have all the best people working on it, and Los Angeles is a major city. Major cities just don't get destroyed by fire."

"Do you have a source for that information?" Nora asks, sounding interested.

"No," he says, "just my forty-six years of life on this planet."

"Oh," she says, disappointed. "Okay."

"Is your mom worried about me?" Patrick asks, climbing down the rickety metal stairs to the safe, familiar asphalt of the parking lot.

"I know she is. She wants you to come here."

"Well, honey, adults often disagree on important things. And in the end, it's only time that can prove one of them right and the other one wrong." He turns and sees Cassidy and Ashley coming out of the building. They're laughing and hugging, and their hair is incandescent in the sun. He can hear Cassidy asking how Ashley started working here, whether she's trained as a nurse or something, and Ashley telling her that actually she just volunteered at a retirement home during high school, doing the weekly bingo night.

"Dad, will you come here if the fires get so bad that they cancel your movie?"

Patrick watches as Cassidy and Ashley exchange a goodbye hug, and then another one. They release each other, and Cassidy begins to walk across the lot toward the white van.

"Dad? Are you there? Are you listening?"

He hears the letdown in her voice.

"No, not that I recall. Sweetie, I have to go. I'll call you tomorrow."

"But tomorrow I'll be doing the beekeeping training all day, so that I can work with the hives." She sounds confused, an unfamiliar tone in her voice—his daughter, usually so preternaturally, frustratingly composed.

"Okay, honey, then the day after that. No problem. Kiss-kiss." Patrick hangs up the phone and walks toward Cassidy. She makes a face that he can't quite decipher—it's either a "What the fuck" or a "I have something big to tell you." And suddenly they both turn to see Ashley calling out, running toward them, holding a large silver briefcase.

"Oh god, you guys, I almost forgot. I know it's a couple days early for Brenda's pickup, but when I got back to the desk I realized it was all packed up and ready, so I thought I would save you a drive up here. I know you're so busy, Cassidy, with your filming schedule and the research for that new role." Ashley smiles a big, toothy smile. Her nose crinkles adorably.

"Ashley, *I love you*," Cassidy says, engulfing her in a hug and holding it, wriggling both of their bodies back and forth and back and forth. "Thanks so much, girl. And remember: burgers next month, when all this filming is done. Don't forget. I'm counting on you. Nose sisters!" She takes the case from Ashley's hand and blows her a kiss, and then, together, she and Patrick walk toward the big white van, pure and bright against the dull sky.

CHAPTER SEVEN

The entire left side of the mountain is engulfed in flames, the smoke rising straight into the sky like a tower, like a signal received by no one. Far from any major road, the witnesses are small-bodied, furry or scaled, their eyes close to the ground. Their tiny limbs carry them through the underbrush as they look for a hole or hollow: a place to wait out the burning, or an unburned place where the air still slips easily into the lungs. In the midday sky, islands of pale blue are visible between the moving, shifting layers of smoke. A dark bird cuts through the shimmering air and disappears around the bend.

Where the fire has already passed, the ground is burning. Small licks of flame rise from the blackened earth, flickering like birthday candles in the dark. An orange color creeps through the black, fading in and out with a pulsing rhythm. The low, earthbound fire moves like liquid across the terrain—some bright, alien liquid climbing hills and tree trunks, flowing upward from the burly base of a coyote bush to hug its slender branches, heating the small, tough, delicately toothed leaves until they bloom with flame.

At the fire's hot, live edge, the flames rear up to touch the unsinged tips of virgin grasses. Fresh matter burns brightest, surging and sinking, the sound of the burn a dull roar, like hunger in the belly of a man who's walked all day. An observer would see intelligence in the way it crawls, seeking new substance to consume, the way it moves in small, tidy increments and sudden leaps. The way it seems to head for the homes, for the cars, for the firefighters standing watch with masks on to filter their air.

At the highway's periphery, a helicopter passes overhead, dropping a sheet of WAT-R on a child-height fence of fire. Where the liquid smothers it, steam rises from the smoldering earth, still hot enough to burn the skin off a hand. The vapor resembles a scale model of the sky-sized smoke clouds overhead: rising from the blistered dirt, a wall of thick, pale translucence, it billows and folds and curls over itself like a body protecting its soft underside. With its frail, opalescent blue tint, it is more beautiful than it should be: if it were ordinary, you would not stop to watch it. But it drifts like a dream on the hot fire-borne wind, a gauzy shadow passing across the unburnt scrub, changing shape from cloud to mist, casting its almost imperceptible blueness on the unburnt oaks crouched tight at the base of the valley.

By the time the vapor reaches Cassidy Carter's seven-bedroom home, its bluish tint has nearly vanished. Traces have settled on the shriveled brown leaves of her dead rosebushes, on the flagstones surrounding the red-clay badminton court. Neither Cassidy nor Patrick senses the presence of an unfamiliar substance in the air as they stand in the expansive backyard, staring down into the empty turquoise-painted depths of the defunct pool. But out in the canyon lands, where the fire rages on, nobody is around to notice that not everything is burning. Though the blaze blackens the grasses and trees and chaparral shrubs equally, there are some plants still standing oddly unscathed, small clusters of ground-hugging green vivid against the ash. Leaved like clover and sprouting tiny, pale-blue flowers, they resemble other low species creeping at the margins of the hiking trail, and yet they are not any of those species. They have no name and no genus, they stir infinitesimally in the wind. When the flames pass over the small blue flowers, they do not singe. In the clearing smoke, they remain sweetly blue, the color of aquarium gravel or adolescent sadness. If you plucked one and held it up to the flame of a match, it would not catch fire. It would stare back at you unchanged, soft blue against the enveloping heat. It would stare and stare until, suddenly, the sharp blue edges of its petals began to melt.

From the northeast, the wind carries the scent of scorched plants, of woody limb reduced to kindling, into Cassidy's backyard. She coughs weakly as she lifts the silver briefcase, and her coughs echo around the empty concrete basin.

"It's not deep enough," Patrick says, backing away from the edge. Looking downward into the perspectiveless bowl gives him a headache, or something worse.

"Live a little," Cassidy says, lifting the briefcase high above her head and then hurling it down toward the hard bottom. The metal clanks dully and bounces once before coming to a rest on its side. She giggles.

"God, I wish you hadn't done that," he groans. "We have to give that to Brenda and Jay eventually, and now they'll know we tried to open it."

"Will they?" Cassidy says. "Listen, did you see how much information I got out of that one trip to the clinic? If we can just get me into a few more of these places, fill in the missing links, crack open this briefcase, I think we'll have a real opportunity to demand some better terms. Then it won't even matter who did whatever to a briefcase."

She strolls over to the shallow end of the pool and climbs the short ladder down into the trough. The heat of the sun bears down on the crown of her head, as she picks up the gleaming case and dashes it again and again against the cool concrete, until the blue paint is chipped on the curved walls and the uniform aluminum ridges are marred by dents and bent lines.

"We can make Brenda and Jay really pay us, cut us a real slice. You don't have to be a PA anymore, Patrick. We could start a boutique production company, writing and producing movies for me to do."

"You'd want that?" he asks, surprised. He should be insulted, but instead he feels amazed. She trusts him, and he hasn't seen signs that she trusts anybody else in her life.

"Why not? You haven't fucked me over yet, and it's been weeks."

He has a vision of himself with his hand on Cassidy's back, steering her away from a flurry of camera flashes.

"Here," he says, "give that to me."

Patrick turns the case over on its side and examines the closure: a double combination lock with three numbers to the left of the handle and three to the right. Whatever force it takes to open one of the locks, they'll have to apply it twice. He takes the long-nozzled lighter from Cassidy's unused grill and flicks it on, holding the inch-long flame over the first set of numbers.

"From the pickup list, we know that they have some sort of relationship with these dementia clinics, with some off-brand WAT-R stores, with what seems to be internet ad-sales offices, and with a factory in Long Beach."

"Be specific," Cassidy responds. "Not dementia clinics in general, just these new Random-Onset–related clinics, Memodyne and ROADMap Inc and MemoryCare. And the factory is some sort of manufacturing plant. From the photos online, we can see the tanks and tubing and stacks coming out the top."

"Right," he says, "fine."

"Is that working?" she asks.

The numbers gleam back at him, the material slightly darker, slightly less shiny.

"Not yet, but it's only been a minute," he says, flicking the lighter back on.

"Forget it. I know something that might work. I did it once in *Kassi Keene*."

On the marble counters in Cassidy's large, empty kitchen, she places the suitcase on its side and brings over a heavy-duty automotive flashlight and a magnifying glass. She shows him how to hold the light so that it floods the right side of the dial, and then she holds up the magnifying glass. Small particles of dust and paint are visible, crammed into the sanitized metal parts. Patrick watches as she begins turning the far-left dial one number at a time, tugging the bit over to the left so that she can see into the gears. She stops turning when she sees a small roughness on the otherwise smooth axis, and she moves on to the next one. She finds the rough spot on the second dial, and then the third, but when she tries to pop the latch, it doesn't release.

"On the show, this only took ten seconds," she says.

"We need to try something else," says Patrick. "Do you have a drill, a hacksaw, something like that?"

"Just hold the light," she says. "I found the right alignment; now we just have to find the right setting."

She slides the three dials up one, punches the latch, up another, punches the latch again. On the third try, it pops open, but the metal case is too tightly made, and they can't pry the top open enough to see inside. Cassidy starts on the right side, repositions the light, squints into the smooth, machined aluminum, seeking imperfection.

"We should get into that factory," Cassidy mumbles.

"That would be great," he says. "But what about security? Who's going to talk to us? Do you know an Ashley over there?"

There's only the sound of the little metal wheels turning, notch by notch.

"What do you think it all adds up to?" Patrick asks. "So they're running some of their other business with resources meant for the movie, making us run around and do errands for them. Why?"

"Ashley said that business at Memodyne has spiked. When she started working, nine months ago, the place was empty, and now they're completely booked. There's a five-hundred-person waitlist for the next open bed. That's what she says. She says there are people trying to get in every day, and nobody's leaving. Except for, you know, a few of them."

"No, I don't know. What does that mean?"

"Ashley says a few of them die. Four or five a week."

"Doesn't that seem like a lot to you?" Patrick doesn't know why this makes him so upset, but it does. "It should be news. People should know about it."

"I don't know—is it an impressive death rate? If you watch people for long enough, they'll die, right? If you gather a lot of people together, you increase the odds of seeing it happen. I'm not an expert." Cassidy gives a slight shrug, her eyes fixed on the lock.

"People don't die because you're watching them; they die for a reason." He thinks again of the green-tiled room, the men and women too far gone to blink for themselves.

"'Everything happens for a reason,'" she replies, like someone quoting from a movie that everybody's already seen.

Cassidy presses the release button, and it won't budge. She starts turning all three dials at once, notch by notch, but the latch won't let go. "Do you want to give it a shot?" she asks Patrick. As he sits down, she leans over his shoulder, pointing to the slight gaps, showing him where to look. Her long hair brushes the back of his neck. Patrick wrestles with the mechanism for a few minutes, but his eyes can't decipher the difference between a rough spot and a smooth one. As he stares into the round, distorted lens, his eye is drawn back again and again to the edges of the magnifying glass, where reality grows smeary. He sees the grain of the marble out of focus, a sort of depthless nebula refracted in the bulging lens, which gives him a sensation like vertigo. Eyes shut tight, he keeps his face pointed at the image but can't bear to look. When Cassidy offers to switch back, he feels nothing but relief.

As she begins the slow work of brute-forcing the combination—starting at 000 and pressing the button, toggling to 001 and pressing the button—he goes to lie down on the sofa. He takes out his phone. For the past few days, he's been checking on the /KassiKeeneTBR_IRL forum, and finds the IRL discourse more inquisitive and nuanced than that of the Revelators, even if he isn't entirely convinced by their conclusions. Where the TBR obsessives puzzle endlessly over the real allegiances of minor cameo actors, the IRLers deal with something much more important: the real world. In IRL, they talked about The Big Picture: the idea that watching *Kassi Keene* was a type of mental training that prepared viewers to turn their eyes onto the world around them. They believed that the town of Paradise Cove was based on a real place—probably somewhere in California, though there was a subsection of IRLers who thought the signs pointed to coastal New England, possibly Maine—and that this real place had been the victim of a major crime that the government was covering up. Some thought the crime was a major toxic-waste spill, others a secret nuclear meltdown on the level of Chernobyl. Or a top-secret CIA experiment, or an alien abduction, or a coordinated effort to sterilize blond men and women. By following the map the show gave them, motivated investigators in the audience could trace the crimes of the show back to their real-life analogues. It made sense that, with a secret so dangerous, the show couldn't be allowed to continue. So the IRLers sifted the celebrity-gossip blogs, looking for clues about

Cassidy Carter and the other actors, the producers, and the writers who had worked so hard, for almost six seasons, to show them the light.

► **BTRlivinthrugivin**

According to <u>this article from last Friday</u>, Cassidy called in sick to work on the set of her new film *Elsinore Lane* and hasn't been seen in public since i.e. no clubs, no shopping, no pap appearances at all. What do u guys think? Personally I never bought the narrative that she was high/ doing coke on the set in front of children/snorting heroin off sports cars/drinking until black out drunk and stealing a plane. One, a single look into that innocent face shows a person w/a very pure heart, as does her behavior in every movie I've seen, including her commercial for sweet potato tortilla chips. Two, it was always clear that the best way to discredit the lessons of *Kassi Keene* was to discredit the messengers. I have known people who struggled with mental illness and have seen that it can come from inside, but also that it can come from outside via substances administered incognito to trigger behaviors. You can make someone go crazy, and not leave a trace. They will never even know what you've done.

I am worried that she has been taken hostage again and is being given memory wipe. Thoughts? What can we do to help her?

↓ **EricBergson01**

I have always felt this myself, but as far I knew was entirely alone in my opinion. Acting is a difficult, rigorous, high-skill business. You don't have a career like Cass has had, two dozen hit movies and a world-renowned television series, while also being a total train wreck. Much more likely that she was under extreme pressure, possibly physical or chemical coercion, from the network and corporate interests that wished to silence the show. If you wanted to take CNN off the air, what would you do? Take out Anderson Cooper. It is as simple as htat.

> ↳ tncb_raphael2
> From your keyboard to god's ears. I pray that someone is taking care of her and forming a barrier between her and those who would hurt her and influence her to hurt herself.

↳ MinorKeeg2021

Wow. I'm astounded. [slow clap] I've never seen somebody chug so much Koolade in such a sort amount of time. Are you insane? You would have to be to think that Cassidy Carter is the victim in this. No one person has done more to derail *Kassi Keene* than her, not just bringing about the original end of the show and dancing on its grave in the press, but personally killing every attempt to revive or spin the show off with her public bad behavior. And if you need proof that she knows exactly what she is doing, and is a govt plant sent to undo the show from the inside, watch this video where you can see that she is pretending to be high, stumbling out of an SUV and falling, making weird moan sounds as she lies on the road . . . but then she turns and gives a wink to the E! camera filming behind her.

> ↳ drx9ovbTT
> They definitely should have cast Dakota Fanning in the role instead.
>
> > ↳ Halokix123
> > OMG. I never thought of this but I love it. Would have saved us all a lot of pain, and we'd probably know TBR by now.

↳ BTRlivinthrugivin

LOL at someone coming on this forum to burn Cassidy Carter. None of this would exist without Cassidy Carter. Kassi Keene would not exist without Cassidy Carter. YOU would not exist without Miss Carter. You should shut your yap before you get moderated right out of here.

⤵ **45VenturaPm**

Go home

⤵ **BTRlivinthrugivin**

Um, no?

⤵ **45VenturaPm**

Sorry I meant to @ MinorKeeg2021!! lol

⤵ **GeneKwok743**

All joking aside, it's incredibly frightening how easy it would be to put something in the water to change human behavior at a citywide or even statewide level. I'm not saying this is the crime TBP deals with, or that this is behind Cassidy Carter's, shall we say, *eccentric* behavior in the public sphere. I am only saying that we place a tremendous amount of trust in facilities we never lay eyes on, much less see the inside of. And in processes that we do not understand, chemistry we haven't mastered. Like Laika the dog, shot up into space on a rocket destined never to return, we know that we live but we do not understand how impossible our lives are, or how fragile.

This is why the show *Kassi Keene* is so beautiful. Yes, there are problems in the world. But finally we have all the clues we need to decode it.

⤵ **WolfWNoMaster**

Just curious, what sort of things could people put in the water? Wouldn't any additive be diluted beyond any efficacy by the vastness of the matter involved?

⤵ **GeneKwok743**

WolfWNoMaster I work in a treatment and processing plant that shall go unnamed and unspecified. Every day I cross a walkway that goes directly above eight major vats where liquid is treated. If I had for example a brick of pure cocaine I could easily let it fall into just one of the vats, where it would be bottled up and sent all over California. Maybe it wouldn't affect you very much, except put a little pep in your step, but it might not dissolve fully and one bottle could get more than another. And if that bottle were given to a baby, that baby could die instantly of heart failure. Same sort of thing if you substitute arsenic, virus, or even just caffeine. Effects could be vast, and difficult to decipher.

In fact maybe you should thank me for not doing anything at all ☺

↓ **HaydenStrange8**

Whenever someone tells you that a so-called "conspiracy theory" is too complicated, too convoluted to be true, ask them exactly how complex they feel reality to be. If they insist on its simplicity, then you know with confidence that they are an imbecile, and can sever the conversation with no guilt whatsoever. But if they admit reality's complexity, the infinite layers of contradiction and indeterminacy that culminate in the cosmic indecisiveness of the quark, then there is no alternative but to consider the more confusing explanation the correct one. The million dollar question may be this one: why do we have so many conspiracy theories in our world? Who benefits from them, both epistemologically and in practical terms, and what one feature links every conspiracy theory you've ever heard? Here's a hint: it starts with a U.

Suddenly inspired, Patrick types the words "Gene Kwok processing bottling facility" into the search engine and turns up a result: Dr. Gene Kwok, senior operations manager at Alamitos Finishing Inc. The address for Alamitos Finishing is an exact match for the address of the mystery factory on the pickup list. He navigates to the IRL forum's messaging function and sends Dr. Kwok a message, telling him that he happens to be Cassidy Carter's manager, and she'd like to meet with him as part of the research she's doing for a new TV series about facilities management. Then he gets up to tell Cassidy the good news, but she's no longer at the counter.

Standing at the edge of the empty pool, Cassidy clutches the silver briefcase to her chest, staring down at something Patrick can't see. His body fills with apprehension, fear that she'll—what?—jump? The briefcase gleams slowly in the hard afternoon light. He notices again that his throat is parched, there's a tender, chapped feeling when he breathes, and all the WAT-R he's drinking doesn't do a thing to help it. She turns toward him, and on her face is a strange smile he doesn't recognize. "Make a wish," she says, and then she hoists the case high above her head and heaves it down into the blue below. There's the sound of a bang, loud as a gun, and then a flutter like birds, birds taking flight, birds in the sky with their wings lifted by the breeze.

Patrick walks to the edge and peers over. Down in the trough, the money forms a shaggy, mossy covering on the painted concrete. It's a carnage of dull greenish-white, some of the bills lying sodden in wet leaf mulch, others fluttering low on the ground or caught up in the wind. A strong gust lifts a couple fistfuls out of the empty pool and carries them toward the gigantic house, dancing in the air. The paper rises up into the air like embers in a fire, and in brief little flashes he can make out faces on the fluttering paper—the faces of white men, all of them long dead.

———

With accidents clogging the 405 and reports of protesters on foot causing disruptions on the 710, Patrick and Cassidy take Highway 1 most of the way down the coast and then switch to local roads. Winds are low today, and the fires burn in place. The voice on Cassidy's maps app gives cool, calm suggestions to re-route, promising seventeen saved minutes if they cut through Torrance's Old Town. They take the shortcut. Through the still-smoky air, the main street is a faded, worn-down color, like in old movies. Cassidy sticks her phone out the window to take a photo of a vintage Fosters Freeze stand as they roll past.

In the ice-cream stand's drive-through lane, a man in his six-ties sits in the driver's seat, staring out at the building. He scours the building's exterior: chipped white stucco, the rainbow-striped awning, the picnic tables molded of royal-blue plastic. He can't remember why he came here. He doesn't think he wants ice cream. He doesn't know anyone else who does. Did somebody send him here? Maybe his children or grandchildren? Warily, he turns the car engine on and backs slowly out and onto the main street. When he is in the shadow of several large, verdant mesquite trees, he begins to relax. He's headed back home, or at least he's pointed in the right direction. The sun on his face is warm, and makes his mouth feel parched. He blinks twice, three times. Then it occurs to him that, on a hot day like this one, some ice cream might be nice. Steep, towering cones of frozen sugar cream, the peak dusted with pulverized nuts and capped with a cherry. He puts his turn signal on. He turns left and left again, until he's on the same road, driving back the way he came. When he sees the old-fashioned blue-and-white sign, his face lights up. Fosters Freeze, a name he recalls from the past. Hadn't he come here sometimes as a child for a root-beer float and a fistful of fries? He puts on his turn signal and turns left, into the store's narrow drive-through.

A few blocks away, a woman turns the faucet. The WAT-R sputters several times, thin and hissing, and then nothing more. She slips on her sandals and opens the door. Even from a distance, she can see that her cube hasn't been refilled: sunlight blazes through the large blue rectangle, setting the plastic aglow. She checks that the seal is tight around the plastic tubing. Only a little WAT-R sloshes around the bottom, hot from the sun, barely enough to fill a bathtub. She's been waiting two weeks for a repair appointment, endlessly on hold with the WAT-R company to complain again about the liquid vanishing from her leaky unit. In Rancho Mirage, less than ten minutes away, the bigger houses receive same-day service from shiny trucks with hoses and nozzles mounted on the side. But in her neighborhood, you're lucky if you hear the voice of a living human being before your phone drops the call, lucky if they read you some sort of number that you can give when you call back a fourth or fifth time. The woman has run her hands over every scuffed inch, looking for the flaw in the plastic, but all she finds is smug, sleek surface. The hole must be somewhere on the bottom, pressed up against asphalt, where it's impossible to examine. With no repair, she's had to pay for delivery twice a week, watching as her money runs out onto the street in dark rivulets, headed for the sewers.

There are other neighbors out on the lawn, approaching their own cubes with wary interest. They stand barefoot on the neatly trimmed grass, in front of poured concrete pagodas and bushes bullied into jelly-bean structures. Nobody knows what it means when the delivery fails to come. They talk to one another across property lines, without setting foot on one another's soil. They agree that the prices have been going up, even though they've been using less WAT-R than ever. They save the shower runoff in a pail and ration it out across the landscaped shrubs. They emulsify shampoo in their palms and work it to lather with the bare minimum of liquid. But the bills are unchanged, or they've crept higher. And at the SuperCenter on Sunset, doesn't it seem like there's more empty space on the shelves, more handwritten signs apologizing for running out of an expected item? Scattered across the tidy green lawns, the robins stand motionless but alive. Sometimes when you're cutting the grass, you have to stop—step in front of the mower, pick up the petrified body in your hand, the tiny heartbeat pounding fast, and set it in a bush or on the sidewalk, someplace out of the machine's path.

As the white van turns toward the marina and the remnants of the industrial waterfront, Alamitos Finishing rears up before them like a fast-food castle, crenellated with piping. An unimpressive cement-colored box with only a fistful of exterior features—window, door, fire alarm—the building lacks a sense of scale, gives the impression of sizelessness. In the parking lot, Cassidy hangs her head out the window and holds her breath, counting how many seconds it'll take for her eyes to discover something other than grayish wall. She reaches twenty Mississippis before Patrick messes up her concentration, fumbling with his WAT-R bottle, dropping the plastic cap on the floor near his feet, and then feeling around for it while he tries to steer one-handed into a spot. The plant is quiet on the weekend, Dr. Gene had said, and the lot is mostly empty. They climb out of the van, stare up at the enormous structure. From a flat roof dense with tubing, a chimney rises into the hazy blue sky, spilling a single, unending column of vapor into the sky. The vapor is thick and cottony, a slow-roiling giant that resembles a tree, and then an umbrella, and then a curving whale. But most of all, from every angle, it resembles a mushroom cloud.

When they reach the entrance, Dr. Gene is already there waiting for them. In a tan suit jacket and brown pants, he has a face awkwardly poised between its actual age and one long ago, when the rudiments of his personality were etched as in wet concrete. Through his forty-eight-year-old features, Cassidy can see both the eleven-year-old boy who won the science fair three years in a row, and the childless bachelor dad whose dreams consist of attempts to lucidly prod his avatar into flight. She knows this type of fan, and knows that he'll be asking a load of questions. As she walks toward him, she watches the expression on his face shift from careful neutrality to an almost unconscious elation; his face smiles without his consent. When she extends her hand to him, he lifts it up toward his lips at first, before pausing and pushing it back down into a standard hand shake.

"Welcome," he says with a slight, overgrown Southern accent, "to Alamitos. It's an honor to have you both here. I know you have many questions for me about facilities management. I hope you'll be willing to answer some, as well, about the mysterious circumstances behind your show's cancellation. I know many Revelators would give their brother's life to be able to stand with Kassi Keene and question her directly."

"Sure thing," Cassidy says with a smile, before turning to Patrick with a scowl. "You didn't tell me he was one of those creepoid forum fans," she whispers into his ear, causing the nervework of his back to blossom with a thousand conflicting sensations that he tries to forget. "You better text our address to someone you trust, in case we never come out of here."

To Patrick, it feels as if they are dignitaries from a foreign country. Dr. Gene gives them each a hard hat and ushers them into a small motorized vehicle to tour the facility. He puts on a spinning yellow light to warn other employees to get out of the way, and he honks the little horn. They zoom through a large lobby where workers in sky-blue suits load large plastic barrels onto hand trucks. Seven or eight reasonable-sized houses could fit into that lobby, Patrick thinks to himself, stacked three high with room for front and back yards. Seven or eight houses like my own, he realizes.

It's been so long since he's seen his home, he doesn't even know how to picture it. He has some trouble remembering what's in it, the makes and models of the electronics, the color of the couch, those little details that don't matter until you realize they're lost.

Trucks drive along the floor of the massive industrial plant, ferrying matter from the entrance bays to far-off destinations in the building's other limbs. The inside of the building feels as big as an outside. Up above, a lost seagull sails through the empty, enclosed space, the gentle color of its body a breach in the industrial gray.

"So fun," Cassidy says as the cart whirs through a broad, seemingly endless hallway. "It reminds me of working on the studio lot, getting driven from the set to the cafeteria for lunch every day. Sometimes my handler would let me drive, even though I was only thirteen."

"In fact," Dr. Gene replies, "this vehicle is a more recent model of the same industrial carts you see in the background of episode nine, season four, when the Paradise Cove volleyball team is playing a game across the street from the Nifty Cola factory."

They stop outside a set of metal double doors separating the long hallway from a room decorated in a more effortfully fun style than the rest of the building. The walls are still laboratory-gray, but a long, glossy, zanily orange bar stretches across the middle of the room, surrounded by upholstered orange stools. On the wall behind the bar are countless bottles of WAT-R, some with familiar labels—WAT-R *Extra*, WAT-R *Pure*, WAT-R *Wildly Wet* (a colorful star-shaped sticker reads "For Kids!"), and WAT-R *Renaissance*. But there are also labels he doesn't recognize—WAT-R *ReGenerate*, WAT-R *Hype!*, WAT-R *Misty Morning Dew*, and the technicolored liquid of WAT-R *Kids Only No Grown-Ups Allowed!* Several bottles marked by colored labels with numbers written on them in neat black Sharpie sit alongside the more polished products. Dr. Gene steps behind the counter and welcomes them to the tasting room, where VIPs can sample the whole versatile range of WAT-R products, as well as treat themselves to rare or discontinued products and new products still in the process of being refined. Patrick senses Cassidy tensing up nearby; he doesn't have to look at her face to know what it says.

"This is really, really thoughtful, thanks," Patrick says, "but she doesn't drink WAT-R. I should have told you in advance, so we wouldn't put you out."

"What do you mean, you don't drink?" Dr. Gene asks Cassidy, laughing. "Are you living like a camel, off the water stored in your back fat?"

"I just haven't tried it," Cassidy says pertly. "I drink the old-fashioned stuff."

"Well, this is the place to try: you won't find a better selection. You know, the old water wasn't very good for you anyway. If you knew what goes on in found water, all the dirt and debris they try to filter out, the secondhand hormones and BPA, the fish eggs and other filthy animal waste—life is a dirty business—you would beg me for some brand-new water, made in a nice clean factory."

"I'm happy to be your guinea pig," Patrick interjects. "I'm from the East Coast, so I haven't been drinking WAT-R that long, but I think the stuff is great. And, besides, if she partakes, we'll have to stop twice on the drive back."

Cassidy glares at him, but nods.

"Okay, then," says Dr. Gene, "lucky man. I'm going to start you off with a taste of our most luxurious product, and then of the special kind we keep in-house. It's too good to sell." He pulls out a bottle that Patrick has seen on WAT-R runs, usually kept behind the counter in a locked cabinet. It has a teardrop shape, and a cap made of plastic molded to resemble a multifaceted gem. "This is our answer to the vintage water market, those glacier waters scraping the bottom of Planet Earth's barrel. It's called *Everpure*." The cap releases with a pop: there's cork glued to the bottom to premiumize the experience. He pulls out a small, perfect glass and fills it with about an inch and a half of liquid. "Glass half full," he jokes, and slides it over. That must be a common joke around here, Patrick thinks. He picks up the small glass and swirls the liquid around experimentally. It sloshes like water, perfectly clear. But maybe what Cassidy says about the stuff has stuck with him more than he knew: he can't explain how, but the slosh seems a little slower than it ought to be, a little sluggish. He puts the cup to his lips and lets the mouthful slip through.

"Doesn't that feel like heaven, like silk streaming down your throat?" Dr. Gene asks. Patrick nods. His mouth feels briefly wet, then normal again. "*Everpure* is triple-milled, strained for a full twenty-four hours in a labyrinthine filter designed with the help of an installation artist from Finland. A series of glass chambers linked by delicate, charcoal-lined tubes, colored to resemble the spectrum of visible light. I can get you in to see that if you'd like."

"We'd love that," Cassidy says quickly, glancing back at him.

"Now, this," says Dr. Gene, pulling a smaller, delicate flask from the shelf and pouring a finger's width into a fresh glass, "is on a different level. This in fact has no level—it is entirely on its own, free-floating in the stratosphere. We call it, simply, *One Hundred*." The bottle bears a small, gold-leaf "100" scrawled in faux handwriting, like a perfect score on a perfect test. "As you know, old water boils at a hundred degrees Celsius, and WAT-R boils at a hundred and four, due to its greater stability. Well, what the media doesn't know, because we try to give them the big picture, not to overwhelm them with facts, is that a tiny percentage of our WAT-R also boils off at a hundred degrees Celsius, just seconds before the rest of it follows suit. What we've done is capture that little bit of liquid, less than a mouse's mouthful from a vat the size of this room, and set it aside for our very special customers. It's the rarest, choicest product from the purest part of the process. It's our 'premier cru.'"

"Fascinating," Patrick says, holding the little glass up to the light. The transparent liquid trembles beneath the bright bulbs. But it's not the water trembling, it's his hand. He lowers the glass and holds it close, gripping his wrist with his free hand, consoling it.

"I'll join you for a toast," Dr. Gene says, pouring another glass and hoisting. "To Mother Nature, who sends us her rough drafts so that we may perfect her grammar!" They clink and drink. The rarefied liquid has a faintly sweet taste, a flavor that reminds him subtly of home, of running out onto a soccer field early in the morning, when everything you see is graced by dew, of the first kiss and the last kiss, of finding that one perfect person you were meant to spend your life with.

"Isn't it bad luck to toast with water?" Cassidy asks.

"It's not water!" Dr. Gene replies, laughing loudly, and after a beat Cassidy laughs too. "I'll show you. Water is the village bicycle. Water has been through the butts of dinosaurs and the blood of the diseased. The water you drink may have been in the mouth of your worst enemy, and you would never know. Water is secondhand, but our WAT-R has never been used. It's pure. It's brand-new. It's a whole different beast, as they say."

"What are the bottles with numbers on them?" she asks.

"A sharp question from a true gumshoe," Dr. Gene says, smiling, in a tone clearly devised for engaging with children. He pulls a new, yellow-labeled bottle from the shelf. "Here we have new products in the process of development. This one is getting good marks. Patrick, have a taste." As the doctor pours the glass,

Patrick feels as though time has slowed. The thin, clear column of water has a static quality, a stillness, it seems to hang in mid-air unmoving—until, suddenly, the pour is done and Patrick is lifting it up to his dry tongue as Dr. Gene and Cassidy watch intently. This one doesn't slide so easily across the palate, nor does it swallow as smoothly as the other two samples. In fact, this one tastes thick and a bit heavy—he would even call it syrupy if there were any hint of sweetness, any hint of flavor at all.

"You like?" Dr. Gene asks.

"It's . . ." Patrick pauses. He sees worry in Cassidy's black-rimmed eyes. "Different. It has a—I don't know—mouthfeel." He swirls his tongue around but can't rid himself of the filmy sensation, like unrinsed soap on the skin. "I feel like it's stuck at the back of my tongue, I can't get it off."

"You're exactly right," Gene says, pleased. "We're developing this for elite athletes, mountain climbers, people who work long days in the sun, and children with bladder-control issues. It's a high-stick, low-evap product that keeps you hydrated longer by bonding deeply with your body at the cellular level. The coating in your mouth is a side effect, but it also lessens the amount of water you lose through breathing."

"It doesn't feel right," Patrick says. "It makes me want to rinse my mouth out."

Dr. Gene looks disappointed but patient. "Of course, our competitor has the advantage of prior market saturation," he says. "But we're confident that customers will adjust to these new textures and, in the long run, come to prefer them." As they board the cart once more, Patrick comments on how large the plant is, so large that seagulls can wander in and fly around the huge space, mistaking it for the outdoors. Cassidy turns and stares at him with some urgent, fervent message in her eyes. He has the uncomfortable feeling that she's checking his pupils. Dr. Gene just laughs.

"You must be mistaken," he says. "An animal in the facility would be a major violation of our manufacturing code, unsanitary and dangerous. We have a security system that zaps them if they enter the containment zone. We've never had a single one make it inside."

Together, they dismount from the cart and walk through a glass-walled skybridge that looks down upon a vast floor dotted with tanks three stories tall. From their vantage point, they can see the tiny bodies of workers in their sky-blue suits. The blue suits check panels on the sides of the units, motion to others across the floor to turn valves on or shut valves off. A constant, percussive oscillation can be heard through the thick bluish glass, a high, anxious sound, like the dripping of a faucet that can't be shut off. For the workers on the floor, the sound is a physical force pounding on the rib cage, tremoring the heart.

"This is chemistry in action," Dr. Gene says proudly, gesturing at everything below. Behind their backs, the manufacturing tanks extend equally far, as far as can be seen, in the opposite direction. "Here, we mix the raw ingredients of water, hydrogen and oxygen, in proper proportion, and apply the necessary energy to bring them together. It's a simple recipe, but a good one."

"So," says Cassidy, throwing her hair over her shoulder and giving Dr. Gene a gamine look, "if I get some hydrogen and some oxygen together at home, I could make WAT-R?"

"Not unless you want to lose your home in a fireball explosion!" he responds, heartily. "When the hydrogen-oxygen reaction occurs, it is explosive. Propulsive. Nobody has ever been able to control it before WAT-R Corp. Do you remember the *Hindenburg,* a blimp filled with hydrogen gas? When it exploded, it made the headlines. What didn't make the headlines was that an amount of pure, new water was also produced in the process, unnoticed amidst the human drama. Nobody else has had the courage to harness a thousand *Hindenburg*s per minute, as we have done, to build the tanks needed to contain it, to discover the substances crucial to containing the reaction and holding it within the realm of human might. Once mastered by inventors of the combustion engine, the explosion drove our vehicles forward. Now it quenches our thirst."

"And what substance is it that you add?" Cassidy inquires innocently.

"Oh, it's a common flame-retardant," says Dr. Gene. "We filter it out in the postproduction. I'll show you."

They follow him out through the double doors and onto the walkway, a narrow path made of perforated metal, hovering above the open vats of cool, swirling WAT-R. As they move forward, Patrick can see the world down below passing through small apertures in the punched steel, each hole reading dark and then light in dazzling sequence, changing as fast as he is moving, which now seems unbearably fast. He's so far from the ground, he realizes, and he loves the ground so much. He grabs hold of the railing and clutches for dear life, but some shivering, buzzing sensation is traveling the metal, and he lets go so the shaking won't cast him into the strange, dark basins below. Cassidy and Dr. Gene are forty feet ahead now, as he lowers his body to the metal surface and lies down flat for maximum stability. He extends his arms out from his sides until he reaches the edges of the metal path. Then he curls his fingertips around the metal rim to remain fixed tight to the surface, to ensure that he won't slide off.

Far ahead of him, he can hear Cassidy and Dr. Gene talking. She nods with a serious, intent expression as he describes a five-year plan, monopolizing the local markets and then slowly raising prices once WAT-R's become a natural, inseparable part of everyday life. Like the frog in the simmering pot, he explains. It feels as though they're talking in another world, another time, a place where Patrick used to live but can now only watch as if through glass, as if it lay in impossible exactitude on the other side of a mirror. With each step they take, his body shakes and the teeth rattle in his skull.

"You know, the producers I work with are in the WAT-R business. They have a connection to this factory; that's why we thought it would be a good place to do my research. Do you know a Brenda Billington or a Jay Arvid? They're fantastic people. I think they have some scheduled in-person pickups? I forget for what."

"I can't say I recognize those names," Dr. Gene says after a moment's thought, "but we have a number of investors who see that WAT-R is not only the future of this region, but also its inalienable present. An in-person pickup would be unusual, but not impossible."

"Do your investors drink WAT-R?" Cassidy asks innocently.

"Of course they do! I really think you should reconsider your 'no WAT-R' attitude," he says. "I see many people afraid of what's new in the world, and they never think about how intolerable they would find the way we as a species used to live. Every single thing you enjoy today is a new thing in the big picture of human history, a violation of the way we once lived: in caves, eating raw mammal in the dark. The WAT-R we make here is cleaner, more perfect at a chemical level, better-tasting. It's better at cleaning, better at plumping our cells, better at putting out fires like that catastrophe up near Malibu. It's even bluer than old water, and looks better in a pool, a fountain, a glass. Aren't we lucky to drive cars now, rather than ride on horse-drawn carriages? I'm sure that the brilliant Kassi Keene, if she were a real person, would see the reason in this."

"I don't have sophisticated reasons," Cassidy says, and though Patrick can't see her face, he thinks he hears sadness. "I can't, you know, argue with you about the things you've been saying. I just feel like we owe something to water. Didn't life begin in water? Didn't we need it so much we grew a skin around us to trap it inside when we crawled out?"

"Is it useful to be so sentimental about a substance? I'm sure it's costly, and not just in monetary terms," he says.

Cassidy laughs quietly. "My mom used to tell me all the time that I had to learn to be less demanding, to be flexible. She wanted me to do more ads, more branding, do more kid roles. I swear, I'd be doing kid roles now if I were still with her—she'll always find a way to get me in pigtails. She never thought I'd be believable as an adult. 'You've got a cute mug, Cass,' she'd say, 'not a beautiful one.' And she hated that I complained, that I wanted to hang out in basements, that I drank, that I'd made my face all bloated the day after partying. She chose every role I did until I was twenty-one, and I had to jump into whatever shape they asked for—happy, sad, sparkly, innocent—the exact moment they asked for it, for years. When I got photographed barfing on someone's car, I had to apologize for it and convince everyone I really, really meant it; when I was messed up and sad because my mom was being a cunt, I had to pretend I felt so bad I let her down; at every single moment, I've had to pretend I want something I don't want or don't want what I really do want: to get enough money and drugs and water to just live on my own fucking terms. I've been flexible all my life," she says, now so quiet that Patrick can barely hear her, "I've been a plastic girl. I don't know anything about how to live. I just don't want to give up and drink the stuff. I don't know."

"Well, don't worry," Dr. Gene says in a friendly way, "let's talk instead about something about which you have expertise. I've prepared some questions about the last season of *Kassi Keene* and ranked them in order of importance, in case you don't have time to cover them all during your visit. This way, at least the most pressing questions do get an answer. Shall we start?" He lifts his hand to the forehead of his grinning face and gives the two-finger salute.

After the tour, Dr. Gene drives them back to the front of the building. Cassidy promises to try to answer his remaining questions when she has time after filming, and Dr. Gene offers to send her a bottle of *One Hundred* on the house, MSRP $475 for a twenty-ounce flagon. The sun has begun to set over Alamitos Beach as they exit the vast building. Smoke from the fires has made the air thick with particulate, and the sky looks fantastical, like a thing cooked up in CGI. Broad, soft-edged stratus formations hang low over the water, glowing in pastel tangerine shades that mirror the sky behind them. Higher in the sky, sheer puffs of thin vapor blaze in vivid violet and red. And in the foreground, a few odd, dense puffs of cloud linger in the air, unmoving and unchanging, their color a pale grayish-blue. As they take off their shoes and walk toward the water's edge, Cassidy looks troubled.

"When I turned back and saw you lying down on the bridge, I thought you were dead or something," she says in a serious tone. "I told Dr. Gene that you're an amateur photographer and like to examine spaces from unusual angles. But, seriously, what were you doing?"

"I wasn't lying down, I was just sitting."

"You were lying belly-down, eyes closed, whimpering. You were clinging to the walkway. Your knuckles were bone-white."

"I was tired," he says, and shrugs hard.

They walk along in silence. They pass one tent, and then another. The tents are set up along the shore, in the soft and mounded sand out of the tide's way. There are duffels and bundles of cloth placed in front of tents, old roller suitcases on their side, and piles of plastic bags tied tight around their unseen contents. There are feet sticking out of some of the shelters as bodies drowse, their heads hidden from the worst of the summer heat. And there are roughshod, handmade stills set up on crates: two bottles set lip to lip with a small can-fire burning beneath, a sheet of glass suspended over a shallow tub of seawater, draining out to an old plastic bucket with sand swirling inside. All of it to separate the sweet water from the brackish, the liquid from the salt. To squeeze a few handfuls of sea for its lifegiving slake.

Suddenly Cassidy stops. She turns toward him about to speak, her hair ablaze in the liquid-gold dying light. To Patrick, it's as though the sun is melting into a puddle in her face. Her skin is a golden liquid staring at him with an expression on its face, but because the liquid keeps moving very slightly, he has trouble telling what that expression is. Is she smiling? He has trouble remembering what that looks like, and what the word even means. She steps toward him, looking into his eyes, searching. Inside his body, his upper skull feels light and squeaky clean. He doesn't feel bothered by anything that has happened to him in the past or that is happening or not happening someplace else. The dissolution of bad feelings, even as the basic goodness of sunshine, blond girl, warm shoulders, bright colors remains intact, feels, to him, a little like falling in love.

As her body begins its lean toward his own, he slides his arm around her waist, the circumference smaller than he imagined, and thinks that he was wrong to believe for so long that the imagination was the solution to reality's disappointments. In actuality, our imaginations cannot, can never, mimic the bliss of the real, the material, the warm, lithe body in your arms at last. Simple things inspire him now, like the smoothness of a cheek or the wetness of an eyeball. The elastic cheer of the *Kassi Keene* theme song. The sky like an upside-down hole you could fall toward forever without ever hitting the bottom. His eyes hurt a little. His mouth is so dry it creaks, and his brain pounds softly against its skull, in rhythm with his heartbeat. With supreme confidence, he bends to her, slides his thumb across her porcelain jaw, brings his lips gently to her face. And then he stumbles backward into a half-submerged rock, pushed off and probably kneed too, if the feeling in his groin is anything to go by.

"Are you fucking crazy?" Cassidy gasps, and the last thing he sees is the surprise on her face, intermingling with purplish motes of fear.

The smoke-gray sectional sofa had been upholstered in smooth Belgian linen and is the lone item of furniture in the stark, grimly white room. Barely used, it still resembles the photo in the catalogue Cassidy bought it from, where the pictures made it look as though it would fit neatly around the infinity fireplace in the main-floor living room. Instead, it had to be installed in the sitting room, the only room she had never figured out a use for, a room whose title always felt like a riddle, another reminder that the house wasn't meant for a person like her, but for someone with a life large enough to fill it up. She can't remember the last time she sat on it herself, or had someone else into her home to sink into its pillowy, undented surface. But now she sips from a low glass of yellowish drink as she studies Patrick, limp and stretched out and still wearing his shoes, and tries to figure out whether he is sleeping or passed out, trying to remember whether there's even a difference.

By the time Patrick comes to on the sweat-marked cushions, the light has entirely left the sky. Cicadas sing in the low bushes outside Cassidy's home, and the room is dark, except for when a car comes around the turn, filling the room with a brief, dizzying flash of blinding white light. She crouches by his head, waves her pallid hand before his face.

"You're alive, right?" she says.

He sits up, looks around him.

"Good. I thought you were drunk," she says. "But you hadn't been drinking. Still, you were swaying and mooning around like someone who had been."

"The kiss?" he asks. He can't keep a hopeful tone out of his voice.

"I'll forget about it if you promise not to infringe on my bodily space ever again." She looks in his direction, but won't look him in the eye. "We'll say you lost your balance."

Cassidy drags a lamp in from some other room and plugs it into the socket. Suddenly he can see the room in its unfurnished melancholy, the white carpet still bearing the marks of a long-ago vacuuming. She turns the light up three notches and stands there, casting a long shadow.

"We need to make a move," she says, and her voice shimmers with an intensity that Patrick recognizes from *Kassi Keene,* which makes him feel like he's part of the storyline, a recurring character. "There's something in all this that wobbles. So Brenda and Jay are collecting money from these clinics, WAT-R stores, and at least one major WAT-R factory. That's steady income, and a lot of it. They've locked down the market in SoCal and they're raising prices, which means they're going to be making more for the same exact product. Why are they dipping into the film business with this half-assed production, collecting all this footage when they haven't found anyone yet to cut it? I called the company that's supposed to do our effects, and they only took one meeting with Jay last year, they have no contract. There's no one on board as editor."

Patrick feels a sudden twist of worry in his guts. He had doubted the project, questioned its quality and their choices, but somehow he had never imagined that it wouldn't produce a film. "Well, that would be fraud, if they claim to be making a movie and have no intention of following through," he says, grasping at a sense of confidence. "We could go to the police."

"How would we ever prove they didn't intend to? I was held hostage once. On a small island in the Ionian Sea, for over a week, by a Russian aluminum man who told my manager they were filming a commercial for sunscreen. For ten days, I had no cellphone, no email, and they kept setting up these scenes with me getting lotion rubbed onto my body by a swarm of foreign models. All they fed me was watermelon and ouzo. After a few days, I said I wanted to go home, but they kept telling me the light was bad, the film got exposed, we needed a redo. Finally, I had to climb out a window and pay a fisherman to ferry me back to Corfu all by myself. There was never any commercial, but because they paid up and anyway there was no way to show the film *hadn't* been destroyed in a capsized boat, there was nothing we could do." The drink, pestered by her restless, gesture-heavy speech, disappears down her throat.

"I can't believe this," he says. "This was supposed to be a life changer. My name on a Hollywood movie. On a Hollywood franchise."

"That's right," Cassidy says, some new awareness creeping into her voice. "They'll never get a sequel made without some receipts for this one—box office, buzz, whatever. They don't plan to make it. They're taking money for it, but they're going to bug out before they're expected to show anything to their investors."

She pulls out her phone and begins pressing a message into the small, bright screen. "I think we have about four weeks before the thing collapses, maybe a couple more if they draw it out a little by declaring some sort of problem with their postproduction vendors. They could hire some film students to poke around at the footage and buy a little time. But listen." She puts the phone facedown on the floor. "If we don't cut a deal now, there are no more deals to be cut, you understand?"

On the floor, the phone trembles, shifting an inch to the right. The little lighted rectangle flares brightly into the polyester fibers, giving them a bioluminescent glow. Cassidy picks it up. "They'll meet with us tonight," she says, looking at the screen. "Do you think you can drive?"

It's after midnight when they make the turn into the long, dark driveway of Billington Ranch. In the rearview mirror, they can still see the orange glow of the fires on the other side of the pass. If the fires get worse and the road closes, they could be stuck at the ranch all night, unable to pass back through the narrow, hilly choke point. But, for now, the winds are blowing strong in the opposite direction, gently guiding the hungry beast back north. When they stand in front of Brenda's door, there's only the warm scent of sage coming alive in the night air. Jay opens the door in a shawl-neck sweater, holding a glass of brown liquid. In the half-light, he looks like a different man, his nose straighter, the shape of his face leaner and tighter and unnaturally still.

"Welcome again," Jay says, his words and his tone forking in two distinct directions. "Can I get anyone a drink?"

"I'll take one," Cassidy says, and gestures back toward Patrick. "And I'll take his, too."

Jay chuckles mirthlessly and shows them in. The spotless modern foyer is not as spare and stylish as it was during the party: now there are steel boxes stacked next to the door, and dust on the sconces, signs of neglect and upheaval. Brenda drifts in, wearing cashmere trousers and a matching kimono top. She leans against the wall appraisingly as they take off their shoes and stand on the luxurious stone floors in their socks.

"You look fantastic, Cassidy," Brenda says in a sort of drawl. "Whatever you're taking is agreeing with you."

"Thanks, girl," Cassidy replies. "My secret is drinking eight glasses of water a day." They laugh at the same time, but not for very long.

On a coffee table as smooth and white as an egg, Jay sets down two tumblers of stiff brown for Cassidy and a glass of something clear and cold for Patrick, who downs it before he can remember to ask what it is. Jay walks around the other side and sinks down next to Brenda, his arm stretched out behind her.

"Would you like to share the special news you said you had concerning our project together?" Jay asks.

"She said it was very important," Brenda says to him with exaggerated seriousness. They share a meaningful look.

"Sure," says Cassidy, taking a long swig from the first glass. "My news is that I know what you're doing. You're not going to cut the film. You're not going to add in digital ghosts and wraiths and a whole CGI-haunted town. You're never going to release this movie, and you're never going to make a sequel. I'd be surprised if you're still in town for pilot season."

Brenda laughs and sits forward. "This is just like that episode in *Kassi Keene* season five, where Kassi confronts Ron Nifton of Nifty Org and tells him she knows they're selling off the Cove's treasured public beach for the development of a members-only boating club. She goes to Nifton Castle and sits on his couch, just like you're doing now, drinking a tumbler full of Nifty Cola."

"If I remember my *Kassi Keene*," Jay says, "Nifton didn't cave."

"And why was that, Jay?" Brenda asks.

"Because what he was doing wasn't a crime—not during the planning stages, at least. It was just good business." Jay sits back and gives an easy, broad smile.

"Your investors might not appreciate the fine distinction between a crime-in-progress and a crime with all the finishing touches applied," Cassidy replies. "What I mean is, if there's one thing I'm good at, it's getting press. I'll tell them everything I know about you and Brenda, the money that's supposed to be going into this movie. You'll be over in this industry."

"Let's understand each other," Jay says. "We can make things difficult for you too, and it won't take us as much effort. As much running around."

"All this posturing," says Brenda, sighing, "is exhausting."

"Okay, here's a question." Cassidy polishes off the first glass and reaches for the second. "Neither of you drink WAT-R, so why do you own so damn much of it?"

"Oh, come on, now, this is ridiculous," Jay grouches. "We invest in growing markets. WAT-R is a growing market. The masses sure like it. And, more importantly, they need it. Which makes it an obvious add to our portfolio."

"Even if it's killing people?" Cassidy asks, her brow arched in full Kassi Keene mode. "We know about the link between WAT-R and ROAD, and it all leads back to you two."

"It isn't 'killing people,' it's 'hospitalizing a certain segment of the population who share common demographics and risk factors,'" says Jay, correcting her.

"He looks ill," Brenda observes, glancing at Patrick.

Sitting in the soft, armless, eggnog-colored chair, Patrick can feel his worldview listing to one side, then the other, like a boat in uncalm waters. The boat is a good metaphor for the conversation happening in front of him. In the metaphor, Brenda, Jay, and Cassidy are on the boat talking, while he floats, suspended, very far below the water's surface. When he kicks his legs, he moves in some direction—maybe up, maybe down, who knows. When he concentrates, focusing his mind with superhuman energy on the voices above him, he can hear the lumps of words and phrases passing dully by him, like currents in the water— now a little warmer, now a little colder. He hangs in the water, not breathing, not drowning, not doing anything at all. And in the metaphor there are fish: long, sinuous snakelike fish with flickering silver fins, octopoids with only two tentacles and six childlike human hands, and a fish with sad, feminine eyes that can't breathe the water. The fish turns toward him with its long eyelashes fluttering and gestures toward its gills, indicating that something is wrong. Patrick feels tears coming to his own eyes as the fish's pain becomes his own; the tears leak seamlessly from his face and join the water around them. He takes the fish in his hands and examines the gill flaps, which turn out to be lines painted on the side of the smooth, gapless fish body. At that moment, he knows exactly what he needs to do. He lines his thumb up with the flank of the sad, sexy fish where the hole should be. Then he pushes it in, the fish flesh warm and alive, the fish screaming like a little girl, thrashing wildly in pain. A dark-red vapor rises up into the clear water. He can't believe he never bothered to learn more about the ocean, when all Nora used to talk about was becoming a marine biologist someday.

"Come on, Patrick, we're leaving," says Cassidy, her voice hot and angry. His eyes refocus. "And we're going on TV to tell the world that Jay Arvid and Brenda Billington are defrauding their investors and WAT-R rots your mind and people like them are getting paid twice: to sell the sickness and to warehouse the people they made sick. We'll drive down Sunset and see if we can find some paparazzi interested in listening to my story."

"You can't do that, Cass." Brenda's voice is smooth and even. "Think about this. What alternative do people have? They can't buy the real stuff, like you or me, and even if they could, the black market would never support all the demand. They're going to have to keep drinking the stuff, but this time with *fear*. Can't you see how cruel that is?"

"When people are dying of thirst, they'll drink gasoline," Jay says, "even if they know it'll kill them. And it's their right to do that."

"Can't you just sit down for a minute and *breathe* and *listen?*" Brenda says.

Cassidy grips Patrick by the hand, tries to haul him to a standing position. He looks up at her and smiles.

"Come on, Cass," Jay says. He fills her up one more time. "Sit down. Finish your drink. Then we'll help you carry Hamlin to the car. It's cute how you guys are working together on this. It'd make a great series."

"We should get them some snacks," Brenda murmurs. "They might be hungry."

"They don't want snacks, they want moral comfort. They want to do the difficult thing and know that, even though it doesn't feel right, they were right to do it." Cassidy watches Jay massage the back of Brenda's neck in slow, comforting circles.

"You know, even if they did get to the media, I don't think

anyone would pick up the story." Brenda speaks quietly now, as if to herself. "What would be the point, they'd say. It would cause mass panic. It would be irresponsible. And there'd be the immediate problem of what people could drink instead. They'd mull it over and decide to sit on it."

"Or they'd mull it over and decide there's just no proof," Jay says. "If everyone in Southern California is drinking WAT-R and still only a few thousand are being treated for ROAD, what does that say about the people who are doing just fine?"

"I don't know if you can even say a threat is something that exists out there in the world the way a house or a tree does." Brenda smooths her hair and resettles it so that it hangs over her opposite shoulder. With one long, slender hand, she strokes it as if it were a cat. "In fact, I think it may be one of the most subjective concepts in our modern culture. If you perceive a threat in the world—a mountain lion crouched before you on a rock, for example—is the mountain lion the threat? How about when that mountain lion is off just being a beautiful creature in nature with not a soul around to see it? Is it still a threat then?"

"It's a conundrum," Jay says.

"It really is," Brenda says, nodding

"Cassidy," says Jay with sudden warmth, "another drink? You look like you could use it."

Sitting rigid and stiff in her armchair, Cassidy is holding her glassful of whiskey in her hand and staring straight forward. She's crying silently, motionlessly. At her side, Patrick's head lolls vaguely forward, as though he's falling asleep with eyes wide open.

"Brenda," Jay says, placing his hand on her shoulder. "The

mood in here is deeply blue. We need to let in some air. Why don't you tell us the story of how your great-great-grandfather bought the ranch?"

Brenda sighs and crosses her arms. "I don't know, Jay. He was such an asshole. We Billingtons don't come off so well in that story."

"It's a great story, bunny." He nods encouragingly.

"Well, okay," she replies. "Don't say I didn't warn you." She takes a long, careful sip of her drink and places it on the table before her.

"So—my great-great-grandfather Eugene Tillington is twenty-seven in 1851, three years after the Treaty of Guadalupe Hidalgo is signed, ending hostilities between the Mexican and American governments."

"Tillington?" Jay asks with mock confusion.

"I'll get to that," Brenda says, rolling her carefully lined eyes. "Anyhow. He's twenty-seven, and a lawyer trained in Boston, he's been traveling west doing work for the railroads and even setting up some town charters in the Dakotas, and he comes over to California because he's heard there's a lot of money to be made there. And for him, there absolutely is. The Hidalgo agreement declares that property rights preceding the treaty should be upheld, but the question is how to establish who has owned what property. The government is a bunch of amateurs, they don't really have records, and a lot of people were given property in strange ways, by verbal decree from the governor and things like that. Landowners need lawyers to establish that they really own their land, and my great-great-grandpa Eugene charges his clients half their property as a fee for securing their little span of heaven. Soon he's got parcels all over Southern

California, beautiful pieces of land with ocean views and citrus. But all those parcels are no good to him, because the land he wants to live on is owned by an old Mexican ranchero named José Benítez.

"It really is a fantastic parcel of land, it's got a good stream and a great view, it's located in just the right part of the hills, where the fog from the sea comes up to visit in the mornings, and so it never dries out all the way and won't catch on fire. Maybe that's why Benítez didn't want to sell. Eugene made him offer after offer, but the stubborn old guy didn't bite, so he had to think of some other strategy. He realized that, in the California Land Commission's eyes, proof in the present meant more than any secondhand anecdotes or documents from the past. So he decided, even though he was a fairly rich man already, that he was going to become a squatter. This was possible because the property was very large, and Benítez was too old to patrol it regularly. He built a little house on the edge of the man's land, and he started raising goats. Goats because he knew they pretty much take care of themselves, and because they leave a trace of their presence—you can see when a place has been grazed by goats.

"So, for months, my great-great-grandfather lives in this little house, when he has a bigger one just seven miles away. He lives like a cowboy, on beans and cornmeal and hot coffee in the mornings, cooked over an open fire. And he grazes his goats, and they disperse themselves throughout the property, munching on the brush, gamboling in the trodden-down fields, getting closer and closer to Benítez's home, where he's got chickens and a couple horses and a little light gardening. And then, one day, Benítez looks out his window and the place is overrun by goats.

They're going after the beans in his garden, the chicken feed, anything they can get their teeth on. And then Eugene walks up calmly and tells him these are his own goats, and this is his own land, and now they have a property dispute going on.

"Eugene knows the workings of these cases very well, and he has connections in the government, well-placed friends who'll testify to having come over to the little house on the property to visit Eugene and his goats. And he has the smarts to get a surveyor who's new to the area, all the way from Ohio, and who doesn't speak any Spanish. So, when the time comes, the surveyor shows up to get everything on record, and both Eugene and Benítez are there to greet him. But Benítez is angry, he's old, and Eugene is smooth. Eugene shows the surveyor around Benítez's house, shows him the chickens and the horses and the goats, shows him how the goats have groomed the terrain as far as you might care to walk. Tells him the names of all the goats and shows how the little bells around their necks play a perfect on-pitch F natural, the starting note for a familiar union hymn. And he says Benítez is the old caretaker he hired, mostly senile, but at the end of his life and therefore entitled to small mercies. Though Benítez is protesting, trying to make himself heard, the surveyor is buying it all, marking things down just the way Eugene wants. It's a victory for Eugene Tillington.

"And then, right as he's leaving, the surveyor notices the metal 'B' on the gate to the property. 'B' for 'Benítez,' of course. But he turns to Great-Great-Grandpa Eugene and asks him, 'What's with this "B" on the gate? What does it stand for?' And Eugene acts all surprised and looks at the papers in the surveyor's hands and tells him, 'Oh no, there's been a mistake. You have my name down as Tillington here, but it's spelled with a

"B." Billington. Eugenc Billington.' And there you have it. That's how we got our name, and how my great-great-grandpa got his land with the help of some friendly goats."

In the van on the way back to Secret Sunset, Cassidy drives and Patrick curls up in the passenger seat, finally able to string a few words together. She's talking to Patrick, but she doesn't know if he is really aware of what she's saying, so she's talking to herself. She says they need to find a scientist, a doctor, someone who can figure out how drinking WAT-R is causing people to lose touch with reality. They need the medical words, the scientific words. Nobody is going to believe Cassidy Carter if she gets on TMZ in a tube top and says all this. Nobody except maybe the *Kassi Keene* forum freaks, half of whom will say this is the prophesied moment, hallelujah, and the other half of whom will say she's a false-flag siren bitch. She says she needs to find a way to get in touch with her sister, tell her not to drink the WAT-R, tell her to stay safe and get out of town. She says she needs to figure out where her sister is living these days. She says she needs to get Patrick back to his family, back to the people who love him. She says not to worry, she won't just unload him at one of those freaky Memodyne human warehouses. She says she'll get him safely back home, no matter what.

As they clear the security gate and take the first turn onto the north wing of the subdivision, Cassidy has the awful feeling that Secret Sunset doesn't look the way it's supposed to. It's too bright for this time of night, and the sky has a strange closeness to it, like something thickening, a ceiling rather than the vast openness of atmosphere. As she turns onto her street, Patrick sees her face begin to glow orange at the edges. He feels his own face and forehead growing warm, inexplicably, like a sudden fever. Little glowing insects come drifting through the air in lackadaisical flight patterns, but it's not insects, it's ash and particles of inflamed ember. As they crawl inexorably forward in the air-conditioned van, toward the smoke and the fire and the scent of carefully chosen interiors going up in flames, Patrick claps his hands tight over his ears to keep out the sound of her screaming.

"Today we bid farewell to the Hula painted frog, a creature that took joy in its life in the Hula Valley, where Israel drained marshes in the 1950s to drive away the mosquitoes." Linden reads from a clipboard in a clear, strong voice, her double braids making her look like a returning camper just promoted to counselor. "Presumed extinct for decades, in 2011 it showed itself to mankind at midday, ten meters from a small pond. Now, with the Hula wetlands toxified and turned to desert, let us say goodbye forever to this rare amphibian, an animal that rose from extinction and then returned to extinction, a living fossil now no longer living."

The room breathes in and out around her in near unison, their eyes closed as they craft a representation in their mind of the intricate and perfect frog, its round, glassy eyes and rust-mottled back. They conjure a feeling of the world as a whole, trembling with life and violence, and in their minds they subtract one vibrating thread from the weaving—this fabric like a net held up to the sun, more hole than fiber. Alison remembers how it used to feel to thrust out an open hand at the right moment and feel the small, adhesive weight of a frog landing on her palm. In the man-made pond behind her grandfather's house, in the ditches running behind the middle-school soccer field, she smelled the pungent freshness of green slime and knew to expect them near her even if she couldn't see or hear their movement. She's sitting straight-backed and attentive, trying to do what she can to feel the sorrowful togetherness that she sees in the silent bodies all around her. She wants to melt into them, but wanting to melt is a self-centered, individual desire, and feeling it reminds her that she has not melted, will not melt for as long as she is thinking her thoughts and not theirs.

It's become difficult for her to feel in rhythm with everyone else, to eat in their rhythm and sleep in their rhythm, since last week's Mourning Report on the Palo Comado Fire. Standing on a creaky old stage where campers used to put on error-ridden performances of *Our Town,* the hastily abridged *Scenes from Shakespeare,* and a clunky stage adaptation of *Camp Do-What-Ya-Wanna,* Linden described the known casualties of the devouring blaze: twenty-three homes, over a hundred missing pets, and unknown precious and irreplaceable wild animals—including possibly a radio-collared mountain lion in its second year of independence, still establishing the canyon as its home. The temperature of the fire at ground level was reported to be unusually hot, a toxic conflagration capable of killing the soil microorganisms and buried seeds that would normally begin the process of returning the canyon to life. With the amount of dense, dry fuel in the fire-adjacent grasslands, there could even be a firestorm, where the fire's inner churn would suck in new air and cause the burn to balloon, fueling a column of smoke and fiery debris that would rain down burning matter miles from the site, starting new fires of its own. Alison can't picture the flames, and the videos won't load on her phone, the trickle of service at the top of See Clearly Peak barely enough for downloading a photo. But as she hangs Nora's tee shirts on the line, as she helps to weed the Earthbridge garden and examines the swollen udder of an Earthbridge cow, she summons the faraway presence of a disaster she can't fathom, happening in a place that she's never seen, threatening a husband that she can't quite picture in her mind's eye. When she thinks of him, the image she calls up again and again is from an old photo taken when they were dating. He's reading a manuscript with his feet up on the coffee table, trying to hold the pages in front of his face to block the camera's aim. In the photo, his face is grinning but his eyes are annoyed: when reading, he hated having his mind reminded of his body.

"Goodbye to the painted frog. Goodbye to the thick-shelled river mussel. Goodbye to the Greenland ice sheet, melting in a twenty-four-degree Celsius summer." They say these words at the same time, a single broad, blurry voice scattered through the old wood-paneled theater. Tears flow freely down faces, as from a loose, unstanched faucet. And with this recital, the report is over, and now it's free-form meditation and unguided mourning for all who care to participate. But Alison's hip is killing her, and she can't stand to sit on the hard wooden floor anymore, her legs pretzeled up beneath her, the jut bones at the base of her ass grinding into the floorboards. She stands, swivels the joint, and tries to rub out the ache. How did sitting cross-legged, Alison wonders, come to mean gentleness, enlighten-ment, and openhearted behavior when in reality the bent, folded legs resemble so many tangles and knots? She can see Nora sit-ting near the wide doors at the back of the room with the other nine- and ten-year-olds, her jaw rigid with concentration, her eyelids fluttering gently. Alison has asked her what she thinks about in her meditations, what she sees and experiences, and she always demurs, saying that the experience doesn't really have any words in it, so she can't translate it into words without betraying the whole thing—but out in the garden, or by the hives, she can hear Nora talking to the other kids, hushed and excited, about her visions.

Over the heads of the seated crowd, Alison sees Linden walk-ing out the side door with her water bottle and yoga mat and goes to find her. She's treading the narrow path through the sunflower patch with a determined, bullish step, as though lost in music coming through her headphones, but there are no headphones and no music. Alison reaches out and brushes her surprisingly hairy arm—the woman's body is covered with a blond down, invisible against her light skin. It is this layer, Ali-son realizes, like newborn fur, that catches the sun during the recitation and makes it look as though she has a whole-body halo, a human figure cut out of light.

"Linden, hi," Alison says, smiling with closed lips. "Thank you for that report. It always is such an important part of the day. Thank you."

"You're welcome," Linden replies serenely. "And my condo-lences."

"My condolences to you too, for your loss both new and ongoing," she responds quickly, the Earthbridge vocabulary still clumsy on her lips. "I was wondering if you have any update on the Palo Comado wildfire."

"From last week?" Linden asks, her eyes flickering infinitesimally right and left, like she's reading on a computer screen. "I'm sorry, no. The pace of disaster has us always moving on, perhaps sooner than we'd like. It's a grave burden to be the watershed of the planet's suffering, the ones born to bid nature goodbye."

"Well, it's personal to me," Alison says, "because my husband is out there somewhere, and it's been hard to keep doing my rootwork here, trying to stay grounded and mindful of the land, while I've been worrying about him."

"Of course, I see," says Linden, her big eyes blinking. "I'm sorry, we don't really have the bandwidth to track individual cases. We're trying to build a bridge between humanity and the earth, not humanity and individual people. Individuals are kind of the paradigm we're looking to break." She pauses, thinking. "But maybe call him? There's a pay phone near Main Meadow, on the outer wall of the woodworking studio."

"I know," Alison replies.

"Oh, you do. Good."

The sunflowers sway around them, their scent warm and dusty and just barely sweet. The edges of their big leaves rub against one another, rasping softly. In a former factory site by their house in New Jersey, a field of sunflowers had been planted to draw the lead from the soil surrounding the old buildings and painted-aqua storage tanks. In midsummer, they grew hot in the sunshine, big black eyes gazing out at the road. Then, a week before Labor Day, the thick stalks were chopped and the mass of plant matter was hauled off to the dump, to decompose atop hard-edged waste from construction sites and junkyards.

"What's it like," Alison asks awkwardly, realizing that she's wondered for a long time, "to put together these reports every day? Is it hard for you? How do you make sense of it all, the information and the data? How do you decide when it's time for a loss to be mourned, and when you need to wait to declare it because there's still something bigger left to lose?"

Linden looks off toward the yoga barn, her face heavy now and weighed down. Only now does Alison realize that the girl may be older than she had imagined, not a college hiatus taker but a woman even older than Alison herself. Is there someone else that she's thinking of right now, a Patrick of her own that she left behind, someone beloved still living in the blood and guts and compromise of the world? "I don't know," Linden says finally, sighing. "I just try to keep it to three."

The Earthbridge trails cut in and out of forest and field, past family cabins and bunkhouses where unattached adults sleep eight or twelve to a room. She walks beneath the thick summer canopy and tries to imagine: That tall oak over there with the thick, leafy crown, bursting suddenly into hot, unquenchable flame. That broad maple on the path, disastrously burning, alive with ember, incandescent with fire raining down from its highest branches. The orange devouring the green, the smooth, satin-sided foliage crackling and curling and falling to the ground to burn upon a carpet of moss. A sleek lizard-colored leaf blackening under the heat of a match. It seems impossible to stoke in herself a genuine fear, an organic urgency. She imagines the highways clogged with people, smoke rushing across the valley, Patrick oblivious in his car, hurtling forward on the highway until the traffic begins to slow and stop and the wall of flame rears up above him. Her breath quickens, her pulse goes fast and shallow—but she's so aware of trying to feel, of trying to worry more, almost like when she took a theater class for elective credit one semester and ended up having to perform a monologue with crying. Her friend Margo told her the trick was to pinch as hard as you could some tender spot, like the areola or the crinkly inner skin of the elbow. Pinch as hard as you could and the tears would come, the feelings would follow. But she stood at the front of the room pinching and all she could think of was flesh, whether it was possible to detach a nipple with the force of index finger and thumb. That semester, she learned that she couldn't feel anything she didn't feel, no matter how she might like to. She tilts her face up into the mottling sun. In the shade of the trees, with the air saturated by the whirring, chiming song of cicadas, it's easier to imagine that fire itself is an impossibility than to imagine it happening at this exact moment, even in someplace very far away.

As Alison crosses the Main Meadow, she sees Klaus waving her over from the pay phone. He holds the receiver against the front of his shirt while he calls her name, then lifts it back to his mouth. "I've got her," he says into the phone. "She'll be on in a second." His face is impassive, a heavy Nordic block of a head, like something he might carve into a reclaimed oak stump—but as she gets closer, she can see, even through the thick beard, that he is concerned. "I think he's in trouble," he says quietly, his hand covering the perforations. "But he won't say." She nods and takes the handset. She's doing dull arithmetic, calculating the time difference, surprised that he's calling her so early in the day, right in the middle of the week, when he would usually be on set and focusing on the film, her calls going straight to messages.

"Patrick?" she says. "What's happening over there?"

"Alison," says Patrick. "It's really you?"

"Who else would it be?"

She waits, but he doesn't answer. The question seems to confuse him.

"Listen," she says, "are the fires still going? Are you someplace safe?"

"I'm in a van," he says uncertainly. He sounds as though he's repeating facts heard secondhand, reaching for words with a familiar shape but an unfamiliar flavor. "Yes. I think so. Let me check."

She hears the sound of rustling, frantic rubbing against the mouthpiece.

"It's a van," he says. "Metal holder, doors that slide, and a lot of stuff in the back. But at least I'm in the front of the van and not the back. So I think I'm still okay."

Alison gazes out at the Main Meadow, where children are chasing one another through the swerving paths; a knot is forming in her throat. "Do you mean the van you rented for work?"

"Work is over," he says with sudden firmness, "forever."

In the background, she can hear a strange mixture of sound: the clutter of vehicles or machinery against an intermittent background growl, and the sound of a muffled voice swelling and sinking in the background, the words unintelligible.

"Patrick, honey," Alison says, and pauses, the endearment

unfamiliar in her mouth. "You need to take a breath and explain to me what's going on. Who's there in the van with you? Where are you going in the van? Are you in danger? Nora and I are worried about you with the fires going on. We haven't heard from you in days. You need to tell us what's happening."

"I can't," he says helplessly. "I can't do anything. Alison, the house burned. The water burned in the basement, the swimming pool was on fire. I saw the bunnies fleeing from the scorching fields into the Kmart lot to huddle beneath parked cars. It smelled like a barbecue restaurant. I know this is real, but sometimes it's like I forget, I peel off of our world like a sticker, and then I'm in no world. Have you ever thought of no world, sweetie? It's worse than you think."

"Who's there with you?" she asks, as gently as she can. "Is it Cassidy there in the car with you?"

"Yes," he says with more certainty, "yes, she is. She's right here, holding the wheel. She wants me to tell you something."

There's a long pause and a lot of scuffling as he struggles for the words.

"She wants you to buy me a notepad," Patrick says at last.

"A notepad."

Alison hears the voice in the background grow louder and spikier, its tone insistent. Out of the corner of her eye she sees Nora head into the middle of the meadow, into the furring of plants and insect life, followed by three or four children who hang on her every word.

"No. A ticket," he says. "For the plane."

"A plane ticket? To come back here?"

"Yes," Patrick says with audible relief. "I want to come all the way back, Alison. I want to crawl back into the old life with you and grow small in its belly, like a baby. A man needs a woman, he needs it like a water needs duck. I've been out west now, to see what I can see, and what I discovered is that it's all on fire and giving off a dark-blue smoke. I saw the palm trees and the bathing-suit beach and the surf-whitened sea, and I looked until my eyes burned down to the nub. There's no paradise here unless you're a bird of paradise. There isn't enough ocean to put out all the flames." His speech is flowing now, the Patrick-like rhythms familiar to Alison. In his novels, there was always a section like this, where one character or another would make a big speech, laying out the themes of the narrative and ending with a rousing call to action. In the Hamlet book, it was the Claudius figure, the stepfather, pontificating on epigenetic theory and the tangled web of succession. In the George Washington book, it was the unlucky boatswain with his soliloquy on the miracle of brotherhood, and the blessed physics by which a boat full of brothers can float atop the river's roof, while a rock just sinks, etc., etc. But this speech unfolding before her reads all out of order, with passages crossed out or missing or entirely unwritten. She can't tell if it's the phone connection or her own frayed nerves, but she can't make the pieces of his speech knit together in her mind.

"You can tell me if you're drunk," Alison says. "I would understand."

Patrick makes a frustrated sound. "Listen, if I could be another time for you, I would. If it were tomorrow and you were there on that lawn, like before, I wouldn't try to stop you, I wouldn't bring you back inside. I would lie down in the dew and hold you. Next time I would."

The noise in the background increases, and the sound begins

to fuzz out. When she hears Patrick's voice again, there's terror in it, and he speaks like a telegram.

"Get the ticket, Alison. It needs to be tonight. I have to go. We're in the fire."

The dial tone is like the ringing of a lone cicada. There's a feeling of crazy, wild panic in her chest, but it has no place to go, and eventually it turns to a numb, tingling feeling in her fingertips. She realizes she needs to get to the public library as soon as she can if she's going to make an airline reservation, and the smallness of the task, the mundanity, feels like a kind of madness. In a small clearing mown into the tangle of butterfly bush and clover, she sees Nora sitting in a tight circle with her friends here, fellow nine-year-olds with serious expressions on their faces. She only knows one of them by name, Appaloosa, whose mother used to work a hedge-fund job in Connecticut. As Alison heads for the bus stop, she plans a path through the grasses that will bring her close to the fervent group. Skirting the edge of the plantings, her ankles brush against the soft fronds and tiny flowers, yellow and blue and swarmed by bees. She slows down as she nears their bent, murmuring heads, and stares straight forward, so that all they'll notice, the ones facing in her direction, is a lost adult with her mind elsewhere, slowly meandering the narrow path.

It's astounding to see her daughter, her familiar, big-eyed, reticent daughter, at the center of this circle of eager listeners. Her daughter, Nora, of a thousand naked baby photos and awkward, forced baths, whose malformed belly button is carved into Alison's memory like the indelible layout of her childhood home, leading this group of oddly straight-faced children. Now she eavesdrops on her daughter's life as she would a stranger's, wishing she could stop to listen but not wanting to break the spell. As she draws closer, she makes her face vacant and her footfall soft. Her daughter's voice is too sweet for the words she's saying, too tender for something so harsh: "The long game of temporary comfort, like playing musical chairs in a burning room, is nearing its end. We've seen the losers holding up shiny trophies of gold-painted plastic." Her sleek brown ponytail, held in place by a flamingo-colored scrunchie, bobs up and down. "People aren't the future," Nora says in a low and serious tone, as the others nod in serene agreement. A couple steps farther, and Alison is too far from her to hear.

Half a mile's walk from the Earthbridge campus, the regional bus makes its stops on a long, nondescript road bordered by shaded ash forest. Alison is waiting with her headphones on, listening to a mixtape on a dusty Walkman she found in one of the back recesses of the admin office. After dinner, when the buildings are empty, she sometimes paws through the boxes, looking for nothing in particular. She's enchanted by the troves of ephemera cataloguing decades of summer-camp obsolescence, supply closets in the rec buildings and locker rooms filled with unclaimed junk that no Earthbridger wants to be responsible for sending to a landfill. For one thing, much of it dates back to her own childhood, and she finds things that she once wanted but never had—like the portable cassette player in her hand, molded from pink and lavender plastic and looking like a massive piece of saltwater taffy. Nora calls it homesickness— with such easy disdain that Alison wonders what definition of the word she's been taught in school. Wasn't homesickness one of the few victimless emotions, a feeling that infringed upon nobody else's right to feel, a thing that you could enjoy within yourself without anyone's even knowing? Didn't it enrich the world, reminding you that there were times other than the despairing present, worlds other than the one we all have to live in?

But sometimes it feels less like she's homesick for the past and more like she's living the past over again, waiting for a bus with New Order blasting tinnily in her ears, just like she did as a teenager in a flat, unremarkable suburb of Denver. As though leaving her house and all the possessions inside it had flung her back to her adolescence, shy and overly aware of how she sticks out. As she boards the bus and takes an empty seat, she imagines herself explaining to a friend, it doesn't matter which one, that it's as if she died in that year of weeping, fasting, and compulsive consumption of news, the year she spent grieving something that everybody around her insisted hadn't died at all. And now, like a video-game character returning to its last save-point, she's been reborn as her daughter's older sister in a never-ending summer camp. Her former life already has a hazy, fictional quality to it, though it feels more real to her with the lights off at night, when she is lying in the bunkhouse and listening to the noisy breathing of eleven other sets of lungs. That life reasserts itself when she checks the credit-card statement, going line by line through the intimate, inscrutable tabulation of Patrick's Los Angeles purchases: $42.07 at Juicy Ladies Cafe, $29.83 at Exxon La Brea, $176.68 at the WAT-R SuperCenter on Sunset Boulevard. In moments like these, she feels that odd feeling from the first year they were married, the invisible threads linking her to every minor thing that he did, the strangeness of this person whose familiarity was so intense and new to her that she couldn't help but point it out to herself many times a day. She wishes he wouldn't keep bringing up the lawn incident, which always makes her feel anxious, guilty, and angry—angry at herself, she assumes, though she's not completely sure.

Outside the window, woods give way to sparse housing, fast food, and short strips of retail, and then the friendly-looking Oswego Main Street with its brick buildings and renovated historical banks. Alison gets off after the bridge and walks three long blocks to the public library, which resembles a castle in white, crenellated and adorned with an American flag flapping proudly at the top. Inside, it's like the library back home in New Jersey: warm yellow wood and mottled carpeting, retirees and the probable homeless. Everywhere, the smell of aging paper. She waves to the woman behind the front desk and sits down at an unused computer. The browser window opens in a slow, fitful sequence. First, the outer box pops up on the screen after a period of whirring; then, slowly, the window begins filling in the starting address in the location bar, then some pieces of text, then a few small icons, and a large, colorful image of the library she is sitting in, which appears one inch at a time in the center of the page. She enters the travel site into the field at the top of the browser and begins searching.

Patrick had said he wanted to leave today, but there are only a few flights left for this afternoon out of LAX and Ontario, and none of them will get him to Syracuse or Rochester. She finds a last-minute red-eye from Orange County to Buffalo that she thinks they could afford and texts him the details. He replies, *Thzzzr35#yxtpxffsehTW$#YHjbq,* and then, a minute later, another message comes through. This one reads: *Thank you. It looks good.* She writes back: *You won't have trouble making this* *flight, will you? It's a red-eye, but it's on the earlier side.* She waits, but there's no response. As she's leaving, the confirmation email pops up on her battered old cellphone: . . . GET PACKED . . . YOU'RE GOING ON AN ADVENTURE!

The return trip is on the same exact bus, and she takes the same exact seat. She leans her head against the window, but it's not restful. The sense of relief she had experienced immediately after purchasing the plane ticket has been replaced by a deep malaise: she keeps turning over Patrick's words from this morning, trying to arrange them so they'll resemble a window into his mind, explaining why he's so desperate to come back east today, after months of delay and defensive rationalization. She doesn't understand why the job is over, why the troubled starlet Cassidy Carter is driving him around in a van, why he can't seem to string three sentences together in coherent order. In the weeks since she arrived at Earthbridge, she's become used to knowing less and less about his life, and the feeling is a little like coming off a drug: a halo of nervousness hovering around every small thing, and a deep current of relief as she begins to sense a subterranean normalcy. She tells the other Bridgers, when they ask, that he's in California caring for a sick relative. She doesn't want to invite a lecture on the unsustainability of the film industry, the relationship between celluloid and peak oil, the role that Hollywood plays in celebrating the human at the expense of all else that lives and suffers. She's begun to understand what it might feel like to live a life without her husband.

It's not ethical to lie to them, but the truth would make no sense in this place. To tell them she has concerns about Patrick's sacrificing so much to work a basic grunt job, to tell them how strange she finds his commitment to *the project* or his defensive-

280 / ALEXANDRA KLEEMAN

ness over simple questions like "You're a writer, why are they making you haul water around town?," would only invite them to question whether being attached to a man like this, a fool still begging to buy capitalism's plummeting stock, was really compatible with an Earthbridge lifestyle. How could they understand her feelings when she doesn't understand them herself? Nora fit in instantly, integrating herself seamlessly into the rotation of youth workshops and work assignments. She plays tambourine in the evening jamborees and serves as a Junior Deputy Mourner during the Mourning Reports, calming fidgety younger kids. On the volunteer wheel for Bridgers aged nine to fourteen, Nora's name appears three times, maximizing her chances of getting picked for a task. Alison, on the other hand, still feels as though she's performing a pantomime of what she sees everyone else doing, her imitation lost among the community's earnest iterations. When the entire auditorium recites the Mourning Prayer in unison, she closes her eyes and finds herself worrying about small, petty things: her rosebushes back home going rotten in the harsh summer sun, their leaves eaten down to lace by iridescent beetles from Japan.

Even in this place, a place chosen explicitly to heal the deepest sorrows she has, she shields a part of herself from view. Peeling and chopping vegetables with five other Bridgers, she answers the questions about what brought her here, whom she left behind, what piece of news or dire prediction was her "burning bridge," the sign that told her there was no going back to life as she knew it. She asks small, polite questions in turn: how long are they staying, what's their favorite task in the rotation, is this carrot too old and ugly for the stew? But when the ends and trimmings are sorted, she's out the door, walking alone back to the bunkhouse to change clothes, while the others are still chatting with one another a few dozen paces behind her. She can hear their laughter, but she stares out at the forest, like one lost in thought. The behavior is reflexive; she barely realizes she's doing it before it's done. It reminds her of being in high school again, leaving the house as soon as dinner was over to walk around with headphones on, in the world but separated from it by a scrim of pop-punk anthems, ending eventually at a narrow canal carrying rainwater runoff out to the treatment plant. She would smoke a cigarette in the tall grass, watching a heron on the other bank stalking prey with vast patience, slowly lifting a long-clawed foot and holding it there aloft for minutes to prove its own stillness. The important part wasn't the cigarette; it was the fact that her parents thought she was out with other kids— friends that they worried about, drinkers and smokers, sex-havers—when she was actually here, doing nothing at all. Keeping something, however small, away from everyone she knew made her feel safe, protected by a secret power.

Sometimes it seemed to Alison that choosing Patrick was a continuation of this pattern. Yes, she loved him and his troves of errata, and the band tees he used to wear when they were going out were cool, but it was also convenient for her to be married to someone whose inner struggle filled much of his field of vision. When he was at work in his office, she could do what she wanted and feel no guilt for not thinking about him at all. He noticed when she was happy, but rarely noticed when she was unhappy unless she told him explicitly, which she explained to herself was better than being held accountable for passing disappointments, fleeting depressions, or feelings of doom. With him, she could hide in plain sight—purchasing a new sectional from IKEA, switching to a cheaper internet-service provider, going to birthday parties for Nora's friends, and telling the other parents about their plan to put in a swimming pool when no such plan existed. She could dream out loud with him about buying a cottage on the Cape when he sold his next book, knowing that it would probably never happen and he would soon move along to some other fantasy. Patrick's belief in the reality of their shared life made it real enough for her to go along with for a decade and a half, and made her doubt nearly impossible for him to perceive.

But all of that was wrecked by the lawn incident. Alison lay in the bath for five long hours as the hot water went cold, feeling the adrenaline travel up and down her body in swells of anger and nausea. Sometimes it felt as though her skull were burning, sometimes it felt as though all the life had drained from her limbs. When she moved them, they shook. She stood up and looked her reflection in the eye. She had never truly gotten used to her face, a face that had been called ugly when she was in middle school and then pretty when she entered high school. Now she tried to focus on the new traces, the lines and spots that marked her age and belonged to her existence as Nora's mother. A patch of shadowy, sun-damaged skin above her jaw on the side where the bright morning light pressed during her commute, a mouth sharper and thinner with a carved-out shape. The person indicated by these signs of maturity could walk out of this room and into the rest of her house without shame. She could explain to her husband and daughter why she had done what she had done and how that behavior was continuous with the rest of her, not a break but an unusual intensification. She knocked on the bathroom door until Patrick came to remove the barricade and let her out. As the door swung open, she saw his face muddled with a mixture of anger and fear, and she began immediately to weep.

That night, the three of them ate microwaved macaroni from thin black plastic containers in silence, as she felt the discomfort of the full, undiluted weight of her partner's scrutiny falling on her over and over. Of course, she saw Patrick looking at her, noting whether she was eating and how much, noting that she wiped away stray tears from time to time. She wasn't trying to cry; it was just physiological now, when and how they seeped out, at all times the tears were softly present within her face, like an ache in the muscle. But even when he wasn't looking, she felt the force of his attention, his thinking about her, the questions he posed to himself about how she was doing and whether another eruption was imminent. Now when she returned home from a long shift at the clinic, having stitched up the lacerated paws of German shepherds and excised benign growths from the armpits of elderly cats, he asked about her day in extensive, progressive detail. Each piece of her response was turned over and scrutinized like a clue, as though she were a crime that hadn't yet been committed. It wasn't that she didn't want him to care, or to worry. Worry was the bridge toll for love—you had to pay for your passage as others paid for theirs. But she didn't want to be examined all the time, searched by his gaze and still not seen.

But there was one night when the scent of damp loam woke her from a deep dream with no images, no sounds. In the dark room, tinged blue by the cold light of Patrick's bedside clock radio, she sensed soil and chlorophyll, the smell of green structures tearing. The thunk of the crowbar digging deep into the

Kentucky bluegrass, dredging the rich earth as Patrick slept next to her like one knocked unconscious. She inhaled the scent that was not there and felt inexplicably happy, her heart full. The physicality of that memory—stripped of the presence of sadness, of desperation, of Patrick running up behind her emitting sounds of panic—was beautiful to her now. It was freeing, to recognize something new: that she felt alive in that moment, plunged into the world. There were other planes of reality that could be accessed, other ways of putting the world in order, which were no less true or concrete. She had accepted that her behavior on the lawn was a sort of stupid self-immolation, but maybe she had unearthed something in herself. Shame made it harder to slip back into her old routines, to behave exceptionally normal as a means of repentance. Under Patrick's surveillance, it was harder to get comfortable, to settle in alongside him and get back to work on feeling happy. In her discomfort, the home turned unhomely, and there was room to imagine a life away from this one, a different logic, a different family.

She fell asleep dreaming of the sea, dreaming in a body different from her own, one lower to the ground and buzzing with totalizing sensation. In her dream, she crawled across the sandy beach and toward the saline bound. Froth moistened her face as she slipped into the saltwater, heaving. It lifted her up toward the surface, buoyed her as she watched the wave in the distance coming closer, growing taller and sharper. When it hit, driving her body deep below the surface, she opened her mouth to scream and realized with shock that she was able to breathe there. Even there, in the dense, chill surf, she could breathe.

———

When she sees the small, nondescript sign along the side of the road, Alison pushes the button to request a stop and climbs down from the bus to solid ground. She walks back toward the Earthbridge gate, checking for a cellphone signal, though she knows she won't find one. Back at the main meadow, she heads to the pay phone and slips two quarters into the slot. She dials Patrick's cellphone and listens as it rings and rings and rings. She hangs up and tries again, and again. On the fifth call, someone picks up. It's a young female voice, sleek and glossy and sounding a bit worn out.

"Hello?" it asks.

"Hi, sorry," Alison starts. "Is this Cassidy? It's Alison, Patrick's wife. I'm just calling to make sure the info for the plane ticket came through. I still have to figure out how he's going to get here from Buffalo, but the plane is the first step. Without the plane, there's no getting home."

"I got it," Cassidy says. "I got the ticket. I'm driving there now." There's a pause. "Patrick is, I dunno, sleeping. Or something."

"Is he okay?" says Alison. "Did something happen to him?"

"I guess you could say he has food poisoning." She pauses. "That's probably the quickest way to explain it."

Alison can hear the sound of the honking in the background, and a siren faintly blaring. "Well," she says, "I'm really grateful to you for taking him to the airport. I don't know how you got into this situation, but it's really a nice thing for you to do. I'm sure celebrities don't do airport runs very often."

Cassidy laughs a tight, bitter laugh. "It is pretty nice of me, isn't it? I should put out a press release to let everyone know I'm not such a bitch after all."

Putting the phone back on the hook, Alison looks out at the campus, at the happy Earthbridgers living seamlessly as one. There's a gnarl in her heart that she can't seem to undo, and thinking about it only pulls it tighter. She walks over to the main garden, where she sees Phoebe and Naomi, two of the women who share her bunkhouse, down on their knees in the rich, warm soil. She asks if they could use any help, and they move down the row to give her some workspace. With her hands on the ground and her back warmed by the sun, she breathes in the mineral scent of earth, like her own sweat after a run along the Charles back in college, the gulls curving in the sky far above. Right at the surface, the dirt is warm and crumbly, but an inch or two down, it's cold, like the chill night air.

Alison grabs the dandelions beneath their tough, tooth-edged leaves, close to the start of the fleshy white root, and pulls up, at the same time taking a trowel in her other hand and digging out the long, stubborn tail. She does dandelion after dandelion, until her eyes and knees and wrists hurt. But the delicate clovers need only a gentle upward tug to hoist them from the ground, stringy little roots dangling with clumps of dirt still attached. She likes weeding the clovers, takes pleasure in how fragile they are and how numerous. As she pulls them up, she sets them in a pile to carry out to the field later on, where she'll leave them out for the rabbits to find.

In the dining hall, dinner is served at six. Pots of simmered beans and carrots, lentil stew, gluten-free pasta with marinara sauce, and fresh-baked bread next to a bowl of butter, everything hot and filling but with too little salt. Alison and Nora slide down the line, scooping portions onto their plates with the shallow wooden spoons. Nora seems quiet to her lately, and when Alison asks she tells her that she's talking to herself inside her head, she forgets she needs to say parts out loud sometimes to let her mother in on the conversation. They sit down across from each other on the long cafeteria benches, and Alison decides to tell her the good news: her father is coming back tonight, leaving on an overnight flight into Buffalo. They'll have to figure out his pickup in the morning—either he can take a bus to Rochester or she'll go and pick him up that afternoon, after her shift in the laundry building. Nora regards her mother with suspicion.

"Why is he coming back now?" Nora asks.

"He's your father," Alison replies. "He can come back anytime he wants."

"You don't know, do you?"

"There's nothing to know. He went to work a job, he was always going to come back, and now he's coming back. Case closed."

"The last time I called him, it didn't sound like he was planning to come back. Did he get fired?"

Alison sighs. "I honestly don't know, honey."

"Do you think Dad will like it here?" Nora asks, her gaze intent. She's still a child, but to Alison it seems as though she sits unnaturally tall, almost at the eye level of an adult.

"He'll learn to," she says with a confidence that extends only an inch or so below the surface, not all the way through. "You know he always said he wanted to get a country house, someplace where he could park the car unwashed and not feel judged."

288 / ALEXANDRA KLEEMAN

"Because," Nora continues as though her mother hadn't spoken, "I don't think he would fit in. He doesn't like to be told what to do. He wouldn't want to sit through the chore raffle. He wouldn't like Vegan Pizza Night. The Mourning Report would be like a punishment to him."

They sit chewing in silence. In the empty corner of the cafeteria, someone starts playing a didgeridoo. A minute later, someone else joins in with a tambourine.

"I saw you talking with your friends today, in the pollinator garden. Are you feeling settled here? Are you happy we're going to be here for a while longer?"

Her daughter glances down into her lentils. "Well," she says with precision, "I think I used to feel like it was immoral to live here as if living here was doing something to help the planet or the other people who are still out there trying to live. It felt like we were abandoning them. It felt selfish. But I see it a little differently now, I guess." She doesn't say more, and Alison doesn't pry. When Nora sees some of her new friends standing by the muffin table, her face lights up. Alison tells her to go ahead and join them.

Walking back to the bunkhouse, she hears the phone ringing outside the woodworking barn. She walks toward it, alone in the hush of the summer darkness, the chiming of the phone just slightly out of time with the pulsing song of the insects. When she picks up the phone, it seems at first that there's no one on the line: she hears the shuffle of air across the input, a sound in the background like cars driving past. And then a girlish voice saying, "Oh my god. You tell her. I'm not telling her."

"Hello?" she asks into the empty phone, the unknown nowhere.

"Alison," says the voice, Patrick's voice, dry and cracked al most beyond recognition. "I can't do it."

"You can't do what?" she says slowly. Dread has a taste in the back of her mouth, like pennies.

"I can't get on the plane," he says. "I can't. I'll never land. I need the ground, I need to feel it. It's the only thing I have. I'm not sure of anything anymore, I can't know that it's there if I don't have my hand on it." And now she hears him weeping like a little kid, weeping as she's never heard before. "I can't go thirty thousand feet up in the air; there's no reality up there, and I'll never find my way back. I'll be lost forever."

At first she doesn't speak, and then, when she does, it's with fanatical, deliberate calmness. She wants to will this feeling into him. "Patrick, it's perfectly safe to fly. And you've never been afraid of flying in the past, so I don't understand why this is hap-pening. Are you okay? Did something happen to you? If you don't want to come home, just say it."

The phone rustles, and then it's Cassidy on the line.

"Mrs. Hamlin? It's Cassidy. I don't think he can explain his situation himself."

"Cassidy. You have to put him on the plane, I don't care what he says."

"I know, and I wish I could, but they wouldn't let him on like this, he's screaming and crying. I thought I could drug him, but then what would I do, push him through the security line? He'd never be able to board on his own." She covers the microphone and says something to him, then gets back on. "There's some-thing huge happening here. People are getting this sort of dementia—they can be any age. There are twelve-year-olds who have it, ninety-year-olds who have it. It comes from drinking

WAT-R, from something about the WAT-R or in it, and everyone drinks WAT-R. I don't, but everyone else does. So it's going to get a lot worse."

"That sounds completely insane," Alison says.

"Too insane to make up," she replies.

"Then shouldn't he come back here?" She feels the phone shaking against her cheek, but then she realizes it's her hands, trembling in the cold. "He needs a doctor. He needs his family."

"I know." Cassidy sighs. "I told him that, and I promised I'd get him home. But he's lying on the sidewalk outside the terminal, and he won't get up. He's terrified. I think he's seeing things that I don't see, and sometimes I think that he sees only a little bit of what's actually there. He has trouble walking on his own, he runs into things." Now Alison hears a waver in her voice, slight, like an error in the connection. "He's so scared. I mean, he's terrified." She pauses. "When someone's this scared, you don't think they're crazy. You think they know something you don't."

Alison stares out into the empty meadow and tries to blink the tears away. Up above her head, the insects dive over and over into the glass shielding the old enameled lantern, blinded by the light and mistaking it for the moon.

"Can you get him somewhere until it clears up? If he just had some time," she says in a begging way, "maybe he could get used to the idea of flying. We can get another ticket."

"I think so," Cassidy says. "I said I wouldn't ditch him." She hesitates. "I'm fucking scared. I've never taken care of someone before. I never had to."

"It's frightening, I know," Alison replies. She remembers newborn Nora, curled red and warm and slightly sticky in her arms. The terror of attaching, the hot, liquid feeling, like tentacles coming out of your chest and wrapping around the little being. "Do you have some family you could stay with? Somewhere you could go that's out of town?"

Now Cassidy's sobs are audible, short and angry and muffled through the connection. "I don't know," she says. "I don't know one single person who would definitely want to see me. I don't know my dad, I don't have a mom. I haven't talked to my sister in three years. What kind of person has nobody they can call to be with at the end of the world?"

"Listen," Alison says. Through the phone she hears a siren, growing near and then far away again. "If you want to find her, you should. She'll want to see you, I know it. Even if you're angry with each other, there are layers below that that are there, just waiting for a reason to feel something good. Trust me." She pauses, reaching for something that'll make it real to the person on the other end of the line. "For months, I've been here at Earthbridge, and I thought I didn't want Patrick to join us. I was afraid he'd ruin this place for me; it's not perfect, but it's better than home. I wanted us to be a family together, and at the same time I wanted him to stay away. But those are just layers. Now that he needs us, all I want is to be there for him."

"Oh my god," Cassidy says.

"What's wrong?"

"He's trying to run away from the airport. He's crawling on the strip of grass in the traffic median. He's going to run straight into all the cars. This fucking maniac."

"Go," says Alison. "Please, take care of him. And take care of yourself. Your life is precious. Your life makes a difference."

But Cassidy doesn't hear her: she's already hung up, and the line's gone dark, dead, the object in her hand just a lump of plastic, molded to hold a voice.

Back in the bunkhouse, she finds Nora asleep, her sleek hair shining in the dim light of an electric lantern. In the other beds, some women are turned toward the wall and sleeping, others are pulling off clothing and changing into loose nightclothes. The room smells like warm bread and incense, and though nobody is talking, it feels crowded and loud with bodies. Alison undresses to her inner layers and climbs into the single-person bed, wrapping her arms around herself and hugging tight, as if she were two separate people and not one person all alone— one person with something to give, and one with the ability to receive. She holds herself tightly enough to keep any sounds of distress from escaping into the hushed room. Her breathing is heavy. When she used to have trouble sleeping, Patrick would peel the shirt from his back and from hers and press their naked upper halves together beneath the covers. Front to front, she could feel his heart beating against her skin, the quick life solid and evident to the touch, the absolute presence of someone who knew her. She's not willing to cry surrounded by sleeping women, all of them still essentially strangers to her. She imagines the tears she's not crying forcing themselves out the opposite way, sliding down her throat, through her chest, filling her stomach with sorrow.

Before they go to sleep, Earthbridge encourages them all to say the Four Earthbound Tenets out loud to guide their sleep along peaceful and harmonious paths. When she read about the community from her home in New Jersey, these little practices seemed to Alison like miracles that had the chance to heal her, fix her once and for all. Now she sometimes wonders whether their real role is not to pay tribute to all this planetary loss, but to sort and codify it, keeping it contained within a series of habits, sayings, rituals. To keep the end within sight, but make it feel livable. Still, what was there to do instead? She doesn't have any better words, or any better ideas. The alternatives were— what?—to chain herself to a bulldozer or to slink back to the suburbs, admitting that its hypocrisy was the one true hypocrisy, for ever and ever, amen?

Alison stares up into the plywood underbelly of the top bunk and closes her eyes to lessen the feeling of emptiness. To fill her throat, she mouths the words silently to herself. *I want to live in the world, not upon it. I want to live in reciprocity, not exchange. I want to give without keeping a ledger. I want to love the earth like I love the person I love the most. Like a person who will never leave me, like a person whose love is always holding me up unseen from beneath my feet.* She knows that it's ridiculous, a grown woman saying silent prayers in a room full of amateur mystics, so she's surprised when a true, tangible peace settles upon her—so sudden that she notices only after it's already happened, so deep that she wonders for a moment whether she took a pill earlier that night and had just forgotten all about it.

The last lights turn out in the bunkhouse, and suddenly there's nothing to see: just the sound of slow, deep breath shuttling in and out around her, and the crickets outside. She thinks of the lake in the dark reflecting the broken form of the moon, the ovaloid shape of the lake man-made and too neat to be real, but full nevertheless of real, teeming life. A lake that does not exist, will not exist, a lake that no longer holds water. What did

Nora mean when she said that people weren't the future? What did the other children mean when they nodded back? What was it her daughter had said, sitting out there in the middle of the field? "The dogs of the faraway future are ten feet tall and hairless, with long, sleek jaws that would reach from the elbow of a full-grown woman down to the tips of her manicured fingers. A soft, saggy muzzle covers a doubled row of teeth, the tail wagging randomly with no memory of what the gesture used to mean. Impassive and unowned, they lope through the regrown forests for days at a time without seeing another creature, they hunt in the naked daylight and dig in the cool creekside cliffs and sleep where they want, sleep without anger or fear."

CHAPTER
NINE

Eyes slip open, and light pours in. Everything before him has the faded appearance of a magazine that's been left out too long in the sun: the sky weakly blue with a runny thinness, a landscape viewed through white gauze. The short concrete walls lining the side of the highway are pallid and hot, baking beneath the sun. In the driver's seat, Cassidy is wearing an enormous black straw hat. She guns the engine, deletes the distance between their van and the laggard sedan just ahead, then shifts quickly into the right lane to pass. It would be disorienting enough on its own, but at this moment Patrick can feel even the wobble of the earth on its axis, a fact he learned about in high-school physics, as a sort of deep-nested vertigo twisting in his bones. The white van lurches, listing to the east on a writhing curve. When he closes his eyes, everything he knows tips forward into darkness. His inner ear quivers. He sweats and freezes at the same time, caught between the heat of the sun beating

296 / ALEXANDRA KLEEMAN

down through the windshield and the refrigerated cool oozing from the vents.

With her phone propped up on the dashboard, Cassidy argues on speaker with voices he doesn't recognize as she forces a path through the crawling traffic, riding the dashed line between two highway lanes. Her driving is quick and sharp, with the jagged quality of a person crying alone in an empty room, heaving air through a tightened throat, trying to give space to a feeling bereft of recipient, a feeling with a beginning but no end in sight. It makes him want to hold her in his arms, to rock her back and forth with incredible tenderness. In his subjective experience of the world, Patrick is feeling the violent newness of the present, an inverse déjà vu that causes him to experience the unparalleled singularity of all of it at once, each moment pregnant with firsthood. He notices each item in its individual, distinct nature as though it might be the last of its kind, the last in its series: the last flash of sunlight through the half-empty water bottle, the last flutter of the protein-bar wrapper in the windshield reflection. Everything he sees makes him want to cry, but the eye won't give it up—the liquid stalled somewhere within, tender ductile tissue inflamed. Outside his window, strange tiered hills rise shelflike above the plane of the highway, resembling a large, sloped staircase. It pricks him: the first and last time he'll ever lay eyes on whatever that was. The firstness is also a lastness. All of this is enough to bring a tear to his eye, and he tries, but there's only a rough, sandy feeling in the corner where the ducts should be. Nothing comes out.

Cassidy instructs her phone to call Toby Olsen, her ex-manager. "I need to find June," she tells him when he picks up the call, his voice many years older than she had imagined and full of wary expectation. "I heard she moved to the desert after the show got canceled, and I'm headed in that direction now, but I don't have an address."

"What makes you think your old, unceremoniously expunged manager knows where your sister lives?" comes the voice through the speaker. "I'm an aged white man with high blood pressure and sciatica, not the White Pages."

"What are White Pages?" Cassidy asks earnestly.

"Just a long-ago tool for keeping people in touch. A little like your swipe-right/swipe-left dating apps."

"I don't expect you to know where she is, but you're the kind of nosy old guy who knows the people who might. Who does June stay in touch with?"

"Well, I can deduce that she's not in touch with you. You know, not to put too fine a point on it, but I've observed that when one person is searching for some hard-to-locate second party, the situation tends to be that the first party is easy to locate, but the second party doesn't, for whatever reason, want to locate them. All the challenge in the task comes from the fact that you're trying to find someone who doesn't want to find you. Are you sure your sister wants to be a part of this search party?"

"I see what you're saying," Cassidy says, mirthless. "I'm a worthless piece of trash and my family doesn't want to know me."

"Hello darkness, my old friend. I'm just saying maybe some critical thinking about your motives and desires may be in order. You could try Hailey—they got pretty close on set. Hair people and makeup people spend a lot of time together, I think they had some sort of Friday-afternoon sushi lunch routine. A dance that went along with it. Besties, I think you would say, in the parlance of your generation."

"June had a best friend on set named *Hailey*?" she says, and skepticism mingles with envy in her voice.

"Sure," says the grainy old voice, "they went for a sushi lunch once or twice a week. They used to bring me back an order of pan-fried gyoza with the sriracha dipping sauce, before I knew about my cholesterol. What a pair of angels."

Cassidy is silent. Out on the highway, a torn sofa cushion sits in the middle of the fast lane. Cars swerve around it, slowing briefly, and then accelerating. Small bits of memory foam litter the asphalt like breadcrumbs.

"Listen. Are you doing okay, kid?"

"Toby," she replies with sudden firmness, "nobody is doing okay."

"What I mean, Cassie, is, do you have someone to look after you?"

"Look after me?" she asks blankly. "What is that? Look *after* me? You mean, like, what, watching someone walk away?"

In three-quarters view, like a medieval painting, the San Gabriel Valley terrain bends and twists to show humans and cars flatly vivid in the foreground, constructions of concrete and asphalt crammed tightly vertical into the faraway plane. Hacienda Heights and Puente Hills, rife with unfinished roofs and bare parking lots, built to be looked at from the ground, for the eyeline of those cruising past strips of retail frontage at thirty-five miles per hour. In the dry, combustible hills, too steep and too dusty to be worth building on, geometric gardens and sprinkler-fed hedges give way to the sound of lizards moving unseen through the parched grass, their only trace the rustle in the lower branches, a trembling in some dusty stretch of calm.

As Cassidy follows the curve of the road out to the desert, the valley fades into the long, brown flats of Riverside, adorned by a sarcastic smattering of palm trees. Out past the highway, terra-cotta-shingled houses huddle around twisting inner streets and culs-de-sac. The development is mostly abandoned: the houses stand empty, rooms with no furniture but what was left behind, carpets marked by depressions where the legs of a love seat once stood. The air is still and hot; the appliances are unplugged or missing. In the backyard of a sand-colored ranch, pale concrete surrounds an empty swimming pool, punctured by short, tough plants with tiny blue flowers growing through cracks in the surface. At the base of the pool sits a thin layer of water scattered with leaf matter and plastic wrappers—rainfall, or the remnant of days when the cavity was filled with brilliant blue WAT-R, dancing in the bright. As the sun bears down hot overhead, a black bird lands on the aqua-colored surface, totters to the edge of the puddle, and drinks. A second bird joins, and a third. And then, at some unseen signal, they take flight together and are gone.

A quick phone call proves that Hailey, a former set assistant with an overgrown hairstyle and bubble-gum voice, is no help at all. Not only does she not know June's address, location, current phone number, or place of work, but she keeps asking why Cassidy is trying to track her down, and whether June knows that her sister is looking for her. "I think she just really wanted to get off grid, you know?" The voice is sugar-sweet and reminds her of the older girls from middle school, the ones who graduated but came back around every Friday to hang out in the parking lot and show off their long teenage legs. "Not just a couple of solar panels on the roof—actually living out where you can't get the news on your phone or find your own driveway without a map. Someplace where even the Bed Bath and Beyond coupons can't find you. Being hard to find was part of the whole desert dream for Junie." The woman calls her "Junie," as if she knows a single real thing about Cassidy's sister.

It didn't matter how long Cassidy and June had been out of touch, how long it had been since June had gently brushed the stray hairs out of the luminous frame of Cassidy's contoured, camera-ready face, or since Cassidy had last felt June's feathery touch cool and smooth on the hot nape of her neck as she barfed into a nightclub toilet. It didn't matter whether Cassidy knew June's current job title or marital status or whether she was still doing the weird monofood diet, with the watermelon in the morning, cucumbers for lunch, and for dinner raw tuna seasoned with just a little bit of lemon and salt, as she had been doing just before they lost touch. Growing up with someone meant you knew them forever, whether they wanted you to or not, and with indelible, bone-aching depth. Trying to rid yourself of someone you had grown up with, someone who had seen you turn from child to unchild, was like trying to pull your own memories out through your eyeballs.

Sometimes she remembers June in the months before *Kassi Keene* was canceled, the last months they were together, working on set each day from seven in the morning until three in the afternoon and then again from six or seven or eight on into the late hours of the night. Cassidy had gotten June hired on as her personal hairstylist for the show's past two seasons, a good way of guaranteeing that she'd always have somebody to go out with on a free night—and an emergency gofer who already knew her preferred brands of yogurt and tequila. It also ensured that June's bank account would always receive a reliable, though modest, influx of cash, since on her own her sister tended to self-select boring, ill-paid jobs, like "barista," and refused all attempts to slip her helpful checks. Maybe it was insulting to have your little sister offer you a month and a half's rent when you told her your car needed an oil change, but in Cassidy's book this was just generosity, generosity and evidence that, however screwed up the tabloids might say she was, she still understood basic familial love.

Her sister made a good hairstylist—even the head of hair and makeup said so—though she was far slower than the others, and Cassidy's hair always took twice as long in the seat. With a serious, almost fretful expression on her face, June would stand in front, blocking Cassidy's view of herself in the makeup mirror. Slowly, meditatively, she would reach for the jar of texture clay, unscrew the smooth lid, and coat her fingertips in a thin layer of the stuff, which smelled of roses and fresh chalk. Then she would rest her ass on the surface of the vanity and bend her shoulders toward Cassidy in the chair, her brows furrowed and close. With an expression of unparalleled intentness, June reached out for one lock of Cassidy's hair at a time, rubbing it gently between forefinger and thumb, twisting it slightly so that each tendril bent toward an organically bouncy, sun-kissed shape. One by one, June would touch her long, intelligent fingers to every piece of Cassidy's hair, rapt and absorbed, barely speaking, and never looking in her sister's eyes. In these silent stretches, Cassidy was free to drink her in: to feel June's short, shallow breath light against her face as her sister hovered close in concentration, to breathe in the warm, clean floral of her sunscreen. To watch this face she knew so well revealing itself to her with its new adult fullness, its new adult roughness, coming as close to her eyes as it had when she was a child and they lay together under a lime-green bedsheet, telling stories with the flashlight on.

From the seat to her right, Patrick releases a low moan of fear. Cassidy follows his line of sight, out the window to the sage-studded fields and the rows of strange white windmills, their heavy blades turning against the background of a boulder-ridden mountainside. His mouth hangs open, and dry breath wheezes through the gap between his teeth. He comes in and out of lucidity, in and out of consciousness, with more time spent unconscious than not. He's had trouble swallowing recently, and his tongue has turned a pale, dusty pink, like the color of an old, hardened pencil-eraser. "It's all right, Hamlin," Cassidy says in a soothing tone. "You don't like the windmills. A lot of people don't. They think they're eyesores. I know they look close, but they're far away. It would take an hour for you to walk to the nearest one, maybe more. They'll never hurt you." She picks up the water bottle from out of the cupholder and pops open the sport top. Genuine water, 100 percent, sloshes inside its plastic embrace, the substance fast and clear and glinting in the sun-filled cabin. Keeping one hand steady on the wheel, she leans toward Patrick and aims the nozzle at his lips, tilting and squeezing so that the mouth-warm liquid splashes into and around his open maw. She dabs his chin with a fast-food napkin, and then turns back to the road.

Patrick gazes in amazement at a diner, or what looks like a diner, with long rows of high-backed chairs upholstered in slippery beige and orange. The fabric is waterproof: he ponders whether that means he's supposed to pour a drink onto it. There are lots of things on top of the table: a squeeze jar of red, a squeeze jar of yellow, little plastic-sealed packets in a shallow white dish. There are two tall plastic glasses of frosty-cold cola, and in his hand a tight little unit of fork, knife, spoon mummied up together in a paper napkin. Patrick thinks of the different ends, different edges of those three utensils pushed up against one another, scratching and rubbing against one another in the snug package, the three things so different they shouldn't even be together—he knows he should probably let them out. Spooning with a knife, he thinks to himself, then immediately forgets what he's thinking. He reaches for the cola, but a thin, pink-nailed hand slaps at his fingers.

"Don't touch that," Cassidy says. "It's the bad stuff, I checked with the hostess. Big Soda is using WAT-R now, it's in the ingredient list."

"I have to," he gripes, reaching for it anyway. "I'm so thirsty." His voice feels like a bit of chewed nut stuck in a crevice of his throat, a particle he can't cough out. She watches him plunge his muzzle into the clutter of ice floating at the top, like a Labrador. Cold liquid swirls around his hot, tight lips, erasing the deep-grooved taste of pennies and plastic and sweaty automobile interior. The cubes bump against his teeth as he drinks, and he sticks his tongue out so that the liquid may slide down faster and more. The sweetness of the beverage, its energetic fizz, slakes something deeper than thirst within him. He looks up and sighs with deep satisfaction: he feels like a man again, a man once more. He could drink another right this second. On the Revelators message board, people whispered that WAT-R had added salts to make you thirsty for your next one, a medicine that stoked the sickness.

Cassidy squints at him from beneath the brim of her black hat, vaguely repulsed.

"Hamlin," she says, "you have to be smart about this. You're already sick. You're not as sick as you could be. You can't keep drinking this stuff, or you're going to end up a vegetable, like those people in the clinic. You'll never get back home."

"You're right," he says sadly, disappointed in himself. "I don't know why I did it. I guess I just wanted to feel like a regular guy again, drinking a soda, and not an irregular guy. Not a vegetable." He rubs his eyes violently, a squinching sound coming from beneath his fist.

"Listen, don't beat yourself up." Cassidy pats his elbow. "I'm just telling you as a friend, I'm not trying to make you feel bad. We want you to make it all the way out of this, all the way back home, to where you belong."

Cassidy is being so nice to him, Patrick thinks. A sparkly feeling in the space between his lungs.

"Wear these," she says, handing him a pair of aviators from the gas station next door. "Just trust me. Your eyes have a weird look to them."

With the sunglasses on, the room becomes dim. Through the dimness, she smiles crookedly at him, and he feels good.

When the waitress comes back to take their food order, she stops, bends slightly, looks under the brim of the wide dark hat, covers her mouth for a moment, then leans forward with an almost apologetic look on her face. "I'm so sorry, but is there any chance that you're Cassidy Carter?"

"There's a chance," says Cassidy.

"I wouldn't have seen you if it weren't for the hat," the waitress says. "Only celebs wear hats like that."

"He'll have a grilled cheese with fries," she responds coolly. "I'll take the spinach-and-goat-cheese omelet. Toast, not potatoes."

"I heard on some TV show that you're not a very friendly person," says the waitress.

"I don't know if I want grilled cheese," Patrick says.

"I'm never sure how long you're going to be with me in the waking world, cowboy," Cassidy says to Patrick, ignoring the woman completely. "So we're getting something that packs up easy, just in case you check out in the middle of the meal."

As the waitress walks away, her thumbs tapping on the screen of her smartphone, Patrick looks out the window at the parking lot and beyond. Surrounding the familiar shapes of curb, sidewalk, and gutter are thousands upon thousands of small silver-green bushes, their shape rough and guarded. The spiky clusters repeat themselves again and again and into infinity, each tangle of vegetation distinct, an unneighborly distance from those around it. The pattern iterates like wallpaper until it reaches the horizon line, where it becomes too small to decipher. In its vastness and flatness, it reminds him of a sea, the underwater part of the sea, laid bare and drained of all its liquid. Enormous silver-sided fish navigate the pebbled surface, drifting above the sand. They cast a hovering shadow as they sift for morsels of food, sucking the stones into their large, open mouths and spitting them back out. From certain angles, it's possible to see through the gaping orifice to a sliver of blue, visible in gaps when the gill opens and shuts. As their bodies turn slowly in the sky, listing like oversized helium balloons, he sees the glint of bright desert sunlight against airfish scales and thinks it looks just like the sparkle you find on top of the sea. The glare hurts his tender brain, his mortal face. A throbbing blindness.

"What are they?" he asks slowly, wonder audible in his voice.

"Which part?" she replies, turning to peer into his eyes through the dark-tinted lenses. "The sage bushes?"

In the back of the van, the boxes lie crushed or dented and the bottles of vintage water from Cassidy's last payment have come loose. They roam free, plastic colliding with glass and the different kinds of water all mingling—crinkly plastic bottles from hotel conferences and sleek flasks of electrolyte-enriched thinking-water, cans of raspberry seltzer and long blue bottles filled from artesian springs: they skitter across the cargo bed from left to right when Cassidy shifts into the right lane, and from right to left when she does the opposite. Either way, they confront Patrick's supine body, curled protectively around himself in the holding area, his legs an obstacle for rolling bottles to negotiate, the vacant space at the center of his fetal position a place where the containers collect and huddle together, faintly clinking.

"Are we where we're supposed to be?" Patrick asks, sitting up suddenly in the cargo area and peering out the two small portholes in the back door. The huddled bottles slide toward the rear door. He sees the highway slipping away behind them, the distance fleeing and yet remaining oddly inert, ever escaping and ever the same.

She turns and looks back at him from the driver's seat. The black hat sits in the empty space next to her. Her face is hot, flushed, with little strands of damp blond hair flattened around her hairline.

"I had to make a decision at the highway fork," she explains. The air conditioning wheezes warm air, inexplicably damp. "When my sister moved out here, did she choose leftward, toward Joshua Tree and Twentynine Palms? Or did she veer right, toward Palm Springs and the Other Desert Cities? Up through Morongo Canyon, or south and east into the Sky Valley? I tried to think about what she might feel when she saw the two signs. She would have liked the sound of Morongo, like some lost land of swirling mists. But she would also have liked the sound of a Sky Valley, someplace serene where you could just lie flat on the ground and watch the colors above you change. In the end, I had to pick an exit. I went with the one to Joshua Tree. She always loved that album."

"Who's your sister?" Patrick asks.

She ignores him. "I'm going to ask around at the New Age food store out there. It seems crazy, but it's a small town, and I have this feeling the acupuncturists or yogis around there might know. I remember she said she'd cut hair out here if she had to, but she wanted to get into something more serious, something that really helped people. Crystal healing and aura repair, stuff like that."

"There are people living around here too," Patrick murmurs vaguely. "Out here in the desert, eating the cactus and drinking the air."

"Why do you say that?" Cassidy asks. All she's seen for miles and miles is the diner, receding in her rearview mirror.

"How else do you think he got out there?" Patrick says. He points out the front of the van at a tall man in a crisp gray suit standing on the right side of the highway, next to a spiny, many-armed cholla cactus. Under the hot afternoon sun, the tall, thin man looks blithely immaterial: no sweat, no wrinkles, no dust on his finely cut blazer.

Cassidy looks out at the vast, unbroken terrain and then turns back to the road, fixing her eyes on the bright-yellow line that divides the traffic in two.

"You should eat your sandwich," she says grimly.

Above the sagebrush expanse, the sky fills with clouds. Soft, cottony cirrus clouds, like the ones Alison described to him over the phone, the ones she imagines when she closes her eyes and thinks of girlhood. Tall, smeary clouds of a saucerlike form, with a shape like a thin oval of petal-white soap dissolving into its surroundings. The clouds are white, like the thinness of a curtain catching the sun. The clouds are soft, like the baby squirrel that fell from its nest and that you are not allowed to touch, like the softness you think when you look at it and not the too-real feeling you have when you reach out with your clumsy, sticky hand. The clouds are quick, like milk spilling in slow motion, melting across the blue at a pace perceptible only if you stand out under the big sky ceiling, looking up and waiting, looking up until your neck aches.

And then there are the clouds that don't move. Hanging in the sky over Los Angeles, but coming your way. They grow larger, which means they're coming closer, but their shape doesn't change at all: the image simply expands. "Plastic," derived from the Greek word *plastikos*, originally referred to the capacity to take form, which was also the capacity for one form to be destroyed in the path of another. Today the word means disposable forks and grocery-store clamshells, rollerball pens and freezer bags—but it was once explosive, reducing materials to their simpler shapes. Stiff and thickly wadded, heavy and faintly blue. A cloud that looks like nothing else at all, a cloud that looks exactly like a cloud, multiplied and reiterated across the horizon. Floating in the sky, as big as a castle and as heavy, they're coming closer every minute. The softer, lighter, whiter clouds pass before them, blown by the wind. But these new ones: they just sit there, unmoving. Like the clouds painted on the ceiling of a casino mall, they appear more real from a distance. They remain still and quietly watching, waiting for their moment to approach, waiting for their moment to show what they really are.

Cassidy walks in the center of the road, dust in her sandals, gathered between her toes. To her right and left, small houses exist at the end of long dirt driveways. A driveway is just the absence of vegetation, a pathway exterminated through the fields of sage and creosote. To her side, a chain-link fence has been set into the beige-colored sand, surrounding a small yellowish home. One group of plants is separated from another. Across the thick, inflexible metal mesh, the plants respire silently, steadily, oblivious to the structures that divide them.

She has a good feeling about this neighborhood. The girl working behind the juice counter told her that not one but three holistic healers live on Sunburst Court, and one of them has a thick, dark, waist-length braid, a descriptor that has fit June at various times in the past. Walking down the long, curving street, with Patrick safely parked in the van behind her, she feels an energy surrounding her that she would call "familiar," a feeling of arriving home that could only mean that June is nearby, since, other than her sister, Cassidy has no home anymore, just a couple acres of rubble north of Malibu and a borrowed rental van. Any of these homes looks as if it could belong to a holistic healer: there are windchimes and stained-glass mobiles hanging from the eaves, rows of quartz-crystal points and amethyst-encrusted geodes lined up along the windowsills. There are brightly striped Mexican blankets and Turkish kilims and lamps shaded by pieces of metal intricately punctured in branching, vinelike patterns. There is a figurine of a big-breasted earth mother, and one of Boba Fett. Any of these things are things that she could imagine her sister owning, and though that un-narrowed breadth might cause some people to grow pessimistic and lose hope, to Cassidy it feels instead as though her sister's presence saturates the air, the way the scent of griddled batter fills every room of the tiny Yucca Heights apartment when your sister makes pancakes on a Sunday morning and your mother is god knows where.

One house calls to her more than the others: the outer walls have been painted a girlish lavender, the front door is decorated with a metal knocker in the shape of a honeybee. June always liked purple. June was once stung in the mouth by a honeybee, which had crawled into a can of cola in search of sweetness. Cassidy lifts the heavy honeybee shape and strikes it three times against the door, but nobody answers. She tries the doorknob, but it's locked. She circles around the house, her hands pressed against the pastel walls, trying to peer in through the windows. She trudges through thickets of lemony sage, her eyes hungry for the clues that lie on the other side of the glass, the woolen wall hangings and macramé plant-hammocks that are manufactured en masse but still manage to look handmade. Her bare legs are crisscrossed by thin white scratches that are beginning to turn red. In the back of the van, Patrick wakes up and mistakes the cargo hold for a windowless, airless jail cell. He begins screaming, but his scream is so loud in the enclosed metal space that he shocks himself back into silence. A salty liquid slides down his forehead, down the sides of his nose, and into his mouth. Blood, or sweat? He barely knows the words, but something about the taste reminds him of heating up leftovers in the microwave, the indefinable, ghostly presence of some unflavored flavor in the food, something unfamiliar that wasn't there the first time. Suddenly the back doors fly open and new air rushes in, making him gasp, making his lungs feel naked and cold.

"Are you okay?" Cassidy says, her eyes wide.

"Thirsty," he says in a rasping voice, but corrects himself: there's a more accurate word. "No. Hot. Hot."

"I'm sorry," she says, and Patrick is surprised to see that she's hugging him, apologizing, and enfolding his shoulders within her thin, sweaty arms. "I won't do that to you again, I promise. I shouldn't have left you in the car. Not even for five minutes. I should know better. I left a dog in the car once on a day like this, and he went kaput. He was a beautiful dog, a long-haired Chihuahua. His name was Tiny."

The lockbox has five dials on it, each of which needs to be turned to the proper number in order to release the key. Cassidy stands before the back door and shouts at him to check the number in the front, the street address. "Five times out of nine," she says, "they'll use the address, even though it's so obvious." Patrick is too far away to hear. Where he stands, he can see a dark color in the sky, descending on the mountain line, the deep purplish-gray like the unmasked color of a bruise, the color it might be below the skin. The short bushes shiver in the breeze, and a scent like his father's shampoo moves through the air, leaving him startled and confused. Cassidy pushes his body gently out of the way so she can see the numbers. "Two-two-three-one-six," she says, turning and walking back. "Come on, Hamlin. I know you're not operating at peak capacity, but pretend, just pretend." He doesn't answer; he can hear in her tone that she's talking to herself. She doesn't seem to believe he could reply anymore, and it's not clear to him that she's wrong.

The lock pops open, releases its key. Inside, the house has an unlived-in feeling, not quite impersonal, but belonging to no specific person. Probably a short-term rental—look it up on the website and book, a 7-percent discount for stays of a week or longer. The sponge is brand-new. There's no toothpaste in the bathroom. That doesn't stop Cassidy from eagerly sifting it for signs of her sister's presence, putting her touch on everything in view. She picks up a ceramic owl and examines the speckled glazc. "Do you think June could have made something like this?" she says out loud, to no response. She likes the thought of her sister learning how to make things out of clay, sitting in some drafty workshop in a smudged apron, focusing on bringing shape into the substance. The way she would smile wide when finishing a task, a favorite smile unfurled in rare and precious moments, always made Cass think, *We did it, fuckers, we got out of that family alive, and now we're thriving and happy, so suck on that!*

She lifts the corner of a runner knit from red and purple yarn, replaces it, grabs a long, flexible-necked lighter out of the kitchen drawer, and flicks it on—once, twice, three times. She opens the freezer door, closes it, opens it again. She's losing patience with these furnishings, feeling more alone every second. The feeling that she's seeing someone she knows, someone beloved, in all this meaningless stuff is harder to conjure as she notices just how much junk there is in this place, how much junk there is in anyone's place, how little it says about the person who lives there. It collects like dust, she thinks, like the skin flakes and single hairs. Stuff sloughs from your life and sits in piles in your house. And then, when you're done, someone gathers it all up, gives some of it away to living people, and throws the rest into the garbage.

The garage is full of plastic-wrapped family packs of WAT-R *Ready2Go,* stacked waist-high and covered with a layer of fine, light-colored dust from the desert outside. She's rarely handled a bottle of the stuff except to refuse it, to hand it back. But now, so far from no-home, so deep in the crowded belly of the catastrophe, she reaches through the tear in the wrapping, her wrist rubbing against flaps of plastic, and pulls out a bottle. The bottle looks just like any other, the ribbing of clear plastic around the bottom half, the flimsy label with a photo of a pixelated river and trees. *Ready2Go* is one of the cheapest lines the company offers, everything about it an afterthought, down to the subslogan: "Water in a small package you can carry in your hand." She tilts the bottle to the left and right, watching the liquid roll back and forth in smooth languor. She unscrews the cap and holds the open mouth beneath her nose, detecting nothing but a faint, almost indiscernible odor of plastic. She reads the warning on the back: KEEP OUT OF EYES AND NASAL PASSAGES. Suddenly she remembers Patrick, remembers that she has to keep checking on him or something could happen. What thing? She doesn't know what to worry about, what to watch out for. Most things. Everything.

She doesn't find him in the kitchen, where the near-empty fridge switches from a cooling roar to a soft idle, cycling in and out through periods of temperature adjustment. She doesn't find him in the living room, standing next to an indoor cactus in a ceramic planter decorated by small multicolored triangles. When she finds him in the bedroom, he is facing the window, looking out to the desert, his hair and body shadowed against the bright, rosy light of the outside. Cassidy says his name—sternly, then softly, then loud enough to call a shout—and still he is staring out the window, unmoving. The sensation of her footsteps, their slight vibration along the carpeting, does not draw his attention. As she walks toward him, one step after another, she begins to feel a strange, cold feeling welling up beneath her heart. She has a vision in her head, a vision of reaching him and placing her hand on his shoulder. He turns around then, at last, but when he turns there's nothing on his face—just the light and shadow of the room, played out over a featureless terrain, as smooth as the inside of a seashell.

She wakes up horizontal, deep inside a headache. The surface is a sofa, a blocky gray sectional. June would never own a hideous, basic couch like this one, she was always finding treasures at the flea market. There's something heavy around her and on top of her. When she twists her body, she can see it's a man; when she twists farther, she can see it's Patrick, his arms wrapped around her waist like they're a long-married couple holding each other in chaste, mundane slumber. He has a surprised look on his face, like a person who's just been awarded a hundred thousand dollars out of the blue. She doesn't remember allowing their bodies to touch, but she doesn't remember refusing either. It's hard to imagine how else she ended up there, her legs braided with his. She tries to push him away, but he's safely on the inner side, and she ends up heaving herself off the furniture and softly, heavily onto the floor. From there, she scrambles to her feet.

"What is this, what did you do?" Cassidy stands glowering down at him, but he seems as confused as she feels. He looks up at her, opens his mouth, shuts it. In his head, he hears the word *Alison,* but he can't say it and he doesn't know what it is. In the melancholic light, the house doesn't look uninhabited, it looks abandoned: the traces of daily life all absent, the things on the shelves and in the cupboards just things that nobody would choose to take with them when they leave. She suddenly understands with awful clarity that this is not where June lives at all.

A buzzing sound comes from somewhere on his body. He points at himself and looks up at her, flustered. "Hamlin," she says disapprovingly, and she leans down and extracts his cellphone from the pocket of his dress shirt. A number with no name attached glows on the screen. She thrusts the phone out toward him as he nods toward her enthusiastically. "No way," she says, "you have to do it yourself. I'm not your secretary, I don't answer phones. Your phone, your conversation." He stares blankly at the small, rectangular brick. "Oh, for god's sake," says Cassidy. She presses the green button to receive the call, and holds the phone close to Patrick's ear.

"Hi, Dad, is that you? Are you there?" says Nora's voice, thin and fragile through the tiny, invisible speakers. Patrick makes a sound like a grunt, but not quite a grunt. "Dad. You can't talk?" He makes the sound again, less loud. "Well," she says with hesitation in her voice, "I guess I'll just tell you. Maybe it won't mean anything to you. Then you can get back to whatever you're doing in *California*." She says the word with adolescent hurt in her voice. The sound he makes in response reminds Cassidy of bleating, a sheep sound from a sheep with its mouth taped shut.

"I had a vision of you, Dad," Nora begins in a serious tone. "You were out in the desert. You weren't wearing a shirt. There were some houses in the background, but they were far away and there were no people. You were crawling through the sand on your hands and knees; you had dust all over your face and your clothes. There was dust in your mouth, and you didn't seem to notice. You didn't seem to care."

Patrick nods slowly. Cassidy whispers to him that if he wants Nora to hear him he has to make a sound.

"As you crawled, you looked up and around you at these prehistoric trees; instead of leaves, they were covered in spikes; their trunks were shaggy like woolly mammoth legs. Trees that had arms instead of branches, arms like a person's, thick and reaching out in all different directions. You were frightened of the trees. But then you saw something before you that seemed to make you happy. You smiled a big smile, and you kept crawling forward. But this time, you were looking up at something. Something up above you. You crawled toward it, holding your hand out toward it—like, I don't know, like you were trying to invite it to come closer. And then I don't see you anymore. I don't see you in any more of my visions. You're just gone."

There's a long, deep silence on the phone as Nora waits, her chest tight, hardly breathing. The sound of the cicadas, buzzing and rattling in the cool upstate night, is faint through the earpiece of the phone. On the other end of the line, in a one-bedroom house in Joshua Tree, Patrick sits half slumped on an ugly gray couch, nodding vigorously, nodding as hard as he can.

At night, the desert landscape is made of low and middling shapes, silhouettes cut from pieces of dense, dark blue. The mountains in the background zag dully like an old row of vertebrae, the creature long dead, its form softened by the attrition of sun and grit and wind. The stiff, dry vegetation looks blurry in the night, the edges gently furred. Above it all, the crescent moon like a long white tooth. In the unseen spaces behind rocks or scrub, in the between-brush, where its coat blends with the white-blue earth, a coyote carries on a conversation with itself, yelping and moaning, answering its call with a long, rising cackle. It multiplies its voice as it crosses the sands, laughing and whining and wailing like a thing with its leg in the trap, broadcasting the presence of a whole pack of loud, hungry bodies. As it passes out of view and into other places, the sounds fade without ever ending. Eventually, the night is quiet again, and still. In the sky, the stars are so many that the darkness seems to be smeared with light.

From the southwest, where the low-lying mountains rear up over the sands, a whiteness surfaces at the dark edge of the peak. It grows and collects there, a space of light color in a field of night. Then it begins to move: a snake of animate fog, scaling the mountain ridge and sliding down the rough slope like a soundless avalanche. As it descends, it spreads, widens, blankets the mountainside in a white that cancels sight. A color that cancels sound. This smooth layer of fog makes the night more silent, more hushed. Birds don't fly within its muffling calm, the big-eyed desert rats don't leave their holes. When the white veil passes over an insect singing on its perch of bramble, the song stops. As the fog reaches the desert floor, it slows for a moment in indecision, considering its next move. And then, like a creature unobserved, it chooses a direction. It turns right, crawling across the dry valley floor, over the rubble of sand-colored granite, over sage and scrub and dry, scratchy thornbush until it reaches its endpoint. When it stops, it seems to grow solid. It sits beneath the cold, hard moon, thickening and collecting, growing murky like a glass of milk, until nothing can be seen but the white below and the dark far above.

———

The morning reminds him of being a child again, waking into a summer day with nothing to do, the joy of remembering this fact, the feeling of dawning, cresting optimism, an excitement for what lies ahead. When he was young, very young, he used to love going to the beach, running along the margin of damp, firm sand, fleeing the perimeter of foaming surf as it came for him, then turning to jump and land feetfirst right in the midst of the swirling shallow. He was taught to wriggle his toes where the sand bubbled with pocks and holes from the life breathing underneath, to uncover the baubles like fat limestone teardrops and place them in the watery pail for eating later. He learned to pack a pail for a sand castle, to turn it over roughly so the sand wouldn't have a chance to rethink its shape. There was the smell of salt, stronger each time the waves came crashing in, and of some lifelike, vital substance he only knew to think of as the taste of a body turned inside out, like when you bite the inside of your cheek and taste blood or cry so heavily that the snot trails all the way to your lips. When he got home, he would stand and pee into the bone-white bowl of the downstairs toilet and recognize the seaside smell in his urine, his body a balloon full of ocean waters and ocean salts, a naked, soft-skinned version of the long-ago fish that crawled up onto the shore with the sea's sweat and tears sealed up in its vessel.

Now, as he rises from the stranger's furniture, he recognizes the feeling of a beach morning, the first waking thought in your head the last you had from the night before. The knowledge that you were going someplace good was a powerful pill that kept you from falling asleep and made your waking sharper. As he looks out the picture window, he recognizes the familiar sight: sand as far as the eye can see, a soft, yielding floor that grows so warm under the sun and feels soft on the skin even though it is made of stone. Yes, the sound is different, he admits to himself as he steps out the front door and into his surroundings. More of a crunch than a whisper, and as he walks the big, round grains don't stick to the soles of his feet, they just fall off. It's a long way to the waterline, he can tell, but that's not unusual. During the busiest summer weekends, there were sometimes so many people at the beach that they had to park in the third overflow lot, not even the second, and the lot was so far from the water that for the first few blocks they walked on pitch-black asphalt, unmarked by even a grain of sand.

The sky turns from pink to violet to a gentle, pallid blue. The beach seems to go on for miles, but he can hear the sound of the surf far off in the distance, a gentle, irregular whooshing punctuated by long periods of silence. A gigantic burr is stuck in his foot, and when he pulls it out, it leaves a bleed. The sand is too large and too sharp on this beach, full of larger pieces that cut at the soles, red-bodied ants that bite and leave a sensation of tiny, targeted burning. The sand is full of bushes and thick, thorn-covered plant lobes. Sometime later, there's still no water, but he finds a road: as he crosses, the drivers on both sides stop to let him go past. It's grown hot and inconceivably bright: some unseen disturbance ripples and dances in the air at the horizon line, and he pulls his shirt up over his head and lets his beach body breathe in the beach air. He can see the faces turn to follow him as he passes in front of their vehicles, he can feel the engine noise thrumming close to his human skin. Dark, broad-winged seagulls circle overhead.

When his feet begin to bleed, he goes on his hands and knees. Even the most distant parking lot is only fifteen or twenty minutes from the sea. From his position close to the ground, he can see so much more: dark, glossy beetles the size of bullets hurry around the base of plants, freezing for a moment as his shadow passes over them and blocks out the caress of the sun. Tracks cross the land before him, little ovaloid dents from rabbits and the multi-toed paws of coyotes. Small, teardrop-shaped birds with a computerlike chirp rush back and forth in front of him, and away into a cluster of low, dry bushes. He's never seen vegetation like this on a beach—except for the strips of coarse, frayed sea-grass on the dunes farthest from the water, nothing much grows where the saline threatens to invade. In the distance, he sees a thousand small, varying shapes that he can't remember the name of. He experiences surprise and wonder when he catches sight of his hands: the skin is an urgent pink, the palms lacerated, marked by dozens of small, mysterious punctures that he doesn't remember receiving. The bright spots of blood buried in his palms remind him of berries in the wintertime, or is it berries in the summer?

It's only when he notices the strange tree that he understands there's something very wrong. The tree is ten or twelve feet tall, the size of a full-grown apple tree. The trunk is too narrow, the upper portions covered with an incomprehensible furring of shaggy brown bark. The limbs are almost as thick as the base, and they end in tough, spiky bursts of green. The tree is impossible, he thinks to himself. He can't imagine a person, a man like himself, coexistent with this tree, standing or crawling next to it, bleeding next to it. It belongs to some other epoch, to gigantic cats with scimitar tusks and dinosaurs grinding the knifelike leaves in their hard mouths. If he is witnessing this tree, something has gone horribly wrong. It's impossible that he should be standing here alive to witness it, impossible that he should exist at all. Either he exists and the world is an illusion, or the tree does and he is the mistake.

Suddenly nothing seems familiar at all. The sky too blue, the air too hot, the sand too big, the ground too grainy. The world tears in half, one side all names, the other side all images, with no point of contact between them. The plants smell like soap, and they are rotten with lizards, darting in and out of tough, knotty root systems. He crawls faster, looking right and left and finding more trees, freakish trees with arms uncannily human, reaching up toward the sky as if in celebration. He recognizes nothing, not the round, spiny plants or the endless brown movers jumping and hopping and flitting in and out of hiding, not the big blue thing or the white things beside it, not the small hot thing that hurts his eyes.

And then, suddenly, he sees something he does recognize: it's the man from the roadside, the man in the suit. He feels the man is a friend. The man smiles like a friend. He wears a double-breasted charcoal-gray suit of a cotton flannel fabric. The suit is not of the moment, but with its sleek cut it will never quite fall out of style either. He would like to call to the man, say hello or ask him his name, to give his own name or comment on the absurdity of his situation, but his tongue won't move, everything in his mouth tube is stuck and dry. Then he remembers his hand. He holds his hand up, turns it horizontal, thrusts it forward. The man in the suit has eyes that crinkle kindly at the edges and a look of calm, diligent authority on his face. A handshake will seal their bond. Patrick crawls forward and forward, his hand straight out before him, he crawls toward the embrace of his new friend, a person he has never met but who is as familiar to him as his own forgotten face.

At the seam of the sea, the only sound is water slapping on shore, steady as a beating heart. Birds don't call, fish don't swim, no voice will raise a cry across the surf. Where the wave throws itself frothing against solid ground, it leaves its thin skin on wet rocks. Dense mists drift across the ocean surface and dissolve, but some linger too long: a cloud as monument, writing in vapor that vanishes unread. In many millions of years, monoliths will rise in the inland distances to form pillar forests of fungi as tall as sequoias, forests to cast shadows where no leaves yet grow, forests to have their soft torsos devoured entire by the first exterminating insects. Until then, in the shallows where the heat of the sun warms the surface, proteins come together and break apart and come together and break apart until they don't. The thick sky lit by bursts of pink and green, the ocean empty to the eye, if there were an eye to see it.

Rafts of foam in the unceasing churn. The only rule is: what lingers will linger.

The animals have no eyes and no ears: they hear with their bodies, each presence a touch. Plantlike fronds rooted in clay, waving in noiseless motion. Flowerlike faces, pliant fingers fanned out around an open mouth. Some crawl across the seafloor a centimeter a day, flat and disc-shaped, mistaken for a shadow on the sand. Heaven could be a fiction told about this place: light soaks the water as living tufts stray into the tendrils of medusas, floating in and out of life. Everything is soft here, and death has the roundness of an embrace. A worm-shaped thing crawling the seabed reaches a colorful polyp and begins to pull it into its mouth. A sensation like tearing travels through the blossomlike body, flashing with lingering bursts of fear. The flesh moves, quivers, folds inward as it is pulled into another's mouth and severed from existence. The pain is a buzzing in the air, not a scream, less like dying and more like coming undone.

As the strange fish struggles onto the coast with fins made for supple water, the sun beats against the unbroken surface of the sea, raising vapor. Heat and light lick at the shifting expanse, the single ocean like the white of an eye, surrounding an island of earth backed like a whale. Stranded in air, the creature lives. It multiplies, lays wet-walled eggs in ephemeral lakes. Its offspring die, but some live long enough to copy themselves again and again on dry ground. Their spines lengthen, their skins grow thick and tough to hide the moisture within. Deep below, the ocean floor is made and remade in hard, liquid fire. At the world's first end, a rock from elsewhere blots out the sky, casting perpetual twilight. And as the armored bodies collapse onto the earth, they are scavenged by small, furry creatures, swarms too numerous to count. The mammals stand upright, the stone comes to a devilish point. But even this new epoch is only a splinter, lodged between long before and longer after.

It begins in a loose circle, each man or woman about twenty-five feet from another, casting long shadows against the hay. Almost the entire town is there, familiar faces holding unfamiliar instruments: rakes, hatchets, poles or sticks, even frying pans. Sarah Irwin, the town's best seamstress, stands squinting into the sun with her pitchfork, and William Beale (who owns the bulk of the county's lettuce land, and organized this brave hunt) waits with shotgun ready to strike the butt against small scared skulls. On a signal from the foreman, they take one step in, then another. Before their feet, the unseen scurry away into the tall grass, fleeing the advancing line. Their terror a rustling in the golden field. Tighter and tighter the circle grows, until all the town could join hands and sing in unison. Until the circumference breaks and folds in on itself, a collapsing star. The rabbits swarm at the center, a convergence of fear and roiling fur, climbing over one another to stay in place. There's nowhere for them to run, noosed in the crowd: the town raises their weapons, clouds above gather and shadow the earth. The feverish heat rising up from the parched earth, the levitating odor of metal as rabbit blood breaks from the bodies and leaches out into the dry California air.

Sitting at the edge of Gratitude Creek with a pad of paper on her lap, Nora tries to sketch the shape of the water flow. At each moment, she works to focus on one point in the stream and follow it with her eyes as it zigs and zags away downstream, like a rabbit running in terror from a dog. The task requires that she move quickly, eyes always on the shifting liquid, quick to dart to its next point of contact—the purpose of the exercise she's given herself is to teach her to dip in and out of flow, experiencing her own uniquely human means of merging with the rushing water. But she's having trouble concentrating: though her eyes and hands go through the motions, the lesson doesn't feel real. Beneath it, something else is occupying all the wordless spaces she doesn't have a name for; after each stroke, she goes back and does it over to make up for being only half involved. The side of her hand is dark with graphite; something prickles the inner corner of her eye. She looks at her pad: it's like the lines are weeping all at once, running wildly from the top down to the bottom of the page. Her dad is gone in some new way today, and it's like there's a smooth, round stone lodged in her chest, cold against her heart. The water she's watched is already traveling far out of sight, leaving her behind, falling back into the sea, mixing irretrievably, irreversibly. The water, her father, the water, her father, the roar so loud and so constant she can't hear herself inside her own head.

———

Cassidy can see tracks leading indelibly into the desert, a trail of footprints arrowing out straight into the vast beyond. A desert walker, full of purpose, headed straight for water that's not there. She stands outside the house that is not June's and squints into the bright. The tread is Patrick's: a heavy, stiff shoe that leaves ridged patterns in the sand. It's not a good idea to go after him, she knows that much: the simplest thing would be to call the closest Memodyne, in Cathedral City, so they can come and hunt him down in one of their clunky green vans. But now that she's talked to his wife on the phone, now that she's learned his daughter's name, she knows it would make her a Bad Person if she let him just get taken away and warehoused with all the others. Looking for Patrick is the *human* thing to do. Or does she mean *humane*? Cassidy grabs a half-full gallon of vintage Poland Spring as she heads out, adding the imprint of her size-six sandals to the unbounded sea of sand. Under the hard, down-slanted desert light, Cassidy Carter barely resembles herself. Her hair is dulled yellow, not gold, and the shadows cut deep across her mouth and under the eyes, making her look like another person, one who wouldn't be recognized on the street, even in the town where they grew up. The sun a white void, the clouds unmoving above.

On Highway 210, toward Calabasas, Horseshoe adjusts the rearview mirror so that the Arm is visible lying unmoving in the back seat, covering his eyes with his hands. Though he's mostly vegetative, Horseshoe watches for those fleeting moments when some familiar life force repossesses the slack, stubbly face. Sometimes he'll speak then, or sit up, or he'll look out the window with an expression of distrust, causing Horseshoe to patter soothingly as to a dog or child, telling him, "Don't worry, bro, that's just a billboard," or "Do you see the waves crashing into the shore? Don't they look so cold and fizzy, like a frosty bottle of cola?" As the surf-glitter gleams in the distance, the Arm sits up, blinking into golden light. He looks around at the scratchy upholstery before registering the world scrolling by outside. In Horseshoe's observation, anecdotal though it is, the Arm always seems to perk up when they're approaching the sea— maybe it's the way the setting sun angles down into his eyes. Or some oceanic drive, a return to the water.

"Why am I in the back?" the Arm says. "It's my car."

"I know, buddy," Horseshoe answers patiently. "But we agreed I'd make a better driver, because I have a higher level of coherence than you these days. No offense meant by that, simply a description of our comparative realities."

"Are we going to the . . ." He trails off, searching for the word. "The beach?"

"I wish we were," says Horseshoe, with a tinge of sadness. "We're headed westward right now, then we take the highway down along the coast, swing east on Twenty-two before Seal Beach, and then back north until we hit the Two-ten. That's the loop."

"But why drive in a loop?" the Arm asks.

"Because that's our plan." His tone is serene, but his eyes are bleary. "You lose your memory, I lose my memory—the freeway remembers for you, it gives direction. You can look around at everyone else and accelerate to their speed, you don't have to know what you're doing, where you're going, just where the other guy is. You remember what you told me? You said nobody's ever really been lost on the highway: even if it's not where you want, you're going exactly where the highway intends." He turns around in his seat to look into the face of his friend, thrusts forward a neon-green Nalgene full of warm, sweet orange juice, hand-squeezed. "I used to play you this recording of you explaining the plan to yourself, but hearing your own voice coming through the speakers really freaked you out."

The Arm takes the container of juice silently, lost in thought. He unscrews the lid and swallows the sugar-bright nectar. Gently, dreamily, he presses the soft side of his hand to his reddening cheeks. "I think I have a sunburn," he says. "Have we been doing this for a long time?" Palm trees along the freeway shake in an invisible wind as the seconds rush by.

"Well," Horseshoe says, "define 'long.' Long in a human time frame, or long in some objective sense? Driving translates reality into the language of the ego. When I drive, anyone I pass is a weak-willed idiot, and anyone who passes me is a narcissistic self-suicider. Driving cuts everything to the size and shape of the self—there's no way for it to be too long or too short, it just *is*. Qualitative terms like 'fast,' 'slow,' 'oriented,' 'lost,' 'safe,' 'in danger' make no sense unless you make it clear that you're using a subjective frame of reference." He looks back expectantly at his pal, waiting for him to chime in, but he doesn't. "If you have someplace to be, any perceived delay causes the length to dilate. But we," he adds with emphasis, "are exactly where we're supposed to be."

"Okay, but. If you told me the number of hours, would I call that number high?"

"The higher the number gets, the better our plan is working," says Horseshoe, looking out the window at a cluster of seagulls, reeling in wide, lopsided circles. The flock of birds, some real, some hallucinated, pass in and out of view as they intersect the strange cloud. A third of the sky is filled with its soft, sloped vastness, the shape as simple as a line in a child's drawing. With its smooth base and its top gently curved, it resembles a whale, and nothing else: the strange cloud leaves no room for interpretation.

"Just wondering," Horseshoe says, "but what do you see when you look at that cloud out there? The big one?"

The Arm squints and leans forward, his breath fogging the glass. "It's a whale, swimming," he says with finality.

"That's what I think too," Horseshoe replies.

They drive in silence, slowing and speeding up. The Arm lies down in the back seat and covers his eyes with his hands. He wants to dream of the girl he met on the highway however long ago—it must be weeks now, or years—but all he can remember are the words: girl, blonde, highway, sunshine. In a half-sleep, he wraps his arms around "girl" and holds it close to him, the sound long and smooth with a languid curl. The dream that follows is as dark and deep as a well in the dry inland plains. It is like turning the radio to a station that doesn't exist: the silence heavy, concrete, containing within it the slightest fuzz of static, which lets you know you're hearing nothing, rather than not hearing at all. When he wakes up, he blinks his eyes and stares into the sun as the glittering blue of the Pacific surfaces up ahead. The ocean reminds him of something, maybe a girl, maybe a highway. The car takes the exit east, then, many miles later, the exit north. They take the exit again and again and again.

As the ocean comes into view once more, the Arm has a sudden revelation: "Are we going in a loop?" he exclaims, sitting forward, intent on the road.

Horseshoe is silent, contemplative. He realizes now that it is the clouds that make it so dark: they cover the sky like a rash, like a burning. He can't tell anymore where the smoke ends and the sky begins, can't see the difference between earth and firmament. If he waits too long, he'll forget the question.

Finally, he admits it: "I don't remember anymore." The turn signal clicks frantically. The horizon line has disappeared. The vanishing point is everywhere. And as night completes its fall, even these distinctions will dissolve into air.

Cassidy notices changes in the pattern of Patrick's footprints, preserved exactly in the sand: thirty minutes in, the imprints stagger forth, wobbly and irregularly spaced. Now and then, she sees a new shape on the trail that could be the print of a hand pressed into the scalding surface. There are holes in the pale sand, the diameter of a snake's torso or the narrow body of a vole. Sharp, rustling movements at the fringe of her sight are lizards fleeing the fall of footsteps. Far from any road, traveling the spaces between clumps of sage and creosote, she finds a baby's pacifier in light-blue plastic and a trail of barefoot prints that end a hundred feet away. She looks around for a body, but there's nothing in sight.

How do things that have lasted for years, a lifetime even, suddenly come to an end? Do they break before they appear to be broken, or do ends come as suddenly as disasters, only without the bang or crash or explosion? After the fight at the Chateau Marmont when June told her that she was quitting her to go become a crystal healer, it was over before either one of them had understood it had ended. But the fury that rose in her every time she read those messages over seemed like proof that the thread of love was still there, red hot and waiting to be pulled at the right moment, to bring June running back into her life. She would pull it if she ever knew for sure that she had hit bottom, if she needed someone to recognize her in whatever state she happened to be in. But there was no bottom to land on, no solid surface to affirm a sensation of doom, just an endless depth around and beneath her, colder and heavier the further down she got.

Thousands of miles away, a beetle navigates the high-pile carpeting in Cassidy Carter's second guest bedroom. The beetle is crawling from the center of the room to the edges, searching for a solid surface. Its glossy carapace heaves slightly left and right as it traverses the sea of beige. If anything, it hopes to find a hole back into the outdoors: the house is a death trap, inedible and synthetic, saturated with the taste of plastic. On the upper floors, the identically decorated bedrooms are photo-ready, beds still tucked tight and topped with ornamental pillows. But below, the wildfire has gnawed through the backyard plantings, blackening the landscaped beds and reducing the rosebushes to branching ash. Flame had devoured the perimeter of the house, igniting dried plant litter and dead leaves in the gutters, melting the plastic siding, and carving a black path from the back deck to the vaulted foyer and bricked façade. There's a charred hole in the back of the structure through which you can see all the furniture inside, like a dollhouse. An hour west under current traffic conditions, industrial piping opens a pathway from the sewer system directly into the ocean. Thousands of gallons pour through every minute, the roar of it muffled in the vastness of the sea. Where the sewer exits, the churn is visible, white with fury and force. But even as the force dissipates and the new liquid begins to join the flow of currents and jet streams, it refuses to mix or dissolve, it won't give up its difference. It descends to the colder depths and collects on the seafloor, caressing the bodies of urchins and crabs in a heavy grip, swaying like the wind.

It leaves you with a strange feeling, watching your own body on video doused with bucket after bucket of ice as your real body blisters and tingles in the heat. June left in April, and in mid-May Cassidy said yes to the strange phone call offering her a week partying on a remote Greek island: free alcohol and airfare and thirty thousand dollars, all for letting a small crew of professional photographers take pictures of her just being herself, having fun, cutting loose in the glittering Aegean waves. June would have told her not to take the gig, would have pointed out that the fee was low compared with how much the pictures might be worth to a tabloid, particularly if something bad happened. But June wasn't around to point this out. At the airport, Cassidy realized that she hadn't packed a toothbrush—for six months, she had been without an assistant, and things like this had started to happen all the time. It was okay, though. She had used a million different things as a toothbrush over the years: a finger coated in toothpaste, a tightly rolled Kleenex, the chewed-up end of a twig, stuff like that. The bigger worry was whether it was a sign of anything, a bad omen about the trip. Ever since she had watched that Buddy Holly biopic starring Miles Teller, she felt halfway certain she might die in a plane crash. She was just about the right age, too, to join the Twenty-seven Club a year early.

From L.A. to Dublin to Athens to Corfu, on a plane so narrow it fit only two bodies per row; she was met by a bearded man who shuffled her onto a ferry, then onto a smaller boat that smelled of mackerel. The smaller boat stopped in the middle of the water to let an even smaller boat pull up alongside it: through gestures and sparse words, Cassidy understood she was supposed to take her luggage and climb over the side by herself. Not a single person had recognized her from the moment she left Athens; the language on the taxicabs and signage reminded her of hieroglyphs on the wall of some crumbling pyramid. Real Indiana Jones shit, she thought to herself. As the boats got smaller, they got quieter too, and the other passengers noticed her less and less. She felt something being peeled from her, the sensation like being skinned. She had spent the majority of her life under constant scrutiny, it made attention like water to her: the medium of life and of buoyancy, the solution to thirst, the unseen, unprompted support. Being outside of the world gaze was cold, like the moment you crawl out of the swimming pool and know the frigidity of air. The last leg of her voyage took place on what looked like a rowboat with a motor strapped to the back, sitting next to an old woman in black carrying a bag of oranges. For twenty-four hours, she didn't speak her name or give a smile. Nobody even glanced at her face.

Brenda plays a little game while drinking her whiskey. She picks up the glass and, before allowing herself a sip, inserts a single gesture—swirling the tumbler once, for example, before lifting it to her lips. On the next sip, she performs that first gesture and adds a second one—tapping the side twice with a long, manicured nail. On the next, a 180-degree rotation. And so on. Curled at one end of the sinuous beige sofa, Brenda swirls her glass once, taps it twice, rotates it in her hand, tips it slightly forward three times with short, sharp movements, brings it to her nose and breathes in the paint-stripping scent, sets it down on the coaster and picks it up again, runs her finger along the entire rim of the glass, swirls it three times, holds it up to the light, swirls it one more time, and then, finally, lets a small mouthful slip past her lips. It burns a tiny fire in the space just above her lungs.

"I'm so bored," she announces, putting her drink down and staring expectantly at Jay, who lies horizontal at the far end of the long sofa.

He sits up blearily. "Did I fall asleep?" He's still wearing his dress shirt, buttoned all the way up to the bulb of his throat.

"It's more like 'did you fall awake.' Jay, you've been such a downer this whole weekend. I wake up on my own, make coffee, drink it by myself. I order lunch, eat it alone, put the other half in the fridge as leftovers. I feel like a goddamn widow."

"I'm right here," Jay says, gesturing around him broadly. "I'm a little tired, is all."

"I'm tired too. I'm tired of planning our life together and never actually beginning to live," Brenda says with escalating drama. "I'm tired of the film, and I'm tired of pretending to be a film producer six to eight hours a day, when I couldn't care less about cutting or keeping a line, getting the audio on mic or adding it in post. I just want to be a woman. I want to climb into a plane and fly to our place in New Zealand and start making it a home. I want to see a fucking wallaby."

Jay smooths a stray patch of hair and leans forward, entering producer mode. His lips glisten in the tasteful interior lighting, invertebrate pink. The tips of his white teeth so bright they seem to glow in the half-light.

"Brenda, bunny, I hear what you're saying, and I want to be there too, together in our future. But you and I both know that there's no more fund-raising, no more movie money after we leave the country. All we'll have is your share of your grandfather's trust, sliced forty ways from Sunday. This is our last big fishing trip, so why would we cut it short? The Vikings, the Polynesian warrior-greats, Genghis Khan—they knew you take in as much as you can to last through the long winter."

"There's no point in trying to keep the movie thing going," says Brenda. "Cassidy's not coming back, and she and Patrick are probably going to tell everyone."

"What makes you say that?"

"Just every single thing they said when they came over here."

"What do you mean, when they came over? During the fund-raising event, you mean? I don't think I said a word to either one."

"The night before last, Jay. What, did you get conked on the head?"

"Thursday night? I guarantee you," Jay says firmly, "that never happened."

"Then what did we do instead?"

His enamel gleams; the smile doesn't waver. After a moment, Jay shrugs. "Look, what is it they say? The lady is always right. Remember that phrase and you'll live a happy life. I'm not here to argue with you, bunny, I'd rather keep my eyes on the prize: seventy-five acres of pristine farmland an hour outside Wellington, an off-grid bunker with a hot tub and indoor lap pool, fully equipped with solar panels and reverse-osmosis filtration system for the well water. A sous-vide machine for me that runs on sustainable geothermic power, and a room for you to do your paintings. One big California king, and no kids knocking on the door on Saturday morning."

"And wallabies," Brenda adds, breaking out in a dazzling smile.

"Wallabies," Jay agrees. "As far as the eye can see."

As far as Cassidy could see, the island was brown, dry, and studded with gnarled black trees: she had traveled thirty-six hours straight only to arrive back in California. Nikos, a dense-bodied man in a loose cotton shirt, collected her from the small dock in a scuffed-up truck with a Mercedes hood ornament. As they crawled up the narrow, dusty roads toward the top of the island, Cassidy saw a block of hulking white squatting on a rock outcrop above them: it looked like a clod of snow, a glacier fixed improbably to the side of the mountain. She rolled down the window to smell the sea breeze and Nikos immediately rolled it back up. "Women shouldn't breathe hot air," he explained.

The white block on the hillside was where she'd be filming and sleeping. Past a shiny steel gate, the driveway led to a bricked courtyard with a single shriveled tree crouched in the center. Four bikinis were laid out on the bed in her room, each in a sparkly, metallic pattern. When she came back down in a cute tunic she had brought, a small group of men sitting and smoking on the terrace called Nikos over to confer. Irritated, Nikos walked over to Cassidy and asked if the swimsuits didn't fit her or what. She said, "I'd rather wear my own clothes," and he nodded and said, "For today, okay, but tomorrow the costumes." The pool was scattered with girls in skimpy tops and thong bottoms who weren't drunk yet and didn't seem to know one another. They stared forward, some on their phones, others silently looking at nothing specific. Necks festooned with leis of fake plastic flowers. Elsewhere, a button was pressed and techno gushed from the speakers. When she asked how many days the shoot would last, Nikos said five days, and then he said six.

The first couple days, Cassidy lay beneath anonymous hands rubbing her body with globs of sunscreen, turning and smiling for the camera whenever they said. She took shots of cloudy liquor and fell backward into the pool, shrieking with laughter; then they'd pull her out, blow-dry her hair crispy, and do it again and again. Slathered in glitter, she took shots from the flat bellies of bored girls, unprofessionals who didn't know whether they should smile or act sexy; she poured the milky ooze over their oiled bodies straight from the plastic bottle, and waited for them to get hosed off, and did it again, with a big toothy grin on her face, until Nikos said they had gotten the shot. She got trashed in the vertical noontime sun and passed out under a blue-and-white-striped umbrella; then the men dumped ice on her to wake her up and make her party again. She looked like a nobody, she realized, as they played the footage back for her. But a few days in, Nikos came with instructions from the men: she was to hold the container of sunscreen up in front of her, smile big, and say with a loud and happy voice, "Party with Eidos!" Cassidy explained to him that product endorsements were a whole other thing, they needed thick contracts and big fees. Because being the face of one cosmetic product meant, for example, that she wouldn't be approached by other brands. It was a future loss of income, so she needed to be compensated accordingly.

Now it became clear that the watchful silence of the foreign men was about power, not language. They came over a few at a time to ask Nikos what was wrong, then turned to Cassidy, saying with childlike firmness, "You want the money, you say the line. We don't pay unless you do the job." Then they shoved the product at her and she gave it back and they put it in her hand and she lifted it high above her head and threw it, then overturned a table littered with glasses and liquor bottles. An area by the pool was covered with thick shards of glass, and she could hear the women fleeing into the house, their murmuring unintelligible but for its tone of fear. Someone held her by the arms and tried to drag her indoors—she gave him an off-center headbutt that bloodied her brow. Then there were men grabbing at her, holding her arms and shoulders and waist, a hand on her face pushing it down and up again. Soon Cassidy was in her room, with the door locked from the outside. When she threatened to call her agent, the police, the secretary of state, they told her to go ahead and call, only her phone got no service. Around ten at night, the sky finally grew dark, and someone unlocked the door for long enough to shove a plate of chicken and potatoes across the threshold. She ate the cubes of chicken and brothy potatoes with her bare hands, wiping them on a towel and looking out the window at the flat blue line of the sea, which moved ceaselessly and imperceptibly in the distance.

Nikos woke her up in the morning, sheepish and muttering

apologies, and handed over a tray of fried eggs, toast, and oil-drizzled tomatoes. It was not a big-budget product or well-funded project, he explained, and everyone thought the terms had been made clear enough in the invitation sent by email. The producers hoped that she would be willing to come out of the room and do the few product shots that were left, as a favor to all of them, at which point they would pay her fee and put her back on the boats with a complimentary case of product to bring home and share with her Hollywood friends. Cassidy Carter listened, nodding and gently smiling, and when he finished speaking, she calmly asked for her fee to be tripled. They could keep the case of their gross, flower-reeking cream—maybe give it to the background girls, who all had a sort of trafficked vibe. Nikos said no way, then he said he'd check with the bosses; she heard shouting in the halls and the sound of feet scuffling against tile. "It's not possible," he reported back. "Then I guess I'll be here in this room until you put me on a plane back to California," she replied. As the door locked again, she wondered why she had said that: Was she truly worried she would screw up a future deal? Was anyone going to offer her deals at all after *Five Moons of Triton*? Was she angry that she had made another mistake, as June had implied was bound to happen given her recklessness, the impulsive spending, the bad public behavior? Or did she believe she deserved a big mistake she couldn't undo, something that would decide for her that her career was over? When she imagined herself with no acting, no endorsements, no paparazzi, all she saw was her own body, smaller than life, sitting alone in her big, generic house.

They didn't deliver any more food that day, and nobody came to check on her. As she thought about their anger, Cassidy grew afraid: who knew what they were capable of, what other people in the world were capable of. Someone rich enough and crazy could buy her and keep her as a human pet. In some parts of the world, she would never be recognized, no alarm would be sounded, nobody would even find out. In the night, when the sky turned a desolate blue, she threw as many clothes as she could into the duffel and tossed it out the window into the garden below. She dangled her legs out the window, testing the proximity to the knotty old olive tree growing close to the side of the building. One sharp inhalation and she let her body fall onto the broadest branch—once this was done, she knew she could find the placements she needed to get the rest of the way down, this tree was made for climbing. But first she stopped to gaze around her: a view over the wall and onto the vastness of the world around it, a view of the steep, twisting hills and miniature boats that made it all look like a found postcard, a postcard from someone she didn't know at all, from someone long gone.

Alison stares into one of the three communal fridges, looking for lemons among half-finished jars of sunflower butter and obscure Tupperwares. When she finds some hard and shriveled citrus, she slices it to float in the pitchers of water she's preparing, one for each end of the five long cafeteria tables. Setting the table is the Earthbridge task Alison volunteers for most often, because it resembles a family dinner at home—scaled up to a hundred, yes, but still familiar. Thick scoops of vegan butter for the bread baskets, a pile of laundered napkins in the bin by the door, all of it in known quantities waiting to be parceled out. For these shifts, they work two to a kitchen, and the other worker is usually someone quiet like herself; together, they focus intently and separately on each action, as though they are each alone in the room.

The repetitiveness of the work is calming, but today she can't stop thinking about the sounds she heard over the phone right before Cassidy Carter hung up: the screeching of implied wheels, the unseen, unknown quantity of her husband's body dashing between them. She struggles to imagine him sick, delirious, dying out there alone, but her mind just keeps conjuring Patrick home with the flu, grouchily demanding homemade soup. There's something terrifying about the absence of images here, those sounds the only trace of a larger mangle, flesh against steel against plastic. Like the problem with WAT-R that Patrick alluded to on the phone, simultaneously alarming and utterly abstract: the substance real and material somewhere utterly out of sight. Alison lifts the cover of the icemaker, thrusts her bare arms into the chill to scoop clattering heaps of ice into pitchers and carry them over to the faucet.

She takes the first pitcher and holds it under the tap, letting the water level rise to the lip. She does the same thing again and again, and she's about to set the last pitcher aside when she notices something odd in the water: it could be something she's never noticed before, but are those suds gathered at the top normal? They seem to linger just a moment too long, the water goes from white to clear, but not clear enough—so she pours the whole thing down the drain and starts again. The new fill is better, calmer and less sudsy, but the water looks different—

bluer than usual? Something mournful in the color? Something wrong? She pours out the pitcher and starts over. She fills the pitchers, holds each one up to the light, and starts again, over and over and over.

When Nora enters, she finds her mother staring down at twelve pitchers full of water and an assortment of glassware, the vessels filled to different levels with liquid. "Sweetie, come over here," her mother calls. "I need you to look at something." Nora comes close. The glasses and pitchers look normal—it's their arrangement that seems strange to her, huddled together like survivors in the aftermath of disaster. It looks like a video she once watched on the internet, where an old man standing in front of a table set with half-filled glasses played a medley of pop songs by running a wet finger over the rims, but there's no music, and no laughter from the studio audience. The man was old in the nineties, so Nora is pretty sure he's no longer alive—just as with most older movies and TV shows, where every adult's performance is like an obituary to itself. "Look at the water," Alison says quietly. "Does it look right to you?" Nora looks at the water, but the water just sits there. She tries to look harder, but her attention seems to drift from the water to her mother again and again, and she wonders if her mother is the one in trouble. How much worry is too much worry, how much sad is too much sad? Her mother's face has deep lines between the eyebrows; Nora can't remember if they've always been there. If all the adults were destroyed, who would she take with her for her survival group? Sometimes at night, as she waits to fall asleep, she assembles a team: Kelsey and Janine, Esther, Otto, and Miguel. Skinny, lisping Thomas. All of them walking the country road toward Oswego, walking without fear on the yellow center line, talking loudly and without thought of being overheard, about how to remake their world.

Cassidy presses her back against the cool side of a boulder, the granite rasping against her skin. Patrick's footprints vanished a half-mile back, but with hours between her and the noplace she had come from, it was less pointless just to continue searching. An image in her mind of a woman sweeping the desert floor with a broom, erasing signs. It's been hours, and the water is nearly gone. But the sun is sinking too, and as the color above grows dark, a chill winds through the desert like a snake. What she felt in the days after escaping over the white stucco wall of the house in Greece was an emptiness, a lightness, almost as if the umbilical cord that bound her to her surroundings had been cut. It felt like a secret had been revealed: the world had ended, and still she hung around, feeling aches in her bones, feeling hunger, digging burrs out of her gauzy cotton blouse. As she wandered through the steep countryside, avoiding the paved roads she thought they might be patrolling, she shed her clothes, her face wash, her luggage, everything except for the passport and wallet. An empty space where hope should be, an empty space where fear should be. And so the feelings of hope and fear drift through that space like clouds through the sky, filling you with temporary fear, temporary hope. This moment is like that one, her fate decided but unknown.

A hundred or so feet away, dim in the twilight, she sees a pattern in the sand. From close up, the shapes are clearly footprints:

a man's dress shoe, smooth and elongated, trailing off into the Mojave. The sky crowded with clouds. She follows the footprints out toward the horizon line, ever present, ever receding.

The fires smolder black and orange in the canyon behind Secret Sunset, unwatched. Ditches have been dug around glowing, smoking earth, a moat to defend the big, expensive houses, their lawns and landscaping still green. The ground is dark, powdery, and fine; pale ashes waft in a breeze from nowhere, and life is already growing back. Nourished by the heat of nearby flames, tiny blue flowers peek through the carbonized earth, their buds opening to face the unearthly light. Across the canyon, a younger fire burns; the trucks use hoses to dampen the ground, and overhead a helicopter releases a tankload of WAT-R to quench the flames. The doused earth hisses, a hot blue mist rises toward the sky. Small blue flowers melting, spreading. "This one is making a run for the freeway," says one firefighter to another. High above the earth, an amalgamation of vapors. The night clouds, dry and immobile, glowing peach and lilac in the darkening sky.

The feel of it on her shoulders is cold, sudden. It takes a moment to comprehend that this is water falling from the sky: desert rain, out of season. Cassidy turns her face up to meet it, the drops heavy, thick, as sloppy as tears. Wetness runs off her brow and into her hair, sombering the blond. The nearby bushes exhale a surreal scent, like dried flowers coming back to life. Suddenly she realizes that this rain will wash away the footsteps of whoever she's been following, will wash away any trace of where Patrick's been or where he's gone. It will wipe from the earth every trace of her own path home. With no way back, the only way is forward. It's like that scene in season five of *Kassi Keene* where Kassi escapes from kidnappers in the middle of a vast redwood forest, only this time the park ranger won't find her in the nick of time, hypothermic and dehydrated. Only this time all does seem to be truly, irrecoverably lost. The strange rain sloughs through the desert floor, carving channels where they never existed before. Loneliness is a blue mist tinging everything it touches. Slender branches shudder under the weight of the sky.

WAT-R enters the opening of a body. It slides over the lips, the tongue, the soft palate, and into the darkness. It leaves behind a tasteless, odorless film, a lip-gloss shine on the living membrane. Inside the throat, the muscles contract and relax, directing liquid down smooth tubes. There's an unusual feeling, the feeling that the WAT-R is lodged there still, fuller than it should be. Solid somehow, unwilling to dispel. In the stomach, the ball of WAT-R crosses membrane walls unseen, traveling the body circuit. Large molecules leach through the perimeter of cells, but some get stuck. Lodged within the brain and liver and heart, the substance lingers like a memory, a memory of nothing. It fills itself into invisible gaps, completing the surface, making each organ gleam like living plastic. What's left over joins the rivers, the streams, the sea, the sky: a residue from elsewhere, a voracious stain, enduring traces of something manufactured, never born.

———

She runs hard into the middle distance, following the fading trail. The rain runs down her cheeks and into her mouth; she wipes it from the hollows of her eyes, but the wet comes back. As the last daylight vanishes behind the ridge, she's not sure if she's still on the path or just chasing gradations of shadow, variations on the incidental. It's raining all around her, but somehow her feet are dry. Far ahead, she sees a silhouette on the dim horizon, perched against rain-hazy sky. As she runs, she calls out to it or him or her, trying to avoid the spiny chollas and outstretched snags of sage and creosote, trying not to scream, trying not to fall. Thin red lines trail her calves up to her thighs; the rain smell is close and warm, like a living, breathing thing. No one ever sees a mirage: they see a real thing and know it to be false, or, more often, they don't. And nothing is more real than that which you reach for and discover is not there.

As she nears the human-shaped shadow, something makes her want to hesitate. Who waits out in the desert, far from any landmark, anyplace with a name, and won't even lift a hand to shield themselves from the falling rain? What type of person? What type of thing? The shape she sees, narrow and upright, could be a man or a figment, a tall ocotillo shrouded in fog. But as she steps forward, she begins to make out the details of the gray wool suit, crisp and pristine though he stands in the downpour. She had been so careful, so disciplined, and now she can't believe what she's seeing, can't believe what's not there.

———

The man is smiling, his hair is dry, he has a kind face—or maybe only a familiar one. A long nose and a jawline as deliberate as a stroke of pen on paper. Cassidy can't place him, maybe he's someone she's seen on TV. As she steps closer, he seems to nod encouragingly, warmly, his eyes some forgettable color. She stops, watching him from across a twelve-foot span of sand and scrub. Neither one moves; no word disturbs the silence. Then, with a small smooth gesture, he lifts his right arm and extends an open hand in her direction. He's beckoning her near. He has something he wants to tell her. The first thing she thinks is how long it'll take the tabloids to get the story: One week? Three? For better or worse, celebrity bodies usually get found.

High above the desert, the sky is crowded with clouds. There's nothing near her, no sound, no movement. She tries to remember a few last favorite things: Tiny the dog in his miniature sailor suit, the lilac flavor of June's hair brushing her lips as they hugged each other tight. Most of it comes back blank, but the space is still there, like a monument to a battle where hundreds of people were killed, the plaque sitting in front of an empty green field. Cassidy remembers that she might cry now, but her eyes feel so dry. Cassidy, Cass, Butch to those whom she held closest. She takes one step forward, then another, another. She looks one more time at her hands. At the sky. There's nothing to do now but step into the nothing. With no fear, no hesitation, she's lost the words for the feelings she doesn't have, she reaches out and places her pale palm in the gray-suited man's long, un-real hand.

His skin is cool to the touch, but he smells like burning.

From the vantage point of the desert sand, daylight flashes on and off a thousand times in succession, strobelike. The stars wheel overhead, a spatter of light rotating beyond reach and nearly beyond sight. For a while, there are automobiles and car-avans, then long stretches of silence. Occasional fires in the dis-tal cities, fierce rains that batter the roofs of untended homes. In the foreground, the cactuses multiply like rabbits, clusters of sharp spines growing dense, leaving only a ribcage-width for the coyote to guide its narrow body through. Nothing lasts until it lasts, and nothing is without its end.

The new flora is plasticky and hard-edged: circular blooms the color of watered-down sky, edging their way into the desert from the coast. There are chunks of concrete rubbled among real rocks, irregular shapes whose texture holds a false smooth-ness. Steel frames where buildings once stood, tiny shards of color indelible in the sand. When the sea rejoins the desert plains, eons have passed and a lone bird lights on the twist of a bough, a bird of a different shape. Pale-skinned whales breach where towering cliffs had stood, reptile-fish flash bright in the shallows. Strange mammals, dark nights. A paw print larger than what they once called a dinner plate. The sun rises and sets in the longer after, without name or recognition.

In the long before, there were rivers that tumbled from the mountain chill into the sweet-smelling flatlands. The water ran cool in the heat of the summer and you could see stones at the river floor, gray-brown and russet, clear and close as if they were laid in the palm of your hand. Where night met morning, the mountain lion would slake its thirst as the deer bent to drink, the same river cupped in the bodies of predator and prey. You could wade shin-deep into the running and gaze down at your own two feet, pale as cave fishes in the morning bright. In the cold, every muscle of the foot felt as if it was outlined in pure, sweet light, the pain like the ache of too much running, too much life. With your eyes closed, you stood there growing colder, growing numb, until the cold was gone and your body was absent too, the feeling of nothing, the feeling of movement, the feeling of being river, of keeping the cycle, of rushing down-stream to the open sea.

ACKNOWLEDGMENTS

Thank you to Claudia Ballard, Alexis Washam, Anna Kelly, Jillian Buckley, and Carrie Neill for the hard work and care that sustained this book. To Sara Reggiani, Leonardo Taiuti, Peter Haag, and Patrick Sielemann. To Joshua Fisher and others at the Jet Propulsion Laboratory in Pasadena, and to my colleagues and students at the New School. Time spent at the American Academy in Rome, Headlands Center for the Arts, Djerassi Resident Artists Program, Kimmel Harding Nelson Center for the Arts, and Brush Creek Foundation for the Arts made it possible to put the words in place.

Thank you to Rosa Handelman, Hermione Hoby, JW McCormack, Maya Singer, Eric Chinski, Rivka Galchen, Liz Moore, Ben Marcus, Nora MacLeod, and Andrew Eckholm for time, effort, support, and friendship. To Terry and Faye Kleeman for their unflagging love, and to Peter, Vilma, and Kara Gilvarry. And to Alex Gilvarry, my first reader and favorite author, thank you for giving me someone to write for.